Enlightenment: Earths

Ken Kirkberry

Ken Kirkberry is a lifelong daydreamer who has finally placed his thoughts into print. Brought up on Sci-Fi, Crime and Horror in both print and film format.
This reissue of the combined Enlightenment books trilogy is dedicated to the recent loss of our much-loved pet dog: Spike

CONTENTS

Title Page

Copyright

Dedication

Epigraph

THE CRASH: 1

BACK TO SCHOOL: 9

STRANGE TEACHER: 20

RESEARCH PARK: 35

ATTACK REVELATIONS: 43

SUPREME COUNCIL: 54

A SPACE TRIP: 68

DUELLING: 88

SUMMER DANCE: 102

POWER OF THOUGHT: 118

KIDNAP: 133

COMBAT TO DEATH: 145

HOLIDAY END: 158

EARTH COUNCIL: 167

BACK TO NORMALITY: 175

THE DIGNITARIES: 189

RELATIONSHIP: 198

EARTHEN AWAITS: 213

THE PALACE: 228

THE CHAMPION: 235

FESTIVE FUN: 245

PARTY TROUBLE: 259

DUEL TRAINING: 267

NEW YEAR DUEL: 277

LOSS OF A FRIEND: 284

NIGHTMARES & TRUTH: 292

REALISATION: 301

REUNITED FRIEND: 310

BIRTHDAY IN SPACE: 321

PALACE RETURN: 336

PRINCES' AGREEMENT: 345

A SHOWING OF POWER: 351

THE CHALLENGE: 358

COMBAT PREPARATION: 368

THE DUEL OF DUELS: 389

THE FINAL BATTLE: 399

About The Author   407

Books By This Author   409

THE CRASH:

(CHAPTER 1)

It was an early June evening; unseasonably the rain fell heavily as the Mercedes made its way through the darkness. The time was after eleven. At the wheel was Kain Saul, mid-forties, tall, with dark hair and defined features, the large S500 a sign of his success. Kain moved the car into the outside lane of the dual carriageway, being wary of the conditions with speed kept to a minimum. Kain took a look to his left to see his pretty wife Jenna, early forties, shorter, slim with long black hair. Jenna was daydreaming following the evening's events, dinner with the Prime Minister at Chequers in Buckinghamshire. However many times Jenna met dignitaries, she was still full of wonderment that a poor Irish girl was mixing with such company. Kain could tell whilst looking at her that she was again dreaming of her privileged life.

In the rear seat was the Sauls' son, Sean Saul, a fourteen-year-old boy, tall and slim like his father but with fairer hair and handsome looks. Sean was awake, playing with his new mobile phone. The Mercedes came up behind a smaller car which pulled aside to allow it through. Sean took a look at the young driver thinking one day, not too long, he would also be driving. All of a sudden there was a bright white light followed by a loud noise. Sean felt the car move sideways, spinning a few times before coming to a halt. Sean sat there for a few seconds, hearing another loud bang although the Mercedes did not move. A scream cut through the air as Jenna woke. Sean immediately spoke. "Mum, I'm ok, I'm ok. How are you?"

Jenna replied, "I'm ok too."

Sean then looked at his father, who was bolt upright in the seat, appearing to be frozen. "Dad, Dad, are you ok?" Sean screamed – his father did not react.

Sean cried out to his father again, however his mother replied, "He's ok. Don't worry, he's ok."

Sean waited for a minute to finally see his father move; having asked both Sean and Jenna if they were ok, Kain said he would need to see what had happened. Kain got out of the car; Sean watched as his father walked around the car to a large shape some twenty metres to the side of them. Sean could make out through the rain and darkness that it was a lorry of some sort. Kain first went to the lorry, opening the door, putting his head inside the cab then coming back out of the cab, heading towards another shape adjacent to the lorry. On approaching this second shape Sean could see his father's actions become more frantic. The more Sean looked he could tell the second shape was a car, probably the one that they had only just overtaken. Sean's heart sank as he heard a loud shriek. "John, John? What has happened to him?" This appeared to go on and on, with his father now appearing to free the person shrieking inside the smashed small car.

Breaking the shrieks was the noise of a siren, blue lights adding some colour to the darkness. Within a minute, Sean's door opened to the familiar face of PC Millan. "Sean, are you ok?"

"Yes," was the reply.

"Jenna, how about you?" asked PC Millan.

"I'm ok too. Please help Kain," begged Jenna.

PC Millan closed Sean's door then went over to the dark shape of Kain. Sean could make out both images scurrying around the car for a few minutes when all of a sudden there were three shapes, the third still screaming for John. As the shapes moved closer Sean shifted across the seat as the door opened and his father pushed a teenage girl onto the seat where Sean had just been.

Kain addressed his wife. "Jenna, watch her. She's ok and best out of the rain. An ambulance is coming." Sean jumped in his seat as the girl cried again then quietened as Kain said something to her whilst holding her head; the girl sat still. Kain and PC Millan both went back to the car and lorry.

Within five minutes an ambulance had arrived, the girl had been transferred to it and taken off to the hospital at Aville some fifteen minutes away and close to where the Sauls lived. Another face had joined the scene, Detective Inspector Cott, also known to Sean as a good friend of the family. Cott put his head through Jenna's now open window. "You two better get into my car, I'll take you to the hospital for a check-up."

Kain from behind Cott interrupted, "No, we are ok. Look, the car's not damaged. We will go home."

Cott replied, "I'm sorry, sir, but it is best."

Before Kain could reply, Jenna had interrupted in agreement with Cott; all three were in his unmarked police car heading to the hospital.

Aville A&E was not busy, the Sauls were seen quickly and Nurse Sal Doogan was on hand to give them the all-ok. Sal was a very good friend of the Sauls therefore her reassurance was enough for Kain to demand his family be taken home. Sean thought his father was being too directive towards Detective Inspector Cott, but noted Cott obliged with no further complaint. Sean approached the A&E exit and could not help but notice the same teenage girl who had been involved in the accident sitting crying, with what Sean assumed was her parents beside her.

As they reached Cott's car, Sean noticed a car screeching to a halt at the entrance. An older couple jumped out, running in – the lady was crying. Sean got into the back of the police car, his mother beside him, Kain in the front.

"We will see you tomorrow, Sal," Jenna said as Sal closed

Sean's door. Turning to Sean Jenna said, "I'm sorry but the young boy in the car has died, the girl was his girlfriend." Saying no more, Jenna cuddled Sean as reassurance. The car pulled off for the short journey home, the rain finally stopping.

Having arrived at the Sauls' home, a large five-bedroom house with double garage, en suites, and Jacuzzi garden room, the house being situated in an affluent small estate on the outskirts of Aville, Sean was put to bed by Jenna after providing him with his special medicine – TDL. Sean suffered from headaches and minor hypertension for which this special drink, a mixture of medicine and apple juice, was regular for Sean to take hot or cold at least three times a day. The hot drink and some further reassurances put Sean to sleep; whilst nodding off he could hear the voices of his father and Cott speaking downstairs.

Sean woke to a lovely sunny morning, a complete contrast to the weather of the night before. Hearing voices downstairs, he put on his clothes and rushed down.

"Hi Sean," was followed by a big hug from the slightly plump bosom of Nurse Sal.

"Hi Sal," Sean replied as she led him to the kitchen table. Similar greetings came from his father and mother. Sean sat down to his favourite full English breakfast with a touch of Irish black sausage on the side. Conversation was light, more around if Kain was going to work and organising a replacement car. This was Sean's chance to pull the conversation back to last night.

"I thought the car was not damaged," Sean asked.

"Not seriously, two of the tyres came off the rims in the spin and some minor bodywork damage at the back where it stopped on the central barrier," replied Kain.

"They make them Mercs strong," interjected Cott, who had now entered the kitchen. "Can I join you for breakfast?"

"Of course," was the reply from Jenna.

"So what happened?" Sean pushed.

Cott replied, "The lorry came down a slip road onto the dual carriageway too fast. Your father managed to swerve past it but spun. Unfortunately, the following Clio was not as lucky, hitting the lorry."

Sean saw Cott turn as if to check what he said with Kain.

"So it did not hit us, but what about the bright light? I swear it was close and I heard a bang!" Sean wanted more.

Sal replied before Cott could. "Sean, what Cott has said is correct. Things always seem different as they happen." This was followed with a big smile and an arm around Sean's shoulder. Sean accepted this but something inside said that even Sal was not being fully truthful. Sean could think no more as he was knocked sideways and a wet tongue was suddenly sweeping his face.

Sean laughed. "Down, Shadow. Down." Shadow was Sean's black and tan Alsatian, and Jenna had obviously just let him in from the garden. Shadow was happy to see Sean; he had stayed next door at the Jameses' last night as the Sauls had been out all day. Sean asked to leave the table; permission given, he was out in the garden playing ball with Shadow. Yesterday's worries were gone for a while.

The rest of the day went fast; Sal had spent most of the day with Sean and Shadow, both taking him for a long walk in the fields behind their house. PC Millan and next-door neighbour Enid James had both popped in to see how they all were. Kain had not gone to work but had arranged a replacement 7 Series BMW. Jenna had decided to make them all a nice meal that evening. Detective Inspector Cott had gone back to the crash scene, hospital, and station to find out more.

Dinner started, Sal, Jenna, Kain, and now Cott all sitting at the table. Shadow had dutifully done as Kain had ordered, resting quietly in his bed in the corner of the room. Sean was still amazed at how Shadow would do as his father said, whilst not always following his or his mother's orders.

After dinner, Sal had suggested to play Monopoly. Kain won as usual; his competitive streak always shone through even with Jenna's occasional, "Calm down," plea.

Sal put Sean to bed, with Shadow sleeping at the end of the bed as usual. This time Sean did not go to sleep straight away, his attention was drawn to his father's and Detective Inspector Cott's slightly raised voices downstairs in Kain's home office. Sean decided to go down and listen. Quietly moving down the stairs, the rest of the house was in darkness although the TV was on in the sitting room – Jenna was watching, Sal appeared to have left. Sean sat at the office door and listened.

Cott's voice: "The lorry driver was ok but definitely not with it."

"Drugs or drink?" Kain's voice was now in the conversation.

"No, something different. He really had no idea of what he was doing or what had happened. Sal will try a more subtle approach with him tomorrow."

"You think that he may have been put up to it? After me?"

"It's possible, it feels strange."

"Then let me deal with him!" Kain ordered.

"Sal will do for now, sir. Leave it for now please." Cott added, "Is Algier aware? Is he coming?"

Sean could not stop himself making a quiet but definite whoosh with his arm and cheering, *Yes*, in his head. Uncle Algier was his favourite person next to his parents, Sal, and best friends Emma and Mush. The office door flew open and Kain looked down at Sean. "What are you doing up!" Kain shouted at Sean, who could not answer.

Before Kain could say anything further the sitting room door had opened and Jenna had entered the hallway. "Kain, leave him. Sean, bed now," was the order as Sean was marched up the stairs by his mother. Sean could not hear his father but could feel his anger as though it was boring through the back of his head.

Sean now lying down, knew what was coming. "What did you overhear?" Jenna asked.

"Nothing," replied Sean.

His mother looked at him, smiled and said, "I'll accept that now, once you go to sleep, but liars will be caught out." Sean thought about replying but was interrupted by a loud snore from Shadow; both he and Jenna laughed. Sean went to sleep.

The next morning was a little tense; Kain, who could be as loving as he could be moody, was giving Sean the moody look. Jenna was keeping things in line, indeed to break the atmosphere she suggested a trip to the local woods and cafe for lunch and Shadow's favourite walk. All agreed.

As they walked Sean was generally ahead of his parents throwing sticks for Shadow to retrieve, when Shadow wanted. Sean looked back at his parents; they were walking hand in hand, and Sean knew they loved each other very much. Following the walk, a nice tea and sandwich in the cafe was had, Shadow spoilt with not one but two cold sausages. They then went back to Jenna's Land Rover Discovery, considered the family car because of the seven seats and general loading capacity plus dog space. As they sat down in the car Sean could not resist. "Is Uncle Algier visiting?" he asked.

Kain, now fully relaxed, replied, "Yes, he will be here Monday."

"I'm at school Monday, the half-term holiday is over," Sean exclaimed.

"You will see him after school. He will stay a few days, I'm sure," Jenna stated. "He has heard about the accident and wishes to see us." Sean sat back with a smile on his face. Uncle Algier was eccentric but great fun and good company; he lived somewhere remote in Canada and had been an explorer of some sort in the past so had many stories.

The rest of the day went well, no more atmosphere. PC Millan and Nurse Sal had popped over for dinner. Sean could not help but think that they had a thing for each other, although both denied it. Sunday was just as easy, the events of the past few days were not discussed any further, and Sean now had two more important things to think about – Uncle Algier, and his best friends Emma and Mush, both his age and in his year.

BACK TO SCHOOL:
(CHAPTER 2)

Monday morning was bright and clear. Sean had said good-bye to his parents and was walking the short distance to the pathway that led through the fields at the back of his house. Past his football club's pitch to the estate that Emma and Mush lived, a few minutes from Aville School which they all attended. At Sean's side was Shadow. Ever since Sean had gone to secondary school Shadow walked him through the fields, past the pitches to the estate edge where Sean would meet Emma and Mush. Shadow would then leave him and return home on his own. This was amazing to Sean but Kain had taught him following an initial three months of joining them in the journey. Shadow also met Sean at quarter past three on the dot in the same place whether Jenna was home or not, unless he was locked in if Sean was to be late or picked up.

As Sean approached the estate's edge he saw the figure of a young girl – petite, blonde mid-length hair, dark brown eyes and a smile to die for. "Hi Sean. Hi Shadow," came the cry from Emma as she ran towards Sean, stopping a metre or so apart. "How are you? We heard about the accident, Mum spoke to your mum. We were going to visit but your mum said it would be best to leave it for now..." Emma seemed to go on but Sean did not care; just looking at her made him feel happy. Somehow he felt jealous of Shadow, who in the middle of Emma's talking was getting a cuddle. Sean thought it a strange feeling.

"You got any injuries to brag about?" screamed Mush, a tall, large, black kid who could not be missed even though he was some metres away.

"No, sorry, no injuries," Sean replied, "but it was some crash." The boys were now both closer. "We were flying along, thunderstorms..."

Emma interrupted Sean.

"Sean, I'm sure that's not true. Your dad would not speed or put your lives at risk. Besides, a boy died so it's not something to brag about!"

Sean stopped, apologised, then said goodbye to Shadow before moving on with Mush and Emma.

"She's a nosey old bat," Mush remarked, pointing to the old lady at number 71 of the same street he lived on. This was normal, every morning the old lady would watch them from her downstairs window, never changing her expression and never once meeting or speaking to them. Mush made a rude hand gesture although not in sight of the old lady. Emma reprimanded him on her behalf. The walk took a further five minutes and they were at the school gates. Sean looked around – a lot of friends waving or shouting Hi, some not so friendly, ignoring them.

"Trekkie, what you up to!" Mush's voice boomed out to a smaller, thin-looking boy. The boy, although in the black and grey uniform of the school, had a Star Trek badge in place of the school badge on his blazer.

"Nothing Mush," was the reply.

Emma went into motherly mode. "Leave him alone, Mush. How was your holiday Jack?"

Trekkie had to think before answering, no one usually called him by his real name. "Nothing much, I did watch all the original Star Trek episodes one weekend and..." He stopped in his tracks.

"What?" Emma asked.

"Nothing," Trekkie replied.

"Go on," pushed Emma.

"I saw a UFO again, this morning on the way to school…"

"That's it, I'm going to mush you." Mush was now grabbing Trekkie round the throat before drilling his fist into Trekkie's head. Although quite playful and not meant maliciously, it did hurt, hence Mush's nickname. "Ouch!" was Mush's next word as he felt Emma's foot hit his backside. Mush let go of Trekkie and turned to Emma, her scowl was enough to make him think, plus Sean had stood by her side with a menacing look on his face.

Mush chose the surrender approach. "I was only having a laugh."

Before any of the others could respond, Deputy Head Professor Smith was approaching with a clear, "Off to your classes. Eugene, stop that now or you will be the first to receive a detention this term." Mush went red; he did not like his real name but worse was to follow.

"Eugene, Eugene, do as you're told, you lump!" Frazier Hamling and gang were next to them. Mush turned and walked up to Frazier face to face. Mush was big but Frazier was as tall if not as broad, more muscle than the slight flab on Mush.

"Boys, stop." Professor Smith was now on top of them both. No more was said as both groups split up, Mush and Sean giving the Frazier gang a menacing look until they were out of sight.

The rest of the morning passed, stories of holidays filled the air, Sean and co. managing to miss the Frazier gang apart from some distant jeering. The trip home was less interesting but quicker as Sean ran the pitch and field part with Shadow, knowing who would be home when he got there.

As Sean ran up the driveway he could see his uncle's old American Mustang in the drive. Uncle Algier left it at Kain's work when in Canada, driving it when in the UK. Before Sean got to the door Uncle Algier had opened it, his tall frame with opened arms for Sean to jump into, Shadow hot on his heels for a hug too.

"Uncle Algier, it's great to see you!" Sean cried.

"It's only been a few months, Sean, but give me another hug," Algier said through a large smile that cut across his chiselled but wrinkled face. Algier was older than Kain by some years.

Once released, Sean looked at his Uncle, whose glasses were sitting on top of his head, the red blazer not matching the yellow trousers and the green scarf even though it was fairly warm. "I like your style," Sean said with a laugh.

"I'll take you shopping then, maybe take that nice young girl Emma." Algier winked.

"Oh good," said Sean, trying to sound convincing. A call for dinner was heard which meant a quick change and clean up for Sean before joining Kain, Jenna, and Algier for dinner.

Conversation around the table was fun, Algier getting his words in a mess as usual, dropping the salt at one point, which was also as common. There was no mention of the crash, which Sean knew would come up at some point.

Having finished dinner, Algier was given a choice to sit with Kain and Jenna or spend time with Sean and Shadow on his PlayStation. No choice – Algier chose time with Sean, much to Kain's annoyance. The evening was a great laugh, Algier managing to get the lowest points on one game that Sean had ever seen. Algier's dexterity skills with the controller at times were worse than Shadow, who occasionally grabbed the controller, moving things on screen with his teeth on the buttons. Time flew by; the fun stopped when Jenna informed them that it was bedtime. Even asleep, Algier made Sean laugh with the snoring coming from the spare room and the not unusual thud as he obviously fell out of bed.

The next few days followed the same pattern – Uncle Algier went to work with Kain, and Jenna was busy in the house and organising both charity events and all the family's private lives. School was fun, back with friends, especially Emma and Mush. The evenings were spent with Algier, Kain, and Jenna playing games or talking, making up stories. The week of the crash was forgotten.

Friday started as usual, Shadow walking Sean to school, the old lady at 71 watching them, Mush and Frazier nearly coming to blows, the only difference being the Friday assembly. Headmaster Professor Holmes stood on the stage to address the pupils and staff gathered. Following the normal welcomes, rule clarifications, came the announcement.

"As you are aware Mr Brune was taken ill over the holidays and unfortunately he will not be here for a few weeks at least. We have a stand-in for Mr Brune's English, Mr Gill." Professor Holmes gestured to his left.

The whole hall took a gasp as a tall, thin, ragged-faced man took to the stage. His suit looked as though it did not fit, his long dark hair and beard was unkempt. However, he smiled with perfect white teeth before saying, "Good morning children, I am Mr Gill and I look forward to sharing the interesting beauty of English with you all. Please excuse my looks, I'm no Brad Pitt, however it is my mind, the knowledge and the inspiration that I can give you that counts."

All of the girls let out an "Ahh," Emma receiving a nudge from Sean in the middle of her "Ahh."

Professor Holmes ended the assembly. Mr Gill started to mingle with the pupils as they exited the hall; most were laughing having spoken to him.

"Miss Cooper, I hear that you are quite the actress?"

Gill was talking to Emma who replied, "Yes sir, I have been in all the school Christmas plays and the summer shows."

"Singing and dancing I hear?"

"Yes, do you do either?"

"Oh no, I sing like a frog and dance like Bambi on ice, but I do appreciate people who can."

"Thank you, sir. As there is no summer show this year because of the dance, if you are still here at Christmas maybe we could work together."

Sean felt that this was an odd conversation. Why was Gill specifically talking to Emma? Why was she so at ease with him?

"Ah, Master Saul, how are you?" Gill was now looking at Sean, his deep brown eyes focussed on Sean's. Before Sean could answer he felt uncomfortable, pressure in his head. This normally meant that he needed his medicine but sometimes it was just a strange feeling, often followed by voices in his head.

The voice he did hear was that of Nurse Sal. "Mr Gill, I will show you to your classroom." Gill responded, winked at Sean then walked off with Sal. Sal worked at the school as the nurse; her hospital job was voluntary and normally only evenings.

"She was a bit ignorant, I was enjoying that," Emma stated.

"No she wasn't, we are late for class. Let's move," Sean said in Sal's defence.

The rest of the day passed with the main talk being of football. Mush and Sean were in the same Sunday team, Aville FC, with Sunday the last game of the season. The season had ended a month or so ago, however, the team that had won the league – their team, Aville FC – played the cup-winning team, SM FC, in a one-off cup match where the varied contributions on the day were given to the hospital. This was something that Kain had set up some three years ago. Sean knew that whatever they made on the day through raffles and burgers, Kain would double the donation.

Saturday evening was strange. The Sauls and Algier popped next door to the Jameses' for dinner. Apart from Enid there was Ged, the father, and Jolie, the daughter. Jolie was also in

Sean's year but generally kept in with the IN girls. Jolie took after her parents when it came to material things; her father earned good money in IT. Their house was similar to the Sauls', albeit slightly smaller – four bedrooms, single garage, an Audi TT, an Audi Q7 in the drive, plus a vintage MG roadster in the garage were obvious signs. The house was perfect with nothing out of place. Although the Jameses' would look after Shadow, he was not left in the house but left in the garden. Enid and Jolie both dressed in designer clothes, usually bright colours, full makeup and hair never out of place. On many occasions Sean offered to walk Jolie to school but was declined; she had to turn up in the Audi sports car as well as be picked up in it.

Enid did not appear her bubbly self and Ged was not as attentive, at one point nearly arguing with Algier over nothing. Jolie was as per normal, 'flirting' with Sean and Algier, for attention. Worst news appeared to be the Jameses' claim of a new life trainer, their third in as many years, something the Sauls paid lip service to but did not take heed of. The evening ended and they walked the short distance home. As they reached their door Detective Inspector Cott pulled up, looking very agitated, Sal pulling up just behind him. All went into the house. Sean could sense that there were conversations to be had but he was not to be part of it. Sure enough, as he went to bed he could hear the adults' voices but could not make out the words. Shadow unusually slept at the foot of the bedroom's closed door rather than at the end of the bed.

Sean was up early; football kit already on, eleven o'clock kick-off could not come quick enough. Algier was full of joy; he did not understand the rules of the game but happily cheered at a goal, sometimes even if it went in at the wrong end!

As it was a home match the Sauls walked to the pitch, meeting Mush, Emma, and their parents at the side of the pitch. As the boys headed towards the changing room, Emma appeared with her father. She shouted, "Good luck!" before they went into the dressing room, she and her father taking their place by the side of the pitch.

Coach Lake rallied his troops before sending them out to battle. A one-nil lead at half-time and Mush saving a penalty was a good start. Algier was virtually singing with joy, mixing up most known football anthems with each other to everyone's laughter. Half-time in the dressing was high spirited, with Coach Lake suggesting that Aville were going to win by three at least; Sean, however, was not as sure, as he felt his head starting to pressure again. Looking to his bag for his medicine, he was disturbed that not only had he forgotten some, in his rush this morning he had not taken any earlier either. Regardless, he took to the field trying to ignore the strange feeling in his head, the voices starting to cloud his thoughts.

Ten minutes in, Mush cleared the ball from his area; Sean received it in midfield. With a flick of the ball to his right Sean was off and running past the first defender. Sean glided past the next defender, in no time he was on his own at the opposition's penalty box; taking aim, he blasted the ball past the goalkeeper for Aville's second. Turning, he waited for his teammates to congratulate him, but they were all further down the pitch than he had thought. Lofty, their short striker, finally reached Sean, giving him a high five before shouting, "Blimey, I never knew you could run that fast!" By then most of the team were congratulating him. Sean trotted back to the halfway line with a big grin on his face; he had scored before but goals were relatively rare for him as a midfielder. Sean waited for the restart but with the joy fading the voices got louder; only the whistle was louder as the game restarted.

Two minutes later and the ball went out for a throw in. Sean turned to see Coach Lake calling him off to be substituted. Sean could not believe it. "Why?" he protested as he walked off past Coach Lake, who did not answer him. Jenna ran up to Sean, put her arm around him, congratulating him, but insisted on him taking a drink of his medicine. Sean took the drink, sat down and looked around. Coach Lake did not look at him, all the parents looked perplexed and Kain had walked over to the other side of the pitch to be on his own. Jenna was talking to each of the other mothers in turn. Sean was confused.

Emma sat down beside him. "After you scored your dad told Lake to pull you off."

"Why?"

"Something to do with your illness, you could have went crazy or something. Coach Lake was not impressed but your dad can be very authoritative so Lake did as he said. Everyone else thinks your dad is mad, you were playing a blinder."

With this Sean got up and walked straight to the dressing room. Sitting alone for a few minutes, the door opened his father standing there.

"I am sorry, Sean, but you have not taken your medicine and you would become hyperactive, possibly injuring you or someone else," Kain said in a low voice.

"Rubbish," replied Sean with a sniffle. "I was playing a blinder, it was an awesome goal and you ruined it!"

"Sean, there is no need for that. I do not expect you to understand but what I did was right for your safety. Enjoy the goal but you have to accept it, I'm sorry."

"No, I don't have to accept it!"

Kain's voice changed. "I have said sorry, I will not say it again. We now must go." Sean wanted to reply but Kain's face and staring eyes appeared to tear into him; he could not speak.

"I'll deal with him." Sal was now present.

"No, I will deal with him," said Kain.

"It may be best to let Sal take Sean home," Algier spoke.

Kain looked at Algier. For a split-second Sean thought that he was going to argue with Algier; instead he said nothing but walked away. Sal took Sean to her car and drove him and Algier to McDonalds, a sure-fire way of keeping them away from the rest of the match and Kain for a while. The lunch was a happy affair, Algier purposely picking the kids' meal to play with the toy to Sean and Sal's amusement.

On the short drive home Sean felt a bit apprehensive wondering how to deal with his father. As they reached the door Jenna came out, giving Sean a hug. She informed them that Kain was at work for the evening and that she wanted time with Sean on her own. Algier took the direct hint and immediately invited himself over to Sal's for the evening, with a clear reference to inviting PC Millan.

A few hours passed. Sean and Jenna were on the couch watching a DVD with Shadow at their feet. Sean thought this was the moment.

"Mum, Dad was a bit over the top today, don't you think?"

"Sean, you know your father he can be very moody. Today was not his best day but he was looking out for you."

"But I felt fine and boy was I quick, it was a great goal."

"Yes, it was the winner in the end so the Charity Cup is Aville's again."

"Shit, I missed the celebration. That makes me angrier." Sean sat up.

"Language. Your father missed the trophy presentation too, I had to do it!" Jenna added indignantly. Both chuckled.

"Was Dad right? Could I really have hurt myself or could he not just give me my medicine on the pitch?" Sean asked.

"No, it takes some time to kick in therefore you would have gone hyper and yes, possibly hurt you or someone else. Your father was right, although he may have handled it better."

"Will I ever get over this, not need the medicine?"

"Yes, age seems to help. It is hereditary, your father lost it around sixteen."

Sean thought, *Of course.* He had been told many times before about his father having the same condition. "Only two years to go then," he laughed. "How long is Uncle Algier here for?" Sean changed the subject.

"A couple of weeks, or less if he doesn't stop giving you fast food." Jenna smiled.

"Sal was with us and she ate it and she's a nurse, so it can't be all that bad."

Jenna generally kept to good, wholesome foods but as with the occasional fry up or BBQ, a visit to a fast food outlet was not the end of the world. Shadow had now climbed onto the couch at Sean's feet; his wishful look outdid his mother's mock angered look to allow the three of them to cuddle and watch the remainder of the film.

STRANGE TEACHER:
(CHAPTER 3)

Morning came and Sean saw his father in the kitchen at breakfast.

"Morning Dad, I'm sorry for yesterday." Sean was feeling the ice.

"Morning, no problem. I'm sorry too," Kain replied.

"My, apologies from you, Kain, you must be embarrassed," Algier, piped up, his smile wiped from his face as Kain glared at him.

"I've booked bowling for tomorrow night, Sean. You, me, and Algier. Is that ok?" asked Kain.

"Great, that will be fun. Uncle Al, will you drop the ball on your foot like last time?" All laughed, Algier was holding his foot under pretence of pain.

Sean went to school; the story of his amazing goal was second only to the climbing popularity of Mr Gill, and all the students were talking about his classes, especially the girls. Sean could not understand this as every time he passed Gill he felt uneasy. Emma was starting to come under Gill's spell, much to Sean's discomfort. Thursday's first lesson with him would be interesting.

Prior to Thursday the only highlight was the bowling with Kain and Algier, as Sean thought it was a laugh. Algier was his usual self, dropping balls, bowling into the wrong lane, however, Sean and Kain had not laughed so much for some time.

The only bad news was that Algier was going to France for a few days on Wednesday, but was returning at some point over the weekend. Kain was going with him. This was not unusual as although Sean could not work out what Algier did, he knew that he helped his father in some way as an advisor. Kain travelled frequently in his job as technical advisor to the government.

Thursday came and lunch time was upon them; Gill's lesson was next. Sean and the gang were at their usual table outside the dinner room at the edge of the playing field, messing around, seeing who could take bits of each other's lunch before Mush went in too hard on Sean – both went crashing to the floor in hysterics.

"So why do they all like Gill?" Sean fired a question at Emma as he got up.

"He appears to be charming, very versed in his subject and has an uncanny way of remembering people, especially somehow knowing things about them that makes it personal," Emma replied.

"Sounds strange. What kind of things?" asked Sean.

"Oh, he said to Zandra to think of a poem, and then recite it to the class but with her favourite actor Robert Pattinson in mind. She apparently spoke beautifully, even the boys had a tear."

"Oh, that's easy." Mush was now joining. "It doesn't take much to know that most teenage girls are in love with Twilight man."

"I know, but he still seems to bring such things into the classroom," said Emma.

The conversation ended as Mush was now trying to vampire bite Trekkie. Walking to class, Sal approached them.

"Sean, your mother forgot that you have a hospital check-up appointment this afternoon therefore I will take you now. Come along."

"I... umm, have I? I mean, how did we forget? I have lessons," Sean stuttered.

"Regardless, we need to go," Sal insisted.

Sean felt strange. Although he disliked Gill he did want to see a lesson; this would put a stop to it, however. His health would be more important so he dutifully spent the afternoon with Sal at the hospital.

Friday's walk to school was full of Gill's lesson. In Emma's words Mr Gill was as good as the playground tittle tattle had suggested; Mush was on the fence but had certainly warmed to Gill. Sean was confused; he did not like Gill but surely all his friends could not be wrong. Lunchtime came and the friends were gathered in their normal place. Gill was still the hot gossip, indeed Sean felt that Gill knew he was being talked about as he could feel his eyes in the back of his head from the other side of the playground in which he was patrolling. Sean noticed Frazier was talking with Gill for some time.

"So, you are shopping with us Saturday, Sean?" Emma had woken Sean from his thoughts.

"Are we?" Sean replied.

"Yes – you, me, and our mums are going to Milton Keynes shopping. I'm buying my summer dance dress, you're getting a suit."

"Oh, yeah I remember. Great, it will be fun," Sean said unconvincingly to Emma.

"Oh Mush, you putting on weight!" came the cry. Sean turned to see Frazier and his cronies walking towards them.

"Yeah, the more I weigh the harder I hit," Mush responded, turning to face Frazier.

"Feeling tough today, Eugenie?" Frazier squeaked, much to his gang's laughter.

Mush moved towards Frazier; two of his cronies stopped him by standing between them.

"I'm going to kick your arse like I did in first year." Mush was starting to lose his cool. Mush had indeed fought with Frazier in the first year, clearly coming out triumphant, however, Frazier had grown since then and certainly was the fitter of the two – kickboxing saw to that.

"That was some time ago, fatty. I'd like to see you try now," Frazier taunted from behind his cronies.

"Leave it out, Frazier. Stop being an arse." Sean was now at Mush's side.

"Oh look, it's prep boy come to help his mate." Frazier and his gang laughed.

"That's not very nice, Frazier." Emma had joined the argument and had pushed in behind the two cronies to be right in front of Frazier.

"Well if it's not threesome Cooper. Don't you know which one you like? Or is it both?" Frazier was on form.

It seemed a split second, then something happened that no one expected. Emma raised her hand and slapped Frazier right across the face – time appeared to stand still. Frazier lifted his hand, at which point Sean struck.

Sean came to his feet. Frazier and his two guards were flat out in front of him. Sean turned to see Emma looking astonished some ten metres from where he was.

"Boys!" broke the air.

Everyone froze. Sal was amongst them.

"What is going on?" she demanded.

Mush thought first. "Rugby practice, miss. Just messing around."

"I am not blind. You two go to my room." Mush and Emma knew she meant them so they moved off. By now all the cronies and Frazier were on their feet; the rest of the pupils were gathering around. "There is nothing to see, please all move away," Sal barked, but no one listened. "Frazier and Sean, follow me."

Both looked at each other but obeyed and followed Sal around the corner into an open hallway. Once inside Sal started. "I'm not interested in what went wrong, but it ends now with both of you claiming that you were indeed practicing rugby, is that clear?"

"What? That idiot hit my mates and me," Frazier protested.

"Really? So you, a kick boxing black belt, and two friends, were sorted by two boys and a girl. That will help your reputation no end, Master Hamling."

"You can't say that, miss," Frazier protested.

"Well I just have. You know, bullies like you sometimes need a bit of their own medicine, so take it and shut up." Sal was going for it.

"You're not a teacher, you're just a nurse. I'm going to Professor Holmes." Frazier went to move but suddenly froze as Sal gave him a look, then moved up close and clearly said in his ear, "You will do nothing of the sort, you were all messing around. Your father is a lovely man, quite the disciplinarian. How would he like it if he finally found out about his son?"

Frazier interrupted. "You wouldn't."

"Try me," was Sal's response.

"Nurse Doogan, what seems to be the problem?" Professor Smith entered the hallway.

"Nothing, Miss Smith. All is resolved, the boys were just moving along."

"I heard that they were fighting," Professor Smith interrogated.

"No, just some horseplay that got out of hand. Wasn't it boys?"

"Yes miss." Sean and Frazier for once agreed. With this, Frazier moved off. Sal walked Sean towards his next class.

"Wow, Sal, you can't talk to pupils like that." Sean broke the ice.

"I can and he deserved it. Sometimes PC has to go out the window, however, violence is not the answer. You could have hurt someone."

"Me? There were more of them, they could have hurt me."

"Of course. Well, you're ok now, but please do not do it again."

"Frazier insulted Emma and Mush."

"I know, Emma should not have smacked him. I don't know what came over the girl but I will have words with her and Mush in a minute. Tell Mr Gnome that they will be a bit late for his lesson." Sal left Sean at the classroom door.

Sean's friends joined the lesson late as expected and it was not until the walk home that they could talk.

"Blimey Emma, that was some smack. Give me five." Mush had no remorse.

Emma ignored the hand gesture. "I should not have done that, thank God it was Sal who saw us otherwise I would have been in trouble. My parents would have killed me."

Then Mush turned to Sean. "What about you? That was some move, all three of them in one hit, they must have moved a hundred metres, like whoosh. That's it – Whoosh Man." Mush laughed.

"Don't exaggerate, Mush. It wasn't a hundred metres but it was quite violent, Sean," Emma pointed out.

"Hey, it was the heat of the moment. I don't know my own strength," replied Sean.

"Look, I'm off to Tom's to play his new PlayStation game but will see you tomorrow evening," Mush was saying as he left Sean and Emma together.

"Tomorrow?" Sean quizzed.

"Yes, we are meeting them in a restaurant on the way back from shopping with their mums for dinner; you have a head like a sieve sometimes." Emma was in teacher mode.

"Oh yeah, I remember," Sean replied just as Shadow appeared by his side. Emma gave Shadow a stroke to welcome him then looked back at Sean. Without flinching, Emma gave Sean a big cuddle, said thanks and walked the short distance to her house. Sean froze for the moment.

Having watched Emma walk home, he gave a start when he saw the old lady at 71 was not only looking out of her window at him, but she smiled. Sean took off, Shadow struggling to keep up with him on the trot home.

Saturday morning and Sean was soon in the car with Jenna, Emma, and Judy, Emma's mum. Judy was younger than Jenna, blonde hair as her daughter but pretty in the same way, no arguments that Emma was her daughter. A few hours into the shopping and Sean was bored; general, electrical, or gadget shops he could stand but not clothes shops – especially women's. In one shop Emma was asked to try on a couple of dresses. To Sean's horror his opinion was asked.

"The black one she just tried on or the red one Emma is now wearing, Sean?" Judy asked.

Sean, now as red as the dress Emma was wearing, looked up. For a moment he stared at Emma, all dressed up. Unfortunately, as Sean had not really taken notice of the previous dress he only had one answer. "The red one," came out.

Emma smiled. "Thank you Sean, I agree." With that she walked back to the changing room, Sean thought that was a close one. Having left the shop, dress purchased, it was Sean's turn; a suit had to be found. Sean did not think things could get worse but they did. Three women suggesting this one, then that one, were stretching his patience. After the fourth shop and tenth jacket he had tried on, Sean finally got the thumbs up from all three.

"Try the whole suit on, Sean, to see if it fits," Jenna advised.

Sean disappeared into the changing room to return fully

suited. The three women all glowed in agreement, this was the suit. Sean looked in a mirror and he actually could agree with them, he did look smart.

"Ok, this is the one. Can I change now?" Sean took his chance to head for the changing room.

Lunch followed, with Sean asking if they were going now. The replies were simple – no, shoes and accessories had to be purchased. By three, Sean had lost the will to live, having gone to the toilet at least twice just to get out of some shops. On return to the women after his second visit they were just about to buy a tie. "That's a bit bright, I'd prefer burgundy rather than a bold red," Sean said as he approached Judy holding the tie.

"Sean, you have to think of the whole look. The tie will work well overall," Jenna threw in.

"Burgundy will go with the silvery/grey suit I just bought and it won't stand out so much," Sean continued.

"Idiot," Emma said as she turned and walked out the shop, Mum dropping the tie and following her.

"What's that about?" Sean quizzed.

"Sean, are you blind? It's the first dance that you and Emma will go to at an age that, well, counts," Jenna explained. Sean thought for moment. Jenna added, "The tie matches Emma's dress."

"Oh shit!" Sean exclaimed, loudly enough for everyone in the shop to hear. "Sorry," he mumbled as he made his way to the shop door. Sean knew his feelings for Emma were changing; the best friend he had known for years but now, finally, with Emma making the move with their parents' help, Sean knew how Emma felt about him.

"Do you wish to hurt Emma's feelings or shall I go back in and buy the tie?" Jenna had followed him. "My advice is to let me buy it," she added.

"Of course, yes please Mum." Sean gave the right answer.

Tie purchased, no more was said, although Sean saw his mother show it to Judy and Emma at one point; both appeared to smile in agreement. Dinner at the restaurant was fun; Emma seemed to be the friend as part of the gang, no strange looks. The mums were also fun, and Mush's mum was nice but a little weird. The meal ended and Jenna drove them home, dropping Judy and Emma first. Emma, saying goodnight to Sean, purposely gave his hand a quick grasp, then disappeared out of the car with a smile. Sean swore that he could see her skipping to her front door.

A few minutes later and they were home; Jenna had already put the shopping away while Sean had made them both a drink and collapsed on the couch with Shadow at his feet. Jenna said nothing but chose a movie channel to end what was a good day, finally, in Sean's eyes.

Sunday saw Sean watching Mush at a small seven-a-side rugby tournament being the highlight of the day; Emma could not make it as she had to visit relatives with her parents but Sean stayed the afternoon at Mush's with Tom playing computer games.

Monday through to Thursday moved on; Emma did not say anything about Saturday but Sean swore she was acting more kind to him, even standing closer at every opportunity. Thursday was to be an interesting day.

Sean entered Gill's class half expecting Sal to take him away, but she did not appear. As they all sat down Gill entered. "What a wonderful day it is outside, certainly makes me feel cheery, how about you all?"

"We are fine, Mr Gill," most of the girls replied.

"Good, we have a love poem on page ten of your books, loosely based on Romeo and Juliet. Spend ten minutes to read it first, then we will discuss." Each pupil obliged, opening their books to read.

"Time's up, what is the poem's main message?" Gill asked.

28

"Some twat gave his life for a girl," Frazier shouted from the back, gaining laughs from all the boys.

"Thank you Master Hamling, I'll ignore your wording but yes, a man has indeed given his life for the one he loves, quite moving." All the girls ahhed, the boys sniggered. "Now think, imagine someone that you love, well, at your age maybe adore. Apart from your life what do you think you could give someone that you had these feelings for? Five minutes. Think, jot down notes." Again, the girls started writing whereas most of the boys looked around.

"Time's up. Miss James, could you share anything with us?"

"Yes sir, I would give the person I loved the biggest car and house that I could find." Everyone sniggered – Jolie had missed the point.

"A bit too materialistic but if that's your way then good. Miss Turner, do you have anything to add?" Gill asked.

"I would give them children," Lisa Turner replied, again to ahhs from the girls, interrupted by a "Come and have my children," from Frazier. All the boys laughed.

"Master Hamling, if you were interested in Miss Turner, which I know you are, then that is not how I would view the best way to show her your feelings." The whole room gasped, Frazier went red. "Miss Turner, I believe that that was a wonderful comment. To have someone's child is indeed a way of showing true love. Miss Cooper, your notes?" Gill had turned on Emma.

"I'm thinking more of a feeling such as warmth, trust, real friendship," Emma stated another group 'ahh' came from the girls.

"Very good, Miss Cooper. Whoever you choose will be a lucky man. Saul, what did you write?"

All eyes looked at Sean. Why had he been picked straight after Emma? Actually, why was he called Saul and not master? Thoughts flew around Sean's head. Then whilst preparing an answer he could see Gill, who was not talking, but could hear his voice in his head. *Let me in*, it appeared to be saying. Again, *Let me in, what do you know?* Sprang into Sean's head. Before he knew, Sean sat there like a trance. At that moment the classroom door opened and in walked Sal; the thoughts in Sean's head cleared and he focussed on Gill now looking at Sal.

"Mr Gill, I wish to have a word with you now," Sal insisted.

"I'm in the middle of a class, Nurse Doogan."

"A word now, outside, Mr Gill," Sal insisted. Gill followed her outside, closing the door behind.

"What the hell is that about?" Mush broke the silence.

"The dragon's being pushy again," Frazier roared out but before Sean could reply the door opened. Gill appeared, looking rather uncomfortable. "Master Saul, you are required to go to the hospital with Nurse Doogan; in future please do not make all your appointments in my class time otherwise you will fail English."

Sean, not fully realising what was going on, stood from his chair and met Sal in the hallway. "I haven't forgotten another appointment, have I?"

"No dear, but we need to get away from here for a while. Come on, let's go." Sal moved off, Sean followed. A short car trip later and Sean found himself at McDonalds again with Sal.

"Mum will kill us if she knew we were here and during school time," Sean declared.

"Don't worry, I'll deal with your mother. How you feeling?"

Sean thought for a moment. "I'm good," he replied, hesitating before continuing, "but my head felt strange back at Gill's class."

"Like, voices in your head? Being precise, his voice?"

"Yes, it was weird. What's happening?"

"Gill is from where your uncle lives, Canada. Although we do not know him we know of his people and they can be troublesome," explained Sal.

"So Gill is here to cause trouble for me?"

"I'm not sure but you need to be careful around him, not let him into your head."

"That's a strange comment. Please explain."

"His people experimented with mind games, mind control, and to some degree it could be working."

"Wow, like ESP or something?"

"Yes, and to a degree it works but it's more of a confidence trick than reality. Think of what and how he was saying things to you prior."

Sean thought, maybe Gill was being clever. He certainly got the girls to say things they would not normally say, out loud at least. "So am I in some kind of danger from Gill?" Sean got to the point.

"No, not danger, but he may still cause trouble; if anything it is your uncle that he is after. It's like clan wars in parts of Canada, therefore Gill could want to get something from your uncle. Oh, your uncle and father are back today. Finish up and we will go and see them."

Sure enough, as they entered Sean's house Kain was waiting.

"Uncle Algier?" Sean asked.

"He stayed in Europe for a few more days," was Kain's reply.

"Dinner, Sal?" came a call from the kitchen.

"Just a little," was Sal's reply, shushing Sean at the same time.

Dinner was finished and Sean decided on an early night as Kain and Sal decided to take Shadow for his last walk of the day. Sean knew that this was when Sal would say something to Kain about Mr Gill.

Nothing was said at breakfast, Kain was preoccupied with his thoughts, but as Sean went to the door to leave for school he said, "I will take you as I need to see Professor Holmes."

Sean saw the look on his mother's face. "Ok Dad," was the reply.

The short car journey was quiet, although Kain relieved the tension by asking Sean if he and the gang wanted to go to his work with him on Saturday. Sean and the gang had been there before and he instantly responded with a yes, and that he would ask them all that day. Kain pulled up outside the school office, said goodbye then walked in. Sean made his way to his first lesson; from the classroom he could see the office entrance and his father's car but obviously did not know what was going on.

Kain entered Professor Holmes' office. Without a greeting he went straight to the point. "Why is Gill here? I want him removed!"

"Good Morning Mr Saul. I'm not happy that you come into my office without an appointment and indeed no manners." Holmes was put out.

"I have no time for this, I am the head of the school governors and you made an appointment without me knowing. That is not how it should happen."

"It was a quick decision, I thought Mr Brune was coming back but he had a relapse and therefore I acted quickly. Mr Gill had great references, you can see his file if you like." Holmes was uneasy but felt he needed to respond to Kain.

"I'm sure he has a great record and perfect references but you did not follow procedure," Kain insisted.

"I had no time, now Mr Saul, regardless of your position both here and in general I am not happy with your behaviour and wish you to leave." Holmes stood tall.

Kain stood to his full height, focussing directly at Professor Holmes. "I wish to see Gill now!" Holmes found himself beeping his secretary to summon Mr Gill. Five minutes passed with no further words spoken, when Gill entered the room.

"Alone!" Kain commanded.

Holmes, white faced, did not answer but left the room. As the door shut Kain turned on Gill, who took a few steps back. Neither said a word for a moment. Kain broke the silence. "What are you doing here?"

"I'm on an information gathering break, no more."

"I don't believe you, I want the truth.".

"It is the tru—"

Gill did not finish as Kain grabbed him by the throat, pain shooting through his head. "Don't fight back. It would be a big mistake." Kain was very aggressive.

"I'm a Vulten protected by a visit passport on their behalf. Hurting me would not be a good idea," choked Gill.

Kain let Gill go, thought, then replied, "As we thought. A Vulten. That would explain many things, including not only the false records but also why my people can't gain the full information about you. So you won't tell me why you are here. Thinking the passport will save you, eh?"

Gill thought. "Vul will protect me as I am one of his. You fight me, you fight him," finishing with a wry smile.

"I understand all the protocols. Grudgingly I respect Vul. However, your closeness to me and my family is outside the protocols so don't be so sure. By the way, you know who I am, therefore follow protocol now in your reply," Kain glared at Gill, whose pain returned.

"Yes sir, I apologise for my manner, however, this is a difficult situation. I have obviously chosen the wrong place for my learnings. I will check with my people and do as they direct."

"If I ask you to leave now, will you?"

Gill drew a breath. "No sir, not until an order comes from Vul."

"You are more stupid than you look. Do you think Vul scares me?"

"No, but you will follow protocol and not harm me until

diplomatic questions have been answered."

"Really? Well, let me make this very clear – I am not happy with you being here, especially around my family. Your dealing with my son yesterday angers me. I will consider whether to take action or not, our diplomats will be in discussion, however, if you so much as go near my family or pull a stunt like that again I will kill you and deal with Vul and the consequence later." Kain threw Gill to the floor, opened the door and walked out.

Sean saw his father come out of the school office, jump in the car and pull away. A few moments later a shocked looking Mr Gill walked out with Professor Holmes by his side. *What could have happened?* Sean thought. The issue was not discussed that night in the Saul household.

RESEARCH PARK:
(CHAPTER 4)

Saturday morning and by ten Mush and Emma were at Sean's door. A visit to Sean's father's workplace was always fun. They all settled into the Discovery; Kain was smiling and obviously in a good mood, Jenna was staying at home. The short journey saw them pull up to the gates, 'Government Research Park' signposted everywhere. 'Authorised Personnel Only' were the other signs. Kain drove through the gates without being confronted, the security guard saluting his boss from inside the box as the barrier was raised. Kain pulled up in his parking space just outside the main office, adjacent to a short airfield which was surrounded by varied hangars and other buildings, including a small tower. Within minutes they were all inside Kain's office; Kain had left to see someone first.

The office was always full of unusual things, Mush had decided to play with a silver tree that was made of small silver ball bearings all stuck together, but they could be moved. "Magic," was all Sean heard so he joined Mush.

"Got to be magnetic somehow." Sean was obviously the more clued up. Emma surprisingly had chosen Kain's chair and was spinning it around with a laugh on her face.

"Young Sean, how are you?" Livia Strom, Kain's secretary, had entered the room with a tray of drinks and biscuits.

"I'm great Liv," Sean replied in tandem with Mush.

Livia was tall, slim, blonde, and tanned with a glamour-model look. Emma, looking at Sean and Mush, said, "Close your mouths, boys. Liv, it's a pleasure to see you again." Sean and Mush closed their mouths.

"Mr Saul will be a few minutes so enjoy these for now. Don't break anything, especially you, Mush. I think they're still clearing up the mess in hangar eight that you made last time."

Mush's pleads of innocence were ignored.

A short while later and Kain walked back in. "I see nothing broken yet." A quick look at Mush created another plea, again ignored. "Let's see... Hangar six will be interesting today – let's go." All three followed Kain to the hangar. Stopping at the hangar door, Kain added, "Ok, as you are aware electric cars and the like are big news at the moment. Well, anything to stop carbon actually. We have been working on something." Kain opened the door.

"Wow!" came a combined cry. As the doors opened, sitting in front of them was a teardrop-shaped car with what looked like solar panels on top and strange not-rubber wheels.

"Trekkie would love this," Mush exclaimed as Kain motioned them to get closer. Close up the vehicle was amazing, not the best looker. Algier's old Mustang parked opposite was definitely better looking but every part of the body was unmarked and smooth. Kain touched the single door as it opened in gull-wing fashion to show space inside for six – two seats in a line of three. Mush jumped in the front next to Kain, Emma sat in the middle with Sean.

"Mush, would you like to drive it?" Kain asked.

Mush shouted, "Yes!" with glee in response.

"Ok, but be careful, it's worth some five million pounds as a prototype." Kain's warning drew a sharp intake of breath from all in the car.

Mush noted the joystick steering panel between him and Kain. "Do I use that?"

"Yes, just like a PC game but be gentle. Forward for forward, left for left, etcetera," Kain said without much worry.

Mush pushed the joystick forward; the car jumped forward, no sound but very jerky.

Kain grabbed the joystick, stopping the car. "I said gently, young man."

"Ok, ok, let me do it again."

Mush took the control; this time the car moved forward. He moved the car out of the hangar shutters onto what was the landing strip. Looking at Kain, he gave it a little more push; the car got faster – no noise, no rush, like a magic carpet. A few hundred metres later and Mush decided to turn, another jolt with all the occupants being saved by their seatbelts from being thrown around the car.

"Slow movements I said," came Kain's cry. "This thing will turn on a sixpence."

Mush took heed. After believing that he had mastered the car, Mush handed over to Emma who drove better than Mush; her softer touch suited the joystick control better. Both had smiles from ear to ear. Then it came to Sean's turn, which fell between Mush and Emma's attempts to control. Finally, Kain guided the car back into the hangar; Sean, although in front, was not trusted. Livia had appeared at the side of the car. "Go with Livia, you two. I need a few minutes with Sean," Kain said.

Once they had left, Sean was sitting there with his father, still both in the driving seats. "It is amazing, isn't it?" Kain said. "Now let me show you something more amazing." He had Sean's full attention. At that point the joystick disappeared inside the console. Sean looked at his father quizzically as he was told to now move the car forward.

"How?" Sean asked.

"Close your eyes, concentrate and think 'forward'," was Kain's reply.

Sean did as he was told; closing his eyes, he thought, *Forward*. The car moved forward.

He could hear his father say, "Try right." Sean thought, *Right*, the car followed.

Kain's next comment was, "Stop." The car stopped.

"Wow," Sean exclaimed. "Thought control?"

"Yes," Kain replied. "Simple commands picked up by electromagnetic wave controls in the car, something we want for fighter pilots in the future."

"Wow," was all Sean could respond again.

Within ten minutes they were back in Kain's office. Mush had done his usual but this time he hasd broken the hanging hook on the signed West Ham United shirt frame that Kain had received that year.

"I'm sorry Mr Saul, I was only trying to read the players' names." Mush did look sorrowful.

"No problem, it can be fixed," was Kain's reply.

Following more drinks and biscuits, it was time to go. Sean thought this was a great day, especially as Kain was in a good mood; he was fun when like this.

Sunday moved on and another week started; Algier was still nowhere to be seen, still travelling was Kain's assessment, probably lost was the wise crack. Sean and the gang could not stop talking about Saturday's visit. Mush purposefully wound Trekkie up about the top-secret car. Trekkie was adamant that he had seen the car on the roads. "Not likely, a five-million-pound motor on the road, no way," was Mush's response.

Emma was getting closer to Sean, moving imaginary fluff from his shirt was enough but occasionally while no one was looking she held his hand. Sean liked this but was not sure of what he was to do in response. Mr Gill was keeping out of their way; at one point Sean rounded a corner and swore that Gill moved in a completely different direction to avoid him. Most notably Gill went sick on the Thursday of Sean's lesson, much to all the girls' disappointment, although thankfully for Sean Emma was coming around to his way of thinking about Gill.

Friday was full of more fun to come; the new Twilight movie was out and Sean and the gang were booked to attend with their mums on Saturday night. Even the boys were allowed to like this movie.

Walking home, Mush dropped out first, his home being a little closer to the school than Emma's. Sean and Emma walked on.

"Mm, thanks, I'll see you tomorrow then." Sean looked at Emma. Emma said nothing but gave Sean a quick peck on the side of his cheek then walked off to her house. Sean froze; a sense of joy came across him, Emma was no longer just a friend and it felt good. Sean skipped along the path merrily, whistling no particular tune, meeting Shadow some steps later. As they walked a little further into the field Shadow stopped and started growling. Sean stopped too. The figure in the distance was coming closer. Some ten metres from Sean, Mr Gill stopped. Shadow took up position in front of Sean between them, not barking but a low continual growl.

"Good afternoon, young Saul. Should that dog be on a lead?" Gill opened the conversation.

"We walk this way every day and no one is around. Besides, he is well behaved and won't hurt you unless of course you want to hurt me."

"Why should I hurt you? I was purely looking at houses in your street I may wish to purchase, so close to the school."

Sean did not normally gloat but his dislike for Gill was strong. "You couldn't afford a place near us so don't bother."

With this, Gill took a few steps forward. Shadow covered the distance swiftly and was now within a metre of Gill, barking. Gill took a step or two back. "Control your dog!" he called.

"Sean, are you ok?" Jenna's voice came from behind Gill – she was running towards them.

Gill, turning, said, "Everything is fine, I'm just having a walk, looking at houses."

Jenna was next to Gill, Shadow stood by her side. "I don't care what you are doing but you need to go now, Shadow has not eaten yet and I'm sure you would fill the gap." Sean was surprised by his mother's comment.

Gill looked at Jenna. "I am not afraid of the dog. Besides, you could not stop me if you tried and he, I can deal with." This was Gill's mistake because as he spoke he had pointed to Shadow, who obviously saw this as aggression so took a leap at Gill, Jenna just catching his collar to stop him making contact. Contrary to his comments, Gill was scared and had moved back further.

"Go, because next time I won't stop him." Jenna had anger in her eyes.

Gill appeared to take a second look behind Sean's shoulder before replying, "Ok but I am going that way." With that, he walked towards Sean. As he passed Sean he gave him a wink, whispering, "Soon you'll know all about it and you won't like it."

Sean turned and watched Gill continue down the path; the figure of the old lady of number 71 was clear to be seen at the other end of the path. Sean walked to his mother then he, she, and Shadow walked home. As they approached their drive a police car pulled up. PC Millan jumped out. "Everything ok?"

"Yes," Jenna replied. "Tea?"

"Of course."

Some minutes later Sean was sitting with Jenna and PC Millan in the kitchen.

"So how did you know there were problems?" Sean again went straight to the point.

PC Millan looked up at Jenna before answering. "Your dad asked me to keep an eye on things, none of us like Mr Gill."

"This is something to do with the clans, Sal told me," said Sean.

"Sal can be a big mouth sometimes."

Sean was shocked. "I thought you liked her?"

Millan went red. "I do but that does not stop her being a big mouth."

"So what does it mean?" Sean was now getting annoyed, there was obviously something going on and no one was telling him.

"Sean, Sal is right. Gill is from another clan, a clan that does not like your uncle's clan. Kain is part of your uncle's clan. Kain has some unfinished business and we fear that Gill is here to bring it all back," Jenna explained poorly.

"Dad lived in Canada? When?"

"I think your father is best to explain." Millan stopped as Kain entered the room.

"Is everyone ok?" Kain asked.

"Yes," was the reply. "Shadow did an excellent job as trained," remarked Jenna.

Kain went up to Shadow and gave him a playful cuddle. "Treats for you tonight." Jenna was already at the cupboard to deliver Shadow a couple of his favourite treats.

"We owe you some explanations, Sean."

Kain was now sitting next to Sean who thought, *About time.*

"Let's eat, then we will talk afterwards," Kain concluded.

Dinner was eaten and Millan left. Jenna popped out to see the Jameses, who she had noted were still acting strangely during the day. Sean sat next to Kain on the couch.

Kain started. "Sal is right. Our clans, if that's the word, have a long, hard history. In early times each would murder each other just for being in the wrong family, obviously now that is not the case. When I left home my decision was not popular and many saw my decision as wrong. The Vultens, so-called because of their family head being Vul, saw this as a weakness and chose to cause further trouble. Frequently in the early years I returned to control the troubles; there is now a peace but one of their clan being in my town is not welcome. Algier and I have been talking to them over the past few weeks, getting nowhere, but Gill's presence is unacceptable."

"So are you are from Canada? Is Algier a clan leader?" Sean was intrigued.

Kain smirked before answering. "Yes, that is a way of looking at it. Certainly I am the blood relative of the predecessors that make up the clans, our family being the head."

Sean thought hard. "Uncle Dain, your brother that you rarely speak about, is he still back in Canada maybe leading the clan?"

Kain again laughed. "Kind of. Look, this I'm sure all sounds crazy, feuds, clans and all, but I promise you I will tell you all on Sunday when Algier is back. You can enjoy tomorrow with your friends because Sunday will be enlightening."

Kain ignored Sean's protests to know then; he would not be pushed.

ATTACK REVELATIONS:
(CHAPTER 5)

Saturday morning and afternoon were slow; Sean could not help but think of what he was to learn. The evening was better, his mind distracted by a good film and Emma sitting next to him. Sean even had the courage to give her a quick peck on the cheek at one point during the film. A surprise was Jolie joining them, invited by Emma's mum who was also friends with Sean's neighbours. Jenna driving, Mush, Emma, and their mums were dropped off first. Jolie was to be next as she lived next door to Sean.

As Jenna guided the car out of town onto the short B road that led to the Saul house, two police cars flew past on the wrong side of the road. "Oh dear," Jenna said out loud before pulling to one side as an ambulance flew past.

Sean shouted, "That was Sal at the wheel!"

Jenna said nothing but the car sped up.

As they turned a bend the blue lights of the emergency vehicles were clearly in Sean's drive; all three occupants' hearts dropped. Jenna pulled the car to a halt behind PC Millan's car that was blocking her drive. All three jumped out.

Their first sight was PC Millan who ran to them. "Everyone is ok. Don't worry, please wait here for a moment." Jenna decided to ignore Millan and started to move past him. Millan grabbed and held her. "Wait here please!"

Jenna stopped, Sean and Jolie by her side. A few minutes passed and Sal emerged from the house. Walking up to Jenna, she said, "Everything is fine, you can go in now. Sweetie, you come with me." Sal was addressing Jolie, who walked off with Sal to Jolie's house.

As Sean and Jenna went through the front door Sean saw Judy James sitting next to her husband, sobbing in the sitting room. Detective Inspector Cott was with them. Jenna caught sight of Kain in the kitchen and went to him. Sean followed. Both had shock on their faces. Kain was bandaged with blood clearly showing through the top of his left shoulder.

"Oh my god!" shrieked Jenna.

"I'm ok, don't panic. It's only superficial. Sal has seen to it, stay calm," Kain responded, but now holding Jenna in his uninjured right arm.

"What happened?" she asked.

"Come over and we'll sit at the table and I will tell you."

All did as asked by Kain.

"Don't panic, all is well; I was working in the office when Ged called from the back door. I got up to say hello when I noticed he was holding a gun. Before I could react the gun went off. Thankfully he is a poor shot but it caught me in the shoulder. I overpowered him and called Cott. Some minutes later Judy came in crying her eyes out. Well, you can see what happened next. Cott has arrested Ged and Sal has sedated Judy."

"Oh my god, poor Jolie." Jenna went to get to her feet but Kain stopped her. "Sal is with her, there is no need to worry. Leave her for now."

Detective Inspector Cott walked in. "The van is here, we are taking the Jameses to the park. Sal will bring the little one, Millan will take you when you're ready."

"No," Kain replied. "Jenna will drive us. Millan can tidy up here."

"Yes sir," was Cott's strange reply.

"No more questions, we need to go to the park now. Jenna,

you ok to drive?" asked Kain.

"Yes, of course. Let's go," Jenna replied.

Sean was baffled. "Why are we going to the park when this is all happening?"

"The Research Park, my work. We will be safer there!" Kain said.

As they all rose Sean suddenly had a thought. "Shadow, where is he? He's not barking."

"He is ok, we think Ged sedated him earlier with some tampered food. He will be fine at the park too. Let's go."

The journey was short especially as Jenna was following Detective Inspector Cott's car with its blue lights still flashing. Sean was confused. Why were they going to the park and not the police station? Would Shadow really be ok?

The gates opened and Sean noticed they went past Kain's office to a building further into the park. Upon reaching the building Sean saw Cott and Sal, assisted by others, taking the Jameses to the other side of the building that he and his family were now entering. The brightness of the building caught Sean's eyes; he had not been in this building before. The walls were a bright white, and the floor a silvery grey. There appeared to be no lights yet all was bright. Sean was ushered to a chair where he sat. Livia was soon with him, offering drinks, which Sean took. Livia then served Kain and Jenna, both now sitting opposite Sean.

Nothing was said until Sal entered the room. "Let me look at that arm more closely, sir."

Kain stood up. As they approached the wall a door slid open automatically and they were out of view. Jenna moved over to Sean, sitting in front of him on the floor. "Sal will give us all something to make us sleep for now; you will take it, and tomorrow, Sean, you will know everything."

Sean wanted to protest but his lids closed. Livia had beaten Sal to it.

Sean awoke in another bright room on a bed that he had never seen the like of before; the blanket fell off him as he moved off the bed and tightened itself to the mattress, ready-made on its own. Sean was perplexed. He walked through the door. Hearing voices, he followed the sounds to find Kain, Jenna, Livia, and Detective Inspector Cott at a table drinking and eating. Kain pointed for Sean to join them. Sean sat down and noticed another figure at the table, Harvey Gwent. Sean was not sure of his job but he knew it was high up in the government, some sort of secret service he believed. It was Gwent who spoke first. "Sean is not aware of anything as yet?"

"No, he will be told shortly once Algier arrives," replied Kain.

"Yes sir, that is fine, then I will keep the conversation appropriate until then," Gwent remarked strangely.

Sal entered and said, "The Jameses are comfortable. How is your arm, sir?" again directed at Kain.

"It is fine, you did a good job. It will not bother me."

"Wow, hold it. Why is everyone calling Dad sir?" Sean asked aloud.

Gwent went to say something but Kain spoke first. "I am the leader of my clan; all here are a part of my clan."

"Is it not time to stop skirting around the truth?" Uncle Algier bellowed from the entrance. Sean could not help but to run to him and give him a big hug.

"Just in time. That is your job, Algier." Kain smirked as he spoke.

"Thanks, then breakfast first and you and me will have a chat, young man." Algier was hugging Sean back as he spoke. All ate; Sean quickly enough for indigestion, but he still had to wait for his uncle to finish.

As they rose from the table Kain called, "Walk outside, it's a lovely day. Oh, by the way, walk Shadow."

Sean turned to see Shadow running through the door. Jumping straight into Sean's arms, he looked fine. Algier grabbed some dog biscuits and led Sean out, Shadow in tow. They walked for a few minutes then stopped at a stream with a small bridge across; the bridge's sides were just the right height to sit on. Shadow found the water and happily amused himself playing in it.

"Where do I start? This will be some learning, young Sean. Are you sure you want to know?" Algier did not wait for the reply but went straight on. "First shock, Sean, is that in our land your father is not just a leader, he is a king, ruler of the land." Algier hesitated.

"Wow, a king? You are kidding!"

"A king. My king, of an area called Saulten, after your family name. Your father rules through me. I am the leader of the Supreme Council which runs the day-to-day of our land on behalf of our ruler, King Kain." Algier stopped.

"You're not joking, are you?" was all Sean could think of.

"No," was the immediate reply.

Sean thought on this. "Canada is a democracy, there are no kingdoms and I've done geography – Saulten does not exist."

"We will not get through this until you open your mind and allow me to skip some parts for now. Saulten exists and your father is its ruler." Sean nodded, Algier continued "Your father inherited the throne when your grandfather died. Kain was about your age. As per our rules, protocols as we call them, Kain could not be the king until he was eighteen, however, he could rule through a kind of proxy in the short-term; I was your father's proxy. I ruled the kingdom on behalf of your father. Although he was king I was able to override many of his decisions. At eighteen your father became king. My role continued as part protector and chief advisor. This is how things should have continued."

"Until when?" Sean piped up, his head still coming to terms

with this information.

"Until we visited England when he was twenty-three and he met your mother. Kain fell deeply in love with your mother; she was different in many ways to Saultens. Although at the time it caused much of a stir, I liked your mother very much. Kain had the support of the Supreme Council for this unusual relationship even though possible marriage outside of his own clan was not common, especially for a king." Algier stopped to give Shadow another biscuit, Shadow immediately returning to the water. It was a hot day.

"All was well until Kain announced his marriage and it became known that Jenna would not move to Saulten. Kain played with the idea of denouncing his throne, which would then have given control to his younger brother, Prince Dain. As you know their relationship is not the best, this was not the option Kain preferred. The wedding was planned and there was still rumblings within the palace and the Supreme Council." Algier was stopped.

"Hold on, we have a palace?" Sean interrupted.

"Of course we have a palace, Kain is a king." Algier continued, "Anyway, before you interrupted me I was saying, Kain then came up with his plan. In basic terms he would live in England whilst I would rule on his behalf, just as what happened prior to his eighteenth birthday. The Supreme Council were uneasy with this decision, however, at twenty-five your father was at the peak of his powers. It would take some very strong people to go against him. I of course was also younger and much respected, which I'm sure helped the situation. By the time of the wedding the agreement was made and your father remained king with me leading the land on his behalf. I deal with the day-to-day small stuff but ask your father when bigger decisions are required. Actually, I think your father got the better deal as he had Jenna and this wonderful land thrown in." Algier gave a chuckle.

"Dropping the kingdom bit in Canada, you really expect

me to believe that Dad is a king and rules some far-off land through you in a kind of medieval fashion?" Sean thought out loud.

Algier thought then replied, "Yes, that is a fair way to put it in basic terms. It works quite well and your father is a great leader. Obviously I help too." Again Algier chuckled.

"So when Dad is away from home on business he actually returns to Saulten to do his king duties?" asked Sean.

"Yes. Not all the time, many times he does actually visit other countries and dignitaries, good friends with the US President as well as our own Prime Minister, as you know."

"Do they know Dad is a king?"

"No, Saulten is not recognised by them. They respect Kain for the great knowledge and wisdom that he has, especially around the work that goes on here at the Research Park, which is why he is a chief advisor to the Prime Minister and a successful book writer."

"Of course, Dad has written a few books on global warming, nuclear weapons, even war, a bit of a celebrity in the brainy people's world," Sean recalled aloud.

Again, Algier chuckled. "Your father is doing more for this planet than anyone. Global warming is real, you know."

Sean was not about to get into that conversation. Shadow had finished playing and looking worn out, was now pushing Sean's legs. "Let's walk back." Sean started to lead the way.

"Does that make Mum a queen and me a prince?" Sean asked whilst looking at Algier, who nodded a yes. "Wow, I'm a prince with a palace, servants and everything. This could be good." Sean tried out his regal voice. "Shadow go forth and tell my kitchen staff to have some food ready upon my return!" Shadow looked at Sean, licked his hand then ran to a bush to do his business. "Charming," Sean cried. "Off with his head."

Algier stopped laughing and suggested a drink would be good; shortly they were back at the room where breakfast had been taken earlier.

"He knows about you being a king, most impressed with me being able to run our land in your absence though," Algier chirped to Kain.

"Do I have to call you sir too?" Sean asked.

"No, Dad will do and I have asked everyone else to call me Kain here unless other Saultens are around. The people here are my friends and family."

"Should it not be Your Highness?" asked Sean in his regal voice.

"Informally, sir is used most often, however, Your Highness or sire is used in formal situations, although I do not particularly like those titles."

Sal made them all drinks and some food. A lighter conversation plus an update on the Jameses were all that was discussed. Sean could just about take the whole idea in, but there were no kingdoms in Canada, this now needed an answer.

"So where is this land that you, I mean we, rule?" Sean asked straight to his father.

Kain looked up. "I think you need to take Shadow for another walk. Sal, if you will please."

"Thanks sir, I mean Kain, leave me the hardest bit. Come on Sean. Shadow, walkies."

Shadow beat Sean and Sal to the door. Sean gave him a look as if to say, "You were dead on your feet a while ago, now ready to go."

Shadow did not acknowledge the look but took off toward the stream again. Sean and Sal caught up and sat where he and Algier had sat earlier.

"So, tell me the hard stuff." Sean looked at Sal, who unusually looked a little uncomfortable.

With a sigh, Sal started. "Saulten is not in Canada," Sean smiled in a knowing smile, "it's... it's part of Earthen." Sal sensed that Sean was still not with it – Earthen meant nothing. Sal looked up, took a deep breath then said straight, "Earthen is another planet." Sean's jaw dropped which was enough for Sal to stop.

"No, you telling me that Dad rules another planet?" As Sean spoke his words got slower as the full meaning of what was just said was starting to sink in. "No, there is no other planet with life on."

"There is, Sean."

"Even if there were, then how did Dad become a king?" Again Sean stopped, thinking through what he was saying. "No, no, you're kidding," was all he could add as the enormity of the suggestion was kicking in.

Sal moved closer to Sean, giving him one of her big hugs before saying, "In your world your father is an alien." Sean's heart missed a beat or two, clearly uneasy with this comment. "Not all aliens have green skin, big eyes, and long fingers you know." Sal added a mock giggle to try and soften the comment.

Sean shot up, pulling away from Sal. "You're an alien too!" he cried. Shadow even looked up at this point.

"Yes, I am an alien. However, I am still Sal, your best friend and second mother as such. Think of me and who I am, what I have meant to you over the years, not what I am physically," Sal pleaded.

"No, I can't take this!" Sean shouted as he ran off down the stream, Shadow on his heels.

Sal left them and returned to the room, reporting the conversation and that Sean had run off. Algier's comment that it should have been left to a man was put down by all present.

"Do you want me to go after him, sir?" Sal asked.

"Kain please, not sir. No, Shadow is with him, he will be ok. Besides, it is getting late, he will not stay away long."

Kain was right, although Sean had stretched their patience,

he returned to the room an hour later. Shadow walked in and collapsed in his bed in the corner of the room. Algier's chuckle broke the silence.

"Sean, come with me." Jenna motioned to the bedrooms. Sean followed, not looking at any of the others in the room.

"Are you an alien?" Sean asked as they sat on the bed.

Jenna flicked a smile. "No, Sean, unless of course Ireland is considered a different planet, which many in England would probably wish."

Sean retorted, "It's not funny, my dad is an alien from another planet. This isn't real, surely."

"It is and you will need to come to terms with it as I have." Jenna tried to be reassuring.

"You married Dad knowing this..." Sean was interrupted.

"I fell in love with him before he told me. I too went through what you are going through now, but it does not change the person you and I love."

"But he's an alien!" Sean cried.

"And what does that mean? He comes from another place yet that does not change the person," Jenna pushed.

Sean thought. "Is it just like a suit or something, like Men in Black?" It sounded silly but Sean was trying to understand.

Jenna replied, "That's a film, Sean. No, what you see is all your father, the same with Algier, Sal, Livia, Cott, Gwent, and Millan, plus others that you have met."

Sean looked up; of course, concentrating on his father too much, he had forgotten all the others. Nearly everyone he knew was an alien, this blew his mind.

"Mum, I'd like to sleep now. Please send in Shadow, assuming he is not an alien dog?"

"Ok, Shadow is pure Alsatian and Earthborn."

Jenna got up to leave but as she reached the door, Sean screamed, "Am I an alien too?"

Jenna walked back to Sean, taking his hands in hers, and said, "You were born here on Earth in England. I am from Ireland, also on Earth, but your father is from Earthen. Yes, you are half alien, if that's how you want to look at things."

Sean moved away and sat on the bed. "Send in Shadow. At least he has not lied to me all my life."

Jenna shed a small tear. "Honey, I'm sorry, I truly am, but there are many reasons as for why we have kept this from you. Given the chance these will be explained but before you sleep forget the word 'alien'. Does it matter where we come from? Think of all the wonderful years we have had together. Who helped you ride your first bike? who taught you to swim? What were your feelings at the time? What does your family mean to you? Sleep, my child, but think of the good as well as any perceived bad."

Jenna left the room. Seconds later, Shadow was on the bed. Sean got in, cuddling Shadow so much that he could hardly breathe. Sean eventually slept but the thoughts in his brain just tore at his whole beliefs.

SUPREME COUNCIL:
(CHAPTER 6)

Morning came and Sean walked into the eating room. Algier, Sal, and Jenna were present.

"Where is Kain?" Sean asked.

"Your father is outside, he has been checking on the Jameses," Jenna replied. "Food is on the table and so is drink."

Sean grabbed a drink, plus what looked like meat, and walked out, feeding the meat to Shadow on the way. From the main entrance, Sean could see his father over near hangar six. Sean walked towards the hangar, passing Algier's helicopter on the way. Upon reaching the hangar he walked to Algier's Mustang and leant against the bonnet. Kain was looking at the prototype car.

"Good morning Sean, and you, Shadow." Shadow had clearly taken Sean's side and stood in front of him as if to guard him.

"Human dogs can sense aliens you know." Sean took a swipe at his father.

"Of course, so Shadow is human then," Kain laughed.

"You know what I mean. He's from Earth."

"You know I can't force you to accept this, however, if you did then you would open your mind and experience many wonderful things. Take space travel – look at Algier's helicopter." Kain pointed as he spoke.

Sean looked at the helicopter. Before his very eyes the red tangible helicopter became a silver tear-shaped spaceship.

Sean could not stop a 'wow' creeping out.

"What are you sitting on?" Kain again pointed.

Sean stood up from the bonnet and turned but did not see the Mustang he expected; he had been sitting on a similar car to the prototype. This was awesome, he thought, before turning back to look at his father. "This is all impressive but it doesn't change the fact that you're an alien and I'm a mongrel of some sort."

Kain laughed out loud. "Oh son, don't be so hard on me or yourself. We are what we are, what your mother said last night is true. I, Algier, and the others love you, we are no different today than we were yesterday."

Livia came into the hangar. "Sir, Supreme Council Secretary Barlo is asking to speak to you."

Kain walked towards Livia. "Of course, I'll speak to him." Kain left the hangar with Livia. Sean turned again and looked at the car; it was a Mustang, now it was not.

"I can't drive your Earthling machines but I like the look of them, that's why I chose the cover. Look again, Sean."

Sean turned and sure enough he was now looking at a Mustang; his curiosity could not stop him asking, "How the hell do you do that?"

"Easy, they are equipped with a Perception Projector. Basically they send out signals which to most humans give the image we want them to see, like a Mustang, when in reality it is an Earthen standard type run-of-the-mill vehicle," Algier explained.

Sean was impressed. "The helicopter is the same but really a spaceship." Sean was now walking with Algier towards the silver spaceship.

"Yes," replied Algier.

"So how come I can see it in both states then, as I'm human," Sean quizzed.

Algier chuckled. "That's simple. You see, we all expect to see the standard things that we see, therefore once the Perception Projector sends a logical image of what we expect the brain asks no questions and you have a helicopter. Now we have started to open your mind, the projection does not work, as you can now expect to see a spaceship as opposed to a helicopter."

They were now standing right next to the spaceship; Sean touched it. "Cool," he exclaimed. Sean continued to walk around the spaceship which although was roughly the same size as the helicopter, was completely different.

Sean had a question. "So you can make anything look like anything with one of these projectors, inside and out?"

"No, they only work on inanimate objects as there is a box of tricks. Look at the roof and you will see a small aerial type thing, you obviously could not fit it to a person. They also have to be of similar size, as the Mustang is to the car and the helicopter is to the spaceship. You could not make the car look like a spaceship or vice versa due to the size and general starting shape, but it is clever. Your dad invented it when he was twelve at school," Algier finished with a grin.

"Dad invented this at school? No way!" Sean needed convincing.

"Yes, the general idea had been around for years but the images would not stabilise, especially in rain for instance, but your father invented the stabiliser and it took off. That's why you Earthlings see a lot less UFOs." Algier explained.

"UFOs are real?"

"You're touching one."

"What about pictures, cameras. They pick up the helicopter, not a spaceship?" Sean asked.

"Similar. The projector sends out the image to film, more recently and easier, digital signals, so they are generally misled."

"Wait, does this fool all humans?"

"No. Most, especially the newer type, however, some humans have more open minds. They expect the unexpected therefore the projection principle fails on them. Your friend Trekkie is such a case."

Sean gulped. "Holy shit, Trekkie has been telling the truth for years. The last time he saw a futuristic car was a few weeks ago when you turned up. He saw your Mustang."

"Yes he did. A clever boy is Trekkie, and no, he is not an alien, just a gifted human."

Sean pondered on this. "How must Trekkie feel knowing what he saw was real and yet we all mocked him? Can I get in and have a fly in the spaceship?"

"Not today but soon."

"Why not now? If I sat inside it would help me to believe."

"Ok, let's sneak a peek." Algier walked along to the middle of the spaceship shape.

"Chief Councillor Algier!" came the shout from Livia by the building. "Please come!"

Algier started towards the building. "Sorry. Another time, Sean. Come with me."

As they entered the building Kain addressed them. "I have called for a communication with the Supreme Council in twenty minutes; we will change first. Sean, you need to be strong. Even without the full knowledge, you will watch and learn as our culture and behaviours differ from what you know." Kain was next to Sean, putting his arm upon him. "I love you." Kain paused. "Sal, get Sean ready as he will see his council."

Sal took Sean to his bedroom. Walking to what appeared to be a blank wall, a door opened to reveal a cupboard with clothes in. Sean wowed again. Picking some clothes, Sal handed them to Sean. "These are appropriate. Put them on, I'll be back in five minutes."

As soon as Sal left Sean stripped then put on the clothes. What was the front was the opening from the neckline to just below the waist. Sean could see no fastening of sorts but as he got into the suit it joined itself together, similar to how the blanket on the bed moved; once sealed the join was virtually seamless. The cupboard door, still open, had a mirror on the inside. Sean looked at himself. He was in an all-white one-piece suit, comfortable fitting with just enough play all round, but not to be tight. White slipper-like shoes with attached sock-type tops, which were now hidden beneath the bottom of the trousers. A gold and silver alternate-coloured belt was around his waist, the gold buckle being prominent, a gold S inside a circle with a crown-like shape above the circle was its shape. The suit neckline, although in a V still had a small collar at the top; both sides of the collar near the V had the same gold S symbol. Sean thought he looked good.

Sal collected Sean and took him to a different room, still the same white walls and grey floor but half dome-shaped in its roof. Kain, Jenna, Algier, Cott, and Gwent were already inside. All were wearing similar clothes to Sean, however, everyone else had single silver belts and symbols, apart from Kain, whose were all gold. Looking closer, Jenna and Kain had short white cloaks to their suits; both had small crowns on their heads, Kain's in gold, Jenna's in silver. Kain and Algier were standing in the centre of the room next to a standalone console, everyone else was at the edges behind them, including Sean with Sal next to him.

"Are you ready Sean?" Kain asked.

Sean felt Sal hold him for reassurance as he replied. "Yes."

"Viewer on."

Straight in front of Kain, a metre or so above his height, an image appeared on the wall, the image was of an older man, dark-haired but greying, round-faced with a large nose.

"Your Highness, your Supreme Council is ready. Do you

wish to start the meeting?"

"Yes, Secretary Barlo," replied Kain.

With this, ten similar-sized boxes filled the dome, all with men in, dressed in similar clothes to Sean. All apart from one looked older, and distinguished in some way. All at once the men bowed their heads and said, "Your Highness."

Kain looked at each box. "I will not introduce you all, as we all know each other, apart from Sean who will pick up as we go along."

"Of course, sire, but may I be so bold as to address our heir?" Barlo acknowledged Kain's nod before addressing Sean. "Young sire, it is an honour to see you. You have grown." Sean bowed to acknowledge the comment, not wishing to talk. "Of course you will not be aware of our customs, however, if you have your father's intelligence you will pick things up quickly."

"Anders, it's good to see you." Kain addressed the older-looking man, round faced, welcoming smile, to the far left.

"And you too, sire. May I be so bold as to address my daughter?" Anders asked.

Barlo went to talk but Kain responded, "Yes, of course."

Sal took a step forward. "Hello Father, you are looking well."

Anders replied, "Yes, my dear, as do you. Do not leave it so long to visit."

"Can we get on with council business?" Barlo was growing restless.

Kain opened. "I have requested this council meeting to discuss here on Earth the most recent events of attempted murder, to both myself and my family."

"Attempts? What a shame," the youngest man to the right threw in with a smirk.

"My brother, I do not take that remark in jest!" Kain turned to look at Prince Dain, his younger brother.

There was a silence, interrupted by Barlo. "I am sure there was no insult meant. Your Highness, please be aware of protocol and address our sire as appropriate, now..."

Kain interrupted, "An apology from you, Secretary Barlo, is not acceptable. Prince Dain, do you wish me to demand an apology!"

Dain moved inn the screen, paused for a few seconds then said uncomfortably, "I am sorry if you took my remark in the wrong way, Ka... sire."

Kain gave a derisory look. "If that is the best that you can do, I accept, but only as I have little time for games. There have been two attempts on my life and the last one saw me shot; my concern and indeed my belief is that a Vulten is responsible, a certain Gaul Gill."

"We have been kept informed of the situation and understand that there was thankfully no serious injury." Barlo appeared concerned. "We are not aware of the two attempts. However shocking that any attempt has been made, we cannot suggest someone's involvement without proof, especially a Vulten."

"I have no proof but I have my feelings that you will not doubt." Kain looked at Barlo, who bowed his head briefly. "The presence of a Vulten, especially Gill who I understand is a drunken, disgraced soldier, so close to my family is also unacceptable."

Dain laughed. "Surely, brother, you should not be concerned of such a minor presence. You are a king and your power must outweigh his. Besides, it was a human who shot you." A giggle ended the sentence.

Kain was about to take the bait but Algier reacted first. "Prince Dain, as Chief Councillor of the Supreme Council I must remind you of the correct protocols and will mark this as a warning. Continued disregard for the rules will remove you from this session and we will not allow your vote if any are required during the session."

Dain shook his head but replied, "Of course, Chief Councillor." The smirk was still present.

"It is correct that a human did act in the last incident, sire. This is surely a simple proof."

"Have you forgotten what I said, Secretary Barlo!" Kain raised his voice, every figure in the screens moved uncomfortably. "I believe that the human, a good friend of mine, was under some form of control, as was the driver of the lorry previously. This control is beyond any human ability or indeed normally Earthens', however Gill's presence and my understanding of his military files that he was working on mind control as a weapon, suggest otherwise."

A grey-haired, very much older man spoke. "Sire, I do not distrust your feelings or indeed how some deductions from a military file you have read can point to the conclusion you make. However, legally this would not be accepted. His presence to you and the restrictions of his passport are of course a fair concern."

"Thank you for your legal comment, Councillor Irnside, but I do not require legal advice." Kain at least bowed his head in response.

"Sire, where are we going with this?" asked Barlo.

"I wish to speak to King Vul directly." Kain's words were met with a sharp intake of breath by all in the screens and those in the hall.

Anders, still smiling, "Sire, if you wish to speak to King Vul with regard to Gill's presence then that can be arranged but Algier or I could question and check such passport details without the need for a personal conversation. To comment to Vul without evidence that one of his subjects is involved in a murder plot would be unwise and not recommended."

"Anders, my friend, of course your remarks are of sense and

I know that you would ask upon my behalf with great diligence, but I must make very clear my anger to the situation and MY wish to deal directly with Vul for MY reasons." Kain breathed, stood even straighter before, coldly saying, "I order the Supreme Council to support my action to speak to King Vul direct."

Again, there were large gushes for air. Algier gave Kain a quizzical look, Anders rolled his eyes, but Dain spoke. "Brother, you cannot be serious, you are ordering your council to take a dangerous action on feeling and wish. You have lost your mind!" By the muted 'mm's and nods of the heads, Dain's statement was agreeable to all.

"Brother Dain, I have had enough of your insolence. Do you wish to challenge me formally or would you prefer that I challenge you?" Kain's eyes appeared to burn into Dain's even though it was but a screen link.

Dain went white-faced; a sweat came across his brow, for he had to choose his next words carefully. "I apologise deeply, sire. I do not wish to challenge you and plead that my insolence does not merit you to challenge!"

"Secretary Barlo, action the vote to support or not my action. The vote will be in ten minutes. I will of course accept your against vote, that being your decision. I also ask for your full honesty in your voting for the remaining councillors but all take account of my feelings towards what is clearly an attack on me and my family."

"I will come back to you in ten minutes as you order, sire. Viewers off!" said Barlo. The dome went back to its normal white.

"Kain, how you are treating your council and you intend to talk to a fellow king is, well... beyond me. To order a vote is of great disbelief." Algier said this with a true look of disbelief.

"My friend, you must trust me. I have been away from Earthen for some time, I missed the last Kings' Council. I need to take this course of action, you must see why." Kain ended then went for some refreshment in the corner of the room.

Sean was not sure of what all this meant but was refrained by Sal from getting involved. Sean noted that his mother's face was that of concern but she too was not getting involved. The ten minutes seemed a lifetime, no one in the hall spoke. Kain stood in the corner stony faced, Algier was deep in thought. Then the viewer came on, ten screens and ten ashen-looking faces were visible once again. An eleventh screen had also appeared with Algier in, even though he was standing next to Kain who had retaken his place in the centre of the room.

"With some trepidation, the vote is ready, sire," Barlo said shakily. With that: "Councillors, vote!"

In an instant all the screens' borders changed their colour. Sean counted seven green to four reds, most notably Anders and Algier were green and Dains was red.

"With seven to four for, the vote is carried in favour of His Highness," Barlo said in a barely audible voice, then added, "For those who have voted against, is there a second challenge?"

Sean looked at the red boxes. The four reds were restless, each looked to their left, and Dain smiled then clearly looked at something or someone. If only Sean was in their room he could see fully what was going on. One man in a red box stood up, again deep breaths were taken.

"Councillor Starn, do you wish to say something?" Barlo addressed the standing figure.

"I wiiiiiishhhhh," Starn clearly stuttered. "I wiiiiiishhhh to express my full concern as to the result and register my displeasure in our king's handling of this situation, therefore..."

To everyone's surprise, Dain interrupted. "Starn, please consider as much the present as the future. I applaud your action as you have taken so far."

Starn clearly looked relieved. "No, Secretary Barlo, I have

said my piece and no further action is required. I will support the vote and plead that my sire accepts my honesty as he requested."

"Your honesty is accepted, Councillor Starn. Secretary Barlo, arrange the call. Viewers off!" With that, Kain turned and left the room without a word to anyone.

The following morning and Sean was walking Shadow with Sal. Sean had slept again thinking about all he heard. He was still coming to terms with everything he had heard, other planets, aliens, and kingdoms.

Sal sat down with a type of picnic basket packed with breakfast items. Now was the time. "Sean, are you ready for more?"

"Yes," replied Sean.

"Earthen is basically the exact mirror of Earth on the other side of the sun. Earthen began some five hundred years ahead of Earth in the first big bang; Earth's was the second. Because of this, Earthen developed in very similar terms as Earth, same water, same weather, same conditions in general, therefore life developed again very similar to Earth but five hundred years ahead. Because we are ahead we as a race developed well in advance of Earth, therefore our technologies are greater. Just think where Earth humans will be in a few hundred or so years if they continue to develop as they are."

"Wow, we will be as advanced as Earthens," Sean said.

"Hopefully not." Sean looked quizzical; Sal continued. "We went through fossil fuels like you and unfortunately global warming. As predicted on Earth the warnings were real but we ignored them, enjoying our freedom, our democracy and greed in the commercial world we were. Sure enough, the planet heated, water became scarce in certain areas, ice caps melted. That is when the great wars began."

"World wars!" exclaimed Sean.

"Yes," Sal continued, "terrible wars, nuclear weapons. Millions were killed, lands were obliterated. For many years we lived underground until we were able to live on the surface again. At this point from a population of billions and hundreds of countries we were down to some one hundred million split into five lands – Saulten, Vulten, Dersian, Ainten, and Biernite as they are known now. Each land became a kingdom named after the king like Saul...ten called after your father's family name. This is where we are today – five kingdoms, five kings, all with around a twenty million population each. Children have been actively encouraged to grow the population over the last few decades. As we learnt from the democratic greed of the past, all-powerful kings with advisory councils are how we govern."

Sal stopped to allow Sean to think. Such a big planet with such low numbers of people. "Is not all the planet inhabitable? Do you have animals?"

"Correct," replied Sal. "Lots of land is inhabitable due to either the heat or there are still contaminated areas from the war or at least dead zones where nothing lives. Our main cities generally have a kind of force field around to keep out the sun and the elements but there are places that you can go out in the air, although not like this, this beautiful clear summer's day with a lovely breeze and a small stream below. You don't know how lucky you still are."

"Accepting all this, if I can, why are you here? Why do you speak English and have so many human ways?"

"Once we developed the Sun Ships, spaceships that catapult around the sun, our exploration took no boundaries. We found Earth and realised it was a copy of Earthen, but some years younger. Our fascination started. Remember, we had a very similar history to Earth, our physical make-up is virtually the same so we went through medieval, Edwardian periods, very similar. We even had the sixties as such, but now all of a sudden there we were, able to revisit our history for real. Imagine if you could find a way to go back to say, just recent history, and actually witness cowboys and Indians, the American Civil War, the Beatles. Would you not visit?"

Sean was starting to fall in. "So you watched what was our present times but saw it as your real history. Like me meeting Colonel Custer – if he existed."

"Exactly." Sal could see that Sean was starting to get it. "Obviously we have moved on since then but just think, whatever time this present is to you, I am effectively five hundred years back in time as such. Not time travel but a freak of the two planets being near identical. And by the way, we have few animals on Earthen; most species did not survive the wars or sun."

"That is why you don't like dogs?" asked Sean.

"Yes, they are alien to us," Sal suggested with a smirk. "But we do have cows, sheep, those kinds of animals which we have reintroduced through a cloning type of process. We eat meat as well as the varied plants we also had to reintroduce.

"Because of our interest in Earth and the similarities of our language anyway, we have adopted your English as our common language. This has been taught in Earthen schools for years. We actually watch your films and TV shows for our sins; Captain Kirk is as much a screen legend on Earthen as he is here, even if we find many parts of the show as funny."

Sean got up and started to play fetch with Shadow, purely to get his mind around everything. Both decided to walk back to the building. They arrived in time for some interesting news:

"Vul will not speak to you unless we are on the space station and his ambassador is present," Algier advised Kain.

Kain smirked. "That is not a surprise. When?"

"He will speak to us tomorrow morning which gives us plenty of time."

"Good, then make the arrangements. We will leave within the hour." Kain left the room.

Algier walked over to Sean. "Good news, you will get that flight in the spaceship you wanted."

"Holy shit." Sean could not help himself. "I'm going on a spaceship."

"Yes, the shuttle ship, err, the helicopter will take us to the space station within a few hours."

"Space station? There is a space station!" Sean exclaimed.

Algier continued, "Yes, the space station is just to the left of the sun, Earth side. The space station, apart from being a laboratory to study Earth also has Sun Ships moored on the side. Sun Ships are great ships that can skim the sun's atmosphere at great speeds. Aboard a Sun Ship, from the space station to Earthen is also only a few hours."

"You mean that we could be on Earthen the other side of the sun within a day or so?"

"Yes," Algier replied. "Go with Sal and she will dress you and prepare you for travel."

A SPACE TRIP:
(CHAPTER 7)

Sean followed Sal, put on similar white clothes as before and met his parents, Algier, and Gwent at the building door. The group walked to the shuttle, clearly no longer a helicopter to Sean. As they approached the side of the silver craft a door opened and a ramp came out. Kain stopped everyone by holding up his hand. "Sean first," he said as he gestured Sean up the ramp.

Sean walked up the ramp and looked in. The walls of the shuttle were the same white and the floor was the same grey of the research park buildings. Sean first saw ten rows of double separate seats, like Captain Chairs. To his right appeared a blank wall but looking along the chairs to his left were two larger chairs and the pointed part of the ship. There was a console in front of the two larger seats but it was the same plain white as the walls, no windows.

Standing at attention next to the two larger chairs were two figures in uniform, similar white tops but with a blue trouser. Both saluted as Sean approached them, Kain was not far behind.

"Your Highness, welcome aboard, especially you, young sire," greeted Captain Shad.

Sean, reading his name on the badge upon his chest just below the S symbol replied, "Thank you Captain Shad."

Kain then spoke. "Good morning Captain, everyone will take their seats and we will leave for the space station as soon as possible!"

The captain bowed and took his seat with the female co-pilot next to him; Sean sat next to Kain in the front two seats, Algier and Jenna, Gwent and Sal filled the other seats.

"Instruments on, joystick control," called Captain Shad.

All of a sudden what was a plain console and walls had varied buttons, monitors, and gauges which appeared around the two front seats. Between the seats a joystick appeared within grasp of both pilots, although the captain took hold of it.

The co-pilot spoke. "Earth shuttle to space station, ready for take-off."

Out of nowhere Sean heard two different voices. "Earth control, ok, clear for lift-off," then, "Space station lift-off authorised."

The captain looked back to address Kain. "Sire, may we lift off?"

"May we have the full front viewer on first, then you may lift off."

The captain nodded, pressed a button, then all of a sudden a windscreen-type viewer appeared just above the console. Sean could see the research building as clear as day in front of it. *Wow,* he thought.

"Secure for lift-off," the captain said as the lights in the spaceship dimmed, the door closed, and Sean noted that a seatbelt had automatically gone around his waist. "Lift-off!" the captain said.

Sean felt the ship move upward, confirmed by the view of the building through the screen disappearing below the console. The ship continued to climb, straight up for some minutes. Sean saw what was blue and green of the land become just blue and white; they were in the clouds. *Wow,* Sean again thought.

The captain spoke. "Course set for space station, prepare for full propulsion in five, four, three, two, one."

The ship suddenly shot forwards and upwards at quite an angle, not uncomfortable but enough to push Sean into his seat. The view went from blue and white then to being filled with what looked like fire, orange and red flashing over it. The shuttle was streaming through the Earth's atmosphere. Once the orange and red lights finished all that could be seen was the black of space and the twinkling of the stars.

"We are in space, at cruising speed and autopilot, secure," the captain called. Sean's seatbelt removed itself and the interior lights lightened.

"Awesome, eh?" Kain winked at Sean. "Jenna, let's get some drinks." Kain walked to the back of the ship with Jenna.

Sean got up and went straight to the captain. Before he could speak the captain said, "Ensign Jeng, take control. I need to speak with His Highness," turning to Sean as he rose from his seat. "Please, Your Highness, would you keep my seat warm for me?"

"Of course." Sean could not believe his luck as he sat in the captain's chair. Sean looked out at the stars; this was space travel. "How come there are no actual buttons?" he asked as he looked at the console.

Jeng replied, "The computer picks up your heat as you place your finger near whichever control you want. We can change our views or what we wish to see like this." Jeng waved her hand over one gauge and touched another, both swapped places. The gauge that was in front of Sean was now a selection of buttons. "They turn varied lights on and off, have a go," Jeng encouraged.

Sean put his finger near one button and the interior lights went off. Someone shouted, "Sean!" from the back of the craft. Sean quickly put his finger back and the lights came on. The button next to it said front view; Sean put his finger near it. He could see that he had turned on some form of spotlight as two bright lights appeared in front of the ship; Sean repeated his action to do the same again. This continued for some time as Ensign Jeng moved certain controls in front of Sean, allowing him to touch them.

Sean was getting a bit full of himself when he asked, "Can I now fly the ship?"

Jeng looked to the back of the ship then at Sean. "Ok, auto-pilot monitor." Jeng then looked at Sean. "You can control the ship from the joystick, however, as the autopilot is watching you it will override if you do something too harsh or indeed change direction too much. Have a go."

Sean put his hand on the joystick. He pulled it back, the ship jolted slightly as if to accelerate but stopped. Jeng laughed. "Too much acceleration so the autopilot stopped you, go again but gentle."

Sean pulled the joystick back, the ship accelerated. Sean pushed the joystick to the right, the ship turned. Sean moved it back to the left, the ship followed. Sean thought this was great and again was left to play with the control for some time, carefully watched by Jeng and the autopilot.

Sean said in amazement. "Wow, does this have lasers?"

"Yes," was Jeng's response.

"Holly crap, can I see them?" Sean was excited.

Jeng looked to the rear then made Sean's day. "Shuttle to space station, we are testing our lasers, please authorise."

"Authorised two shots, low power, test mode," came a voice from the control panel.

Jeng pushed some buttons then addressed Sean. "Ok, so I will press the release button, a dummy target will fire forward, your laser sight will pick it up. When it goes green around the target you press the fire button below it, just like a computer game – ready?"

'Yes, am I ever." Sean could not contain his excitement.

Jeng pressed a button. Sean could see a small light object fire out in front of them, the now visible laser aiming screen started to track it, the crosshairs went green and Sean hit the fire button in front of him. Two bluey white light streams fired out together from the ship, meeting at the same point, hitting the target that blew up in fire before disappearing.

"Great shot, number two release."

Again, another dummy target was released, trailed, and extinguished in the same way as the first. "Excellent, you are a true marksman," Jeng chirped.

Captain Shad was now back. "I think that is enough fun. Your Highness, may I have my seat back please?" Sean moved from the chair with a big grin on his face.

As he walked back Algier shouted, "Well done, young man. I still remember my first laser shot."

Kain, now sitting, responded, "I too, you blew up my father's car!" All laughed.

Sean decided to sit next to his mother for the remainder of the trip, her reassuring words keeping his excitement down to reasonable standards.

Not long later, "Secure for space station approach and landing," the captain said. Lights dimmed, seatbelts fastened.

The ship moved to its left. Speed slowing, the viewer started to darken; they were looking and heading towards the sun. The temperature in the shuttle appeared to get hotter but not by much. Sean could see a shadow shape even in the darkened viewer. The shape got bigger as the space station got closer.

"Earth shuttle to space station, we are coming into dock," informed Captain Shad.

"We have you, allow auto guide," came a voice.

"Affirmative," said the captain.

The shuttle moved closer to the station, which shaded the

craft from the sun, the brightening front viewer allowing Sean to see the space station clearer. A hatch opened and the shuttle went through into a landing bay. With hardly a movement the shuttle was docked. Kain stood up and headed to the door, Sean went next to him followed by the others. Jenna gave Sean a cuddle and warming smile from behind him. Kain looked at the side of the ship and the door opened and the ramp came out. Sean saw that to the side of the ramp were soldiers in the same white and blue uniform of the shuttle crew, four abreast, weapons at arms. Kain led the group past the soldiers through a small tube-like corridor to what was obviously a meeting room and a welcoming committee.

"Welcome, King Kain." A blond-haired, middle-aged man, very tanned, addressed Kain with a bow. "I am Commander Strik of the space station."

"Thank you, Commander. There is no need for any other formalities, please lead us to our rooms."

With an, "Of course, Your Highness," the commander led them all out of the room, along corridors, all the same white and grey theme. Everyone they passed bowed to them. They reached another room; as the door opened tables, chairs, and a large window to the stars were visible.

"Food and drink has been laid on, I will leave you with your people and see you tomorrow unless you need me – please call." Commander Strik bowed and left them.

Another man came up to them. "Your Highness, it is a pleasure to meet you." He bowed at the same time. "We are at your service."

Kain replied, "Thank you," and beckoned them all to sit.

Drinks were given out and hand food available; there were many servants to wait over the small party. The room had about twenty other people present, many spoke to Kain and Algier; lots of greetings and small talk, all were briefly introduced to Sean.

After an hour, Sal said, "Come on, Sean." As she rose from the table Sean followed her to a corner of the room, his view fixed on the stars outside the full-length windows.

Sal said, "Viewer on." The wall lit just in front of where they were standing. "Here is what we are on."

Sean could see a picture of what was obviously the space station that they were on. One main cylindrical centre body labelled the Hub, on one side there were five square arms coming from it, each labelled with a different kingdom name. The other side had what looked like a big sun screen which was the side facing the sun.

"Each arm is part of the kingdom that it is named. Ours is called the Saulten Wing, as you can see," Sal was pointing at the obvious. "Each kingdom has full control of their own wing and you will normally find people of its own race in it. The Hub is multi-race which holds the crew. The crew is mixed race from any of the five kingdoms, however, the commander and the command crew are only one race, in this case the Dersian people. Each kingdom runs the command crew for six months at a time in order. The commander from whichever kingdom reports to the five council secretaries and ultimately the kings whilst on their rota. Commander Strik is a Dersian."

"Can we move around the ship?" Sean asked.

"Yes but we tend to stay in our own wings. The central Hub has bars, shops, and everything. You can go there but most visitors don't, therefore it is mainly only the crew there." Sal was pointing out the various parts on the viewer.

"So what goes on up here? Surely not this many people go to and from Earth," asked Sean.

"Apart from being the transfer point for Earth, the station acts as a laboratory, test centre, a military base, and a base for travel to other planets." Sal continued to point as she spoke.

"Wow, you travel to other planets? Are there other aliens?"

"Yes, we do visit other planets, although Earth is our main focus. As yet we have found few that could be able to sustain life as we know it, no aliens seen as yet."

"It's time for bed." Jenna was standing by Sean.

"I'll leave you with this to dream on." Sal had pulled up a picture of a large spaceship, similar to the shuttle but much larger. The main body in silver was triangular with the same two half cylindrical tubes along the bottom and wing shape on its sides near the bottom. Battleship, as it was labelled, had a few more parts coming from it that appeared to be aerials, communication satellites, and guns.

"Are they big guns?" Sean cried out.

"Yes, but not a discussion for tonight." Jenna led Sean to a room where he slept.

The next morning with breakfast finished, Sean, Kain, Algier, Jenna, and Sal were all heading to the Hub. Upon reaching the end of their corridor a door opened. Flight crew soldiers were at arms either side of the door, ten each side in a line. All bowed as Sean, Kain, and the others walked through. Behind the line of soldiers were other people generally just watching. Sean looked around, they were walking across a circular floor some fifty metres wide, and around the floor on the outside were varied doors. As they reached the end of the floor they reached a walkway to the central cylinder that was only a couple of metres wide, therefore the soldiers stopped, allowing Kain's party to move on their own. Sean stopped in the middle of this walkway which was actually a bridge leading from the outer ring to the internal ring, which was a large lift shaft. Sean looked over the barrier; the drop below and above was ten floors high. Both the bottom floor and the top floor were filled in, however, Sean noted the ants (obviously people) moving on the bottom floor.

Sean felt a gentle push from Jenna so he continued to walk. As he walked he could see a similar-size party walking on another bridge to his left. They were tall, dressed in black, dark-haired with many having beards. As they approached the lifts the tall older figure in front bowed and smiled at Kain who acknowledged the bow with a tip of his head.

"That is Secretary Seth, he is a Vulten, the head of their council just like Barlo, although we have Algier's chief councillor position above Barlo." Kain informed Sean, "I'm surprised that such a senior figure is here," as they entered their lift.

The lift stopped, the doors opened, and Sean walked out onto what was obviously the space station bridge. The external view of the stars or virtual black side hiding the sun went all around the circular walls. There were many consoles and chairs with varied flight crew sitting or standing, the bridge looked a busy place.

"Good morning," said Commander Strik. "You know Secretary Seth?" Strik was introducing Seth to Kain.

"King Kain." Seth had a smile on his face. "It is good to see you again, and of course you, Chief Councillor Algier, looking older."

Kain and Algier nodded as they chuckled.

"Queen Jenna, as beautiful as ever." Seth allowed a longer lower bow for Jenna, who smiled in acknowledgement. Seth looked at Sean, he was tall at least two metres in height. "You must be the young prince." With that he placed his hand out for Sean to shake, Sean obliged. As Seth touched his hand he could feel something in his head; the thoughts ceased as Seth removed his hand.

"You are acting as the Ambassador Secretary Seth?" asked Kain.

"Of course, only the highest authority for a king," replied Seth.

"Commander I, Algier, Sean, and Seth wish to use the communication deck on our own first," Kain ordered.

With that Kain, Algier, Seth, and Sean were led to some stairs between the lifts. Taking one flight, they entered from the floor another room that was fully dome-shaped, again a mixture of stars or black could be seen. Strik left back down the stairs, the floor closing above him.

Kain was direct. "Secretary Seth may I be open, honest, and direct without the formalities?" Seth nodded a yes. "You are aware of the attempts upon my life and the presence of a Vulten named Gill who I believe is involved?"

"We are aware of this, however, Gill's involvement is not proven."

"That may be the case but I believe that he is." Kain looked direct at Seth. "Regardless, his presence annoys me and I hope that King Vul understands this."

"King Vul may accept your annoyance, however, if Gill has the correct passport and approvals then he will not be concerned."

"Don't treat me as stupid, my friend." Kain's voice was lower. "I know he will have all the right passports, they can be forged although I note your formal lack of assistance in supplying copies of both the passport and his personal file as Algier has requested."

Seth looked awkward. "We are doing our best to provide you with the details requested but we have to check them first. Presently we see no issue with his passport. Again, you are making accusations, not fact."

Kain walked towards the ship's window, braced himself, turned, then looked at Secretary Seth, not saying anything. Sean could see Seth physically start to sweat. Kain spoke in a commanding voice. "Do I assume that Vul and his council are behind Gill because of this lack of assistance? I and my council are in full support of the path I wish to take. I will not refrain from dealing with Vul in any such way as I need to, that needs to be very clear."

Seth wiped his brow. "Of course, my friend, but I must warn you of approaching King Vul like this."

"Why?" Kain said in a loud voice. "I am his equal and I will address Vul as I feel fit. I and my family have been threatened by Gill's presence, I have indeed been shot, I have no patience on this issue."

Seth waited before he replied. "Of course, where do you wish to go with this with King Vul?"

"I wish all of the requested information on Gill, full approval to investigate Gill." Kain paused. "An acknowledgement that if required I or my people will remove Gill."

"I'm sorry Kain," Seth looked again awkward, "King Vul will not agree to you dealing with a Vulten, neither does this follow protocol..."

Kain interrupted. "I am not interested in protocol. I repeat, I have my council's full backing, plus I am prepared to duel if necessary." Kain approached Seth. Within a metre his eyes were fixed on Seth, whose whole demeanour had changed – he looked frightened. "You have an hour before the call. Algier, Sean, let's go."

Sean followed Kain and Algier back down the stairway. Upon entering the bridge Kain headed to some seats away from most of the people and sat down. Sean sat next to him, Algier stood in front of them, motioning all others to leave them.

"Pushed the point a bit." Algier looked at Kain. "You had better hope that Seth relays your anger and intent to Vul in the right way otherwise your bluff could be called."

Kain did not respond. No one spoke further, just drank from some drinks that Sal had finally brought over. Kain was in deep thought; Sean felt he was piecing it all together but was not sure. About an hour later they were summoned back to the domed communication room, however, this time Jenna, Sal, Gwent, and some more of the Vultens were present.

The first viewer was Barlo, followed by Anders who winked at Sean and Sal – no one else was present. Barlo started to go through the formalities when a third viewer lit up followed by a fourth.

"Councillor Barlo, stop, let's get to the point." The obvious Vulten in the third screen spoke. Again, long dark hair, short beard, chiselled features, but dark piercing eyes. "Kain, are you well?"

Kain bowed. "Yes Vul, I am."

"Good." Vul looked around. "Councillor Algier, it is a pleasure, oh and of course, Queen Jenna, you know I still have a place for a fifth wife if you wish." Vul finished with a wry smile.

"It is a pleasure to see you again, King Vul." Jenna returned the smile. "I am only human, one husband is plentiful for me." Both Vul and Kain laughed, everyone also gave a quick ha ha.

"Kain, I have been briefed of the situation. Our councillors seem to be making a big deal of nothing." As Vul spoke, Seth and Barlo both moved edgily. "The files on Gill and his passport will be with you after this communication. I assure you that I or my Supreme Council have nothing to do with any breach of protocol, if there were I would deal with it." Seth and the figure in the fourth viewer both bowed their heads.

"Thank you, Your Highness." Kain nodded.

Vul continued. "Secretary Seth will stay with you for two weeks as my advisor. During this time you may investigate Gill but any course of action or information must be agreed through Secretary Seth, who will keep us all within protocol." Everyone appeared to let out a sigh of relief.

"King Vul, again I thank you for your understanding in the matter. Secretary Seth will be most welcome on Earth to oversee investigations. He will be updated of all events when practical and included in any agreed action."

"Kain, I must remind you that any action taken against one

of my subjects must be agreed by me!" Vul raised his voice.

"I am aware of protocol and fully plan to adhere to it, however, if for reasons of time or indeed need deemed by me, then I will take the appropriate action as I see fit and deal with all consequences after!" Kain was just as loud, all appeared to now hold their breath.

"My friend," Vul appeared to want to lower the tension, "I am aware of your feelings, attempts on your life and your family's. Maybe your human side lends you to be close to such contempt. I have agreed to assist and if your feelings are correct then I may agree with your actions, but I must ask you would consider any action that would embarrass or annoy me. Is that clear?"

"Understood," Kain replied, bowing.

"Viewers off." Vul was gone.

"I wish to have a communication of my own, all leave but Sean, Algier, Sal, Gwent, and Jenna," Kain directed.

The room emptied quickly, leaving those Kain had requested plus Anders and Barlo on the viewers. "You may speak," Kain finished.

"Kain, you may have pushed Vul a bit further than necessary." Algier was first.

Barlo seemed to be spurred on by this. "Sire, is there a need to take direct action against Gill? We can work with the Vultens."

"I hear your advice but do not wish to take it, I have now made myself clear and I have the Supreme Council's backing. Barlo, Gill's passport location so close to my living area must have been approved by us as per protocol. Who approved it?" asked Kain.

"Mm." Barlo thought. "As we have not received the passport details from Seth we have not looked at who authorised it."

"Rubbish, you know as well as I that the passport will

be correct. Surely you have already checked our side?" Kain pushed.

All of a sudden a third viewer opened. Prince Dain was present. "You will find my signature as authorisation, I am sure."

"Why am I not surprised?" Kain gave a mock laugh.

"Brother, your mocking gets tiresome..." Dain stopped himself in his tracks.

Kain stood straight. "More disrespectful remarks, I will deal with you direct!"

"Of course, sire, forgive me. You know I hate the paperwork side of things. Signing this, signing that, it is not my strong point. The Supreme Council should check everything for me before signing, my signature is a mere formality to most things."

"Am I to take this as complete incompetence of you and my council?" Kain stated. Barlo and Dain looked very uncomfortable.

"Sire, I will deal with the issue from here." Anders had joined in. "If they are forged, incorrect, or against protocol, I will advise you personally."

"Thank you, Councillor Anders. Barlo, Anders is in charge of this investigation at Saulten. Make sure he has all the files and your full support, viewers off."

No one said anymore; the trip back to the wing and comfort zone was quiet. Back in their room, Kain announced, "We will not leave until after dinner, there are some people I wish to see first. My subjects will do well to see me. Gwent, you will make the arrangements for Secretary Seth to return to Earth with us. Sal, you will take Sean to the duel room." Kain walked over to Sean, putting his hand on Sean's shoulder, "Sean, I have purposely kept you involved in everything, you are bright and will pick up many things but now you must learn more." With that, he smiled and walked to the door.

Jenna went over to Sean. "Are you ok? Your head must be

buzzing darling:" Her words were followed by a cuddle.

"I'm ok, Mum."

"Sal, inform Kain that we will stay longer, at least the night. I need time with my son before he is shown any more," instructed Jenna.

"Are you sure, ma'am? King Kain was quite specific," Sal replied nervously.

"Tell Kain what I have said, we will remain here longer." With that, Jenna took Sean's hand and headed out. They walked without speaking for some time until a door opened and they entered a room very similar to Earth – colourful, plants, etc.

"This is like home," Sean stated.

"Yes, it is. It is an acclimatisation room for Earthens to sit and experience Earth-like qualities – plants, water, even our type of seating." Jenna sat on a picnic blanket on grass. Sean sat beside her.

Jenna put her head back and smiled. "So are you with it so far?"

"Kind of. Not sure about all this medieval talk, duels and the like, but love the gadgets. Why do you – we – not live on Earthen in the palace?"

Jenna chuckled. "Amazingly love conquered all. For all your father's faults he is a wonderful husband and our life on Earth is good. All the earthly things, good friends, countryside, air – real air – you don't get much of that on Earthen." Jenna continued. "Since you have now met the Earthens, all their protocols, it is middle-aged. I don't want to be Ann Boleyn."

"Hope not. Look what happened to her!"

"Son," Jenna was now holding his hand, "all so far is a shock but the next lessons from Sal will provide more of the picture and you will understand further. Like I did. Don't judge your father on the Earthen king he is but the father we both love."

Sean chatted with his mother further; he felt more comfortable in what seemed like home, Earth.

Sal entered the room. "I wished I had married Kain, as he would not have shouted at you as he did me, just another night did not go down well."

Jenna laughed. "Sometimes I do think you should have had him, his royal ways can be tiresome!' Sean was perplexed. "Let's have some fun," Jenna continued. "The bar!" With this, all three stood and Sean followed Jenna and Sal to the Hub again, but this time entered what was clearly a more relaxed bar area. More interestingly, a greater mix of people.

Sean also noted Captain Shad and Ensign Jeng had joined, not in uniform but clearly armed. Jenna called, "We'll get the table, you get the drinks," as she, Sal, and Jeng went off, leaving Shad and Sean. Shad walked Sean towards the bar area and ordered drinks.

"Should we be here?" Sean asked.

"Yes," was Shad's reply. "This is a very highly respected bar. Most here are councillors, senior figures and the like, so we can be here. Even Kain would drink here sometimes."

"Then why the guards?" Sean looked at Shad's gun.

"Wherever you go, you are still royalty so you should have protection, especially your mother who is not Earthen."

"Mum seems to look after herself, certainly Dad does what he's told and he's a king," said Sean.

Shad chuckled. "Yes, I'll give you that one." He started to lead Sean with the drinks towards the table the ladies were sitting at.

It was clear Jenna and Sal knew Ensign Jeng better than her being a crewmember, although as it appeared Jeng had been on Earthen more recent the gossiping was a strong part of the conversation. Sean looked around, there were clearly a lot of people, many with similar features. Sean was starting to make out the Saultens, Vultens, indeed he started saying to Shad which each were and was praised or not for getting it right.

At one point as Sean was talking to Shad, Shad froze. Looking up, all Sean could see in front of him were four women, all very pleasing to the eye, he thought. The first spoke to Jenna. "Hi, how is cousin Livia doing?"

"Hi Louisa, long time no see. Yes, Livia is fabulous, really enjoying her time on Earth," Jenna responded. Sean fell in. These were Dersian, again with the mainly blonde hair (although one was dark-haired) very tanned skin tone, and well, stunning. Sean realised why Shad had frozen.

"That's great. I really should pop down and see her someday. Your son has grown into a handsome young man." Louisa was now looking at Sean; he knew he went red, but smirked in acceptance of this compliment.

Jeng saved Sean. "Look, why don't you all sit here and talk? I need to show Sean something." This was agreed and Sean was soon sitting a few tables away with Jeng only.

Jeng started. "Your mum likes the Earthen wine, but it's good to see her let her hair down. Mind you, I think we have stranded Shad with six beautiful women." She giggled. "Watch this. Viewer on, show Earthen."

With this a 3D Earth-shape planet appeared, floating on top of the table. As Sean looked closer, although it was blue and green with clouds around, the continent shapes were not that of Earth.

"This is Earthen," Jeng informed. "Very similar to Earth. Saulten is like your Europe, all in one. Dersian is Asia, Ainten is North America, and Biernite is South America." Sean could see the resemblance to Earth.

Jeng continued, "Vulten differs in that it has two lands, what would be your North and South Poles. King Vul lives in the North, Secretary Seth in the South, ruling on Vul's behalf. You can see less water coverage than Earth and if you see along the Equator there are hundreds of miles either side that this land is the dead zones – basically vast deserts of little life – thereby this and the seas providing natural borders to each kingdom."

Sean could only say, "Wow," again.

Jeng continued explaining more parts of the planet and some ideas around the people. In her words, Vultens were awful, still warrior-like, cold like their lands. Dersians were blessed with looks, shallow but warming. Biernites were laid back and friendly but tended to follow the Vultens easily. Saultens were lovely, autocratic rule followers but had the most influence on all the kingdoms, except maybe Vulten. Aintens were the best – smart, charming, and doers.

Sean was a little surprised. "Aren't us Saultens the best?"

Jeng replied, "No, I'm an Ainten, which is why we are the best." Sean was a little shocked. "If you are an Ainten how come you work for Dad and are friends of Mum and Sal?"

Jeng acknowledged, "Your father is a great leader, much thanks in the background to Algier who everyone loves, even the Vultens. Therefore, Kain is open to involve all. Once you gain his trust then regardless of race he will love and protect you. I, as many people do, respect him and happily, dutifully work for him. As does Livia a Dersian, your PC Millan is a Biernite."

Sean used his favourite word. "Wow."

"Indeed, young people like myself all over Earthen see your father as the person who can take Earthen forward. Outside of protocol that he has to adhere to, his acceptance of all people of all races is applauded. Hell, he even married an alien!" Jeng laughed, knowing Sean would pick up on this word.

"So generally, on Earthen races don't mix?" asked Sean.

"That's correct, the other kingdoms are less tolerant, so for instance Millan couldn't go out with Sal in his homeland."

Sean interjected. "I knew it, I knew they were a couple!"

Jeng laughed. "Hope I've not let the cat out the bag, I have an Adonis of a boyfriend myself in Saulten, he is a Dersian."

Sean looked at Jeng, taking in her youth, maybe mid-twenties and very pretty. "You will have to tell me about the Earthen youth one day, but first Mum said something about Sal and Dad?"

Jeng laughed. "Sal is a little younger than your father but because of the closeness of his father to Councillor Anders, an Ainten, Kain would see Sal many times when young. It was thought that Kain and Sal could be the first non-kingdom royal marriage. I'm not sure they ever actually dated but as you can see are very close, but your mother changed all that."

"Wow," Sean repeated again. "Mum really stirred things up. Wait, does that make Sal an Ainten?"

"Yes, her father Anders is the only non-kingdom-born on a Supreme Council in all of Earthen, again your father's openness." Jeng clearly respected Kain. "We were starting to fully involve ourselves on Earth, having studied it for many years, but still did not fully understand your cultures. Your mother was a breath of fresh air – fiery, not over concerned about royalty and protocol – speaking your mind in front of kings can be dangerous without the right character and of course two powerful men behind you, Kain and Algier."

Sean was thinking about how proud he was of Mum, then asked, "You talk of power but not in a role way. Dad is obviously powerful as a king but the way you say things suggest something else, something more personal?"

Jeng responded with some thought. "Yes, there is more but this is not for me to say," then changing the subject, "I can tell you about the night when your mother danced with King Ders when King Vul tried to move in. Of course King Kain decided the pleasantries were over and took his wife from them. Three kings all upstaging one another over a human woman. Jenna took it in her stride when…"

"Nothing." Jenna had interrupted, wiggling her nose at Jeng. "I think it is time for bed, young man." Jeng and Jenna laughed, as Sean was led back to his bedroom. Jenna was there to say goodnight.

"Mum, how do you do it? You seem to control all these people and yet you're human." Sean asked.

Jenna smiled. "I may be human, but I have the Irish glint in my eye. A bit of Irish fire and a lot of Irish charm and luck, the Earthens have no chance. They think they're superior, NOT!"

Both laughed aloud and Sean went to sleep.

DUELLING:
(CHAPTER 8)

Sean woke; although there was much going in his head he walked to the breakfast area with quite a step. In the breakfast area Sean was greeted by all, his father specifically. "Take your time, there is no rush. Someone has changed our schedule," he said, glinting at Jenna, who just smiled back.

Kain continued. "I have arranged some meetings this morning so Sal can still show Sean the duel room." Before Sal could answer the door opened and in walked her father, Councillor Anders. Sal immediately jumped up to welcome her father with a big hug.

Algier spoke. "Welcome, Anders. That was a quick flight from home, but glad to see you." He shook Anders' hand.

Kain spoke. "Welcome, my friend. Maybe you should have some time with your daughter then we can meet." Looking at Gwent, "Have Ensign Jeng take Sean to the duel room but fully brief her first." Gwent nodded and left the room.

All sat down, ate, and drank with small talk. It was clear that Anders, Kain, Jenna, and Algier got on very well. Sal appeared happier around her father. Some ten minutes passed when Ensign Jeng entered the room, addressing Sean. "Looks like me again, let's go."

Sean followed Jeng through the varied corridors of the spaceship. As they got to a door with 'Hub' written above it they were joined by Captain Shad. "Morning Sean. Being a prince, you need more protection so I'm with you guys."

All three entered the Hub; most of the people were in uniform. All dutifully bowed or saluted Sean. After a few further corridors and a lift ride they came upon another door with 'Arena' written above it.

Jeng looked at Sean. "You ready?"

Sean nodded – Jeng opened the door. They walked a short distance then the room opened up before them. Sean looked around, it was not a room but as the name suggested, an arena. The arena was about the size of a football pitch in total but oval in shape, with many seats higher up than the flooring with what appeared to be glass between the seats and the arena floor, which Sean was now standing in the middle of.

Looking around, Sean asked, "What games are played here? I see no goals or nets."

Jeng smirked. "Follow me."

Sean followed Jeng to the other side of the arena, entering another short tunnel that led to what was obviously the changing rooms. Jeng went over to the white walls; waving her hand, a cupboard-type door opened. Behind this door were varied bodyguard pads just like those used on Earth in kickboxing. Jeng reached in, checked some sizes then threw some over to Sean. "Put them on."

Sean put on some elbow and kneepads then a belt around his waist, which went slightly down his front, more around the rear. "A bit big round the butt," he called.

Jeng laughed. "Now the head guard."

Sean obliged. Fully kitted out, a mirror appeared on one of the white walls. He walked over and looked at himself. Catching a glimpse of Jeng in the same mirror, he realised she had also dressed in the protective gear. He turned. "We are not going to fight, are we? This looks like kick boxing gear."

Jeng replied, "Let's see."

Sean followed her back to the middle of the arena; Shad was standing on a platform above the tunnel they had just entered, within the arena and in front of the glass-fronted seats.

Jeng started to circle Sean. "Come on then, hit me."

Sean laughed. "We are not going to fight."

Jeng carried on circling about a metre from Sean. Her build much smaller but similar in height, she then lunged and with one motion took Sean's legs from him; Sean fell to the floor on his rear.

Sean got up. "I'm not going to hit a girl!"

Jeng struck again and Sean ended on his rear for a second time. "Very noble of you not to hit a girl but you are in a duelling arena, fight or be thrashed!"

Sean got up and took a defensive stance, watching Jeng as she circled. Shad shouted across, "She is a trained military combat expert, you won't hurt her so fight back. Besides, you both have protective guards on." He added, laughing, "Now you know why the bottom pads are bigger."

Sean thought for a moment, stood taller, then pounced, striking Jeng's legs, forcing her to the floor. "Oops, sorry." He could not help himself.

Jeng said, "Ok, but don't drop your guard." Sean hit the floor again, Jeng now standing above him laughing.

Sean got up but this time looking at Shad, his back to Jeng. "Shad, are you sure I can hit her?" before he got a response Sean turned and pounced at Jeng. Sean did not know what happened but instead of flooring Jeng he was now some metres away from her on his backside again.

"How did you do that?" Sean exclaimed.

"Come and get it," was Jeng's response.

Sean got up, walked closer to Jeng and started circling her. Jeng went to pounce, Sean dummied then went to counter but again he ended up on his rear a few metres away. Shad interjected. "Jeng, stop playing with him. Stand still and show him."

Jeng stood still, lowered her arms and said, "There, that makes it easy. Go for it."

Sean carried on circling, was he really going to attack a girl who was clearly ready just to be hit? Then came the shock, without going towards Jeng or her to him, Sean felt something hit him in the stomach. He flew backwards, ending up again on his rear but now some metres away.

"How did you do that?" Sean cried.

Jeng said, "Stand up."

As Sean stood Jeng, moving towards him but still some ten metres away, lunged her arms forward and Sean again flew through the air, this time ending flat out on his front.

Sean turned and sat up; Jeng and Shad were now both standing beside him.

"Telekinetic energy, you would call this on Earth," Shad advised. "Jeng was using her head, her thoughts, not physical."

Sean stood up. "You are kidding me," he stated.

"No," was Shad's response. "You can do it as well, just think. Jeng, stand still." Sean could see Jeng standing a few metres away, arms down, looking a bit apprehensive. "Move her," came the taunt from Shad. "Use your thoughts, look at her."

Sean focussed on Jeng, then in his mind he thought, *Push*. Jeng shook. Sean did it again, Jeng shook more. Jeng suddenly fought back, moving her arms to direct the energy. Sean instinctively moved his to stop her. Both now circled each other, trading 'jabs' but from a distance of a few metres. Sean was amazed; he could see the air distort between them. If Jeng raised and directed her right arm, Sean would raise his left and the air between them appeared disturbed. At this point Jeng put both arms together and Sean hit the floor.

"Being beaten by a girl and you're a prince. You are useless." Jeng goaded the fallen Sean.

Sean thought for a minute then as he started to rise he

flipped round and threw his thoughts at Jeng full on, before getting to his feet. Jeng flew across the floor, landing in a heap some thirty metres from him. Next Sean hit the floor but this time could not move. Shad was above him, clearly pinning him to the ground.

"Sean, I'm going to let you go slowly but you must calm down," Shad said, standing over him. Sean nodded yes and could feel the force lessen until he could sit up.

"Good," Shad said. He was now walking to Jeng who was clearly sitting up and moving.

Sean stood up and ran to Jeng. "I'm sorry, I'm sorry, are you Ok?"

Jeng got to her feet. "Wow, young man, that was some force. But yes, shaken but fine." Jeng's smile had come back to her face.

Sean stated, "I didn't mean to hurt you."

Jeng reassured, "You didn't, just winded, but my pretend goading did the trick. A bit of a temper, young man."

"My turn now please." Sal's voice was clear as she entered the arena.

Sean responded, "I'm not duelling you. Besides, you are not kitted up."

"I'm not here to fight but to talk to you, come on." Sal started towards the changing room area.

Jeng grabbed Sean's arm. "You're lucky. I wouldn't fight Sal, but hey, you did well."

With that, Jeng and Shad left the arena. Sean went to the changing room. Sal helped Sean to take off and put away the protective gear, then from another unseen cupboard door opening got them both drinks.

Sitting beside Sean, Sal started. "Now you have it, basically, we have advanced in our bodies as well as technology. We are telekinetic – our minds are our power as much as any physical power we may have."

Sean started to click. "So when you talk about power you mean this force from within?"

"Yes, if that makes it easier to understand."

"So, this is how humans develop?"

"Yes. Earthens have mind control, telekinesis, indeed we are superior in many physical ways. Our reflexes are quicker, we are stronger and faster than humans."

"Wow, like superhumans?" Sean quizzed.

Sal laughed. "Not quite, we are just that bit more advanced all round, however, our basic anatomy is the same as yours, therefore we can be hurt, we do bleed, we can be killed."

Sean thought for a while. "If I acted like this on Earth then I would be like Superman?"

Sal repeated. "Not exactly, as you can be hurt. However, yes, you would be faster and stronger than humans, maybe Earthlings is a better word."

Again, something clicked in Sean's head. "My goal the other week when I flew through two or three players, no one could catch me. I was using my Earthen powers."

"Yes, which is why you understand now that Kain had you taken off."

"Yes, but why have I not used my powers before?" Sean thought harder. "No, wait, the fight with Hamling and his cronies. I floored them, that was my power. How come I have not noticed this before, just these odd times?"

Sal gasped for air, held Sean by the shoulders, but with her head slightly bowed said, "TDL, your medicine, it weakens your power. TDL is a drug used on Earthen to sedate people, sedate powers. As an example our police forces have TDL needles, our prisoners are on TDL all the time..."

Sean interrupted. "What, I'm a criminal? Wait, you have been drugging me for years telling me I'm ill when I'm not."

Sean stood up. "I can't take this. All my friends, my family, have lied to me, drugged me. No." Sean turned and walked out, Sal crying behind him.

Sean walked around for some time, oblivious of the people and the stares around him. Although not listening, he could feel voices back in his head. Every now and then he would look at someone who would cower their stare from his gaze. As he turned a corner a familiar voice cried out, "Sean, come here please." Sean knew his uncle's voice. Rather begrudgingly, he walked towards Algier. As usual Algier did not fail to surprise him. "Let's have a beer," was said, as Sean was led into a strange-looking bar.

Algier sat down, gave his order to the waitress and looked Sean straight in the eyes. "You are right. We have all lied to you and drugged you. But is it not obvious why all the people that love you did this?"

Sean thought. "No." He decided it was not time to talk.

Algier waited until the beer came before speaking again. "Drink it. It's Earthen beer, you are too young and I'll be locked up but who cares? You don't." Algier took a swig of his beer, which was clearly too much at once; he started coughing and spluttering. Sean laughed in his head and put a hand out to ease his uncle.

Algier chuckled. "Drink yours, it may loosen your tongue."

"You must know how I feel." Sean went defensive.

"Let down, I understand, but for once I'll blame your mother. Think. How could an Earthen boy be brought up on Earth without being controlled? Hell, you would probably have been a mass murderer at two just because someone nicked your dummy." Algier was trying.

Sean decided to give Algier a bit of slack. "Yes, I didn't think of that."

Algier swigged more beer. "Many sacrifices were made when your parents decided to live on Earth, not telling you who or what you really are is a big one of them. Again though, were you not loved? Many a child would have wished for your upbringing. Hell, now is where the hard part comes because now you know you will have to grow up and learn to control your powers. Sometimes naivety can be bliss."

Sean took a swig of the beer, noting it was quite nice. "I need to think on this. Can we go back to our room? No, the Earth room with the grass please."

Algier gave a smile took and led Sean towards the Earth acclimatisation room, leaving Sean to his own thoughts. Sean sat on the grass for what appeared to be hours, his brain trying to take in all he had learnt over the last few days.

"Sean, how are you?" His mother's voice came from the door as she walked towards him.

Jenna sat down next to Sean; she knew he did not want to talk so a big hug was provided as they sat on the grass. Sitting there, just holding hands was enough, not speaking until Jenna led Sean back to his room to rest.

Sean surprised himself and slept well; again, upon waking he entered the breakfast area seeing his friends and family. No one spoke as he took some food and sat down. Sean ate, the room was in total silence. Sean caught a glimpse of Sal, who did not look as tidy as she normally did, indeed she looked unhappy.

It was Sean who broke the silence. "Sal, I'm sorry for making you cry yesterday."

Sal's face lit up as she replied, "That's Ok, it was a lot to take in."

Kain stood up and announced, "We are going home now, let's get ready to depart."

Gwent piped up. "Sir, I must remind you that Secretary Seth will be coming with us. Maybe you, Jenna, Sean, and I should go first, allowing Sal some more time with her father and Algier time to prepare Seth – we don't want a powerful Vulten free on Earth."

Kain agreed and within the hour and with very little talk, Kain, Jenna, Sean, and Gwent were on the shuttle back to Earth. Sean still playing the moody silent game, although Jeng's "Want a rematch?" nearly made him lose his guard and chuckle.

Within minutes of landing all were in cars and driven to Sean's house, Sean going straight to his room. His thoughts were disturbed by a knock on his door. "Go away!" Sean shouted, but to his surprise the door opened and Shadow came flying in, pinning Sean to the bed, smothering him with licks. Sean giggled and hugged Shadow, noting PC Millan was now with him. "So don't say thanks for me looking after him. Gee, does he eat!"

Sean laughed again; PC Millan gave a smile. "I know it sounds corny but all will seem better in the morning now you are home." With that, he left.

Morning did come and this time Sean ate breakfast on his own, Detective Inspector Cott was in talking with Kain. Sean went to the garden with Shadow; Jenna sat at the garden table near them. "You can't ignore us forever."

"I know." Sean sat next to his mother. "It is a lot to take in but yes, I can see now why you all had to do what you did."

"Good, then maybe we can move on. Dad wishes to teach you more about your powers especially now on Earth, this will start later today."

"So I'm not going to school? I would like to see my friends," asked Sean.

"Tomorrow," was the reply.

Kain came into the garden, Jenna went back inside. "So the last part of the puzzle, Sean. Not only can you project force with your brain, you can also read, or at least attempt to read minds."

Sean was shocked; Kain got to the point. "The voices in your head are either you picking people up or people trying to get into yours, like Gill did as an example."

"Wow, so you... I mean we can read minds?"

"Not exactly, although some very powerful Earthens are believed able, it's more of a communication tool. Sean, look at me and let me in."

Sean looked at his father then felt his voice in his head. "Let me talk to you?" Kain's mouth was clearly not moving.

Sean replied, "Yes."

Kain, again without moving his mouth, said, "Try it by thinking it, don't use your mouth."

Sean obliged. "Yes, I can hear you. Can you hear me?"

"Yes, excellent. Again, a bit of focus and you can communicate like an Earthen." Kain then started to ask Sean silly questions such as 'what is your dog's name?' which Sean answered. This went on for ten minutes, both communicating but neither opening their mouths.

Kain finally spoke with his mouth. "I believe you have got it. Let's talk as humans."

Sean, also with his mouth, replied, "Ok, but there is a catch?"

"Yes, of course. If people can get into your head to communicate they may try to read your thoughts or even control you. As I've said, this is not common but possible which is why the first thing you learn is to block out people's thoughts."

"Show me?" requested Sean.

"Ok, I'll try to talk to you and all you need is to say no, but focus the no against my voice in the part of the brain you are hearing it." Kain carried on. "Let me in, let me in...?"

Sean heard the first few attempts but as he focussed more Kain's voice faded.

"Wow, that was easy!" Sean exclaimed.

Kain laughed. "Yes, it is a basic natural defence mechanism

in our brains, with time you will automatically block everyone out without actually thinking about it, or the need for TDL. TDL not only reduces your brain power out but also stops people from entering your brain, hence why Gill could not easily get into your brain as TDL stopped it."

"I get it, although drugging your child in many countries, err, planets, must be illegal." Sean took a verbal swipe at Kain.

"Not if you're a king because you make the laws." Kain made Sean laugh as even he did not have an answer for this. Again, Kain asked Sean to try some more, either blocking Kain or communicating to him. Sean was getting quite good at this.

"Wait, if you can read minds and us Earthens can block, what about humans? They can't?" Sean was now talking with his mouth.

Kain responded, also verbally. "That is correct. Earthlings are easy to communicate with, read basic feelings, if not thoughts, which is why we again automatically turn this off. First for privacy, second is sanity. Do you really want hundreds of human voices going around in your head? I don't for sure."

Sean thought. "But when you want to it must be great, I mean say arguing with Mum or persuading her to do something..."

Kain gave a big laugh. "No, no, don't go there. Do not ever use your powers to woo a woman or even understand them. A relationship based on espionage is not going to be a long one. Besides, once your mother was aware of this function I taught her some basic tricks and actually even she can be quite effective in blocking people out. Worst is she lets you in then nags you to death..."

Jenna interjected, "So you are doing the mind reading bit?" A pretend scowl was across her face followed by a chuckle. "Sean, Dad is correct. Do not use that particular power unless necessary, certainly not on friends and definitely not on Emma!"

Sean thought for a moment. Getting into Emma's mind could be fun. His mother's look stopped his thought. "Oh no, of course not, never. She nags verbally, let alone in my head."

Jenna shrugged her shoulders and went back into the house. Sean thought about reading his mother's mind when Kain interjected. "Don't even try, not only has Mum learnt some basic defence, the locket she always wears has a blocking transmission device – the one defence weapon I can give her."

Sean asked, "Defence? I know someone in your head is not good but how can it hurt...?" Sean did not finish his sentence when a sharp pain went through his head then stopped.

"If you can get into someone's head, then like that you can attack. Sorry, I hope that didn't hurt too much."

"Holy shit, you actually were able to hurt me."

"Yes," was the response.

Sean continued, "Can all Earthens do that?"

Kain rose to his feet. "Again, possibly yes but it comes back to our power. Who is the most powerful? Brain strength being the ultimate prize."

Sean looked up at his father; at full height above him Kain did look like the powerful king he was. "Yes Father," was his only response.

Kain ended the training session with, "I have things to do. Mum needs groceries so go shopping with her, and Millan will be around to watch you. We will carry out some more training tonight and tomorrow, then at the weekend we will put more effort in, but you are a natural."

Kain left the garden and within the hour Sean was at Tesco's with Jenna. PC Millan was obvious, trying to watch them from a distance without been seen made himself more visible but Sean knew PC Millan knew this. Sean could not resist playing a few games. As some people went to pick fruit up Sean would push the fruit onto the floor, chuckling at their shocked response. Jenna's look stopped that fun.

As Sean rounded one aisle he virtually bumped into Derek Mill, one of Frazier's goonies. "Why are you not at school, Master Mills?" Jenna had asked.

"I'm ill, Mrs Saul," was the response.

"Can't see your mother or father?' Jenna pushed.

"Mum's at home, I'm just picking something up for her, she said fresh air was good for me." Derek was trying.

"Really? So she is ill and off work too?" Jenna pressed.

Derek was caught. "Mm, no. I'm meeting her after school... I mean work, bye."

Derek walked past Jenna and Sean. This was Sean's chance, a quick thought and he had kicked Derek up the rear. Derek jumped and knocked many of the crisps and biscuits off the shelf he was passing. Sean laughed, but was then dragged away by Jenna, who now out of sight in the next aisle also laughed.

"Sean, that is naughty. Stop it now." Jenna returned to the shopping.

After paying they sat in the small Tesco café, PC Millan joining them. Jenna had rumbled him and said, "If you are that poor at surveillance then just walk with us." All three sat down, sipping at their drinks.

"Was that you on Master Mill?" PC Millan knowingly asked.

"Yes," was the reply. Sean knew he was busted and continued, "How come I can now use some of my powers?"

PC Millan laughed so loud others looked over quizzically; a fully uniformed policeman sitting at the table drinking was an unusual sight, let alone laughing aloud. PC Millan dropped his voice. "Since you have been coming aware we have dropped your TDL dosage so your powers are now able to be used."

Sean, just as quiet but still direct, "A uniformed cop telling me drugging by my parents is ok, that is still weird." All three chuckled. They knew Sean had the message clear now, even if he was making a point of it for fun.

Sean enjoyed the rest of the evening with his father, playing what was now called mind games. Sean was a quick learner. He was advised Sal, Algier, and Seth would be on Earth tomorrow. Seth would be staying in the still-empty James house. On this point, Sean was advised to say that Ged was having work issues and had taken an early summer holiday with his family. Make no big deal of it was the main stance.

SUMMER DANCE:
(CHAPTER 9)

Sean was up and out the next morning, racing Shadow to the path end. Sean won as Shadow at one point had just stopped. If a dog could look perplexed he did, because although Shadow was slightly faster, Sean nearly keeping up with him at full pelt was strange.

Sean was at the path end early. To his shock, the old lady of 71 had come out of her door, walking towards him. Standing just in front of him, she gave a welcoming smile. "I'm Saulten too, a friend of your father."

Sean fell in. "You mean you're not a nosey old b... I mean lady, but a Saulten watching me?"

"Carnell is my name and yes, I am doing my job watching you. Shadow is good but you never know when you may need help."

"Wait. That morning with Gill, he was scared of you?" Sean said.

"Not exactly." Carnell started to explain, "Earthens are scared of dogs, they can't get into their brains plus Shadow in his collar has a similar thought cloaking device as your mother's, and a tracking device-cum-alarm. Once Shadow went into fight mode the unit sensed this and alarms went off everywhere. Your mother and I responded."

Sean threw a sigh. "Now I'm bugged by my dog, does this ever end? Serious, surely Gill would not be scared of a dog and, with respect, an old lady."

"I may be old but I am ex-military and a professional duel champion on Earthen, so I maybe rusty but can handle myself. Mix this with a barking dog, a screaming human, and the possibility in all the excitement of waking up the most powerful Earthens son's power – I think you get the picture."

Sean giggled. "Wow, my sincere apologies, Mrs Carnell. Looks definitely can be deceiving."

"Sean."

Emma had shouted as she and Mush were heading towards them, both stopping some six metres from the old lady and Sean. The old lady turned, looked at them, and turned back to say to Sean in his head, "I'll walk Shadow back, he is my friend and often sneaks into my house once you disappear out of sight for a sausage, he loves sausages. I'll join him with your mother this morning for breakfast." With this, Mrs Carnell started towards Sean's house, Shadow at her side.

"Blimey, what was that all about...?"

But before Emma could finish Sean had engulfed both his friends in a big hug. "It's great to see you both."

Mush, now freed from Sean's embrace, "No, come on, what happened there? The old hag was talking to you."

Sean snapped back, "Her name is Mrs Carnell and she is not a hag, she is a sweet old lady."

Emma only repeated, "Blimey," before Sean turned on her. "I expect better from you, respect for your elders."

Emma was quite taken aback. She could not recall when she had ever actually been derogatory to the old lady but had to accept she didn't stop it either.

Mush had had enough and now was on top of Sean, drilling his head, Sean knew this was play fighting and allowed it to happen, both ending up on the floor, laughing loud. "We will be late," was Emma's only response to this horseplay.

Upon entering the playground talk was full of the Summer

Dance the next evening, the last day of school. Sean had forgotten but Frazier had not.

"So you three going together? A threesome," came the goading from one of his cronies.

Mush stood tall. "Sean is with Emma, I'm taking Zandra. Are you taking baby Lisa or you going as a gay boy band with your cronies," followed by a bellyful laugh.

Frazier was angry; pushing aside his own guards he squired up to Mush. "Not now, Eugenie, but I will have you!" With that, Frazier and his cronies moved off.

Emma remarked, "Mush, you go too far."

"So what? He's a... Good morning Miss Smith." With this, all went to their classrooms.

At lunch Zandra joined them. She was a pretty, rounded Asian girl, Philippine by birth but had lived in England since the age of four. Zandra started. "So Sean, we heard the Jameses' dad had a breakdown over losing his job, took it bad, but your dad is helping them out?"

Sean said, "Yes, Dad and Ged are close so in his hour of need he stepped in."

Zandra pushed, "So why did you miss some days off school?"

Sean thought. "Oh yeah, the pressure got to me and I kinda overdosed on my medicine, so I was not well."

"So, no police cars and ambulances at your place last Saturday." Trekkie had joined the group.

"It was a bad breakdown. Dad called Sal who turned up and of course PC Millan followed her." Sean cringed inside; he was not ready for that question.

"I don't get it with that Sal, she's like your personal nurse?" asked Zandra.

"She is a relative, so yes, we are very close," Sean responded off cuff.

"Hey, let's leave this. If a friend and her family is in trouble we should not tittle tattle over it." Emma had saved Sean. "Besides, Sean does not know about Mr Gill. He has also left, out of the blue."

Sean was now back, more comfortable. "Wow, that's news. What a surprise. Any idea why?"

Mush joined in. "No idea but worse, we have Miss Smith for English and we are late." Conversation stopped and they all went to class.

Deputy Head Professor Smith looked uncomfortable. Although she was a very accomplished teacher she normally liked to run and organise things rather than teach. The lesson was going well; the one thing Professor Smith had was respect from the pupils, even Frazier would not try it on when Professor Smith was about. Fifteen minutes in and all were asked to read a short chapter from a book. Professor Smith then asked Sean to step outside with her, passing a comment about him not looking well.

Sean, now standing in the corridor with Professor Smith right in front of him, was uneasy. "I haven't done anything," he offered up.

"Really?" was Professor Smith's reply. "So why were you off school for the last few days?"

"Did my Mum not call?" Sean was definitely now uncomfortable.

"No, I thought you could tell," Professor Smith pushed. "After all, flying around in spaceships is not the normal activity of a young boy."

Sean relaxed. "You know? Don't tell me you're an Earthen?"

Professor Smith replied, "Saulten of course, great friends with Marla, your grandmother. An outstanding woman and queen was she."

A happy thought shot into Sean's mind. Rarely had he heard his grandmother's name, nor indeed was much said about his grandparents in general. However, he only had fond memories of her visits. He had not met his grandfather, who had passed away before he was born – "Thank you, Miss Smith. You are also spying on me." Sean gave a laugh.

"You are a prince, one day king of our kingdom. Your protection has always been planned and in place – my job is here at the school, sire."

Sean was a little startled, this lady that he was wary of for many years was actually working for him. "Wow," came his favourite word. "Thank you again. You calling me sire is a bit unnerving."

Professor Smith smiled. "Ok Master Saul, shall we get back to the lesson?"

The next day was to be a big one; last day at school before the summer break and the summer dance in the evening. Sean having had another evening's training with his father, was full of confidence, although the 'remember, do not use your powers on Emma' instruction from Jenna was clear in his head.

The walk to school was fun, Sean waving to the old lady at 71, much to Mush's annoyance. Emma was quizzing Mush over his relationship with Zandra. Mush got really upset when Emma suggested he was no Twilight actor. Mush thought of mushing Emma but wasn't feeling brave enough. Besides Mush could tell Emma was only joking.

Talk in the playground was about the dance, who was with who, who would be wearing what – which would be quickly followed by half day, whoop whoop!

Frazier unusually was keeping out the way of Sean and the gang. Zandra was with them most of the time; Sean was happy for his friend. Indeed, Zandra was making an effort to get on with Emma, which was working. At break time Emma and Zandra were talking; the thrown glance at Sean and Mush kept them thinking. Sean at one point thought, *No, I'm going for it.*

He turned to look at Emma when he felt a clip behind the

ear. "Hi Sean!" Sal was standing next to him. Sean wanted to hug her there and then but realising where he was, gave her a big smile. "Hi – how did you know?"

"I saw the look in your eye."

"Oops, don't tell Mum," Sean pleaded.

"Of course not," Sal added as she walked off to her room.

"What's that all about? Hang on, you were looking at Emma in a funny way, she must have seen that... You soppy so and so." Mush pushed Sean, laughing as he did. Mush added, "So remind me what you doing over the holidays?"

Sean was caught short. "Mm, I err..."

Emma once again saved him. "We are off the first week then our families are having a joint holiday at Sean's dad's Tuscan holiday home." Sean had forgotten. Emma added, "Gee, Sean, if only you had a brain."

Sean thought, *If only she knew.*

"Wow, we had a great time there last year if you recall," Mush remembering when all three families had indeed holidayed there last year together. "Shame Dad has booked us a villa in Florida with my uncle and aunt."

"Oh yeah, they have those two young bratty kids. Bet you're there to childmind." Sean chuckled.

"Don't worry, I have a plan. I'll Mush them in the first few days then be barred from being left alone with them. Boy, I wish I was with you two."

"It will be strange without you but you will enjoy Florida, the rides are great," Emma added wisely. "What are you doing, Zandra, for your holidays?"

"Oh, we are going home to the Philippines to see some family, but I wish I was going to Florida with Mush." Zandra's comment made Mush flush – Emma giggled. Sean behind both the girls' backs made a gagging motion to Mush. Mush decided direct action was needed and set chase after the now running

Sean, much to all-around amusement. Sean could sense that a public mushing would go down well, however, for some reason Mush was never going to catch him.

In the safety of the school final assembly, many teachers present, Sean felt courageous enough to stand next to Mush. Professor Holmes took to the stage. Starting with the usual welcomes, he moved on to some awards. Sean at this point turned off, best pupil, most helpful, etc., were never coming his way. His ears did prick up when Emma's name was mentioned, Sean had forgotten the earlier part of the term; she and others had gone on a singing trip to Salzburg for a pre-halfterm school share initiative. Emma was the school 'choir' team leader for the event. Emma went up to the stage and accepted a small bunch of flowers from Miss Gould, the singing teacher. Sean and Mush led the applause. As the awards came to an end Professor Holmes turned his attention to the coming evening's events.

"Year eleven prom, be back at the school promptly for 5pm for transport to your prom. Please behave at the special but secret venue." Laughs came from most of the year eleven boys. "No drinking, which includes the year eleven rugby boys." Laughter met this comment from all present.

"Year ten students, please ask your parents to drop you off in the back car park to keep away from all the limos as the Summer Dance will be on the back field, thank God it's a beautiful day!" Professor Holmes ended with, "Enjoy your holidays!"

The pupils and teachers all started to leave the hall, their last 'lesson' was actually in their form rooms just to tidy up things, checking if they needed anything for any school homework, by 1pm it was time to move. Sean, Emma, and Mush got to the pathway quicker than usual, Emma in a rush, saying she had to have as much time as possible to do her hair. Mush suggesting they didn't have all day did not go down well. Sean found himself alone at the path when catching out the corner of his eye, spotted Shadow standing just inside the old lady's open door. Sean, checking no one was looking, walked towards the door. As he approached Mrs Carnell came to the door. "Come in, have a quick drink?" Sean entered the house.

Sitting at the kitchen table, Sean could see why Shadow obviously enjoyed there. Two sausages cut up and put in a bowl for him to eat, Sean guessed some had already been digested. "I won't hold you too long as I know you have the dance, but how are you?" Mrs Carnell asked.

"I'm fine, I'm coming to terms with it all now. To be honest I am amazed at how many people care for me, although that's my position right?'

"Of course much of it is part of your role, royalty and all that. However, much more is about you, your father and mother, and how they generally treat people – respect is too small a word."

Sean's thoughts were now changing. "This actually means that one day I will be king and will have to fill the shoes of my father?"

"Yes, that should be the way it goes, but hopefully a long time from now. Your father is not old and anyway, us Earthens tend to live on average ten to fifteen years longer than Earthlings. By then I'm sure you will understand all our ways and make the right decision for you, your family, and our people."

Sean started to now feel the enormity of the situation. "Do you think I'll be as confident, driven as my father was when making his decision?"

Carnell smiled. "Yes, I see the young Kain in you, you are your father's son."

Sean thought. "But with my mother's fire?"

"Yes, the unknown. Your mother, bless her, has a lot to answer for. Although probably not said out loud, many on Earthen consider her a hero, someone to look up to. Earthen still has many male dominance traditions as you can tell.

Shame Jenna is not Earthen, she would make a great queen as a leader rather than a queen to a king."

"Wow, I guess a queen of their own right has not happened on Earthen?' Sean asked.

"No, definitely no, totally unheard of. If a king dies it will go to his nearest male relative. In the unlikely event there is no one then it would go to duel for the Supreme Council members or families to fight for," Carnell said, a little agitated.

"This duelling is it to the death?"

"In professional terms like I did, no. Think boxing with rules, etcetera, the aim being to overpower, not injure or at least seriously injure. If, however, a duel is called, then yes, it can, almost always is, to the death."

Sean had to think. "The mix of such high tech and intellect, and yet you have such barbaric rules and ways. Suppose that's how kingdoms work."

"Yes, quite the contradiction but it is our ways."

Sean looked Carnell straight in the eyes. "Dad, has he ever duelled to the death?"

Carnell was uneasy, walked away to top up her tea then upon returning, "Yes, although as king he can have proxies depending on certain rules. But yes, he has duelled himself."

"You are saying Dad has killed someone?"

"You have to think of this in a different way. He is not a murderer but he has to rule, taking good and bad actions for him and his kingdom."

Sean pushed. "So is that why he is seen as so powerful? He has defeated many at duels?"

Carnell looked up, sighed, then said, "You will find this out, better me than anyone else. Here goes... When your father first started dating your mother, to say it was frowned upon is an understatement. Worst, when he stated he was to marry and consider living on Earth. Kain had enemies within but also the other kings, sensed a chance to maybe overthrow him. King Vul and King Ain were especially mocking of the time, both having been stoked up by Prince Dain. You must understand the pressure your father was under. Story goes that a Kings' Council was called to discuss the affair, attended by the five kings, their Supreme Council secretaries, Algier in Saultens case, with the only addition being Prince Dain. The other kings saw Dain as a weakness to Kain and Algier, and also claimed that as the heir to Kain's throne had a right to take part. It appears during the meeting that things got a little out of hand, King Ain being led on by King Vul and Prince Dain overstepped the mark. I believe he insulted Kain and Jenna. Try telling 'sticks and stones' to a hyped-up king. Kain responded – King Ain, who was a few years older than Kain and just as physically matched, apparently threw down the duel challenge, personal, meaning him and Kain. Everyone thought this was a bluff; Kain on the other hand did not. Being young and new, he accepted the duel."

Carnell moved in her chair, taking a sip of tea. "King Ain was now lost, his bluff being blatantly turned around. I'm sure he thought he could handle this relative upstart but having never previously duelled, we believe he would not relish the event. Apparently, King Vul sided with Ain, and then Prince Dain said something to King Ain. King Ain went for your father there and then, slamming him around the council chamber. Kain lying on the floor with all thinking the fight was over, stood up, anger in his eyes, looking for revenge. I believe at this point all the kings and indeed the councillors thought enough was enough and tried to control Kain. No one can explain what happened next but only four kings left the council room that day."

Carnell took a breath. "Ain's younger brother took over the Ainten kingdom. Thankfully he was not his brother biggest fan, obviously an Earthen sibling thing." Carnell chuckled. "His secretary at the time, Anders, was very influential in controlling the new King Ain and the general situation. How one king in front of four others plus six powerful councillors was able to take the life of another has never been explained, but the power of your father has been unquestioned ever since."

Sean sat quietly. "So Dad is as barbaric as all the others?"

"No, he did his duty. King Ain made the challenge, technically Kain had to oblige although I'm sure that if it didn't explode as said, they would have come to some diplomatic agreement after."

"From what you said Uncle Dain provoked this?"

"Yes, as rumour suggests. Your uncle is a two-faced, untrustworthy person, a disgrace to your family's history. King Sharn, your granddad, was a great leader, and his father before him."

Sean sat still. Shadow was now at his legs, pushing as if to go. "You will be late, Shadow is restless. Maybe you should go now," suggested Carnell.

Sean got up and walked home with Shadow. His thoughts were a mess, how could he look at his father now? A murderer or a great king?

Sean entered the kitchen. Jenna gave him a knowing look. "Carnell told you about Kain and King Ain, I hear." Carnell had obviously called Jenna.

"Yes, it's a lot to take in."

"I know but you have to take it into context. Being honest, if King Ain's first 'shot' was successful your father would have been the one that died. It was self-defence, is the way to look at it." Jenna was trying to help.

Sean sat at the table. Of all he had heard this was probably the hardest to take in. Jenna let him sit for a while then disturbed him. "You may not want to hear this but you have a dance to go to and a certain young lady to impress." Jenna banked on the Emma card working.

Sean got up. "Yes, of course. I will put this to the back

of my mind." With that, Sean went upstairs to get ready. A short time later Sean was in the Discovery being driven to the dance, Jenna at the wheel, cursing all the limos now blocking the road to the school.

Sean laughed. "Proms, hey. Thankfully we don't have to turn up in such things."

Jenna replied, "Some do. Jolie had a limo booked and I know Mush's dad has loaned a Mercedes from work to take him and Zandra."

Desmond Green, Mush's dad, was the salesman who sold Kain every Mercedes he had owned over the years. Jenna finally guided the car to the back car park, looking at Sean, stopping him before getting out. "You look handsome, young man. Do not mind game Emma." Then placing a kiss on Sean's cheek she let him exit, then drove off.

Sean's first sight was a bunch of girls all dressed up. *Wow,* he thought. *Are they really girls at my school? No, they can't be.* "Hiyer mate." Sean turned to look at his friend Mush, who was all suited and booted. Sean took a second look. "Wow, you scrub up well," is all he could think of to say.

"Not as good as them." Mush's reply caused Sean to look around again; Zandra was standing next to Emma who had just exited Emma's mum's Volvo. Even though Sean had seen Emma in the dress before, she was obviously not as made up and hair done as in the shop. Both boys were gobsmacked.

"So boys. I hope you can dance?" was Zandra's welcome.

"Shit, we have to do that." Mush looked very uncomfortable.

"It's a dance, idiot. What else are you going to do?" Emma threw in. "Hi Sean, you look smart."

Sean was on the spot but could not stop. "You look beautiful."

Emma blushed. Zandra added, "Come on, you lump. Get me a drink." Mush followed Zandra's command, leaving Sean and

Emma together.

"Thank you." Emma gave Sean a peck on the cheek then led him to follow their friends.

The start of the dance was usual, all the boys somehow standing near the food and drink. Strong rumours that Frazier was filling the non-alcoholic punch with whisky were abound. All, however, enjoyed tasting it. The girls all seemed grouped together eyeing up each other's dresses. Although this was a garden party under a big marquee, most were dressed as if going to a ball, although some had very fancy summer dresses on. Most of the boys had suits, few dickey bows, or jacket and trousers at least. Trekkie was wearing a suit, which definitely had a Star Trek uniform look about it. Although he received some gibes he did not care. Frazier had indeed turned up with Lisa Turner; Emma commented on what a nice couple they looked. Mush questioned her eyesight.

Not long in and the music started, the girls having now mingled back with the boys. Terror came across Mush's face as the first dance was called, grab your partners. Unfortunately, Mush's terror was warranted. His slow dance with Zandra was awful; it stopped a minute or so before everyone else's as he had stood on her foot at least three times. Sean was more successful with Emma, allowing her to lead and enjoying their closeness. By the end of their dance Emma was leaning her head on Sean's shoulder. The music stopped. Sean looked into Emma's eyes. "Git," was not the word expected but thankfully it had come from Mush, now pulling him away.

"What?" Sean shouted.

"You had lessons. I bet that's why you were good." Mush was jealous.

"I may have had some advice from Livia," Sean responded.

"Livia, you danced with that babe? Never."

"Yep, I did, and now thinking about it, wow." Sean's face

lightened until he felt a dig in his ribs. "That's worse. I'm not jealous of Emma but dancing with Liv, holding her, oh my god. Let's get a drink." Mush virtually pulled Sean to the punch bowl. Both took a sip or two and both definitely agreed there was something other than fruit juice in it.

The evening moved on. Dancing was a bit easier as all were fast numbers, so no embarrassing holding or foot stomping was required. The punch had been replaced by a new untouched bowl, courtesy of Professor Smith. The teachers, although discreet, still ran the event. Mush, somehow knowing in advance that the punch bowl was being swapped, managed to over fill his last glass prior – a toilet break was needed. Sean, waiting near the mirrors, checking over his tie, shouted to Mush at the urinal. "Are you finished yet?"

"Yeah. Boy that stuff is strong, I could pee for England." Both laughed as Mush was at the sink next to Sean washing his hands.

Their fun was cut short as Frazier and four cronies entered. "Eugenie, how did you get a date?" was Frazier's first cry.

Sean turned. "Frazier, this is not the time or the place, it's meant to be fun. Besides, if something happened now it would be too obvious. Come on, we are all dressed up."

"Blood won't show on that stupid tie," one of Frazier's cronies called.

Sean held back. "Let's go," he said to Mush. They went to move from the sinks when two cronies pushed them back, clearly now in their faces.

"We are not going to hurt, you're right, too obvious. However, a toilet hair wash is on the cards. Who's first?" Frazier and his cronies all laughed.

Mush had had enough. "No. If you want it, go for it. It's time to stop this." Mush stood tall, he did look menacing.

Frazier yelled, "Get him!" Two of the cronies went for Mush, their mistake. Mush was not taking prisoners; within a second he had both pinned against one of the cubicle doors. The other two forgot about Sean and went for Mush. Sean made a movement, both were sent flying before they got to Mush.

Sean turned on Frazier. Frazier tried a kick, Sean pushed it off with no trouble and now was looking Frazier in the eye. Without talking, Sean was in Frazier's head. "Call them off now!"

Frazier had no chance, his head was spinning and he could not move.

Sean ordered again, "Call them off!"

Frazier was now terrified. "Yes, yes, lads stop, stop!" he screamed. All the cronies stopped. They could see Sean at the throat of Frazier who was literally shaking in total fear. Mush took a step back; even he thought this was too deep.

"Get out and I'll let him go," Sean commanded. The four cronies obeyed, leaving the toilets. Sean released his grip on Frazier. "Enough. No more." Frazier nodded in agreement. Sean stood back from Frazier, who caught his breath then ran out of the toilet.

"Holy shit, Sean. How? What...? That was scary.".

Sean looked at Mush. "I have my dad's temper, it was time for them to grow up and fight like a man or flee like the stupid kids they are."

Mush was taken aback by this comment. "What you on about? Bit deep, they were only going to toilet dump us, it's not life or death."

"You didn't think that when you pinned those two to the cubicle door."

Mush thought. "You're right, I did lose it but man, I need a drink." Both checked their clothing and hair then went back out to join the party. Thankfully no one else appeared to have seen the fight in the toilets. The evening continued; Frazier and co. kept a long distance from Sean and Mush. Finally, it became a party atmosphere, Trekkie's moon walk being the best bit, then the final dance.

Sean took Emma to the floor, much to her surprise; his hold was a bit tighter as they went into the dance. Emma was beautiful, her smile melted Sean's heart. The music stopped and they kissed on the lips for the first time. Boy and girl becoming a man and a woman in that few seconds.

Jenna picked them up, dropping Mush and Zandra first. Upon dropping off Emma, Jenna appeared to have to make a quick call. With Jenna out of the car Sean went for a second kiss, it was as good as the first.

POWER OF THOUGHT:
(CHAPTER 10)

Next morning Sean's house was full; Cott, Millan, Sal, and Algier were present. The talk was about Secretary Seth next door who was bored being trapped in this "Useless Earth house!"

Jenna had what could be considered the worst idea of her life. "Let's take Secretary Seth out. Seeing Earthlings, mixing with them would be good." No one else seemed to agree.

"Good," Jenna continued, "give me five minutes," as she disappeared off to the home office, returning five minutes later. "Tickets booked, we are off to the local theatre for the show tonight," was the instruction.

Kain, even for a king was courageous. "Jen, I'm not sure..."

This rebuke was dealt with swiftly by Jenna. "Sal, you book that restaurant for 5pm. Let me see, eight of us, we'll eat before the show." Sal acknowledged with a nod and then left the room to make the call. Kain was about to go for a second try; Jenna's look stopped him in his tracks.

"My dear, do you think this is wise?" Algier was braver than he looked.

"You think so? Well mine and Sal's bit were the easiest. Not only are you telling Seth but you need to get him into some Earth clothes."

Kain shrieked with laughter, joined by Millan and Cott. "I've changed my mind," he said. "Off you go, Uncle. Good luck."

more laughter followed.

Algier left, finally providing a derisory look at Jenna before exiting. Kain said, "Ok Sean, let's do some more training." He obviously didn't want to get involved any further in this ludicrous plan.

Sean, Kain, and Shadow were in the garden. Having warmed up with some mind games including some soft duelling, they moved onto more thought control. Kain called Shadow over, without opening his mouth. Shadow obeyed and did all his tricks on command from Kain. Shadow sitting, playing dead, and even waving without anything obviously being said tickled Sean.

Kain then spoke properly. "Generally we cannot speak to or at lesser brains as our communication is two-way, you need to be telekinetic on both sides for a proper connection. Having said this, some Earthens can indeed communicate with lesser beings, humans aside." Kain's try of a joke missed the point. "Anyway, I and some others have managed to at least try, Shadow and I being a good example."

"So you are actually talking to him and he to you?"

"Don't be silly, I can't talk dog but because I can access his mind he responds, obeys more easily than a general verbal command. I can also feel his feelings more and can sometimes pick up, say, where his pain is. I once diagnosed a toothache long before the vet." This was a strange but fun achievement King Kain was sharing.

"So can I learn this?" asked Sean.

"Let's be gentle, focus on Shadow and ask him to fetch his ball. Don't talk."

Sean looked at Shadow. *Fetch your ball boy, go on*, he kept thinking. Shadow was now looking at Sean moving his head from side to side, that quizzical look again. Sean kept on; he thought he had won as Shadow rose and started walking. Sean's triumph was short-lived. Shadow, instead of walking to the open garage where his favourite ball was, actually walked to the fence, cocked his leg, did his business and then settled into his kennel for a nap. Kain was in hysterics; Sean gave in and laughed too.

Sean asked, "I understand our powers now, so assuming there are more Earthens on Earth than just here in Aville, how come they don't abuse their power and become presidents or something?" Sean stopped and thought. "Oops, hang on, maybe they have." Kain also laughed, getting the point about America's new president.

Kain explained, "That is my main role here on Earth. All kings agreed that Earth needed watching and studying therefore by decree visas, passports and processes were set up and one person was to lead all Earthen efforts on Earth – yours truly. So I am officially the Earthen Earth Secretary, a bit of a mouthful I know. My job is to control and monitor all Earthen activities on Earth, plus and most importantly, help the Earthlings develop, especially around protecting their planet. Our goal here is to stop Earth going the way we did."

Kain stopped, then continued, "We try to mix in, not dominate. We want Earthlings to learn, led cooperatively, as we know that even with our greater powers their will would not take to being ordered or forced to. Remember, they outnumber us by millions – no, billions – so not a small number to upset or worse, to go to war with."

Sean thought. "Ok, I get that. So what is in it for us, I mean Earthens, to worry about our Earth?"

"For all our intelligence. We are not as good as Mother Nature, therefore by trying things here – some known, some experimental – we hope to be able to change things on Earthen. A good example are certain plants, animals such as cows, we had to reengineer them for life on Earthen. It sounds silly but we have three to four hundred years to stop this Earth becoming Earthen. Mother Nature is a bitch."

Sean was a bit taken aback by his father's profanity and indeed honesty, but he got the point. Sean decided another question was needed. "So what about Earthens abusing their powers?"

"My – our – role is also to police and enforce the discreet protocol on Earth," Kain went on. "As you know we are faster, remember Ensign Jeng?" How could Sean forget? "Well, if she was in a race with Usain Bolt she would beat him by a second at least."

"Wow," came Sean's reply. He decided he liked Jeng very much but wanted to continue the conversation. "So let's say Jeng, sorry, an Earthen, does break the rules and does beat Bolt. Hold on, back the bus up, is Bolt an Earthen?"

Kain laughed. "No, unfortunately not. He is just a very gifted athlete. So let's assume Jeng did race Bolt. For the story let's forget she is a woman and wouldn't be allowed. So, Olympic final Jeng versus Bolt. Bolt does a PB at 9.7 seconds, coming second to Jeng in 9 seconds flat. The world goes crazy, however, the varied Earth council members and I realise she is an Earthen. The joy will not last long as she is surrounded in a drugs scandal, medal revoked, and never heard of again."

Sean fell in quick. "That would do the trick, the time would be obliterated from the records and no harm done."

"Exactly," was Kain's response.

Sean thought some more. "I have heard of discredited athletes so this does happen?"

"Not always. Some are humans being humans and real illegal drugs are at play, but yes, the Earth council has dealt with many issues. Remember not just sport, but even scientists. We still argue over providing a cure or at least control and longer living for cancer. Certainly someone just coming up with say a HIV vaccine tomorrow would also cause questions."

"Wait, if you can cure cancer or HIV then you have to do it.

Millions die from this."

"I did not say we can cure all of these but yes, there are many things we can do. However, our goal is not to take Mother Nature on again. This time we will work with and gain a better, more sustainable outcome. There will sadly always be losses in any such journey."

Sean did not accept this. "No, that's not right, that's not what I expect of you. Maybe you are the cold-blooded murderer people think you are."

Kain rose to his feet. "Son, I think you are learning, now you are not. Be open minded, do not judge so easily."

Sean rose to his feet. Without opening his mouth he threw an expletive at Kain. Next thing Sean knew he was waking up on the sofa with Sal next to him. "What happened?" Sean asked.

"You pushed your father too far and he, well, simply put you in your place. Two back flips and twenty yards in the air, I hear. Luckily no injuries," Sal explained.

"Dad attacked me?"

"Yes, and he will do so again. By no way was he out of control or attempting to hurt you, but he made his point as king."

"That's no way to end an argument." Even Sean thought these words were funny coming from his mouth.

"There is no argument, you sometimes have to accept what is," replied Sal.

"Where is Dad now?"

"Getting ready to go out. Mind you, the grilling Jenna gave him was enough. Don't think he would do that again."

"Again? Wait, has Dad ever hurt Mum?" Sean quizzed.

"No, never. She is the one person he has never used his powers on, or at least not to that degree. Love and Mother Nature are the only two things that control Kain."

"So you saying he doesn't love me?"

Sal did not need to answer, Algier was at hand. "In your words... you can be a right asshole sometimes, young man." With that, the wink was enough to calm the situation.

Before leaving Jenna heightened Sean's spirits further by reminding him that the mums, Emma, Mush, and Sal were all going out together tomorrow as a goodbye to Mush who was going on holiday the day after. This nugget of news did brighten Sean's spirits and he decided to watch if not take part in the evening's events, giving his father a wide berth.

The first laugh was seeing Secretary Seth dressed up in Earthling clothing, not just because he looked awkward in them but was clearly in Algier's supply of clothing. Someone should tell them that tartan green pants with yellow shirts were more suited to a golf course than dinner and a show. Worse was they were both wearing virtually the same, but Algier's blue to Seth's green.

The restaurant meal was just as fun, Seth ordering the waitress around. She finally giving in and saying, "I'm not your servant," went down very well. Boy, the poor waitress was unaware of how close she was to being killed. Sal as usual did a great job in calming the situation down with both Earthens and restaurant staff and management. Kain had to leave a big tip.

The show, a musical called Jersey Boys, Sean thought was good. Secretary Seth complained about all that wailing. Algier was continuingly asked to sit down by those behind as he got into the spirit of the show. Sean had to admit, knowing how powerful these men were, their comic release was even better. Algier having a nightcap with Seth next door, Sean was now left with Kain and Jenna. "Off to bed now," he tried.

Kain wasn't having any of it. "Sean, today was unfortunate but you must know our ways and customs. I am an Earthen and a king. That will come out."

Sean felt a little uncomfortable. "Yes Dad, I know." A big hug to his father settled it and Sean went to bed a bit less stressed if not truly happy.

Jenna, as usual, was driving the Discovery full of all Sean's favourite people. Mush had made him laugh, forcing his bulk into the smaller rear boot seats with Sean. "Not sitting with the women," was his reasoning. Now at the shops, he and Mush people watched as the women (Sean was now calling them) could not pass a clothes shop without going in, leaving he and Mush outside. Mush's ploy being to remind them all of his clumsiness, all had accepted the plan on those grounds. The odd shop Emma did stay outside to spend time with her friends.

Lunchtime came. Mush chose Nando's so Nando's is where they went. Jenna surprisingly stated she did not understand this theme, as if she was eating out she expected to be served upon, not get up to effectively serve herself. Judy and Daphne (Mush's mum) pretended to take the mickey out of Jenna, posh so and so was quite close but Jenna took it in her stride. Again, Sean wondered if this was just a pet hate or did Mum occasionally remember she was a queen and expected to be treated that way? *No,* he thought.

Next came the news, "Your film is about to start so off you go you three, we are having a liquid lunch," followed by, "Sal, you're driving." Jenna was on a roll with her queen impression.

Emma, Mush, and Sean were left at the cinema, the summer action-packed blockbuster. Tickets in hand, *Result,* thought Sean. Although they had pre-booked tickets Mush wanted a drink and sweets. Looking at Sean and Emma, he volunteered to queue up and buy all three.

Sean was now alone with Emma who broke the silence. "Friday was perfect, thank you." A peck on the cheek followed.

"Wow. Yes, it was great, you were great," Sean nervously responded.

Emma said, "Great, mm… beautiful was the word I recall?"

Sean went red. "Yep, and I meant it." This correct response gained a peck on the lips. With this, Sean held her hands. They were showing their affection clearly in public, although at one point Sean saw Mush look backwards, he let Emma's hand go. Mush finally returned fully loaded. Sean asked, "Why didn't Zandra come today?"

Mush genuinely looked saddened. "They left for the Philippines yesterday."

"They – she – will be back. It's only a holiday," Emma said in her supportive voice.

"Yeah she will." Mush led them to their seats.

The movie was good, Sean holding Emma's hands at the right points but joining Mush in the cheers when appropriate. Mush was loud at the cinema. Straight after the film the mums were there. Sean had seen his mum drunk before, today she was tipsy but she, like him, needed to let off steam. Judy, Daphne, and Sal were great with Jenna and all had a wonderful time.

Dropping the Greens off was a bit embarrassing. Jenna deciding to hug both Daphne and Mush, planting a kiss on his cheek, saying something like, "We will miss you, young man." Worse, before Mush could wipe away the kiss Emma had joined in, hugging first then a peck on Mush's cheek, copying Jenna. Daphne laughed, bid her farewells then followed Mush in, who had moved quite quickly for a big lad. Sal and Judy laughed; Emma and Judy's goodbye was easier as they were to be seen again. Another lovely day was over.

The first day of the holiday Sean woke late; he and Shadow were going for the 'who could stay in bed longest award'. Sean lay there looking at Shadow sprawled out at the bottom of the bed, every now and then raising his head to look at Sean. Just past eleven o'clock Sean thought, *Here comes a record, just ten more minutes.* His record attempt was thwarted by a loud knock on the door.

"Get up you two lazy so and so's, or no breakfast!" Jenna shouted.

Shadow gave in, falling off the bed in reaction to Jenna's scream. *Damn*, Sean thought. Yes, he had beaten Shadow so was the longest, but as both were now not in bed the record time would not be beat.

Sean walked to the garden where Jenna had made a basic picnic on the garden table. "It's a beautiful day and I need some air," was her defence. Sean could see that Jenna was still suffering from a hangover, taking every opportunity to drop things or make a noise to wind her up.

"Strange, no one is here." Sean realised they were indeed on their own.

"Millan is outside in his car, or a tree I think, being covert surveillance. The rest are at the Research Park." Jenna could talk.

"They seem to be having trouble finding Gill?"

"Yes, all that brain power and tech but still useless!"

Sean smiled. He liked his mother like this, and at that point Jenna's mobile rang. During the call Sean saw Jenna's face drop, although a "You are joking!" comment did not suggest it was not that serious. Jenna completed the call. "That two-faced idiot, your father's brother, is visiting and staying here. I'll get his room ready."

Sean until recently had quite liked Dain but having seen recent events he was coming around to his mother's feelings. A shout from the utility room made Sean laugh. "Have you seen the toilet bleach? I think I'll make his bed smell nice." Followed by, "Remind me to buy some arsenic coffee." Jenna was on a roll.

Sure enough, by dinnertime Kain, Algier, Cott, and Dain arrived home. Talking about two-faced, Sean looked at Jenna who upon Dain's entrance went up to him, embraced him and said, "Lovely to see you Dain, hope you are well," although

Sean swore her fingers were crossed.

"Pleasure, my beautiful sister-in-law. How are you?" Dain was playing the game, Sean could see his eyes were not matching his words.

A simple "All good," was the response.

Dain looked at Sean. "Wow. You have grown, my young nephew. How are you?"

Sean copied his mother. "All good." He caught the smirk from his mother.

Jenna went straight to the kitchen to prepare food; Sean sat with the men in the living room. Small talk went on for some time then something strange happened. Shadow, who had decided, having lost the sleeping competition, to sleep all day in the sun in the garden, now entered the living room, immediately stopping in front of Dain and growling at him. Sean recalled Shadow had done this to Gill, albeit a bit more aggressive.

"Remove that dog," Dain ordered.

"Why? He has seen you many times before with no issues. Shadow, what's up?"

Shadow looked at Kain but returned to growling at Dain. Dain learnt forward and shouted at Shadow, "Go! Go, stupid dog."

This had the opposite effect as now Shadow started barking. Dain went to raise his hand, Sean jumped to his feet and Dain was pushed flat back into the sofa. "Leave my dog alone." Sean was now next to Shadow and ready to fight with him.

Kain ordered, "Stop, all of you. Shadow, garden!" Shadow whimpered but obeyed, Kain's will was too much for him. "Sean, go and help your mother!"

Sean also obeyed, although he caught a comment from Dain just as he was leaving the room. "You can't let him do that, he's dangerous, he needs to control his powers."

Kain had the final say. "He is my son and protecting his loved ones. Lucky for you I didn't decide to protect him. How do you fancy taking on the three of us?"

Although Jenna had not seen what had happened she had overheard it; as Sean entered the kitchen she did not speak but gestured to look out the window. Shadow was on the grass eating the biggest bone Sean had ever seen. Jenna laughed with Sean.

Dinner was less eventful; uncle and dog were kept apart. The men went to the home office, but this time Sean was invited.

Kain started proceedings. "Why are you here, brother? We can handle this ourselves."

"I feel ashamed that I have allowed Gill in by incorrectly signing his papers." Dain was trying to sound apologetic.

"I have not forgotten your error, maybe a reshuffle of my council is required," said Kain, passing a glare at Dain. "Cott, this Gill search has been going on too long. Where are you with it?"

"Sir, Gill is very clever or maybe being supported, as any or every lead we are getting is leading us up the wrong path."

"Am I to think you are incompetent, Detective Inspector!"

"My sincere apologies. We are doing all we can, sir." Cott was visibly shaken.

"Then do more. Get out of my sight and only return when you have some real news!"

Sean was shocked at Kain's tone to Cott, they always appeared close. Cott had no response but left.

Algier responded, "Kain! You are going too far." Again, Sean was shocked. Algier was rarely that assertive to Kain.

This approach backfired as Kain turned on Algier. "My family is at risk and you believe I'm going too far? If subjects fail me I will take action, whoever they are!" Even Sean took a deep breath.

Algier was not finished. "And you class me as your family or a subject!"

Wow, go for it, Sean thought.

Kain gained back some composure. "You are my family, my apologies." Then he turned on Dain. "However, you are looking more like a subject than a brother!"

Dain looked very frightened, but before he answered Harvey Gwent entered. "Sire, I have some bad news." The room went quiet, Gwent continued. "It would appear that Gill has five recruits, our intelligence suggests. All mercenary ex-soldiers, have somehow landed on Earth, most Vultens but one Saulten, he being Swartz."

Kain sat down, taking this new information in. "Swartz is a threat, are you sure he would work with Vultens?"

Dain looked more comfortable. "Swartz was your friend at school and military training." He quizzed, "Did you not duel quite seriously when young?"

Kain responded, "Yes, Swartz and I have, though he is strong... Regardless, how has he got here? Is your department totally ineffective!" Kain was now back to brother beating.

Gwent asked, "Regardless of how they are now here, sire, shall I call reinforcements?"

"Yes, but do not be silly, I want this discreet. Earthlings should not see our battles. I want Ensign Jeng to be Jenna's personal guard. Sean," Kain was now addressing Sean, "we will be around you but I have shown you how to defend at least. Your power is good so do not be worried, although I will ask Sal to stay close. Gwent, make the arrangements."

Sean was quite happy; he had taken a shine to Jeng, her being around more would be fun. He actually thought of asking for Jeng to be his personal bodyguard but decided a different track. "Why Jeng, may I ask?"

Algier answered. "Jeng is a remarkable young lady. Top of her power class, very agile, very alert, plus gets on with your mother."

That's it, Sean briefly thought. *Emma, you're dumped. Let's go Jeng!*

The meeting ended and Dain was allowed to stay, although the atmosphere was tense. Poor Shadow was banned to the garden.

Thankfully the next day most were busy, Dain spending much time next door with Secretary Seth. Sean decided the garden and Shadow were his best bet of fun. Sean also decided to train himself by moving varied objects; he was quite adept at this now, and not everything smashed to the floor. As his confidence grew he looked at Shadow. *Maybe,* he thought. Sean stood and focussed his efforts on Shadow. Slowly Shadow lifted and was a metre off the floor doing his quizzical look. He was then moved from side to side gently. Sean was in full control and thought Shadow was actually enjoying this. Upon hearing the back garden gate open Sean lost concentration for a second. Shadow, who was now some four metres off the ground, was falling. Sean froze; just as Shadow was about to hit the floor he stopped. Sean looked up. Jeng was present and now clearly controlling Shadow to a soft landing.

"Oops," Sean could only mutter as he ran to comfort Shadow, who thankfully did not appear to have realised the danger he had been in.

"You are an idiot, Sean. You could have hurt him!" Jeng was rebuking Sean.

"I was in control and got carried away. I won't do it again." Sean was defensive.

"Don't experiment on living things, did you realise he was so high that drop would have broken his legs?" Jeng stated.

Sean thought and was now cuddling Shadow. "You are right jeeez, I'm a prat. Sorry Shadow." A tear came to Sean's eyes.

Jeng sensed Sean had got the message. "Great powers, great responsibilities and all that, get the point. Anyway, come here." Sean got a hug, Shadow joined in, followed by Jenna who had heard Jeng from the kitchen.

"So you are here as my bodyguard," Jenna stated.

"Yes ma'am," was Jeng's formal reply.

"Great. Drop the formalities, let's start thinking shopping or fun strategies for this week before we go on holidays." Jenna stopped to think. "Actually you could come on holiday with us, that would be different."

"Yes ma'am," was Jeng's formal reply, after which Jenna grabbed her arm to have a wine together. Sean wished he were old enough to drink; he would have happily drunk with Jeng. His daydream was broken with a dig in the arm. Sean turned; Emma was next to him. Sean smiled whilst embracing Emma.

"Who's that with your mum?" was the question from Emma.

Sean thought. "Family friend, knows Mum. How are you? Want to walk with Shadow?"

Emma's reply was, "Yes."

Sean and Emma spent the afternoon walking in the fields behind his house, Shadow by his side; neither of them talked about much, just enjoying the sunshine and each other's company. Upon returning home Emma was invited to join them for dinner. At this point there were only Jenna, Jeng, Emma, Sean, and now Sal present. Some of the talk Sean swore was alien, shopping, makeup etc. – what was all this about?

Emma, although by far the younger female in the room held her own and did appear to get on with 'Cousin' Jeng as she was now labelled by Jenna – visiting from Canada of course. Emma did appear to get on with Jeng. Sean obliging said yes, provided drinks, and generally just waited on all the women.

Emma took a phone call and said she had to go home. Sean offered to walk her, with Shadow of course. As they were walking Emma was in a funny mood. "So I saw you looking at Jeng. She has got to be in her twenties or even thirties, way older than you."

Sean choked; boy, girls pick things up. "Err, twenty-two I believe."

"Oh, she looks older," Emma retorted with a little snarl.

Sean didn't agree. "No she doesn't, she actually looks younger." The dig in his arm suggested this was the wrong answer.

Then Emma said something strange. "So who is the best looking, err, I mean over me, Jeng or Livia?"

Sean stopped in his tracks. Emma was jealous, he had to answer this correctly. "You are all different in your own ways." Sean didn't get away with it as a harder dig in his ribs said this was the wrong answer. Even Shadow appeared to take a few steps from Emma.

Sean thought quick. "I mean for their age, I mean over twenty and all that but of course you are." Sean thought he had saved himself, even ending with his best smile.

'Liar." Emma turned on him. "Liv is gorgeous – tanned, flawless skin, shining blonde hair, Jeng is very pretty and knows how to hold herself."

Sean did not understand the last sentence but got his head back in gear. "Look, does it matter what they look like? You are my girlfriend and beat them all." Right answer. Emma swooned and planted a real smacker of a kiss on Sean's lips. Sean was relieved. At the path end, "Ten o'clock tomorrow, don't forget. See you," was Emma's goodbye.

"Ok, night," Sean answered, but had forgot. Searching his brain all the way home, he could not remember. Before going to sleep all was revealed as Jenna reminded him to get up early as they were going to Chessington World of Adventures the next day. How could he forget?

KIDNAP:
(CHAPTER 11)

The next morning Sean was up and ready. He, Jenna, Sal, and Jeng were in the Discovery, shortly picking Judy and Emma up for their day out at the theme park. It was a great day, Jeng was fear-free, any ride she was on, Emma putting on a brave face, joining in. Sean knew she was not liking them as much but was not going to be beaten by Jeng. Sean's only mistake was getting his mother on one ride, explaining it was not as bad as it looked, being sent to Coventry for an hour after by his mother suggested otherwise.

Over a cold drink, Jenna caught Sean in a quiet moment. "Jeng and Emma seem to be getting on, it's good for Emma to have a slightly older friend instead of you and Mush all the time. She is becoming quite the young lady." Sean was not sure what his mother was after but did get her point.

The day out ended happily; all were tired. With Emma and Judy dropped off Jenna, Jeng, and Sean headed home. Although no lights were flashing Sean saw PC Millan's police car in their drive together with Detective Inspector Cott's unmarked car. All three hearts dropped a bit; all made their way quickly into the full living room.

Kain acknowledged them first. "Hi, the news states a train just past Milton Keynes has come off its tracks, at least ten believed dead, many injured." Sean, although saddened was unsure as to why this would cause such a stir. At this point Secretary Seth appeared with Algier.

"You called, King Kain?" was Seth's opening line.

Kain went to speak then stopped. "Look at the telly." The nine o'clock news was on.

Reporter on the screen: "I'm reporting from just outside Milton Keynes where a train has derailed, at least ten dead, many injured as reported by our news desk. With me is a witness, please tell me what you saw."

A man came on the screen and stated that he saw four strange-looking people by the track that appeared to be making pushing movements when the train derailed. The reporter questioned the pushing movement bit. The witness explained, "Well, they were some metres away so they weren't actually pushing it, but maybe they had put something on the tracks expecting it to happen. I don't know but it was strange and they looked strange."

Kain turned the TV off. "I think we know where Gill and his friends are, or at least were."

Cott responded, "Cowards picking on poor humans, they had no chance."

"You and Sal need to get up there and assist, plus find out what you can," Kain instructed.

Sal got up and left with Cott. Kain turned on Secretary Seth. "If this is Gill and other Vultens, involving Earthlings in such an obvious way breaks all protocols, meaning the Earth Council and I can take direct action."

Seth thought. "I am here to oversee justice for my king's subjects regardless of their actions." Kain went to respond but Seth added, "My friend, I also understand a Saulten called Swartz is with them as well?"

Dain decided to interject. "Secretary Seth, with respect, Vultens or Saultens, they cannot cause such obvious distress on the poor Earthlings. My lord Kain is right and they should be punished to death if caught." Even Kain looked surprised at his brother's support.

Seth raised an eyebrow. "Remember you the Earth Council, although led by King Kain are still accountable to the joint Supreme Council and ultimately the Kings' Council."

Kain went into Earthen mode. "Secretary Seth I, we, are aware of our responsibilities as the Earth Council. However, you forget I am taking this as a king not an Earth Council Leader due to its direct closeness to my family." Sean could tell, as king or at least in king mode, his father was a power freak.

Seth looked at Kain. "My friend, again you make this point. I am but a councillor and cannot stop you as a king, but only advise you to be wary of any consequences if you push protocol too far."

Algier interrupted. "I'm sure King Kain is aware of such consequences and will carry out the correct actions when required. Until then, my friend, can we concentrate on finding these criminals?" Algier showed Seth to the door whilst talking.

Sal decided to be brave. "Kain, I mean sir, you are obviously troubled by this but must keep calm. You and your family have many protectors. Gill and his gang are no match."

Sean took a step back and hid slightly behind his mother, expecting Kain to explode. PC Millan had actually moved closer to Sal for support. Kain looked at Sal, then to Jenna. "My friends, I am sorry for my actions but I am now tiresome of this snake in the grass Gill and his entourage. Ten humans are dead for our issues, not theirs. Forgive me but this needs to stop." Kain left the room followed by Jenna.

"Wow," was Jeng's response. "King Kain scares the shit out of me!" Quite an unexpected line but at least caused all in the room to laugh.

Sean was woken early the next morning by Jenna, who took him downstairs to hear the 6am news:

Terrible traffic accident near Northampton on the M1. Fifteen cars and two lorries, at least three dead. Two people, adults, seen running from a motorway bridge seeming to throw something on the motorway below, is this related to the train accident yesterday...?

Kain was in a foul mood. Gwent was present at the breakfast table. "Sir, do we need to tell the Earthlings? Six Earthens on a destruction spree... it's inconceivable. What they could do?"

Kain responded, "They obviously want us to feel pain. You go with Algier and Seth to Northampton. You know our fellow Earthens there, find Gill and his gang!"

Gwent responded and left with Algier.

Kain motioned for PC Millan, Prince Dain, and Jeng to go to his office, Sal to stay with Jenna and Sean. The three remaining ate and drank with very little conversation. Upon return Kain gave his orders. "Sean and Jenna, you will go to Mrs Carnell now. Take Shadow, Professor Smith will also be there. Dain, Millan, Jeng and I need to go somewhere." No one argued, Jenna collected Sean and they went dutifully off to Mrs Carnell's with Shadow.

No words were said until they were in number 71. "You look anxious, my dear." Mrs Carnell spoke to Jenna.

"I know, I also know my husband. Would he be that silly?" For once Jenna looked confused.

"What, Mum, what do you mean?" Sean was now worried.

"Not silly, but stubborn," Professor Smith interjected, then wiped a tear from Jenna's eyes.

Sean jumped up. "Someone tell me what's going on!"

Mrs Carnell said, "We think your father took a call from Gill earlier threatening to kill more Earthlings unless he met him with no others in tow."

Sean sat back down. "You mean Dad is meeting Gill, on his own?"

"Yes. Earthen pride, especially kings, struggle to turn down a direct challenge." Jenna was teary eyed.

"He has Millan and Jeng with him." Sean sounded confident, then thought. "Wait, Gill has five others including that Swartz guy?" Sean thought further. "Surely Dad will call others, he has an Earth force or something?"

Jenna sat next to Sean and hugged him. "Sean, surely you get their culture now – medieval. Your father could not ignore a direct threat and his macho king position."

"They are going to fight, even duel?" Sean was for the first time both worried and scared.

Professor Smith spoke up. "If they meet then that will be the outcome. Remember your father has much power, Millan also, and that Jeng, well, few would want to take her on."

Sean was taken aback by such honesty from someone about fighting, no, even death, murder even. He sat quietly, holding on to his mother. All of a sudden there was the noise of a smashing window and smoke filled the room. Sean grabbed his mother and headed for the door followed by Shadow. As they exited the rear Sean felt pressure on his chest; he tried to respond but could not. Next, he was on the floor. A man was over him; Shadow was barking and hit the man full force with a jump at his torso, causing him to fall. Sean turned and focussed on the man on the floor below Shadow, then felt a pain in his neck. Turning, he saw a woman's face grinning over him. As he blacked out he saw Shadow been thrown in the air.

Emma was walking along her street catching what she thought was a commotion at number 71, not taking it all in, she saw Sean thrown into the back of a van, two figures then jumping into the cab. Emma had no idea what was happening jumped onto the back step of the van, holding on to a ladder on one of the doors. The van sped through the estate roads onto the now country roads, ignoring all traffic laws. Emma found all her strength to hold on. The van turned off the main road onto minor country roads before entering some gates to what was obviously a farm or something. As the van slowed down Emma jumped off then hid in some bushes to the side of the track she was now on.

The van did indeed stop a few hundred metres up the track, next to a strange-looking door access. Emma, keeping close to the bushes and trees along the path, moved towards the structure, now seeing three people getting out of the van, opening the back and taking Sean out then into the building. Emma settled behind an old tractor some metres from the entrance Sean had just been carried into. Surveying the scene, Emma could see that the entrance was quite small and there appeared to be no structure behind it or indeed very little buildings around. Looking closer, Emma could see the entrance was a dome shape and around it were some four other domes, although they did not appear to have doors.

Emma went for her mobile phone; the phone that was always in her jeans pocket was not there. *Damn,* she thought. It must have fallen whilst she was on the van. Where was she? What was going on? Emma sat for a while then heard another car coming down the lane. Hiding more, she looked out carefully. Three more figures got out of the car and entered where Sean had been taken – one was limping, being carried by the other two. After what seemed like an eternity Emma saw a figure come out of the entrance and walk around the two vehicles, appearing to take some air then go back inside. The clothing of this figure was strange, Emma thought. Certainly military-looking but not anything she had seen before.

The evening went – the inhabitants each seemed to come out for air, chat, but all went back in through the door. It was now dark and Emma saw the opportunity to try and take in more of what was going on. First going to the dome shape of the entrance, then moving to the next one, this had a window which Emma carefully looked through. She could not make out how many figures but there were mainly men or at least one woman, all dressed strangely. Emma moved on to the next dome, peering carefully through its window. Although lit looked empty, a bedroom of some sort. The next was similar, however, the fourth had the shutters over the window. Emma slowly and carefully opened the metal shutter; her heart jumped. Sean was on a bed not moving.

Emma had to think, maybe she could run and find somewhere and call for help. How far was she from anywhere? She thought she was mad but remembered seeing car keys in the car still. Although she could not drive she had been lucky to have taken part in some junior driving track days so had some idea what to do. Emma had to hide further as one of the occupants had come out of the building and shut the metal shutters on all the domes' windows. Emma waited further. Feeling it was now late, she was to go for it. Slowly, walking bent over towards the car, taking advantage of anything to hide behind, now fifteen metres from the car and no cover.

Emma took a deep breath then ran – jumping in the car shutting the door. *Wow*, she thought.

On the passenger seat was a mobile phone. *Please please be unlocked*, she thought. Her luck was in, the phone was unlocked. Emma went straight to the messaging. The only number she could remember was her mother's, texting, 'Mum this must sound strange, I'm ok but you must give this phone text to PC Millan or Kain immediately and follow its signal'. Pressing send, she let an internal whoop. Delivered.

Hearing a door open. she sat up. Figures were coming out of the door towards her. Emma started the engine, crashed a gear then hit the throttle. She felt the acceleration and buried her foot more, and then all of a sudden there was noise but no movement. Emma kept hitting the throttle but the car was going nowhere, then its engine died.

"Get out of the car or I will kill you!" came a cry.

Emma looked out of the window. The car was surrounded by a number of people but they appeared lower than her. She looked out the window again, she and the car were in the air. The cry came again. Emma opened the door and looked down; she and the car were off the ground… the car jolted and hit the floor. Emma was pulled out and carried into the building screaming.

Sean woke up, looking at the ceiling. Where was he? As he sat up, the room, a dome with very dirty, old, white paint was around him. Sean felt very drowsy as he moved his legs off the bed he was on to sit up straight. His heart missed a beat. "Emma!'

As he tried to stand up he fell to the floor. Not giving up, he crawled over to Emma who was laid on the floor at the other end of the dome. Upon reaching her Sean took her in his arms. "Emma, are you ok? Please speak to me."

His face brightened as Emma started to come round, enough to open her eyes and say, "Sean." Sean hugged her further.

Then the door opened a woman entered. "Hi Sean." Sean focussed and the woman pulled back. "Feisty, eh? Here." Sean could not stop the needle being placed into his neck. He did not pass out but the drowsy feeling increased. The woman laughed and left.

Some time passed and Emma had helped Sean back to bed and he was sitting up. Emma had found water and was rubbing his forehead with a wet torn cloth. Sean asked, "How the hell did you get here?"

"It's a long story but what the heck is going on?"

Sean replied, "That's a longer story."

"Are you ok? They are drugging you?"

"Yes, they are drugging me, I'm guessing high levels of TDL, my medicine." Sean looked at Emma. Where could he start, he decided not. "I'm sorry but we are in danger, these people will ki… hurt us."

Emma looked worried. "Now you're scaring me. Were you

going to say kill us?"

Sean evaded the question. "How did you get here?"

"I saw them putting you into a van and jumped on. We are in some strange underground place…"

Sean interrupted. "Did you jump on at the old lady's house? Did you see my mother or anyone?"

"No, just you being thrown in the back of the van. I just reacted and jumped on the back, ending up here then got caught outside… They lifted the car I was trying to escape it was off the ground."

Tears came to Sean's eyes. "Did you see my mum?" he asked again.

"No."

With that, the room felt like it moved, with things being thrown around and the light blowing. The door flew open and two people entered. Emma was thrown aside as they both focussed on Sean. Sean looked up; the two figures moved back then Sean fell unconscious on the bed.

"Give him some more." Another needle was pushed into Sean's neck, both left.

Sean awoke. He was on the bed with Emma lying beside him, holding him. Emma looked up. "Good, you're awake. You were breathing. Don't know how but I must have slept."

Sean looked at Emma, she had obviously cried herself to sleep. "Emma, I'm sorry you are in the middle of this. It's not your problem but, Dad, Algier, Gwent, everyone will be looking for us, I'm sure we will be ok." He added, "Are you sure you didn't see Mum, the old lady, or even Miss Smith?"

Emma gave the same response. "No."

Sean sat up abruptly. "I will kill them!"

Emma sat up. "Sean, you are scaring me. What is all this talk?"

Sean looked at Emma. "It is too long a story but you need

to know these people are not normal, they can do things with their minds, they will hurt us."

"Did they lift the car up with their minds?" Emma asked quizzically.

"Yes, they are al... soldiers trained in mind technology so can do telekinesis." Sean really did not know how to explain any other way.

Emma thought, *Not sure what you mean but they certainly were not touching the car and had no equipment.*

Sean held Emma and looked straight in her eyes. "We are in danger." With that, the door opened and Gill entered with two others behind him.

"What a delight, Miss Cooper. Quite a pleasant surprise," Gill said.

Sean jumped to his feet. "You touch her and I will kill you!"

Gill took a step back, looking at the two behind him. "Are you sure you have the correct dosage?"

The response was, "Yes, any more we could kill him."

Gill looked at Sean. "You do have some power, but although uncomfortable, I can deal with you. Any more attacks, however minor, and Miss Cooper will be the first casualty."

Sean thought then reluctantly relaxed. "My mother, what have you done to her!"

Gill thought for a moment. "I'm not going to tell you. However, your girlfriend, although bringing the matter forward has given us an opportunity, especially now with two hostages, one being a petty Earthling. You will see your father soon." With that, he and the two guards walked off laughing.

Emma looked at Sean. "What is that nut talking about? Did he say Earthling? Why do you keep asking about your mother?"

Sean evaded the Earthling comment. "Mum, Mrs Carnell, the old lady I mean, and Professor Smith were in the house with me before I was taken." Sean stopped. "And Shadow. I'm going to kill them, every one of them." Sean started to kick the now closed door.

Emma went up to him. "You are scaring me, Sean. Please calm down. I need an explanation."

Sean went to respond when the door opened again – Gill. "Your father has agreed to meet, so enjoy your last minutes together, and remember, anything you do before Kain gets here and she goes first."

Sean squared up to Gill. He did not say anything but Gill gave an evil smile and left.

"What the hell is going on?" Emma was crying.

Sean held her. "Look, hopefully the TDL will wear off and I will protect you, you will be fine, I promise."

Emma calmed down but was clearly lost in all that was going on. "Did Gill say your father would be here soon?" Sean nodded. Emma continued, "Look I have no idea what is going on but I have these." Sean turned around as Emma pulled a small clear box of pills from her jeans pocket.

Sean took the box. "What are these?"

"Your mother gave them to me. She said that if I was ever alone with you and you were hyper the green ones are TDL and would control your illness."

Sean looked up. "And the red ones?"

"Well she said only give them to you if you were very ill or in serious trouble." Emma had no clue what she was saying.

"Wow, the red ones, they have to be an antidote to the TDL. They have to be." Sean smiled. "Did Mum say how many to take?"

"Err, one unless serious then two," Emma replied.

With, that Sean threw three down his throat and swallowed, looking at Emma. "Look, there will be some strange things, I can't explain now but ignore whatever happens and stay by me. I will protect you."

Emma could see Sean's demeanor change, her only response being, "Ok."

COMBAT TO DEATH:
(CHAPTER 12)

A half-hour or so later, the door opened. Sean did his best to appear dozy. He and Emma were led out to the edges of a circular quarry. Both were led down and stopped in the middle where they were tied to a stake in the ground around their wrists. Gill gave the order, "Positions please."

Four of the five moved back up onto the quarry walls. The fifth stayed with Gill but then addressed Sean. "I am Swartz. I was a friend of your father at military school until he busted me and I was court marshalled and sent to jail." Sean looked at his tormentor; he was big, well over two metres tall and just as broad.

Gill was smiling. "It took ten Earthens to control him and unheard of amounts of TDL to suppress him. Are you not one of the few people on Earthen that professionally duelled with Kain and won on many occasions?"

Swartz laughed loudly. "Yes, revenge will be sweet."

Sean heard a car engine, then some fifty metres above them three figures emerged – Kain, PC Millan, and Prince Dain. Swartz jested to Sean. "Here come the cavalry, enjoy your death."

Kain called, Gill beckoned him down. Kain and party obliged and were soon stood in front of Gill, Schwarz, Sean, and Emma – she was now looking very white.

Kain looked around, noting the other four on the quarry sides, then addressed Gill. "So you feel you have a chance. A king, a prince and a police duel master?"

Gill replied, "We outnumber you two to one, plus we have an old friend."

Kain looked at Swartz. "And I was the one who stopped your death sentence…"

Swartz interrupted, "But left me to rot in jail!"

Kain remained calm. "Are you ok, Sean and Emma?"

Sean replied, "Yes."

Emma's was, "I don't know."

Kain looked at Gill. "You are prepared to die today?"

Gill looked uncomfortable but responded, "Six ex-military against three who need to protect two useless souls. I rate my chances."

Kain circled. "Then so be it. Take your positions."

With this, Gill and Swartz moved to their positions; now all six aggressors were equally distanced apart on the walls of the quarry. Dain and Millan took position either side of Sean and Emma. Kain looked at Sean. Without opening his mouth, he asked, "Are you able to protect you and Emma?"

Sean responded, again without talking, "Yes, I've had some pills. my power is growing."

Kain smiled. "Then protect you and Emma."

With this, Kain turned and took his position up, creating an even triangle with Millan and Dain around Sean and Emma.

There was silence when Sean heard a whoosh and a crackle, then more and more. Sean could see the frenzied air around him. Kain and the others were still but Gill's people were moving around, aiming force at what was clearly now a protective bubble that Kain, Millan, and Dain had set up. This went on for a few minutes then stopped.

Swartz shouted out, "Kain have you become human? Fight like an Earthen!"

Kain did not respond but looked at Sean. "Are you ready? Can you protect you and Emma?"

Sean thought a simple "Yes."

Kain looked at Millan and Dain, both nodded, and with that Sean put up his shield. The larger one around them dropped. Kain, Millan, and Dain were moving; clearly the fight was on. All combatants were moving a few feet either side, directing their blows through arm movement – Sean kept his shield up. Millan made a hit and the woman aggressor hit the quarry wall then fell ten metres to a lower cliff. Millan took a hit but composed himself and fought back.

Kain was clearly focussing on Gill and Swartz, each taking a blow but recovering. Then suddenly Dain hit the floor. Millan responded first and fired out to Dain's slayer – the two he had been holding hit him hard and Millan fell. All went quiet; Kain was kneeling and had set a protective bubble around himself, Sean, and Emma. Sean looked at his ties and willed them off; he and Emma were now free.

"Emma, stay beside me. Do not move." Emma held on to Sean. "Dad, I'm fine. I can handle this!"

Kain responded, "Wait, but remember protection especially of Emma is your main goal."

Sean stood straight, Emma behind. Out of the corner of his eye Sean saw one of the aggressors fly into the air and hit the quarry wall. On the top of the quarry was Jeng, who had now turned her attention to the other two. Kain shouted now; the protection bubble dropped and Kain hit Swartz hard, knocking him to the floor, then concentrated on Gill.

Sean looked at one of the others; thinking of his mother, the aggressor had no chance, his body virtually splitting against the wall. Jeng took out the other aggressor, her speed and agility getting her so close it was nearly like punching him.

Sean turned. Gill had gone defensive, a clear protection bubble around him. Kain stopped sending blows at him. Jeng was at Sean's side. "Go to your father. I'll protect Emma."

Sean turned and walked the short distance to his father, who had now stopped bombarding Gill, who dropped his guard and stood to address Kain.

"Many years of Earth living have weakened you, Kain. Our plans were nearly successful, however, cheating with an unknown player is not good protocol," Gill shouted.

"You are correct, such actions in a duel are underhand and not protocol. However, do you think attacking my family, having kids caught in the middle can be considered a duel? No, this is war!" Kain was now standing. Sean swore he looked metres taller but was very menacing.

Gill stuttered. "Sooo beee it, I will not give up as you will show no mercy."

Kain replied. "No one but my friends and I are leaving here alive..." Kain suddenly flew to his right, hitting the ground. Sean looked up. Swartz was on his feet, attacking Kain with Gill joining him. Sean thought hard and hit Swartz square on – Swartz fell.

Kain stood up and called, "Enough!"

Gill was raised into the air. Kain was not using his hands but just moved his head to the left, Gill's floating body followed. Kain looked to the right, Gill followed. Kain looked up then down quickly; Gill lifted some ten metres higher in the air then came flying towards them, hitting the floor a metre from Kain.

Kain started to take a step towards him when Swartz rose again. Kain simply raised his right arm, and Swartz disintegrated. Kain was now on top of Gill who was murmuring but not dead. Kain raised his leg, stamped down, the murmuring stopped.

Jeng was the first to talk. "You ok Sean?"

Sean said, "Yes, Emma?"

As he looked at Emma she looked totally lost but managed, "I'm ok."

Sean walked towards her and hugged her. Kain turned to address them. Sean swore there was fire in his eyes; the anger, power or force whatever it was, was evident. "Jeng, check Millan."

Jeng moved to Millan, Kain to his brother. Within a metre of his brother Dain moved and sat up. "What happened? Is it over?"

Kain stopped. "You are not dead?"

Dain was now standing. "No, no, but I was hit hard, unconscious. What went on?"

Kain's expression changed. "Brother... I will deal with you later. Jeng?"

Dain interrupted, "Jeng, where did you come from?"

Ignoring Dain, Jeng holding back tears. "I'm sorry, he is gone. If only I were here earlier." She was kneeling and holding Millan's body.

"It is not your doing. You carried out instructions and fought well for someone so young. As did you, Sean." Kain then turned again to his brother. "You call yourself a prince?"

Dain's response was inaudible but was clearly apologetic in some way. Sean heard then saw a car pull up at the top of the quarry, then heard the news to brighten his heart. "Jeng, take Sean and Emma to Jenna." Sure enough, one of the figures exiting the car was his mother.

Sean reached the quarry edge first; ignoring Algier and Sal, he only had eyes on his mother. "Mum, Mum! You are ok." Although the hug he gave her did nearly kill her. Jeng and Emma had caught them up; both now joined the hugs of Sean and Jenna.

Sean caught Sal's eye then stopped; his heart fell. "I'm sorry Sal." He was now hugging the crying Sal.

Algier took control. "Jeng, take Sean, Jenna, and Emma to the Research Park. I will tidy up here."

Jeng headed towards the car. Algier was now holding Sal and leading her down the quarry side. As Sean got into the back of the car he swore he heard another scream. Jeng threw him a knowing look; Sean remembered his father's words that no aggressor was leaving alive. Jenna and Emma were now next to Sean in the back. The car pulled off, passing another car coming that had Secretary Seth, Detective Inspector Cott, and Harvey Gwent in. All was silent in the car apart from tears. The trip was short and soon they were in the research facility.

Livia was making drinks; Sean, Emma, Jeng, and Jenna were seated on one big sofa. Emma finally could not hold her tongue. "What the fuck just happened!" Definitely an unusual expletive for her.

Livia came over. Holding Emma's head, she appeared to whisper something in her ear; Emma fell unconscious, just as Kain had done to the girl in the car crash, Sean recalled. Livia smiled at Sean. "Emma will be fine, she needs to sleep." With that, Livia picked up Emma and took her to one of the bedrooms.

Sean looked at his mother. "Mrs Carnell, Smith, how are they?"

Jenna wiped a tear. "They were very brave. Sorry, Mrs Carnell did not make it. Professor Smith is alive and in hospital here on the base and doing well."

Sean also wiped some tears. "I was so awful to Mrs Carnell."

"I know. Whatever has gone on, you are just a child and will do what children do, but be proud. Although this may sound silly, Mrs Carnell died serving her king and fighting for her friends. If there is a heaven she will be happy smiling down on us, as will PC Millan."

"How did you get away?" Sean asked.

"I was not their target, it was obviously you and your father they were after, indeed Gill while tying me up said that his masters would enjoy seeing me deal with my son and husband's death. Gill had called your father as a decoy so as he could kidnap you whilst being less protected. He must have thought that a subdued you would have strengthened their chances, your father would have needed to concentrate on protection." Jenna looked up. "You know I have never wanted to be an Earthen. I hate their ways but at that point, seeing you and my friends being attacked, I would have wished to have been one." Jenna cried, Sean just held her.

Sean noticed Jeng was missing, but was now coming back in the door. "Be careful with him, he took a big hit." Sean's face lightened up. Walking slowly in behind Jeng was Shadow. Sean ran to his dog, carefully hugging him as he was clearly in pain. "Sal seems to be good with dogs as well as people. I'm going to bed," Jeng finished.

Shadow was licking Sean and although subdued was clearly ok, if not injured. Jenna joined them both on the floor. "It seems that when Shadow hit the floor they thought he was dead so left him."

Sean, still smiling, then thought and stopped. "Is this wrong? Two people I care about have died and yet I'm happy over a dog."

Jenna looked at Sean. "No, don't be hard on yourself. Life, as you have now learnt, especially Earthen, can be hard. You must take terrible downs in your stride and enjoy the ups; besides, Shadow is one of the family." Sean felt less guilty and continued to hug Shadow.

Sean finally slept, albeit on Shadow's large dog blanket with him, waking only to see Algier looking quizzically at him. "I really don't understand this attachment to an animal." Defensively, he added, "But of course Shadow is a family member."

Sean laughed and joined the others around the couches. Kain sat next to Sean. "Well done, you were very brave. It is good you remembered the pills we have been advising you about in the heels of your shoes."

Sean thought, *No what a fool of course he had the hidden pills all the time!* "Yes dad," was Sean's subdued response.

Jeng announced, "Secretary Seth is ready for us now, sir."

With that, Kain and Sean rose and headed for the door. Sean stopped. "Where's Sal? Is she ok...? And Emma?"

Jenna took him by the arm. "They are ok. Sal is looking after Emma, don't worry. Let's go."

Jeng, Jenna, Sean, Kain, and Algier entered the communication room, joining Gwent Cott, Seth, and Dain.

Seth welcomed them then spoke to Kain. "I have briefed my king and he will now join us, as will the other kings and their secretaries." With that, four kings and four councillors plus Barlo appeared in viewers on the wall.

Algier addressed all. "By now you have all been provided details of the events that led to yesterday's troubles and the clear outcomes. May I have your thoughts please?"

No one wanted to start the conversation, then Kain did, looking at King Vul. "Sir, my humblest apologies for the direct actions taken against your subjects. I personally take full responsibility for them, my people were only following orders." Sean could not but note the calmness in Kain's voice.

King Vul looked a bit taken aback. "I appreciate your apology, but actions meaning the death of five of my subjects plus others from other kingdoms, surely an apology is not enough?"

Kain responded, "King Vul, you are correct. No words can replace life, however, I from the start clearly made you all aware of my disgust and that if I had to I would take action." Kain was still smiling.

Secretary Seth made a pretend cough. "Sire, if I may, the taking of another kingdom's subjects is clearly against protocol.

However, there are definite extenuating circumstances which I believe if challenged would consider recent actions as self-defence or defence of defenceless others. Not forgetting that King Kain also lost subjects, as did King Bier."

A screen to King Vul's right shuffled in his chair, obviously King Bier. "Yes, we lost a good man, indeed Millan's father Rane has spoken to me. Obviously he is very sad over the death of his beloved son. Algier, thank you for making the arrangements to have his body returned home for burial. Rane, a noble man, recalled how his son was very happy working with King Kain on Earth. He would never have been allowed to be with his love even if in Biernite. Rane was gracious in his thoughts for King Kain and his ways. Not wishing to create friction, but I too have lost a subject and unfortunately the main aggressors were from Vulten. Any Kings' Council vote and I would support King Kain."

Kain acknowledged King Bier. "Thank you, I second the bravery of Rane's son Millan, he will be missed."

All eyes were now on King Vul. "We are not having a Kings' Council or vote, this is purely exploratory discussions. If for suggestion this was taken seriously, by say, myself, what would be your response, King Kain?" Even Sean thought this was a poorly hidden challenge.

Kain thought but remained calm. "I would fully understand the suggestion made but with respect do not see what the outcome of such would gain anyone. Surely even you, sire, would wish to see no more bloodshed?" Kain did not say anything or drop his smile but he clearly gave King Vul a look and actually moved towards King Vul's viewer, a strange but unnerving move.

Secretary Seth joined. "Your Highnesses, within protocol I am sure that some compensation could be made by Saulten, as regardless of their actions Vultens were killed without our king's agreement."

Algier cottoned on. "Yes, of course. We will provide the appropriate compensation to the deceased families and something to the Vulten people."

King Vul was listening but focussing on Kain, who was now virtually in front of his viewer but still smiling. King Vul replied, "If protocol allows this and appropriate compensation is made, then yes, I see no need for further action. Viewer off!"

A cloud seemed to lift from the room; all the remaining viewers apart from Barlo's went off.

"Secretary Barlo, please make the arrangements and be generous to the lost ones' families. Viewer off."

Kain was now looking to those in the room. "Gwent and Cott, you have much to do here on Earth to cover the recent events." Gwent and Cott turned to leave when Kain called out, "Cott, I am sorry for berating you during the events."

Cott looked a little shocked but responded with, "Yes sire, thank you," before leaving.

Kain turned to Secretary Seth, shaking his hand. "Thank you, my friend. Have a safe journey." Secretary Seth bowed and followed Gwent and Cott.

"Dain." Kain's voice now changed. "I am not certain or happy with your actions..."

Dain tried to interrupt with some again inaudible apology about being knocked out but Kain focussed on him, clearly mind hurting him.

Algier jumped in. "Kain, you have no proof!"

Kain let Dain go. "Begone with you, go home!" Dain said no further and followed Secretary Seth out.

"Jeng, you will receive our Medal of Honour, the youngest ever to be awarded this, I'm sure, but more importantly my thanks and promise of undying support for you and your family, who I'm sure you wish to see now."

Jeng approached Kain and even gained a peck from Kain on

her cheek. She turned, smiled and waved at Sean, then left.

Kain walked up to Jenna took her arm. "Let's walk, I know a bridge with your name on." Both giggled, smiled at Sean and left.

Sean looked at Algier. "Crikey, what's come over Dad?"

Algier smiled at Livia, who was now also leaving the room. "Come, let's sit," he said to Sean. "It would appear that maybe your father had indeed lost some of his power. From what I know he would have dealt with all six on his own at his peak, although Swartz would have maybe tipped the balance. Sadly, to Millan's loss it does appear the battle of such magnitude has awoken his brain. Maybe they were right; many years here on Earth did make it stale." Algier thought further. "Actually, if you notice we do not use our telekinetic powers all the time, as resting it, indeed saving it, is deemed good, so possibly your father's power has been dormant for many years but clearly is back now."

Algier took a sip of drink. "Clever Earthens can sense power. Secretary Seth is such. He sensed Kain's re-found power and I'm sure pre-warned King Vul that a challenge was not best." Algier laughed. "I would have loved to have been a fly on the wall for that conversation." Again Algier laughed.

"And Uncle Dain, what is Dad's displeasure about him? If you're injured, you're injured."

"As you say, the jury is out on that one." Sean was a little taken back by this reply. Algier continued. "The small matter of Dain signing off Gill's Earth permit. Accident, my arse. Did I get that Earth saying right?"

Sean giggled. "Yes."

Algier continued. "I'm not sure a prince should go down that easy and clearly not hurt. Who has the most to gain if both you and your father were killed yesterday?"

Sean was shocked. "Really? No, his brother?"

"Position and power mean a lot to many an Earthen, indeed

even Earthlings. By no way would I condone such actions if true but it must be hard playing second fiddle to a king, even if he was your brother." Algier cleared his throat. "Is there not a certain young lady you would be best to see?"

Sean stood up, smiled at Algier and headed to the door. Upon exit he could see a spaceship that had obviously just landed. Seth, Dain, and Jeng were getting on board. Sean went red as Jeng, seeing him, blew him a kiss and waved goodbye. Sean waved, or at least he thought he had as he did feel frozen on the spot in a good way. Coming off the spaceship were a man and a woman – it was Councillor Anders and Sean assumed his wife, because Sal had joined them. All were now in a big huddle.

Sean walked to the sofa room and Emma was sitting patting Shadow. Livia approached Sean and whispered, no messaged in his head, "Sal has worked some magic and poor Emma does not recall anything over the last few days, but thinks she has just been hanging out with you and Shadow. She is looking forward to the holiday though."

Sean was beyond questions or even astonishment. Could Sal really clear Emma's mind? Who cares? But he did approach Emma gingerly. "You Ok?"

"Yes, why shouldn't I be?" was Emma's reply. "Although I feel a bit strange but Sal told me the bee sting was probably something more, so my drowsiness or foggied memory over the last few days will clear."

Sean could not help but say, "Wow... Let's go to the flight tower and look out, it's a wonderful day."

With that, both friends headed towards the tower, climbed the many steps and were now sitting legs over the side but holding the lower railing. The views across the English countryside were amazing. Shadow, although now ant size was obviously barking at them from forty metres below. Emma laughed.

Sean looked at Emma, pulled her close and kissed her on the lips.

HOLIDAY END:
(CHAPTER 13)

Shadow was darting towards his prey, eyes focused, when he suddenly hit something, twisted in the air and landed on the grass. "Ouch!" Followed by a laugh, Mush was also lying prone on the grass.

Sean Saul looked at his friend who was now sitting up with Sean's Alsatian Shadow circling him and licking him. Sean gave a laugh and as he walked towards the two of them, "You ok Mush? Shadow hit you hard?"

"Your fault throwing the Frisbee between us, Shadow couldn't resist it." Said Mush still laughing.

Sean now at Shadow's side, "You ok?" Holding Shadow's head, he was asking Shadow without talking. Sean stated, "He's ok, no thanks to you, you lump," With that Sean gave Shadow a treat. Shadow took the treat and moved to the side of the lake they were at to eat it.

Mush, still laughing, had got up and walked the few metres to the bench where he sat down. "Have a drink." Sean sat next to his friend both taking in their drinks; it was a late summer hot day.

"Been a good holiday. You and Emma had a great time in Italy, she doesn't stop talking about it."

"Yeah, sounds like you had a good time in Florida. Mushing your cousins in the first week worked."

Mush giggles, "Yep didn't have to look after them after that, did all the rides on my own."

"Did you miss Zandra?"

Mush looked up, "Yeah but we've seen each other a lot since. We are at Alton Towers next week as a treat before we go back to school. Staying in the hotel there."

Sean thought, "How come you didn't invite me and Emma?"

"Emma is right about you, brain like a sieve. You're away with your dad picking up the new car ordered through my dad then Paris or something." Mush was obviously clued up.

"Of course." Sean was up to speed. "Shit that means I miss Emma. She is back Wednesday from her acting course up north." Mush responded with a shrug of his shoulders as both boys picked up their rucksacks and headed home with Shadow in tow.

Mush had to go home as some relative was visiting for dinner. Sean entered his house that appeared empty. "Anyone here?" He called.

"In the garden." Was the reply from his mother Jenna. Sean went to the garden and sat at the wooden table; Jenna was taking some washing off the rotary arm. "Don't help then!" Jenna taunted.

Sean sat still. "Dad late again?"

"Yep." Was the reply.

"Mine's a coffee." By the time Sean had made the hot drinks his mother had joined him sitting at the kitchen table.

"Dad seems very busy at the moment, is he still tying up the events of a few months ago?" Sean asked quizzically.

"Yes. There is a lot to both cover up and resolve, but time and diplomacy will help. How are you holding up?"

"I'm OK. I know I've come to terms with the alien and power stuff but fighting and death still bother me."

Jenna moved next to Sean, giving him a quick cuddle. "I am sorry we could not hide anything further from you. Time will help heal things. Sal is doing well."

Sean could see the slight tear in his mother's eye. "Millan was a good guy and Mrs. Carnell...I'm sorry I didn't get to know her more. I think the holiday helped Sal, although she joined us late. You and Uncle Algier have been great with her." Jenna smiled as Sean continued "I'm worried about Emma she is having flash backs."

Jenna wiped her eye, "Emma is a tough young lady, and her sessions with Sal are helping. Actually, I think they are also helping Sal, giving her a focus. Yes, it is a little concerning that Emma is having these flashbacks, her confusion is worse."

"So, would it not be better to tell her?"

Surprisingly Jenna gave a little jolt as she tensed her body before responding. "I'm not sure that would be a good idea. Certainly, their protocol will have something to say. We cannot tell everyone about Earthens."

Sean caught on, "Stupid protocols, surely some of us humans know about the Earthens. Anyway, if I want to tell Emma I will, I'm a prince..."

"You sound like your father." Jenna interrupted. "Even though you are a prince you have to follow protocol."

"Why Dad doesn't, well not always."

"I'm sure it would be a great opportunity to ask your father while you are away this week with him picking up his new car and attending that Earth council meeting in Paris. I am glad I'm not going, although I love Paris? Father and son time is what is needed." Sean, Jenna and Shadow ended the day watching a movie. Kain came home late.

Sean woke thinking it was a shame this was the last Monday of sleep before school next week. This time it was Kain's turn to wake him, no door opening but Sean could feel him in his head. "Get up both of you." Shadow was also now alert, "Picnic with friends remember." Sean needed no further pushing and within minutes he and Shadow were washed and, in the Discovery, ready to go.

Jenna made the short drive to the woods. Parking near the BBQ area they all got out of the car. Shadow was spoilt as he ran towards their friends Daphne and Desmond Green with their son Mush being his first target, followed by Judy and Harry Cooper. Sean could not help noticing that even Shadow looked perplexed that Emma was not present with her parents.

Sean, Mush and the dads all started playing cricket while the mums were cooking the food. Shadow was an excellent wicket keeper. Many balls (tennis balls) strangely missed the bat and ended up in his mouth whilst Kain was bowling. Upon walking to the food table Sean could not help but think to his Father "Cheat!" The pain in Sean's head suggested Kain was not accepting this allegation, albeit his wry smile gave the game away.

Food and drink aplenty Jenna started. "Shame Emma is not here. I am sure she is doing great at the acting academy?"

Harry Cooper was first to respond, "Yes Emma FaceTime us last night. I think she is up for the actor of the week award. Her skills take after me, dealing with people and all that...oh and her mother's looks of course."

"Thank God for her mother's looks" Desmond was up for baiting. Judy smiled at Desmond who received a top up of the summer wine he was drinking. Desmond now wanted to play. "So, I hear some money bags bought the Jameses house next door to you?"

Kain bit, "Desmond you know I bought it. You're Green by name but not by nature," All laughed. Kain continued. "Seriously though, yes I bought it. It will be an investment in the long term although initially I'll rent it out to my company for the short term."

Harry could not help himself. "Kain you never seem to surprise me. There will obviously be some kind of tax advantage there?"

Kain knowing his friend was an accountant, "Yes. Does any-one know a good accountant?" only Jenna's "boys!" stopped the laughing and ribbing getting out of hand.

Daphne asked, "Is it right the Jameses are now living in America?"

Kain replied, "Yes I have connections there and was able to find him a job."

"Oh, so you will help the James' get a job but not us your best friends?" Harry chuckled.

"Harry. I would be happy to get you a job if it meant you moving miles away, shame America would not be far enough." Again, all laughed at Kain's response.

At that point Sal's car pulled up. Before she joined the group, Sean heard Judy say to Jenna "Poor woman, PC Millan pass-ing away, even courageously in the line of duty is hard." Sean knew that PC Millan's sad death was passed as a car accident; he apparently was chasing some known drug dealers. On this point Sean also remembered that Mrs. Carnell's death had been passed off as old age.

Sal joined the group, clearly feeling the warmth and sup-port they all gave her. She joined in the banter and some of the games. As the day ended, Jenna offered Sal to stay the night and she accepted. Sean, Jenna, Kain and Sal found themselves around 11pm sitting in the garden having a drink together.

The next morning with Kain and Jenna busy packing, Sean saw the opportunity to talk with Sal. They both offered to walk Shadow to get out of the way. Kain's protest as to why he had to pack yet Jenna packed Sean's case was ignored. Sean found himself sitting next to Sal on the bench near the lake.

"Are you Ok young man?" Sal broke the ice.

"Yes, I am fine, more importantly, how are you?" Sean went into mother mode and gave Sal a hug.

"It's hard. I and Iain were close, and we were thinking of making it more public." Sal's stare stopped Sean from speaking although he could not stop a giggle. "Look I deal with this type of thing all the time in my job, so I need to take my own advice. Talking about a lost loved one, spending time with friends is the best medicine."

"You are brave."

Sal returned the cuddle, "So you want to know where things are going and more importantly how Emma is?" Sean was shocked. "You reading my mind?"

"Sorry couldn't help sneaking in. Look who knows where things will go, this summer's events have certainly raised issues on Earthen. The Kings seem to have accepted the reasons but still, subjects died. Your father and Dain are stretched further, Dain is playing a dangerous game." Sal pondered for a moment, "Emma is strong minded, I am keeping her sane at present, but it is hard. If you are planning to tell her then please get Kain onside first."

No more was said; by 5pm Kain and Sean were on the plane to Stuttgart. As part of the Mercedes package they went business class, were picked up by a Mercedes driver and dropped off at a small but nice boutique style hotel. The evening meal was time for Sean to talk with Kain. "So, what's going on you seem very busy with Earthen things?"

Kain thought for a moment, "Unfortunately all the events have opened up some scars of the past and some intrigue for the future." Kain picked up on Sean's look before continuing, "Look you know how the Kings operate and how the Councils, indeed Saulten, is compared to the other Kingdoms, so political power games are taking place."

"I don't really understand politics but what about people, Uncle Dain?"

Kain shrugged his shoulders, "That fool. If I could prove his definite involvement in the events, I would deal with him."

Sean again looked at his father. "Yes, I'm sorry but if I had to kill my own brother I would, certainly in defence of you and your mother."

Sean took a deep breath, "Wow, I am sorry you really do have a lot of responsibilities."

"Yes, I do but I also have good people around me. You will learn there is a lot in the saying keep your friends close but your enemies closer. I have changed Dain's council responsibilities. I have put him in charge of facilities...more specifically bogs and drains as you would call them." Both Kain and Sean laughed at this. Kain continued, "Your other question, Sal told me, Emma." Again, Sean flinched. "The Earth Council would need to authorise such an exposure. Even then it can be dangerous."

Sean interrupted. "I know if other humans found out then it would have to be dealt with."

Kain changed his expression, looked straight into Sean's eyes and without moving his lips said, "You know if an Earthling tells on Earthens initially they are ridiculed. If they are important or make a public fuss, then they would be dishonored in some way." Kain stopped.

Sean took this in, "That explains many of the UFO sightings or abduction stories not being believed. Even famous powerful people being brought down as mad and their stories ridiculed."

Kain continued, but now talking with his mouth, "They are the easy ones. A famous writer been shown as a drunk or a politician being disgraced by being tied up with adultery allegations rather than finishing their alien theories."

Sean was falling in, "So you and the Earth council are behind these cover ups?"

Kain was a bit uncomfortable but nodded then shocked Sean to the core. "We also plan disappearances and...deaths if they get too far out of hand." Sean sunk in his chair. Looking at this man in front of him who he loved so much but realising more and more the decisions and actions he had and would take scared him.

Sean looked up, "So if say I told Emma and she or her family told the world, made a big song and dance about it you would...kill her?"

Kain stood up to leave the table then turned. Sean felt his head hurt then heard his father's voice clearly in his head. "Yes, the Council would authorise it if it were the last course of action."

Sean felt like he wanted to be sick but sat alone for a while deep in thought. Upon entering his room, he saw his father was awake and reading in bed. Sean got into his bed turned over to look at his father in the opposite bed then said out loud, "I hate your Earthen ways." He then sat up and looked at his father. Without opening his mouth said, "If Emma needs my support then I will need yours. You will never treat me, Mum or Emma as Earthens." Even Kain could feel the power in Sean's thoughts.

The next day was lighthearted. Both Sean and Kain had clearly made a point to each other; this was after all a father and son-bonding trip. The Mercedes chauffeur picked them up as planned and by 9.30am they were in the factory reception area. The reception had some exhibits including the latest Mercedes F1 car; both took opportunities to be photographed next to it. The tour of the factory was interesting. At one-point Kain was asking questions about the robotics. The guide invited an engineer colleague to answer but even he was amazed, offering Kain a job on the spot.

After a quick lunch they were in the showroom looking at Kain's new car, a silver E Class Estate with all the toys. Pictures and niceties over and they were on their way heading to Paris, some six-hour plus drive. Sean finished setting up the mobile phone connection and then started to play with the entertainment system. "Wow, I can watch a film whilst you see the sat nav both from the same screen." Kain laughed, "Suppose it's no big deal on Earthen but it is here!" Sean made his point. Thinking further, "Dad, with all your global warming stuff how come you drive a big Merc. Even if it is smaller than the last one?"

"You got me I'm a hypocrite." Kain sniggered. "Look I am all for stopping global warming etc. but Earth has some time to work it out. Remember we want to teach Earth not direct it. Besides this is smaller than my last one. The extra space for Shadow will save me some earache, Mum moans when I don't put her seat back." Sean chuckled. Kain continued, "This is the largest but most ecofriendly petrol engine they do. Hybrid or electric are not here as yet in a useable way, so I am making sacrifices. When ordering I really wanted the AMG model."

"Hypocrite. By the way I know it's a long journey, but we are going some speed."

"You see the gadget box on the dashboard I put there before we left?" Sean acknowledged. "Well it is a portable Perception Projector. I have set it up to project to any radar or camera, even toll bridges, to show the countries Police Chief Commissioner's car and registration. We will not be slowing down or stopping for anything." Kain laughed as sure enough at that point they approached a toll that opened instantly and let them through.

"Once home it will be fitted discreetly in the car, as there is in Mum's car. Funny we have never had a speeding ticket or fine of any sort."

"Wow, but what if we get stopped?"

"Do you not think I could deal with an Earthling Policeman? I can be very persuasive you know."

Sean replied, "Hypocrite," again as they both laughed.

EARTH COUNCIL:
(CHAPTER 14)

The miles in the car were covered with both comfort and speed. The time gained benefit was instead of the expected late-night room service bite to eat was turned into the opportunity of sitting down to eat in the plush Parisian hotel they were staying at. Around 11pm instead of suggesting bed Kain surprised Sean, "Let's get a night cap in the bar. I'll sneak you some wine, the fizzy stuff you like."

As they entered the hotel bar Sean wondered what the commotion was, the bar appeared full of men jostling around someone. Kain approached the group stood tall and said, "Sorry Gentleman this lady is with me." Amazingly some six men looked at Kain then all moved away from the bar to reveal Livia Strom sitting there. "I was having fun Sir!" Livia spoke but rose to greet Kain and Sean with a cuddle before they found a table and sat down.

"All organised for tomorrow?" Kain asked.

"Yes Sir. And how about you young man. Ready to meet the Council?"

"Of course, can't wait."

They continued with some small talk. Sean was allowed to drink some more wine. He knew his parents allowed him it in moderation and were teaching him rather than banning him from drinking it altogether. A short plump man came over. Kain stood, shook his hand and said something in a foreign language, the recipient laughed.

Looking at Sean the plump man spoke. "I am Councilor Robares," lowering his voice said, "The Earthen Councilor for France, how are you young Sire?"

Sean realised they had been speaking French but had to respond in English. "I'm fine Councilor, your hospitality is great."

Robares smiled, "I think you will find it is Livia who arranged all this. Kain may we talk privately?" Kain did not respond but he and Robares moved to another table on its own in the corner.

Livia advised, "Tomorrow we will have breakfast together. Your father is having some private meetings prior to the main one at eleven, you can help me set it up."

"Sounds great but yes of course." Sean was being sarcastic.

Sean and Livia had breakfast together whilst Kain was busy eating with others. Livia led Sean to the meeting room that was a typical Earth room some twelve seats around a wooden table, with other seats placed around the room behind them. No white walls or viewers although the window looking out to the Eifel Tower was such a good a view Earthen could not even try to beat it.

"So, let's get started," Livia was removing what looked like PC Tablets from a box, Sean now holding one looked closer. It looked like a tablet, about A4 in size but the screen was clear and had rounded edges, the back was white but very thin. "The electronics are in that coating very discreet but works the same as an Earthling tablet." Livia said, "Tell it to turn on."

Sean said, "Turn on," the tablet came to life with a very clear welcome page similar to a Microsoft or Apple PC. "Ask it for notes, then say type and type something." Livia continued instructing.

"Notes," Sean said, the screen reacted instantly and a page like a typical clear white note pad was on view. "Notes, hello Paris," the screen followed Sean's voice perfectly writing

'Hello Paris'. "Wow." Sean was back to his favourite word, "So do I have to tell it to write? That wouldn't be good in a meeting."

Livia smiled, "When in the meeting you think it and it types what you think, no noise. Each tablet is tied to its user's voice or thoughts as yours has already been set up for you and only you can write on your tablet. However, if another person allows you to access theirs as I would as the meeting secretary then you can project to my screen by saying, 'project, meeting secretary,' then what you want." Livia was now holding her own tablet.

Sean thought, then in his head said, "Project, meeting secretary...I love you," his tablet printed the words on his screen. Looking at Livia's smile suggested she had received this, her answer now showing on Sean's screen confirmed this, "Be careful young man I thought you were accounted for. I can text straight from this screen to Emma's mobile if you like!" Sean went red.

"Obviously the projector works in the same way, try it." Livia continued.

Sean looked at a box of tricks in the middle of the table. With his mouth, "Projector project to wall screen." The projector responded by placing his screen on the wall space in front of him, which was there for normal Earthling computers. Sean started playing with it asking it to project on the ceiling, then the floor. This was great fun.

His fun was stopped some ten minutes later when Livia said, "Thanks for your help we are ready now." Sean stopped what he was doing; Livia had placed tablets on the table in front of each chair together with drinking glasses. "Oops, sorry for not helping you," Sean let out.

Kain entered the room with some men, all appeared to be Earthen judging by their look although they were dressed in Earthling professional clothing, suits, ties etc. Kain sat down in the middle of the table, the other nine seats taken up by varied council members, all male Sean noted. Livia ushered Sean to sit at one end of the table, which was actually a pointed oval shape. Livia sat at the other end facing him, both having five councilors now either side of them.

Kain started, "As Chief Councilor for the Earthen Council I welcome you all Councilors. Before we start I apologise for my son's humour, please clear it." Kain was looking out of the window on which Sean had projected a picture of Shadow doing his business on the Eifel Tower. Sean went red, Livia saved him, and the picture was cleared leaving the Eifel Tower to be seen in its full glory.

Kain continued, "That was my son's introduction, please could each of you introduce yourselves." With this each Councilor spoke in turn, advising their name and country they were responsible for; Sean noting Robares was France with most of the main ones announced covered Germany, Russia, Italy, China and the USA.

"Livia has provided a full agenda. I though wish to start the meeting making a couple of points." Kain continued, "First the events of early this summer. Thank you all for your support and efforts to control this both here on Earth and at home on Earthen. We will discuss some of the details later as per the agenda, but I must reiterate that I am happy with my and my people's actions." Kain could not help being a King sometimes. "The other is the agreed planned visit by some dignitaries' children to my son's school and my home later this Earthling term. I am happy and fully agree with this visit but do wish to make sure all controls and agreements are in place. My apologies Councilor Toal but that includes those with your King."

Sean watched as who was obviously Councilor Toal acknowledge Kain's comment. Toal must be a Vulten he thought. With this the meeting started in earnest, Sean, although not fully taking in everything found some details of interest; he found the Earth Council were a lot less volatile than the Supreme Council he had previously experienced.

Lunch came and Sean could talk to Livia. "So, these dignitaries, why my school. Why a normal secondary school." Sean thought, "Actually having been to private school previously why am I now in a public secondary school?"

"Slow down. First your school is perfect as out of school they will have your parents, Sal and everyone to support them and in school Professor Smith and a new planted Gill replacement who is on our side plus of course you. Now you are aware of your powers and responsibilities you can help educate, mmm watch them."

"As for why a secondary school the same is for them as for you, first when you were young your mother like all mothers wrapped you in cotton wool therefore, a smaller more controllable private school was right for you. However, with no disrespect for your human friends their intellect is no match to yours, you will pick things up easily. Your, and the dignitaries placement in a normal school is not specifically academic but more about mixing with Earthlings. That is your and what will be the dignitaries learning."

Sean thought on this. "Snobs," was his only plausible response deciding to eat the biggest chocolate muffin he found would hide him from having a further discussion about class. He personally thought Emma and Mush was his equal.

The meeting ended but the names of the dignitaries were not released, as this was tomorrow's agenda. Livia reminded Sean to put his suit on and come back down to help her have the restaurant ready that they were all eating at. The Le Jules Verne on the Eifel Tower. Sure enough, Sean and Livia headed off before the main party to check the table and food orderings. Sean could not help but laugh, the French waiters had no chance with Livia who had them eating out the palm of her hand. "Yes Mam."

"Of Course, Mam." Whatever Livia asked they obeyed; the

French have good taste in women.

The meal was a bit too formal for Sean's liking, but he managed to get through the three, or was it five courses? The earlier chocolate muffin was definitely not his best move. All of the councilors had their wives or partners with them, again Sean could not help but note their general friendliness to each other. With the last dish down Sean agreed to get some air on the balcony with Livia.

Livia gave Sean a flattering smile. "So, come on then. Here we are in the city of love, you a Prince and me if I do say a beautiful woman." Sean went redder than he had ever been before, thankfully Livia was only kidding. "Sorry, you are a little young for me and besides you will be like your father, Emma is a lucky young lady."

Sean between blushes managed to say, "You are...I mean yes of course but seriously you are stunning...I'm not aware of you having a boyfriend?"

Livia laughed and tossed her hair. "Look it's not just the Earthen men that can have fun. Remember we Earthens will live some ten maybe twenty years longer than Earthlings so our fun time is twenties to forties. The average age for Earthens to marry is forty as opposed to Earth, which is closer to mid-twenties. So, I'm a single and happy woman enjoying my time. We too, like Earthen men, are not frowned upon if we have more than one partner."

Livia looked at Sean, "Sorry does that shock you?"

"No, no it's just different."

"Actually, I have a man in Norway who I'm close to, plus a good military friend on Earthen, among others." There was a glint in her eye as she said this, "Now get to the point this is not about you and me?"

"No," Sean quizzed, "Are you reading my mind?" Livia shrugged a no, "Well you and Dad, even Sal and Dad I mean, I don't know."

Livia chuckled, "Sean surely you know your father by now, he has and always will only love your mother. Others have tried, hell he's a King but no he is unlike most other Earthens especially kings." Livia let Sean take it in, "You have heard about Sal and even me probably being suitors. I'm sure I speak for us both in saying given the opportunity yes maybe it could have happened but no we are close friends, loyal subjects to both Kain and Jenna." Livia added with a mischievous smile, but it does not stop us having fun. When we dance, which we will in a while, take a photo and send it to your mother and see what happens." Sean was not sure but thought, 'ok why not.'

Sure enough, the dance started, Kain first danced with Livia, followed by Sean – picture messages sent. Sean watching from the side saw Robare clearly over dancing with Livia and Kain dancing with one of the other wives when Sean received a response – 'Kain the spare bedroom is ready for you. Sean the local children's home has spaces and you're booked in for tomorrow.' Sean looked up at his father who had obviously seen the same message and whilst laughing gave Sean a wink.

The meeting was reconvened in the morning. Sean was not taking much notice until they got around to discussing the dignitaries. Councilor Toal spoke, "From my Kingdom we will have Prince Det, youngest son to King Vul. From Biernite we will have Princess Gabrielle. She will have King Der's granddaughter Kiera to assist her." Toal looked at Sean, "Young Sire for your information Kiera is a good friend of Princess Gabrielle as they have schooled together in Saulten. They are your age, just turned fifteen as you have however, Prince Det is slightly older at nearly seventeen."

Kain asked "And the chaperones?"

Toal informed, "Prince Alex, Prince Det's older brother plus Ensign Jeng. The replacement English teacher is our own Vulten Professor Stein. He will be with you at the start of the term to settle in and make plans with Professor Smith."

Kain thought, "Professor Stein is an excellent choice as is

Prince Alex. We, no I will keep an eye on Prince Det...I'm sure King Vul will accept this."

"Of course, Sire, my king is fully open to these learning's and his children will behave as requested." Toal advised.

With the meeting ended Sean and Kain went to their room, packed and left the hotel. The car journey to the Eurotunnel was quick and with little traffic on the English side, they arrived home early evening. Their arrival met by a loving embrace from Jenna and with Shadow.

BACK TO NORMALITY:
(CHAPTER 15)

The next day Sean could not wait to see Emma. Having chosen to meet at the lake bench for midday Sean was on time. Even Shadow had been bathed that morning, both looking good Sean thought.

"Hi!" Emma shouted as soon as she saw Sean. Sean meeting her halfway gave her a cuddle and a kiss, Shadow joined in with a wet tongue to both of their cheeks.

"I missed you. How was Manchester and the acting?" Sean asked as they both sat, Shadow sent off to the water with a treat.

"It was great. I got the 'Actor of the Week' award." Emma was proud.

"Wow. I heard. You are really good."

"So, when I'm rich and famous, and an Oscar winner like Glenn Close I might consider still dating you," Emma was mocking.

"Watch your head doesn't fall off, being so big." Sean giggled even though he was now being jabbed in the sides. Then worse Emma knew he did not like being tickled, so she obliged, and both ended up on the floor in fits of laughter. Shadow joining in was good apart from he was wet so both Emma and Sean were also wet. Standing up they started to walk towards Sean's house.

"How are you, your head?" Sean was direct.

"I'm fine." Emma thought. "It's strange, the things come into my head like flashbacks. I even thought I saw PC Millan sadly die, yet I was never in his car so couldn't have been there. Sal is great though, each session I come out more relaxed, even if still confused."

Sean had to think, 'It must be hard, and you have no idea why you are having these dreams?"

"No. Sal says the sting I got must have caused some kind of hallucinatory response. I must be allergic to bee stings."

Not much more was said but Sean did not like the idea of Emma being lied to, even worse, being mind washed by Sal. Having reached Sean's house Emma spent the remainder of the afternoon cooking with Jenna - Sean and Shadow being chief tasters. Emma left around 10pm, and Sean thought this had been one of the best days he had had in a while.

The next day an evening meal out had been planned for the kids and mums; the dads were going for drinks at the small social club that Sean's football team was based from. Sal arrived half an hour early. "I'm not ready." Jenna shouted from upstairs. "I'm doing my hair."

"We don't have that long," was Sal's response. The door slamming upstairs ended that conversation. Sal sat with Sean, Sean seeing his chance, "I'm a little concerned with you brain washing Emma."

"I know, but I need to for both her sanity and so as to not break protocol. Your father has explained the possible repercussion if an Earthling tells about an Earthen. We have to be very careful who we tell."

"Would Dad really..." The look on Sal's face answered Sean's question, he continued, "How long can you keep it hidden?"

"OK, as you are aware us Earthens have power however, we also have differences in intelligence or use of our powers. Soldiers and Kings are all about aggressive power, moving and breaking things with their minds where I as a nurse can actually mend things." Sean looked confused. "So, let's say Kain broke your arm. I with my anatomical knowledge, that's medical training to you, can actually repair the break and re-join the bone just by thought."

"Wow!"

"I can stop bleeding, clear blockages, many other minor things through thought or precise direction of my power. This also allows me to understand the brain more. Again, my training allows me to pick the exact spot in your head to either repair or hurt."

Sean shot up, "Ouch!"

Sal laughed, "You got that?"

"Did I! That hurt! I thought I should be able to stop attacks like that?"

"You can, but you did not expect your friend to do it." Sean flinched again. "Stop it! Or I will fight back!"

Both were now laughing. Sean asked, "So you have the same powers as me but can target them more effectively or accurately?"

"That's a good way of putting it. So, when I'm talking to Emma and she says something I feel where in her brain the thought came from and close it. She forgets but it would not be permanent."

"That means at some point we will have to deal with Emma knowing." Sean stood tall. "I will protect her against anyone!"

Sal saw Jenna enter the room, "Oh Jenna I thought you were doing your hair?"

"Ha ha very funny, let's go." Jenna was at the door.

At the restaurant all were recalling their holidays. Judy Cooper reminding 'the kids' that they were all now fifteen. Emma had her birthday in Italy; Mush's was also in July whilst in Florida. Sean's was late August, a week before going to Paris, so Emma had missed his birthday meal.

The remaining few days of the holiday were fun, Sean, Emma, Mush, Zandra and Shadow spending as much time together as they could. Sean commented positively on Mush about his growing relationship with Zandra. "It's all right," was Mush's manly response.

The first day back at school came. Although Sean was now deemed to be able to look after himself, Shadow continued his guard duties to school. Upon reaching the end of the path Sean looked at Mrs. Carnell's house. "Shame, I'm still embarrassed about not talking to her." Emma was at Sean's side. Mush missed the point. "Silly old bag was spying on us..." He stopped talking as somehow, he fell over. Sean just shook his head.

As it was the first day at school with only the higher years present (the younger years had an extra day off) there was an assembly. Professor Holmes took centre stage; again, Sean was not listening but caught the, "Be nice to the new younger students tomorrow..." blah blah blah, Sean thought. "First of all, Professor Smith is present, thankfully getting over her illness." Holmes nodded in Professor Smith's direction. "As you are aware sadly Mr. Brune has taken early retirement therefore, we have another English teacher Professor Stein." All the pupils laughed, Professor Holmes continued, "Please introduce yourself."

Professor Stein was old, slightly stooped with a good crop of black and greying hair, a moustache and glasses. The other students had obviously picked up on the likeness of look and name to Einstein, Sean actually thought this was probably no mistake; Professor Stein had obviously modeled himself on Einstein. "Children, wonderful children." Professor Stein was addressing them. "I am privileged to be here. I am sure we all will learn together..."

"You're the teacher, ouch!" Came from Frazier Hamling, Sean saw Professor Stein was not as gentle as he appeared, after all, he thought this was a Vulten.

Professor Stein smiled, "Yes I am however, whatever age you are there is always opportunity to learn young man," with this the pupils all laughed.

The remainder of the day went without issue; Frazier had obviously decided to leave Sean and Mush alone. During the afternoon break Sean was asked to attend Professor Smith's office on the pretense of explaining to her about the football schedule for the school team that Sean and Mush also played for. As Sean entered the office, he saw Professor Stein was present.

"A pleasure to formally meet you young Sire." Stein held his hand out and shook Sean's hand.

"Likewise, Professor." Sean responded, "Did you not break protocol earlier on Frazier?"

Stein chuckled. "Brat I'll have him for dinner if he wants it that way."

Professor Smith reprimanded, "Stop that Albere. "

Stein responded, "It is just some fun Glad."

"Professor Stein it is Professor Smith whilst on these premises!" Professor Smith gave him a look.

Sean waded in. "No, really your name is Albere Stein and your look, you are copying our Einstein?"

"Of course, I have. For a human your guy was so intellectual and charismatic. On Earthen my main subject is Human History and culture so being here is 'awesome' as you would say." Stein ended with a wink at Sean as he exited.

Professor Smith spoke, "He is a lovely man, how he is Vulten I don't know but he will be protective to you and our visitors. He worships your father for what he is doing here on Earth." Sean gave Professor Smith a quick hug before going back to class.

The rest of the week went without problem. Sean was forgetting all the Earthen troubles. The start of the football season and weekly matches for Aville FC were a welcome point for Sean to release some energy, although he still had to take TDL before each match just in case he got carried away.

The following weeks all passed quickly. Emma was missing a few times as the Christmas play was not far away. She, Professor Smith and Professor Stein were heavily involved in the production. Sean warmed to Professor Stein and was delighted to hear that Stein and Uncle Algier were friends. One of the stories Stein told Sean about Algier, Sean bagged; it would come in useful at some point.

Sean's relationship with Emma was strong. They, Mush and Zandra went out quite often together, and the 'mums' were appearing to take a back seat. Life was bliss, Sean thought to himself most nights whilst stroking Shadow at the end of the bed. Only Kain's business at work and trips away were disruptive to this.

The Monday before half term soon came, school went well and talks of who was doing what at half term had started to fill the playground. More importantly was who with whom!

Sean said goodbye to his friends and playing with Shadow he made the short stroll home. Upon entering his house, "Hi Mum!"

Jenna was on him. "Make your own dinner. Dad will be home shortly. I'm out." With this she was gone. Sean thought 'what has got into his mother' but dropped the thought as he could now have PlayStation time with her gone. Sean was getting into the game when he heard his father from downstairs. "I'm cooking I'll call you in a while!"

"OK" Sean got on with shooting aliens...

At just the wrong moment an ear-piercing alarm went off. Sean had to put the controller down then run down the stairs to see his father fanning the kitchen fire alarm to stop it, which it thankfully did. "So, your cooking, what is that smell?" Sean laughed.

"Yes, your mother...never mind, give me a hand."

Some twenty minutes later Sean and Kain were sitting at the table looking at burnt sausages, chips and beans.

"Look he's enjoying it!" Kain was pointing to Shadow who was clearly full of sausages and had retired to his cushion at the edge of the kitchen diner.

Sean smiled, "So why are you in the doghouse with Mum?"

"Ahh," Kain confessed. "Well you see we nearly always have Christmas with your grandparents." Kain paused he could see Sean was thinking positive thoughts about Granddad John and Grandma Elise, Jenna's parents. Sean jumped. "Get out of my head!"

Kain laughed. "Then listen. Unfortunately, with the dignitaries coming I, well the Supreme Council and I have decided it would be a good idea to go back to Earthen with them as a kind of debrief, all the families together."

"You are such an idiot for someone so brainy Dad." Sean could not resist a taunt.

"So, two visits to Earthen for you."

"Wow, of course I'm going to Earthen with you next week!" Sean exclaimed.

"Blimey you remembered I am impressed," Kain chuckled. "Are you looking forward to it?"

"Yes. Although I don't like how you, I mean Earthens act. To see another planet has to be amazing." Sean thought further, "And I can shoot more lasers!"

The evening ended and Kain played some video games with Sean. Shortly after Kain went to his room Sean heard his mother come in but no conversation, Dad was definitely in the doghouse.

The next morning at breakfast Jenna was not talking to either of them. All Sean got was she had been around Sal's with Livia the evening before however, as he and Kain went to leave

Jenna shouted, "Have a good day. I will!"

Sean looked at his father, Kain shrugged, "Whatever it is it will be expensive."

That evening the dinner was Shepherd's Pie, one of Sean and Kain's favourites. Jenna was smiling, Kain was uncomfortable. At the dinner table Kain went for it, "Lovely dinner Dear, so anything I should know?"

Jenna gave a big smile; there was a glint in her eye, "Nothing really but I may have some news."

Sean gulped. "Mum come on what?" Jenna gave Shadow some leftovers. "That's it, tell me please!" Sean shouted. Jenna rarely fed Shadow from the table.

"Well I'm off to Ireland next week to see my parents. Lovely friendly Cork, beautiful weather forecast for this time of year. No Earthens, oh sorry, except one of the nicer ones, Sal is coming with me." Jenna was now smug.

"Oh, you are not coming with us to Earthen." The look Jenna gave Kain for this question was a definite 'No'.

"What do you mean 'us'? Sean could come to Ireland, after all he will see Earthen at Christmas!" Jenna's tongue could cut granite.

"No, you can't make him choose between us?" Kain was brave.

"I'm not. This is not a test just a simple choice and no one will hold it against him." Jenna added under her breath, "Unless he chooses Earthen."

Sean cringed. "That's not fair I am being forced to choose!"

"Not how I see it. Earthen is just a formality to meet some spoilt brats who you will want to get away from in a week I'm sure." Jenna was not giving in. "Anyway, sorry Dear I know seeing Earthen is important but it's not long to Christmas. Why don't you think about it tonight and tomorrow then let us know?"

Sean looked at Kain for support - support was not forthcoming. Sean thought all night, he loved his grandparents but seeing Earthen...Sean was not happy about his mother's actions although he loved her dearly.

The next morning you could cut the air with a knife. Kain was keeping well clear of Jenna who was infuriating him more by doing her Mary Poppins impression, singing and smiling all over the place. Kain left early.

Jenna walked Sean to the back gate, cuddled him and said, "I am sorry you are in the middle of this but sometimes we have to keep your father's feet on the ground. Anyway, I am sure you will make the right decision. You will have a great day at school." Jenna followed this with another hug and a peck on his forehead. Sean slightly protested, "Mum, don't!" Jenna laughed.

The day was going well, lunchtime brought the subject of half term up. "What are you doing for half term Zandra?" Emma asked.

Zandra replied, "I'm here most of the time but have some family visiting mid-week for a couple of days, my cousins from London. What about you Mush?"

"I was hoping to spend more time with you." Looking at Zandra.

"Ahh, come here." Mush got a peck for the right answer.

Mush looked to Sean, "You off to Canada with your dad to see some relatives?"

Sean was a bit hesitant. "Yes, that's the plan, what about you Emma? Aren't you going to Manchester to see a play or something?"

Emma gave a big smile. "Manchester has been rearranged. It is a show by some of the people I met in the holidays but it's on for a few weeks so we will catch it nearer Christmas. I'm visiting relatives instead."

"Good, which ones?" Sean was struggling to remember

Emma's relatives.

"Well they're not exactly my relatives...I'm going to Ireland with your mum and Sal."

Sean nearly fell off his chair. "What? You are going on holiday with my mum!"

Emma had a bigger smile. "Too right, a girly thing. Besides I've met your grandparents many times and get on well with them."

"No, that's not right, you can't visit my grandparents without me."

Sean had no idea until Emma enlightened him. "Who said you are not going? Apparently, your father's trip is more business than pleasure so surely Ireland with me is the better choice. We will have a craic of a time?"

Mush laughed, "Looks like you're snookered. Seems like Ireland it is then!"

Sean chuckled. "Actually, I wouldn't want to be anywhere else, although mums a bitch!"

"Sean, how dare you! Your mother is wonderful!" Emma was now hugging him.

The evening was easier than Sean thought; his mother had clearly out maneuvered his father. As Sean was going to bed Kain caught him. "She played the Emma card?"

"Yeah sorry Dad but going to see Granddad and Grandma also helped."

Kain smiled, "No hard feelings, but I'll get her back," with this he laughed.

By the Saturday Kain was driving them all to the airport, he was dropping them off at Stansted before leaving for Earthen himself. As Sean was exiting the car he said, "Thanks for your understanding Dad, enjoy Eart...Canada". Jenna's, "Love you!" Was a simpler goodbye.

Hire car sorted at Cork airport and they were soon at the

Loclin farm of Jenna's parents. A fair size estate that had the usual cows, chickens and ducks but mainly horses. Granddad John Loclin was not a farmer as his predecessors were but had rented out most of the land as a stable and paddocks for other people to use – a popular and financially rewarding business with less hassle in the Loclin's retirement. Sal and Emma were welcomed with open arms; Sean could sense Jenna was extremely relaxed. Sean was reminded of how he was their favourite grandson, not hard as he was the only one!

The week took shape, playing on the farm during the day. Jenna loved horse riding; Emma was learning. Evenings were spent mostly in local pubs come restaurants with the odd visit to Cork for shopping. The visit on the Wednesday was most interesting. With the women in a large department store, Sean was sitting on a bench at the side of the River Lee, and Granddad John had gone to get some coffees.

"Frightful young man served me." John was saying whilst sitting next to Sean. "He insulted me saying something about being skinny. I know I have a belly but…"

Sean interrupted. "Granddad he was talking about a skinny coffee not you."

"What's that? I didn't think coffee was that fattening. Do they take the milk out or is skinny with no sugar?" John was looking quizzical.

"No, they…it doesn't matter it's too complicated this coffee stuff now." Sean laughed. At least Granddad had remembered his cappuccino correctly, "So how did Mum meet Dad?"

Granddad John smiled. "Unlike my Father, God bless his soul, I was not into farming. At a young age I joined the Garda. With the farm being so close to the city I was able to commute most days. When I met your grandma, she loved the farm, so we moved in with my parents, your mother was born on the farm…"

Sean sensing this could be a long conversation interrupted,

"Your stories of Mum and the farm are wonderful, but Mum and Dad?"

Granddad John took a sip of his coffee. "Well I was quite senior in the Garda, a Chief Inspector at the time, one of the youngest ever....sorry, I digress. Your Mother was now what... early twenties? And her youthfulness had given in to the charms of the city, strong willed your mother. Anyway, to help her out I got her a part time job helping me organising events. On one event we went to London at the Houses of Parliament, lots of big people there, the Prime Minister and the like. Your father was there in his advisory capacity; well to cut a long story short it was love at first sight. Your father is many things, but his wooing of Jenna just blew her mind, she was putty in his hands."

Sean asked, "Mind games?"

John had a smile, "No Earthen tricks just good old fashion love."

"You obviously know about Dad and Earthen?"

"Obviously not at first but yes of course soon afterwards. Hell, I had to attend two weddings you know it's my job to give my daughter away." John was chuckling.

"So, you have been to Earthen?"

"Yes." John's demeanor changed slightly. "Wonderful technology, open spaces and yet an awful, barbaric culture, such a shame. That is why we rarely visit there; our farm is a million times better. Indeed, apart from your father, Sal and of course Uncle Algier...did I tell you about the time we went fishing..."

"Yes, many times but you have never spoken about Earthen."

"Yes, of course, we have deceived you for so long. I apologise."

"No need to apologise, deceit runs in the family." Sean chuckled. "So, with all this king thing and many wives and children how come I am the only child?"

John took a deep breath. "Anatomically Earthens and humans are basically the same so making babies..."

"Granddad!" Sean interrupted again.

"Anyway." John continued but with a tear in his eye. "Although you were obviously possible and born healthy it does appear a powerful Earthen baby in a human mother caused complications. Sadly, your Mother cannot have any more children after your birth."

A tear came to Sean's eye also. "Wow, I hurt mum that's sad."

John put his arm around Sean. "Don't be, these things happen. Regardless of the pain Jenna, Kain, I and your grandmother have a wonderful Son and Grandson that has brightened all of our lives for what fifteen years now?"

Sean felt good inside; "I hope he is not telling you about my youth!" Jenna had joined them at the bench.

"No darling!' was John's response, "But I could if you want me to?"

Sal, Emma and Grandma Elise had now joined them. Emma somehow sensing Sean's slightly subdued mood held his hand as they walked to the car to return to the farm. That evening Jenna went to tuck Sean in, "I'm fifteen now Mum!" Sean stated.

"So, I won't then, shall I go?" Jenna had just sat on the bed.

"No, you stay, Ill pretend you're Shadow." Sean thinking it was a joke got it slightly wrong.

"So, you are calling me a dog. That's nice!' Jenna giggled.

"Granddad told me about my birth and you not being able to have any more children. That's sad."

Jenna was holding back a tear. "Yes, it is, but I have you. What more would I want?"

"A cuddle?" This worked Jenna gave Sean a big cuddle. Sean asked, "So I am the only Earthen and human mixed child?"

Jenna sat up and was a little more serious. "I believe so,

well certainly legally. There are rumours of unspeakable acts by some rogue Earthens, they would be executed if found out. Your birth, as is our marriage, is watched closely by the Earthen Councils. They could not understand why physically it went wrong therefore, Earthen and human relationships are frowned upon and mixed babies banned, if not feared – I nearly died with you at childbirth." A tear was now in Jenna's eye.

Sean sat up and cuddled his mother.

THE DIGNITARIES:
(CHAPTER 16)

Emma gave Sean a big hug. "Thanks for the holiday it was great, and you Mrs. Saul, I mean Jenna and Sal." With this Emma exited the car and into the welcoming arms of her mother at their door.

Livia who had picked them up from the airport continued the drive dropping all off at the Saul's house. Sal was straight in the kitchen; Jenna started to unpack already with Sean helping to carry the bags upstairs. "Dad will be here tomorrow?" Sean asked.

"Yes, I mean no, we will be meeting that lot at the Research Park first. Algier will be there, I've missed him." Jenna informed.

"Me too."

The next morning Professor Smith dropped Shadow back, Sean taking him for a walk with plenty of treats before putting him in the garden to leave with Jenna and Sal for the Research Centre. After parking they walked to what Sean had now called the eating room but was more like a large lounge come dining room. As they reached the door, they were engulfed in the arms of Uncle Algier.

"I have missed you guys, been busy on Earthen. Are you ready?" Jenna's look suggested not.

They entered the room and Sean saw many figures, all stood upon his entrance. "Jeng please." Was the command from Kain standing in one corner of the room. Sean was nearly taken off his feet as Jeng gave him a big hug. "Hi yer...oops Your Highness." Jenna got the same welcome, with a slightly more restrained hug.

"This is Field Officer Daved." Jenna whispered in Sean's heard, "My boyfriend." Sean, remembering Jeng's previous comments about her Dersian boyfriend being an Adonis, noted they were true. Young but fairer haired Orlando Bloom came to mind, Sean was jealous.

"Prince Saul this is Prince Alex." With this Prince Alex bowed and shook Sean's hand. "A pleasure to meet you Sean." Sean could see Alex had the Vulten look, tall; dark haired, chiseled features but his demeanor was certainly not that of a Vulten Sean expected. That said Sean noted Prince Det was.

"Prince Det, this is Prince Saul." Jeng was still introducing.

Prince Det was slightly older than Sean and similar in size but was in a full uniform of sorts as opposed to his older brother's Earthen but more casual attire. Prince Det made eye contact then in Sean's head, "Hello". Sean pushed back with a clear, "No!" in his own head.

"Prince Det Stop that!" Kain was on them; Prince Det looked up at Kain and moved away from them. Kain went on to introduce the other two dignitaries. "This is Princess Gabrielle."

Princess Gabrielle was Sean's age, dark haired, pretty and made up. She reminded Sean of Jolie James his ex neighbour. "Hi." Sean said.

Princess Gabrielle was more formal as she curtseyed to Sean. "It is a pleasure to meet you Prince Saul. I very much look forward to this experience and opportunity you and your father King Kain have given us." Princess Gabrielle turned and approached Jenna. "Your Majesty it is an honour to meet you again and I look forward to your company and guidance."

Sean could not help thinking that if all Earthen Princesses were like this maybe...however, Sean came back down to Earth. "I'm just Kiera a kind of princess, my grandfather is a king though."

Sean was now looking at Kiera. A definite Dersian, beautiful, blonde and tanned, dressed in Earthen casuals but with lots of flesh showing. Sean could not help himself, "Wow!" Came out of his mouth. Jeng saved his blushes. "At least Kiera is not a princess so we will let you get away with that welcome." All in the room laughed.

The remainder of the afternoon was small talk, excluding Prince Det who was not the conversational type. Sean got on well with the two girls; Gabrielle was charming, Kiera was, Sean actually didn't know because every time he looked at her his head was a blur. Some time in, Livia asked Sean to help her get something with her before they were to journey home.

Sean followed Livia to a big walk in cupboard, Livia looked busy but not finding anything. "It's not here I'll find it later." Was her opening line. "So, what do you think of Kiera?"

"She is definitely a Dersian."

"Yes, she has my looks."

"Yes, you are beautiful too."

"I'm not looking for a compliment. Kiera resembles my looks because she is my niece."

Sean froze, "Hang on if Kiera is King Ders' granddaughter and you her aunt then what does that make you to King Ders?'

Livia stood tall, "I am his daughter, Princess Livia of Dersian."

Sean took a gasp of breath. "Wow, you are a princess as well!"

"Yes."

"Sorry but how does a princess become a secretary. No offence."

"No offence taken." Livia continued. "I have four brothers all wanting to be king. Although I love my Father, he is a typical Earthen king and the boys came first. My father's attempts to marry me off to Kain failed as in that I fell in love of Kains ideas and even Earth. So, I happily moved away from Earthen and all the princess crap using my mother's maiden name." Livia hesitated, "By the way on Earthen you can choose how you are addressed. Vul is King Vul but your father chose Kain as opposed to King Saul although his full name is King Kain Saul. Anyway, I am very content working and living here on Earth."

Sean looked at Livia; he felt the honesty and passion in her voice. "Wow, true belief can lead to sacrifices."

"Very well put. I, your father and others follow our beliefs, that is what will truly make you happy inside - as of course love can."

"Can I change my mind, you being a princess and all that..." Sean stopped, Livia now laughing with him.

The rest of the day passed without much concern although the dignitary's first sight of their new home next door to the Saul's was interesting.

"How do you live in such a small area?"

"It is so crowded."

"I want my Palace!" Were a few of the comments made.

Sean noting at this point his house was big for Earth standards, wait until they see the town let alone London!

The Sunday was as interesting. Sean saw Emma and Mush at their football match, the dignitaries not allowed to attend as yet. However, they were taken on a guided tour in the Discovery to see certain points, the school and the town. Sean was right, the girls thought it was quaint but smaller and more congested then expected both in housing and road terms. Prince Det announced it was awful. "Get me out of here!" Was his cry, Kain dealt with it.

Monday came and Sean was at the back of his house, Jenna had joined him and Shadow. Sean knew she just wanted to be nosey. Daved and Prince Alex were first out - they also were being nosey. Jeng followed with the three in tow. Sean was eyeing them all up in their Earth school uniforms – Det looked smart, he obviously preferred and looked grand in a uniform. Gabrielle was perfect again managing to make the look feminine but studious. Kiera, Sean took a gasp, he had never seen so much flesh in the uniform legs....

"Get that beast away from me!" Det demanded.

Sean took note, although they had seen Shadow the day before it had only been through the window as Shadow had been sent to the garden, not his fault just safety. Shadow was slightly in front of Sean and Jenna looking at Det and giving a low but obvious continuous growl.

"He is not a beast. He is my dog." Sean was defending Shadow.

"Move him or I will!" Det was closing in on Shadow.

Sean grabbed Shadow's collar, moving in front of his dog. "Or you will do what?" Both boys now eyeing each other up. Sean let Det in and each other's thoughts were exchanged.

"Shadow manners!" Sean turned and his mother was grabbing Shadow's collar from him. Jenna continued, "Let's get some sausages maybe today is not the best time for you to walk." With this Jenna pulled Shadow back towards the house. No more was said as all four headed down the path. Gabrielle leading with Det next to her. Sean could tell she was clearly talking to him, probably advising. Kiera was initially just behind them when she stopped and caught Sean's arm then continued walking with him. As the group reached the path's end Emma met them. A brief shake of Gabrielle's hand followed by a shake of Det's hand but with a quizzical look saw the first introductions.

"Hi, I am Emma," with that Emma grabbed Sean's arm and pulled him to her side, forcing Kiera to drop her grip on Sean's arm. "I am Sean's girlfriend." Emma followed this with a peck on Sean's cheek.

"I am Kiera." Kiera responded with a big smile but a glint in her eye. "I have heard about you; funny you are not what I expected." With this she walked towards Gabrielle and Det who were now shaking Mush's hand.

Scowling Emma looked straight at Sean, "Holding her arm what's that all about?"

Sean fumbled, "I err...was just being welcoming, it wasn't all the way..." There was no point, although Emma continued the rest of the journey holding Sean's arm - it was too tight for his liking.

Once at the school the same welcomes were seen. Gabrielle was engaging, Det was the complete opposite and Kiera, well Sean thought he did not realise how many boys were actually at his school.

Once in the form room their form teacher Professor Stein did the formal welcome. "As you are all aware, we have three kind of exchange students, please come to the front of the class." Det, Gabrielle and Kiera obliged. Stein continued, "They are not exchange students in the sense here to learn actual lesson details. However, they are here to learn our ways, which is why Det Vul is older but will be in your classes... Master Hamling anymore sniggering and I will detain you."

Sean looked around and Frazier was looking uncomfortable. Mush unusually broke the tension. "Sir do you not mean detention not detain?"

Sean looked at Stein who was still focusing on Det. Sean threw a "Professor?" Into Stein's head which was enough for him to focus back on the class. "Of course, Master Green. Yes, detention is the correct word, maybe you should take this English class?" Everyone chuckled.

Professor Stein went on to introduce Gabrielle Bier and Kiera Ders. Frazier got another brain burn for wolf whistling upon Kiera's introduction. Formalities over and all the pupils were getting their bits together, although in the same form class not all pupils attended the same lessons. Mush was in a sports coaching class next, which Sean was not. Mush caught him before leaving. "Det's a dick, Gabrielle is lovely, Kiera is hot but don't tell Zandra I said that!" Mush winked and left. Sean could not help agreeing with Mush's summary.

The classroom was now emptied but Sean held back to talk to Professor Stein. "You can't use your powers on Earthens?"

Stein chuckled. "Oh, that imbecile Hamling. I was not hurting him, but I note your point. Prince Det on the other hand is going to be difficult. Good luck you are with him most of the time young Sire." Stein winked.

The rest of the day and indeed the week followed suit. Gabrielle was loved by everyone and had been invited onto every school group and out of school events. At this point she was declining saying, "Part of the exchange is to get to know our family friends the Sauls more, so no out of school activities allowed." Kiera had been asked out more times than Sean could count. Even Frazier who was still with Lisa Turner as far as Sean knew was pushing. Det was not popular but definitely interesting - unfortunately all his responses were monolithic however, in his defence he was controlling his temper. Their friend Trekkie although not appearing to have long conversations with Det was however very intrigued by him. Trekkie could sense something but did not know what.

The Friday lunch break was fun. Sean, Emma, Zandra and Mush were sitting on one side of the table, and the dignitaries were on the other - facing and talking to the throng of people around them.

"So shallow." Zandra spoke. "A smile from Gabrielle and all the girls love her. As for that Kiera and well the boys, thankfully you two are acting as adults."

Mush replied. "Yes. Let's get some water." As he guided Sean to the water fountain. "Zandra is right but hey they are both..." Mush looked around to check they were on their own.

"Gorgeous. I want to talk to them but Zandra would kill me. I'd have Kiera you could have Gabrielle."

Sean laughed. "Come on don't think like that, besides I might fight you for Kiera." With that Sean was mushed. Mush drilled his fist into Sean's head, although the other pupils were now looking at them and laughing. Sean did not fight back. Mush had to keep his reputation.

The highlight of the weekend, apart from the Sunday match, was Sean, Jeng, Alex and Daved going bowling. An agreed respite from the dignitaries arranged and allowed by Jenna.

The bowling started. Sean was good. Alex got the hang of it quite quickly but surprisingly Jeng who had bowled before was not on her game. Daved joined in the bowling however, his body language showed he was not interested and was taking part half-heartedly. At one point, Jeng bowled the bowl clearly heading to the gully when it suddenly changed direction then hit the pins - a strike! Sean approached her. "That's cheating, you can't use your powers."

Jeng smiled. "Sorry but I don't know where my brain is today. Besides Alex, for a new starter, is beating me." Jeng was competitive.

"Look I'll show you on your next turn." On Jeng's next bowl Sean did as he said, guiding Jeng on holding the bowl and how to release it down the lane. Sean noted Daved looking at him whilst doing this. Alex on the other hand was supporting him and even asked for help on his next bowl.

The game ended, Jeng won with Sean saying it was his coaching but really feeling Jeng had continued to cheat even if a bit less obviously. Sean was second and Alex third accepting this being his first real go at Ten Pin bowling, he would beat Jeng next time. Daved made no comment.

Sean grabbed Jeng holding back before they left. "Daved doesn't like me, or is he just strange..." Sean remembering he was Jeng's boyfriend added, "I mean confused by it all?"

Jeng chuckled. "Neither. He is a soldier and maybe he can't get his head around being so close and informal to two princes. He leaves on Monday; he is back on duty on Earthen".

With Field Officer Daved leaving on the Monday, the next week seemed to fly by, as did the following with very few issues at school. However, the crowd around the dignitaries was beginning to niggle Sean. Midweek of the following week with only three full weeks to the Christmas break school talk was about the coming Christmas period. Emma was all about the Christmas play; her time at breaks and even lunch breaks was taken up by preparation. Although Emma was an actor, she also enjoyed the production and design. The only exception to Emma's acting was the varied clubs she attended after school. The reading club most Wednesday evenings was one. Kain had allowed Gabrielle to attend this on her own with Emma along with some of the play preparation. Kiera was still being kept on a short lead as was Det. Shadow was not being kept on a lead at all. Sean making sure Shadow did the school walks every day and regardless of the dignitaries' visits to the house Shadow was allowed in. Sean knew this annoyed Det, but he did not care.

RELATIONSHIP:
(CHAPTER 17)

The weekend saw Sean, Jeng, Livia, Sal, Jenna, Alex and the dignitaries visit London for the day. The train was chosen to add to the experience; Jenna's look at Kain as he dropped them off at the station could kill. 'Chicken' was the word used, Algier driving the other car laughed, he was going golfing with Kain.

The train trip was ok, as they were travelling quite late it was quiet, all got seats. Upon reaching Marylebone things became a bit taught, the dignitaries did not like the crowds. Det had to be persuaded nicely to get onto the tube. Once at Oxford Street station the crowds were better but still irritating. However, the cultural look of the buildings and feel of London helped as all the dignitaries focused on this rather than the people.

A successful visit to Hamleys brightened their time; after all they were kids at heart, including the adults who also played with the toys. The walk to Piccadilly Circus took ages; Kiera loved the clothes shops, as did Gabrielle. The group finally looking at Eros was smiling; Sean noted Det was trying to smile. Jenna was fraught trying to keep the group together as the boys obviously not enjoying the cloths shops announced.

"Livia, will you and Sal take the girls to other clothes shops, Jeng, I and the boys will look at Leicester Square and Trafalgar Square. Meet up in two hours to eat before we go to the show.

Livia you know the restaurant in Covent Garden, you booked it."

This was agreed and the group split. Sean caught his mother for a second, "So why you not with the girls?"

"Even I need a break from Kiera, she is a pr...I mean teaser. Her flirting when trying things on, it's embarrassing." Jenna laughed.

Jenna's choice was successful and the boys plus her and Jeng enjoyed the two squares. Sean even jumped on and around the Nelsons' Column's lions with Det. Sightseeing over they were all in the Covent Garden restaurant for dinner, this also went well although space and crowding complaints came back again. The crowding not helped by the amount of bags Gabrielle and Kiera had with them, the London shops did well on this visit. Jenna was right as even during the meal Kiera was pulling clothes from the bags to show Jenna and Jeng but either holding them up close to her chest or legs depending on the type of clothing it was. Every male in the restaurant could not help but notice. For once Sean and Det agreed as they both winked at each other.

Dinner eaten the group were off to see Wicked the show; again, Livia had excelled with excellent seats. All enjoyed the show, Sean had to explain to Det that there were no green humans and the show was fantasy not history. Gabrielle really enjoyed the show, and for an additional treat in the Limousine, now taking them home, Gabrielle managed to sit between Kiera and Sean.

"That show was magnificent, so imaginative, and the songs catchy." Gabrielle was talking to Sean. "I can see why your Emma loves acting. Emma is a lovely girl, is it serious between you both?"

Sean was taken a little aback, as Gabrielle was being quite direct, he replied, "Yes."

Gabrielle looked at Sean. "Shame as a princess and a prince

we would be a good match. Still when you are on Earthen, I will show you some of our sights, we will have fun." Sean had that funny feeling again, but he did not respond.

The following week followed a similar pattern. Det had lost his manners again, Sean stopping many a confrontation. Thursday lunch break saw Sean catch up with Emma, "Hi" Emma spoke as she gave him a hug. "Missing you I've been busy."

Sean hugged her back, "I know it's a big thing but I'm sure the play will be great as usual."

"Shame you won't be seeing it; it will be the first one you have missed." Emma caught Sean's confused stare. "Idiot, you are leaving for Canada next Friday, the Friday before the Monday show. How your father can get virtually an extra week off before Christmas is unbelievable. It pushes his authority as a Governor. Lucky you!"

"Oh, I'm sorry, I like your shows."

Emma smiled. "Gabrielle is not that bad actually, strange but very polite, she has an air about her," Sean giggled. "What you giggling for?"

"Nothing." Sean continued to giggle, he thought if only he could tell Emma.

"Remember I'm not here tomorrow, I and Professor Smith are visiting the prop and costume store to finalise the clothing – the shop is donating the equipment as usual…your mum set that deal up if you recall." Sean nodded, finally not giggling.

The next day, Sean was missing Emma but still had the crowds around him. Sitting at lunch he was joined by Kiera, who obviously noting the absence of Emma sat quite close.

"Your father has agreed for us to go out this weekend. Our last here on our own, no chaperones." Kiera was advising Sean.

"Really, wow, I mean good it must have been hard tied in at home or with us all the time. I thought seeing our culture was key."

Kiera sighed, "Safety. We were told to keep near people who could watch us. I understand why, although at home I ignore it. We also slip out windows, drink and get home late on Earth en you know."

Sean laughed, and then Frazier was standing at the table beside him. "Hi yer! How you doing?" Frazier was addressing Sean.

"I'm ok." Sean could guess where this was going.

"Hi Kiera. So, your last weekend here, how about a date and I'll show you how to party?" Sean was right Frazier was going for it. "The new Shake Bar in town is the in place to start, and then a mate is having a party in the evening. No Parents."

Sean could tell Kiera was tempted, although her reply was not as he expected. "Thank you, Frazier, I would love to go to the Shake Bar...actually I am already, Sean is taking me." With that Kiera grabbed Sean's arm and gave him the biggest smile she could. Sean even knowing this was her weapon could not fight it and replied, "Yeah, of course."

Frazier gave Sean a look. "Oh ok. Well I'm there around three so if you are there then think about the party, maybe we could go after."

Sean felt uncomfortable the remainder of the afternoon, Mush was on Sean's back. "Idiot what will Emma say?"

"I'll take Emma as well." Sean thought he had this in hand.

"Emma is in Manchester all weekend seeing her friend's play she missed in the half term remember." Sean's heart sunk upon hearing Mush's words.

"Shit, mmm, it will be ok Dad will say no anyway." Sean was now comfortable. This feeling did not last as early that evening Kiera, clearly playing up to Kain over dinner, got his agreement for her to go to the Shake Bar, not the party. Sean was gob smacked and immediately WhatsApping Mush to tell him of his father's decision and asking what he should tell Emma. Sean chose to ignore his friend's reply and the advice to not go. After all Emma would not know, even if she did, she would understand it was just a laugh, he thought.

Half two Sean, Kiera and Gabrielle were being driven to the Shake Bar by Sal – Det, Jeng and Alex was going Laser Blast in Hemel. Sal stopped the car. "Have fun you guys but behave!" All three acknowledged this and were soon walking through the marketplace to the town centre shopping mall. Even though this was December it was very mild, Kiera's short skirt stood out, men and women noticed. Somehow this actually made Sean feel proud; here he was walking through the town with two good-looking girls at his side. This feeling was heightened as they approached the Shake Bar. It was clearly the new in place for the Aville youngsters; even outside the bar there were many kids. Sean knew many of the faces, some from school, others from football. Trevor Sales was the SM FC Captain who Aville FC had beaten in the cup earlier that year. Trevor acknowledged Sean with a wave. Sean waved back but thought it strange as Trevor was talking to Frazier, Sean did not think they knew each other.

"Hi ya mate!" Mush and Zandra had joined Sean and co.

Upon entering the bar, it was busy, Mush looked around, "Too busy let's go!"

Kiera said, "No, wait," she and Gabrielle walked over to a table of three boys; both spoke to them then whispered something in their ears. All three boys downed the remainder of their shakes, smiled and left. Gabrielle and Kiera had the table. Zandra looked at Sean and Mush, "Great we have a table. Look there is six main Shake types so get one of each."

Shakes in hand the boys joined the girls at the table, Gabrielle, Zandra and Mush one side, Kiera and Sean the other. Sean started to enjoy himself, they all tasted a bit of each shake before agreeing who would drink what. Gabrielle getting the Banana Bomb that all thought was the best but somehow her diplomacy won. The bar being American themed had a jukebox with individual selection controls on the tables. Zandra was warming to the girls as they discussed and selected tunes to play. Both Gabrielle and Kiera hardly staying in their seats as they 'bopped' to each song.

"Hi Mush, Hi Sean." Trevor Sales was at standing at their table. "This is Alice my girlfriend." Sean and Mush both replied, "Hi."

"Sean you were amazing in the final. We will get you back as we have been drawn against you in the cup at an earlier round in Jan."

"Thanks. Yeah I don't score many but that was a good one."

"Your penalty save was excellent. I thought that changed the game Mush."

Mush smirked, "Thanks. Yeah I enjoyed that one."

"So, Sean I thought you were dating that Cooper girl?"

Before Sean could reply Kiera grabbed his arm and responded. "Maybe he has changed his mind?" Sean turned his head to protest to Kiera, Kiera seeing this movement kissed him on the lips. Sean froze, Kiera staring in his eyes.

"Ouch!" Sean screamed looking to his attacker, Mush now standing was grabbing him.

"Come on I need a wee!" Sean did not protest as Mush was pulling him away.

After going to the toilet, the friends were standing at the washbasins, Sean turned on Mush, "What did you do that for?"

"Are you mad? You were kissing Kiera!"

"No, I wasn't, she kissed me!" Sean protested.

"Unbelievable, what if Emma found out...or is it true are you and Emma split?" Mush had an open-mouthed astonished look on his face.

"NO, NO." Sean stated clearly. "That minx...Emma will be ok, anyway she is not here she won't know."

"And all our friends won't tell her." At that point both boys' WhatsApp message beeps went. Mush was first to read it. As he did the toilet door was opening, Mush turned, pushed it shut on whoever was trying to get in and shouted an expletive. Addressing Sean, "Look at WhatsApp, you're a dead man!"

Sean pulled out his phone; the message said. "Sean Saul's new girlfriend?" Was above a picture of him kissing Kiera. Sean's heart dropped. "Oh shit, this is the football group, Emma will see it!" He thought, "I'm going to kill Sales!"

Whoever was on the other side of the door shouted, Sean looked up, the shouting stopped. Mush shouted, "Calm down, Calm down! Jeez, let's think."

Sean did not want to calm down, but his friend's grip was tight on his shoulders. Mush said, "Look let's go. I'll get the girls; you go to the square and get hold of Emma. I'll buy you some time. Don't get involved with Trevor!"

Sean nodded. They opened the door, and on the floor just outside the door was a young boy, clearly dazed. Mush checked on him. "He is ok, somehow he had fallen over." Sean realised he had to control his temper. As advised by Mush he went straight out to the square, ignoring as best he could the stares and sniggers from the kids who knew him and had obviously seen the chat.

In the square Sean's fingers were typing, SMS, WhatsApp and Facebook all direct to Emma. "I'm sorry, it's not what it looks like." There was no response. Mush had called Sal for an early pick up and surprised them both by saying Sean was staying at his tonight, some new game to play.

This worked; Sean was soon in Mush's room and had at least calmed down. This was some four hours later, and Emma had not responded to him. Sean was ignoring the chat string, so Mush was keeping him up to date.

Mush thought, "Look didn't Emma have a meal or was seeing the preparations before the show? Now she will be in the show, you won't hear from her for hours. Let's play a game." Sean gave in and they played, the game taking away his thoughts. He and Mush had fallen to sleep literally whilst playing it.

Mush woke first, "Any news?" Mush was at the side of Sean's bed. Sean looked at his phone. "No not yet. I'll try again." Sean's fingers working overtime.

The boys had breakfast then made the short trip to Sean's house. Grabbing Shadow, they went walking. An hour later, still no response. "I'm sorry mate but it's football, we are at home, we need to go."

Sean thought, "No tell them I'm ill, I'm not playing..." Sean stopped his mobile had pinged. "I'm not talking to you, stop messaging me, go away you..." Sean's heart sunk as he read the message from Emma. Sean showed Mush the message.

"Shit you are in trouble. I'll tell the guys and will see you later." With that Mush left.

Sean sat for a further half hour; Emma was providing no more responses. "There you are I thought so," Jenna was approaching Sean. "Mush says you are ill?"

Sean looked at his mother, "Yes, I think the milkshake didn't agree with me. I am not playing today..."

Jenna sat next to Sean, "Really?"

Sean looked at his mother, thought then replied. "Yeah, can I go home please? Oh, and I need a day on my own."

With this they headed home, Sean gained his wish, Jenna clearly directing any actions away from Sean who spent most of the day in his room with Shadow - the only breaks being when he took Shadow out.

The next morning Sean virtually ran to school leaving the dignitaries but not Shadow in his wake, he so wanted to see Emma. Upon approaching the path end he was disappointed as only Mush was there. "Emma is in early doing her play stuff." Sean was not reassured. The day remained as bad, apart from the looks, odd jibe and sniggering behind his back worse was Emma found every reason to avoid Sean. Even in the classes they shared she sat next to someone else. Sean knew this was the worst day of his life.

That evening Sean ate in his room, again Shadow being his own preferred company until Jenna entered. "So, you going to tell me what is going on?"

"Nope!" Sean continued to play the game on his phone. Jenna pulled the phone from his hands; Sean went to protest.

"Don't be so ignorant I want to talk to you! So, what is it with you and Emma?" Jenna looked at Sean. "Judy has called me apparently Emma is in bits, putting two and two together and...well?"

Sean dropped his head, "Emma thinks I've cheated on her. I kissed Kiera."

Jenna looked shocked. "Oh, honey you never." Sean's look said he had. "Why, I thought you did not like her?"

"I didn't kiss her, she kissed me, but someone got a photo and Emma won't listen. I don't like Kiera, look!" With this Sean pointed to his phone. Jenna opened on the chat screen, taking in the detail including the picture. "I hate this social media, when it's good news all is well but this, this is unbelievable."

"What have you said to Emma?"

"Nothing she won't talk to me!"

"You have tried to talk to her not just this messaging rubbish?"

"Yes, at school but she is ignoring me. What do I do?" Genuine tears were coming from Sean's eyes.

"Look it's simple," Jenna hugged Sean. "When it's the right moment." Jenna stopped, gave Sean a quick peck on his forehead then continued, "I love you." With this Jenna got up and left. Sean sat there, he could not help but feel better, and he did love his mother but did not see what she was telling him.

The next day at school was just as bad. Sean took one opportunity and actually stood in front of Emma stopping her going somewhere, her scowl was enough for him to surrender. That evening again Jenna spoke to him, "Anything?"

"No," was Sean's response.

Wednesday was no better. Sean had tried Zandra and Mush as icebreakers but was not winning, and Zandra, although liking Sean, was on Emma's side. That evening whilst walking Shadow, sitting in his favourite spot Sean was joined by Jenna. "Tomorrow is our last night before we go to Earthen on Friday, have you spoken to Emma?" Sean's negative response saw a shrug from Jenna then a, "Leave it with me." As she walked off.

Sean's call, "Mum I'm old enough to sort it myself!" Was ignored.

"Never when it comes to women are you old enough." Sean could see Uncle Algier was now passing his mother but heading to him. Sean was met slightly later with a big hug as they both sat on the bench. "I have just got here. I have to help your father with the dignitaries, getting them ready for home." Algier said. "Women troubles eh?"

"Yes, what do you know about women!" Sean bit.

Algier looked at Sean "Prickly eh. I'll ignore your inference but will answer it. I in my younger years remember being your grandfather's brother was a prince just like you. Obviously better looking." Sean could not help but giggle, he knew Uncle Algier was actually his father's Uncle, Sean's Great Uncle. "Anyway, the women could not keep their hands off me, an Earthen Casanova...don't be shocked remember in Earthen many partners even wives are accepted. I'm sorry if that disappoints you."

"No. I now understand your ways, so?"

"Well I enjoyed my youth, noting youth on Earthen is up to thirty say in equivalent to Earth years. When you are older, I will tell you some stories however, needless to say I caught the women drug. By the time I was forty I think I missed the point. Sadly, I did not see partners just conquests, this is why I never married."

Sean was a bit shocked but liked his Uncle's honesty. "But on Earthen you can have many partners, so surely that was perfect for you?"

Algier chuckled, "When I said I liked the conquest, I meant the conquest. Unfortunately, although I knew I would not be king, your damn father being born saw to that," Algier winked at Sean. "I was tied to my job. Even though my brother was a great king he needed my diplomacy skills. The travelling, well, allowed my other passion."

Algier went a little red and Sean gave him a cuddle. "I'm not judging you Uncle, but I'm surprised as all I see is love in you. You would have been a great husband and father!"

Algier looked up, "You are right but probably only until the next conquest came along. So, if I am no good with women, what did your mother advise?"

"Nothing really, she just said I would know at the right moment?"

Algier laughed then putting his arms around Sean he gave him a big cuddle then kissed him on the forehead saying, "I love you young man."

Sean thought, again he felt good, and then he felt it. "Of course, that's what mum meant. But when?"

"I'm sure your mother has this in hand, can we eat I'm hungry?"

Sean and Algier went home and ate. Sean was feeling better but his mother's; "It's in hand" was frustrating.

The morning came, Sean and the dignitaries were off to school for the last day together. Sean thought Shadow had an extra spring in his step but had to stop him at one point from peeing on Det. Sean looked at his dog, maybe he is Earthen he does know things...

Again, Emma was not joining them, the same at break although Sean could see Emma was with Professor Smith and Sal a lot. Lunchtime came and went; Sean was advised he might see Emma in the last break. Break came and Sean headed to the common room area, five minutes in and no sign of Emma, Sean was growing impatient.

At first Sean ignored the growing commotion in the corner but when he heard, "Oye Mono!" Being called by Frazier he knew this could be trouble – 'mono' had become Det's nickname due to his very short responses or indeed lack of. Sean approached the group - Frazier was clearly goading Det. Then strangely Frazier put his hands around Gabrielle. Sean thought to say something when Frazier fell to the floor. Sean looked at Det, and he was clearly using his powers on Frazier. Sean had to stop him, so he threw a, "No," at Det, who ignored him; Frazier was on the floor in pain. Sean gave a big, "No!" To Det, then he felt pain. Det was focusing on Sean, this was not playing, this hurt. Sean had enough and went for Det. Det shook but was not going down, Det fought back, the pain in Sean's head became more severe. All of a sudden Det stopped, Sean looked surprised but got another pain in his head with a clear, "Stop it!" Sal was in his face looking very menacing. Sean tried to stop her, but Sal was hurting him. Sean said in her head, "I will fight back!" Sal responded, "Good then I will drop my defences, go ahead hurt me!" This was enough to stop Sean however he felt; he was not going to hurt Sal. The pain gone; Sean took in the situation. Professor Stein had Det; Professor Smith was also focusing on Det. All the pupils were looking stunned, Frazier, still on the floor but sitting up holding his head.

"Everyone except Det and Master Hamling to their next classes now!" None of the pupils disagreed with Professor Smith. "Det you go with Professor Stein, Master Hamling with me!"

Sean went to turn when Sal added, "You are coming with me;" Sean was indeed led to Sal's first aid room.

"I'm not hurt!' Sean started.

"I know but what were you thinking attacking Det like that? Especially in full view of humans"

"Det was hurting Frazier."

"And now you support Frazier Hamling?"

"No, I mean yes, whether I like Frazier or not Det can't hurt him like that. Is he ok?'

"Yes, he will be fine. Your intervention has probably stopped serious injury."

"Well that was my job to protect people from the dignitaries. You can't tell me off for doing what I was expected to."

"I know. We just need to make Kain and Vul see that. You were over the top it was nearly a full-on fight."

"Kids fight on Earthen surely?"

Sal made the point. "Yes, but not two princes in front of humans!"

"Did anyone see?"

"No, because there was no physical attack. I'm sure they will be confused so that side should be ok."

"Emma," Sean recalled, "I was to speak to Emma!"

With this Sal smiled. "It's in hand just leave it for now. By the way Jeng is picking you up from out front after school, go with her. For now, you are not going to the last lesson you will stay here and help me...do an inventory of things." Although this was a strange statement Sean did as told.

At three on the dot Sean went to the front of the school to meet Jeng. Mush stopping him said, "I hear your headaches were back, so you had to spend time with Sal. You ok pal?"

"Yeah I'm fine," Then Sean thought. "Look I won't be seeing you until after Christmas. Sod it come here." Sean gave his friend a hug. "Easy mate." Mush said as the hug went on a bit, "I'll miss you to, but you need to sort Emma."

"It's in hand."

"Is it really?" Mush was looking at the drive; Jeng had turned up in the James' MG roof down calling for Sean.

Sean got into the car, without talking he said, "What are you doing? This is not helping."

Jeng smiled and replied in his head, "Just having fun, don't worry." As Jeng started to pull the car out of the drive she could see the boys looking at them. Near the gates Jeng gave a big smile and waved to all around, Sean sank in the seat.

A short journey later and they were in a car park of a nice but remote pub. "Dinner?" Was Jeng's comment as she got out of the car, Sean followed. They entered the pub, Sean looked around, it was quite empty, probably too early as this was a known and well-reviewed pub come restaurant in the area. They walked towards the bar, Sean stopped, "Professor Smith what…" as Professor Smith stood up and moved towards Sean, Emma was revealed standing beside her.

"Good afternoon Sean. Jeng our table is over there." With this Professor Smith headed towards a table. Jeng gave Sean's hand a little grasp and without speaking said, "Good luck." Jeng then joined Professor Smith.

Emma looked at Sean. "Hi," Sean did not answer as the waitress led them to a table over the other side of the restaurant. Both sat for a while, both uncomfortable, both having ordered and received their starters before even speaking to each other.

"I'm sorry," Sean said apologetically.

"So, I hear."

"It wasn't like it seemed."

"I bet it wasn't."

Sean was uncomfortable, and clearly not winning. The waitress taking away the finished starters gave a brief halt in what was not a conversation. Sean thought, he took both Emma's hands in his on the table then virtually stood to lean forward, gave Emma a kiss on the lips and said, "I love you." Sean felt Emma instantly relax and could have sworn her hands got warmer.

Her smile was radiant as she responded, "Come here you fool." They were both now half standing but embracing each other over the table. "Eh hmm." The waitress with the food interrupted.

Both chuckled and the meal was eaten in good humour, at every opportunity at least one hand was being held by each other over the table. Sean thought again, he pulled out his mobile, wrote something on his mobile then showed it to Emma. "Emma and I are together regardless of the rubbish being said. If any of you trolls want to take it further come and talk to me direct otherwise shut up!" It was the best Sean could think of to end the chat. Emma smiled. "Not my choice of wording but telling everyone you are with me is what counts." Emma's simple hearts emoji reply was enough.

Food eaten; they were both in the back of Professor Smith's car for the trip home. Upon reaching Emma's house her mother was at the door. Professor Smith getting out of the car said, "I need to say something to your mother."

On their own in the back of the car Emma looked at Sean. "I love you too." With that she embraced Sean, closer, warmer than ever before.

EARTHEN AWAITS:
(CHAPTER 18)

Friday morning came, without much packing Sean, Jenna and Kain were in the car being taken to the Research Park where they were to travel to the Space Station then onto Earthen. The dignitaries were on another craft, Sean, his parents, Algier and Sal on his. Sean was not that bothered about the shuttle; he was more interested on Earthen to follow. Sean sat behind his parents, noting Jeng was up front but not Commander Shad, a younger looking pilot sat next to her.

"This is Commander Jeng. We will be leaving for the Space Station, breaking there before onward travel to Earthen." Sean looked as Jeng threw him a smile. The trip to the Space Station was noneventful, although whilst having a drink at the rear Commander Jeng approached Sean. "Did you say Commander Jeng?"

Jeng looked at her uniform then remembered Sean had no idea of the inscriptions or badging. "Yes. I had your father promote me. Medals and awards although very pleasing do not pay the bills!"

"Well deserved." Sean was pleased for her.

As Jeng headed back to the controls she shouted in Sean's head. "Youngest ever and only female Commander!"

Upon arrival on the Space Station Kain advised it would be a quick turnaround, only an hour's comfort break. Jeng, still smiling, took Sean to the corner of the room. "Table viewer on." A 3D screen appeared in front of them. "Show a Sun Ship."

The image showed a spaceship, similar to the shuttle in shape but with no obvious wings and more bronze in colour.

Jeng continued. "A Sun Ship has no viewers and is made of a different material than other ships. In simple terms it's...skin is probably the best word is molten. By that I mean inside it is solid, but the outer layer continually mixes with the Sun's rays. This chemical reaction turns to heat which then through the engines into propulsion and speed. A Sun Ship will surf around the Sun in just over two hours, meaning as we will only be going halfway, we will be on the other side in about an hour."

"Wow, I can't imagine that kind of speed."

Jeng thought, "Let's go back a bit. In simple terms Earthen only has itself, its moon, just like Earth, and the sun. Generally, we see few other planets however, once we conquered our Moon we then focused on the Sun and found other planets behind it. Technology and all that we were soon surfing the sun and discovering the full solar system and obviously Earth. The Earthen Space Station is smaller and more basic than this as it was only a station come building platform. The Earth Space Station being also some one hundred years later is more modern, bigger and caters for a laboratory, holiday venue and obviously a station point for Earth."

"So, when the first Earth Ship got around the sun and saw Earth, what did it do? Did it land on Earth?"

"No. Sun Ships cannot move far from the sun, they only transfer us from one station to the other however, they can pull cargo." The 3D picture now showed a large cylindrical shape behind the Sun Ship. "Once we decided to investigate your side of the sun, we built parts on Earthen, shipped them to the Earthen Space Station then transported them to this side, eventually putting the Earth Space Station together."

Sean was back to, "Wow," even a, "Cool," came out at one point whilst Jeng was teaching.

"I'm sorry we don't have enough time to give you all the technical details. To be honest I only fly these things so I'm probably not the best to teach you, but it works, and you will be on Earthen by tomorrow morning."

Sean thanked Jeng, he thought her simplistic approach was best, but wow he really was not only going to surf the sun but would soon see Earthen. The group were called and again led through varied corridors until they were at a hatch. The hatch opened and Sean looked in. The inside of the craft was very similar to that of the shuttle although the seats were four across not two. Sean was led to the seat next to his mother, Algier to his right and Kain next to Algier.

As Sean took his seat Jenna leant over, "It will be quick. I suggest you take one of these and listen to some music."

"No, no more drugs." Sean laughed to his mother. Jenna shrugged her shoulders, as she leant back in her chair the helmet that was above her came down and covered her head, although open at the front. Sean sat back, the helmet above him lowered onto his head and the four-point seat belt came across him tight. Algier looked at Sean and winked.

Sean heard Jeng in the helmet. "Welcome on board the Sun Ship. We will be leaving immediately and will be at the Earthen Space Station on the hour...Sean, only you can hear this one." Sean chuckled at Jeng's voice. "The visor will come down, whilst surfing you cannot leave your seat however, if you ask for music you will get music, if you ask for a drink a tube will provide you one. If you wish to get sick then ask for a sick bag, basically the bottom of the visor will open, and you will be able to get sick into a kind of bowl in front. Hope you took the pill Jenna gave you." Sean could only think, 'Crumbs!'

Sean felt the Sun Ship move; all was gentle until about five minutes in when Jeng was on the intercom again. "Commander Jeng to all passengers, we will be engaging main thrust and the surf will start. I will count down shortly." At this point the helmet visor came down and all was black in front, Sean said, "Cool."

Jeng announced, "Surfing in 5, 4, 3, 2, 1." Sean felt as though he was kicked in the stomach, the Sun Ship sped forward and just kept accelerating. Now with his body tight against the seat and the harness even tighter Sean felt a little more comfortable. Then Sean felt a definite lean as the Sun Ship was clearly leaning into the sun for its curved voyage. Nothing changed, the feel of continued speed and tilt did not stop, all was in darkness. Sean was feeling queasy, but he was not going to call for the sick bag.

Eventually Sean felt the craft was slowing and straightening upright. A minute or so later and his helmet lifted as did his seat belt, Sean let out a deep breath. Jenna looked over, "I need the facilities, why don't you go with me?" Sean got out of his seat and followed his mother to the toilets at the rear, his legs hardly holding his weight. "I'll take that cubicle; you use this one." Jenna instructed. As soon as Sean was in the cubicle, he said goodbye to his breakfast, twice. Having stood and cleaned up as best he could. Sean opened his cubicle door - Jenna was still there.

"Did you go to the toilet?" Sean asked.

Jenna smiled, "No. I didn't need to, you get used to it after a few journeys, but I thought you could do with some moral support. See that green liquid, swoosh it in your mouth, spit it out then drink a few sips and swoosh again. You should have taken the pill I offered."

Sean did as told, drinking what was mouthwash seemed strange, but it did the trick. Sean felt better in his throat and gut not just his mouth. Both returned to their seats for the less adventurous trip to the Earthen Space Station. Upon exiting the Sun Ship Sean could see the Earthen Space Station, as Jeng had advised it was smaller. Its insides looked as though it had not been completed, air ducts even wiring visible.

The time on the Earthen Space Station was short and all

were shortly accessing the Earthen Shuttle. As Sean went to sit Jeng stopped him, "I have no Co-Pilot, would you like to help?"

Sean followed Jeng straight to the front of the craft and sat next to Jeng in the Co-Pilot's chair, "Do I need to do anything?"

"No, it's more about the view, I will leave the viewer on."

Following the formalities, they were moving, Sean did not keep track of the time but played with any button he was allowed to. After some time Jeng spoke, "Sean look." Sean did as asked, seeing the shape of an Earth coming towards them. "Earthen." Jeng advised.

Sean was fascinated and watched, as this Earth got bigger. He could see the Earth similarities; the general clouds, the black/brown of the land and the blue of the sea. As they got closer, with Jeng's direction Sean could make out the Kingdoms. Four main areas similar to Earth's with a north and south pole of which there was less white but more land, the overall surface appeared more land than sea. The burnt equator was obvious, like a long black stripe connecting the blue seas. Sean let out a, "Wow!"

As they got closer the colours and land definition became clearer until eventually all went an orangey red as they entered Earthen atmosphere. A further, "Wow!" As they were now in Earthen air space. Sean noted even at this height and descending Earthen looked similar to Earth. Sean jumped as a message came through the intercom, "Fighter Patrol to Earthen Shuttle we are guiding you." With these two viewers either side of Sean and Jeng appeared. Looking at these viewers Sean could see two spaceships, similar shape and colour to the shuttle but with more defined and larger wings although overall a smaller craft. Underneath and above the wings were weapons and the pilots were inside a glass cockpit similar to an Earth fighter jet. "Are we in danger?'" Sean asked.

"No, they are Saulten military craft and are here as a guard of honour as well as protection, we have a lot of Royalty on board you know." Jeng teased.

"Wow!" Sean was in awe as he was seeing fighter spaceships up close and in flight.

As the now three in formation craft descended to what Sean thought would be normal airplane heights on Earth, he heard Jeng say. "Shuttle to PA I have orders from his Highness to approach at low height, the guiding craft will stay above us."

"PA to shuttle, this is confirmed please lower to one thousand meters." With this the shuttle dropped quickly and was soon crossing the land very low. Sean looked out all three viewers; he could see land, trees, grass, everything similar to Earth. Further along Sean saw buildings; most were detached, all appearing to be the straight rectangle type white exterior looking buildings as at the Research Park. Sean saw an area approaching that appeared more built up although most buildings were detached just closer together, with more roads but few structures of height.

"Is this a town?" Sean asked.

"No this is the outskirts of Saulten City, very shortly we will be over the centre," Jeng explained. "Now you know why we call it Canada. Earthen has lots of land but with few people therefore we have more land with our properties and no need to build upwards. Indeed, you will find virtually no skyscrapers on Earthen, generally the highest building is five floors high."

"So, no flying cars or lots of advertising as in most Sci-Fi films?"

"No, they are awful we have space and culture!" Jeng giggled.

Sean kept looking out, the buildings did get closer and denser and there appeared to be no advertising, traffic lights or signs it did appear uncluttered. "Wow!" Sean could not help himself but shout as the shuttle, passing over some greenery, came to a halt in front of a building and descended to land. The building was the same colour as all the others with mainly rectangular shapes but had varied domes or semi domed glass or transparent roofing. The main part of the building being some five storeys high had a domed top; each corner had towers slightly lower in height but again with half domed tops.

"Wow, if that's the airport I'd love to see the rest!"

Jeng laughed, "That's not the airport, it is your palace."

"What?" Sean was stunned, "This is our Palace, and we live here?"

"Yes, PA is Palace Airport, it is a big building and we have landed in the Palace ground."

As Jeng completed her sentence Sean felt some hands on his shoulders. "Yes, it looks amazing, but it is Earthen so do not get carried away honey." Jenna was next to Sean and was guiding him to the shuttle door. With Sean standing between Jenna and Kain the shuttle door opened. Sean saw what were obviously guards standing at arms either side of the path leading from the shuttle ramp, the guards were fifty along and five deep all with weapons.

As they exited the shuttle, whilst walking down the ramp, Sean saw two figures at the bottom of the ramp clearly waiting to meet them. One was Secretary Barlo and the other an older, uniformed man. Both bowed then shook Kain's hand followed by a bow to Jenna. Sean could see that beyond the soldiers were other people oddly the men to the left and the women to the right.

"I am Military Chief Norment young Sire." The old man in the uniform addressed Sean whilst bowing. "Would you like to inspect the troops?"

Sean replied, "Yes." With that Military Chief Norment was leading Sean and Kain along the lines of the troops. Kain shook as many hands as he could, in some instances speaking to the soldiers, some he obviously knew. Sean copied the hand shaking and did his best to look regal. As they were nearing the end of the line Sean had noted that his mother and the main party were over to his right talking to the mainly female side, Sean was led to the left side.

"Sire so good to see you King Kain," Councilor Anders was greeting Kain, Sean noting he received a brief embrace from Kain not just a handshake. Sean was next and the brief embrace was a hug although the, "Welcome young Sire," Was similar to Kain's. Two to three other now obvious council members welcomed Sean, shaking his hand, although they introduced themselves Sean was not taking in their names.

"Really, do I have to welcome you?"

Sean looked up; he was eye to eye with his Uncle. "Uncle Dain I don't know the protocol for Princes meeting each other?"

"Good, then I will not welcome you." Dain was talking through his mind. Sean could feel him in his head, then, "Ouch," he felt a pain in his head. "Sorry Sean that was me, brother be nice or else!" Kain had just interrupted their mind games.

"Of course, Sire." Dain was unsettled, "And I welcome you again...and of course you young Sire," With that Sean threw a, "Pratt!" Into Dain's head before following his father.

Kain led Sean to a square vehicle, which had no sides was about thirty centimetres off the floor but on wheels. On top of the vehicle's floor were five lots of three aside poles with small seats on top and another pole with handles just in front. Kain leant against the middle seat holding the handle in front, Jenna was next to him on the other side, and Sean took the seat next to Kain. As others filled the rear the vehicle moved slowly but with no jolting along what was a road. Either side of the road was other Earthens in differing dress, not military or predominantly white in colour, Kain and Jenna waved to them.

Although the vehicle moved slowly, they were soon at the palace entrance. The external doors were large and opened similar to how they would on Earth, outwards towards the approaching Royals. Once inside the first doors, a short walk along a corridor, a second but more ornate set of doors of similar size opened. Upon entering the next room Sean looked around, it was the hallway. The room was big, rectangle with many doors either side and at the end with an atrium style roof clear to the sky. In the middle of the hall was a large long table adorned with food, drink and plants, no chairs. At the sides of the room were smaller tables and chairs, Sean noted again the colour was the same white walls; silvery grey floors however, mixed in with the obvious plain white Earthen furniture were the odd Earth sideboard or couch.

The party started to split, taking food and sitting or standing in different areas. Jenna pulled Sean to one side, "Look this is the informal welcome, so I, you and Dad will need to mix and mingle. Thinking about it stick with me." Sean could not take in all the people but with lots of pleasantries, all bowing to him he enjoyed it, grabbing the odd drink helped too.

"This is Palace Master Wort, he with his wife Lans run our palace household and staff." Jenna was giving Wort a big hug. Sean was engulfed by a big embrace, hardly able to breath. "Young Master Saul, my have you grown!" A large, plump old lady was smothering Sean.

"Lans you are killing him." Jenna was smiling, "Remember he is a Prince, we are in public."

"Nonsense, I have not seen this young man since he was three." Lans was unrepentant and gave Sean another hug.

"Do not be so prim my Dear." Kain was with them, "Wort and Lans it is good seeing you again." With that Kain embraced both.

Jenna whispered in Sean's ear, "They are both over one hundred years old and Lans was Kain's nanny, like a second set of parents. They also helped look after you when you were here obviously at a very young age. Why don't you have a break, see Jeng in the corner."

Sean smiled and headed to Jeng who was in sight but within an arched open side room to the main hall. "Mad out there, your mother and father will be shattered with all the handshaking, troubles of being a royal I suppose. Let me show you something."

Sean looked around; the room was small with no furniture and the plain white walls. Jeng called, "Centre table and chairs." With that a table with four cylindrical chairs came up from the floor. Each chair had a small back, which was at ninety degrees to the table. "Let's sit."

As Sean approached his chair it seemed to sense his height so as he sat its height was perfect for his legs. Sean looked to his left and saw Jeng sitting correctly in line with the table, Sean tried to move his chair, but it would not move and remained at ninety degrees to the table. "Take a little weight off with your toes then move and the chair will turn." Sean carried out the instruction and the chair turned. "It senses your weight and once you take a little off it you can turn allowing you to sit under the table or walk away from the table." Jeng explained.

Now standing next to the chair Sean asked, "So what if I don't know where the chairs or table are, will they come up on me?"

"No watch." Jeng was now standing next to her chair, "Down." And the chair sunk into the floor. Jeng then stood where the chair had been, "Up." The chair did not rise. "Again, sensors in the table or chair know you are on it so it will not rise, or as in the case of the table if it senses weight on it such as food it will not lower."

"How do I know where the table and chairs are in a room?"

"You can use your powers and sense them again you do not have to talk you can mind connect or if you look closely the outline of the furniture on the grey floor will be white, or grey on the white walls so as you can see if you do not wish to use your mind."

Sean looked, "Yes I can see the lines, so this applies to cupboards or other types of furniture?"

"Yes, look, see the line on the wall, seat cupboard open." With that the wall cupboard opened to reveal four chairs, the same as those at the table. With one hand Jeng pulled a chair from the cupboard, the chair moving effortlessly. Jeng spun the chair around then sat on it, "Move me!" Sean walked over and pushed the chair it did not move, Sean tried again and again but the chair did not move. Jeng advised, "I'll press down with my toes and take some weight off then push." With this Sean pushed and the chair with Jeng on it moved. Sean then continued to twirl Jeng around, Jeng deciding she was getting dizzy tried to stop but did so too quickly and fell off the chair in a heap of laughter, Sean also laughed.

"There are people watching, what do you think you are doing!" Field Officer Daved was addressing Jeng.

"Leave her alone she is with me!" Sean went into defence mode.

"And you a prince, have you no decorum!" Daved said.

"Field Officer Daved is there a problem?" Sean saw Daved turn, Kain was asking.

"No Sire, my apologies." Daved was stooping so low he nearly hit the ground Sean thought.

"Then you must have duties, leave, now!" Kain was in King mode. With this Daved still stooping left, Kain looked at Jeng, Jeng went after her boyfriend.

"Come on Sean, that's enough fun. I'll take you to your room." Jenna was ushering Sean along. Finally getting to the end of the hallway, many people wishing them good evening,

Sean and Jenna entered a lift. "Four." Jenna stated. The lift went up, it was a glass lift and as it stopped Sean could see into the hall below through the atrium roof. Looking up he could see the shuttle in front, lots of grass and trees either side of the road or path they had been on earlier which lead to what appeared to be a wall and gates in the distance.

"The palace has a wall about a mile square all the way around. The palaces drive leads to the palace gates then off to Saulten City a few miles outside. We are now on floor four of five." Jenna turned and the doors opened to a square room with a door on the other three sides from the lift door where they were standing.

"This is the main secondary bedrooms; left is Dain's room. Right is Algier's room, straight ahead is your room."

"I have a room?"

"Of course, you are a prince." Jenna was leading Sean to his door.

"Where is your room?"

Jenna giggled, "Ours is the fifth floor above. It is a suite and the size of well all your three rooms, plus a dome to see the sky and stars."

"And we live in Aville, your suite must be bigger than our school!"

"No, not that big but yours is not that small either."

Sean was now looking into his room. It was large and empty looking, the same white and grey colours as elsewhere but a half-domed shape glass side ran the length of the room in front of them with a full terrace. "Wow, this is all mine?" Sean exclaimed.

"Yes," Jenna replied, "To the left are doors to two guest rooms each with bathrooms. This room is your day room, desks, tables whatever, they can be seen when and as Jeng demonstrated. Terrace first." With that Sean and Jenna walked across the room and stood on his terrace. "So, your main views

224

are to the rear, again lots of grass and paths, then gardens and trees before the palace wall. Beyond that you can see the hills and mountains. To our sides there's mainly land however, there are some buildings."

Jenna allowed Sean to walk and take in the views. "You will notice there is no force field up so the sky and the sun can be seen clearly. It is winter here just as on Earth although it's seventeen degrees still and sunny, the sun will set shortly. In the summer we can hit thirty to forty degrees when the force field is raised, and you can see a slight disturbance in the air where it is."

Again, Jenna let it sink in for a while, "Come on the best bit." They went back through the main room. "You have viewers, TVs and everything, look at the room schematics at some point. This door leads to your bedroom."

Again, the room was the same colours and had the glass to one side however, although there was an Earthen bed at the centre of the end wall there were some clearly Earth furniture in the room as well, Sean looked at the cot.

"That is your cot from when you were born," Jenna was standing next to the cot, gazing into it. "You obviously will not recall it but..." Jenna was now in a daydream. Sean looked around further, not only was there Earth furniture but also some toys. Jenna sensing Sean was looking around walked over to the bed, sat on it then pulled from the middle a claret and blue teddy bear. "Mr. Hammer, he was your favourite, obviously called after West Ham." Jenna had a happy tear in her eye, now cuddling Mr. Hammer.

Sean sat next to his mother "So why the support for West Ham?"

Jenna recalled, "Blame Granddad John. Like a lot of Irish people, they support premier teams, and my dad wanted to be different so chose West Ham United. The first ever football match your father attended he was taken by dad to West Ham and it stuck. Anyway, follow me."

Jenna led Sean into an adjoining room. "Your dressing room, the cupboard is normally left open so you can see your clothes, note there are Earthen and Earth clothes your size already."

Sean thought, "My clothes, my toys and cot, does no one else come here?"

"Of course not, you are a prince, and this is your room." Jenna thought, "Actually quite often when I visit, I sneak in and cuddle Mr. Hammer. Anyway, this is your bathroom."

"Holy crap this is bigger than my bedroom at home!"

"Double shower, Jacuzzi bath everything, just leave the shower and bath settings on W for water not FB. I'll explain FB tomorrow, this way." Sean followed his mother back to the main living area. "Desk and chair cupboard open." With that an Earthen white desk came out from the wall and Jenna was moving a standard Earth office type chair out of the cupboard to use against the desk.

"Sit!" Sean sat. "The room schematics are on the viewer over there, viewer show Earth FaceTime." With that the viewer in front of Sean looked just like a PC at home. Jenna took out her Earth mobile, "FaceTime call Mum," with that her phone rang, she answered it and Sean could see him on the wall viewer one side and his mother's face through her phone on the other side just like Earth. Jenna carried on, "It will work exactly like at home, it will have what you would call satellite delay, not much but it comes in handy. Room - Earth Canadian lodge interior." With that all the walls turned to look like the inside of a Canadian lodge, Sean's screen looked as though he was in a lodge.

"Cool so I can FaceTime Emma and Mush and they will think I'm in Canada?"

"Yes, we are about an hour and a half in front of UK time, side clock UK time." The viewer followed Jenna's request and a clock was showing Earth UK time appeared to the side of the viewer. Sean looking at the time said, "I better call them now."

"Change first dear, the setting looks authentic but a crown and white top with crowned S's may be hard to explain. But yes, call them, see you in the morning."

By the time Sean had changed his shirt and returned to the desk Jenna had left. "Viewer call Emma Cooper." Within a minute Sean was looking at Emma, "I miss you already." He said.

"Ahh, me too, you got there quick?" Emma was smiling at Sean.

"Yeah....tail wind. Can you hear me ok, what about the picture?"

"Yeah fine although a bit of a delay, long way Canada must be satellite delay."

Sean chuckled; he was millions of miles away not just thousands.

"So, what's it like there?"

Sean started to describe as though he was in Canada, snow and all that. The hour or so he was talking with Emma flew by, Emma calling it to a halt. "I miss you and could talk for hours but Mush would appreciate a call as well." With a joint "love you!" The call was ended, and Sean was soon talking to Mush. Again, time flew by, only Mush's mum shouting, "Go to bed!" Reminded them to end the conversation. Sean went to bed, catching a Star Trek episode on the viewer above his bed before falling to sleep.

THE PALACE:
(CHAPTER 19)

Upon waking Sean showered and wondered whether he should try the FB setting...no better not. After dressing he had no idea of the time so took the lift immediately. As the doors opened and Sean exited, he bumped into his Uncle Dain.

"In a hurry. Not surprised breakfast is almost finished" Dain mocked.

"I'm a teenager and a prince so can do what I want, my time is my own." Sean looked scornfully at his uncle as he was walking away.

"First corridor on the left fourth door on the left nephew!" Dain shouted as the lift doors closed.

A few minutes later the door opened, and a man's voice asked, "What are you doing in the cupboard young Sean?"

Sean turned to see Wort standing in the doorway, "I got lost, or someone...never mind, it's a big cupboard though!"

Wort laughed, "Follow me."

Upon entering the obvious breakfast room Sean saw his mother sitting but his father walking towards him with Algier. "Good morning sleepy head, we are off to the Council and will catch you later." Sean stopped his father and said quietly. "Dad, Dain he is strange, but will he hurt me?"

"Strange," Kain chuckled. "No that is normal for him. Do not worry he is scared of me, and for that matter you, he has sensed your powers. Do not be scared of him, he is the one person you can push around."

"Good morning Sean, I will have a word with Dain," Algier winked as he left.

"Always working," Was Jenna's welcome. "Still that means a whole day with your favourite person."

Sean looked around pretending. "Nope I don't see Shadow."

"I'll ignore that. Do you like my clothes?"

Sean looked, this was a strange question, but he knew the right answer, "You look great Mum."

Jenna's look suggested it was the wrong answer. "I am not looking for compliments, I am wearing jodhpurs so that gives you a clue. Lans can we have a takeaway please?"

With that Sean followed his mother, Jenna pointed out a few things as they walked but said she would concentrate on the main areas for now. Sean although lost could tell they had moved to the rear of the palace. Jenna opened a door and they were in the swimming pool area. Two pools horizontally next to each other with a glass wall looking out to the gardens, both pools were fifty metres long.

Sean exclaimed, "Wow! Not one but two pools, why?"

"First, four floors above us is your room, if we go outside then we would see your terrace above...yes your room or apartment is bigger than two swimming pools. Anyway, the furthest pool is standard water, chlorine just like Earth however, this pool," The pool Jenna had now approached and sat on the side of, "Is FB or Fluid Bearings." Sean joined his mother, sitting next to her by the side of the pool. Looking in he could see it was not water but clear looking balls. Jenna put her arm in, swished her arm around then pulled out some fluid bearings.

"Oops slippery bug...I mean, see they are basically clear balls about ten centimetres in diameter coated with a fluid making them very slippery."

"So, like a ball pit in an Earth play area?"

"Yes, exactly apart from as you can see you can move in them easily, actually you swim. No different to water once you are in you will go to the bottom, so you need to tread water."

"Wow!" Sean swished his hand in the fluid bearings. "I don't seem to be wet?"

"Exactly, you can jump in, swim then get out and dress. The fluid also cleans and is good for your skin. Hence, we have fluid bearing showers and baths, although, different size fluid bearings." Jenna informed.

"I'm going to fluid bearing shower every day from now."

Jenna chuckled, "It is the quickest way but does not really wash hair that well, and I still prefer a proper bath or shower. By the way the fluid bearings are no different to water in a normal swimming pool they recirculate through the system, cleaned so you don't pick up someone else's dirt." Jenna now standing put her leg on her son and pushed, Sean toppled into the pool. Sean went to the bottom before thinking to swim; as he started to rise, he stopped about halfway still inside the fluid bearings. Sean realised that not only could he see through the fluid bearings but although immersed he could still breathe.

'OMG' he thought. There he was fully clothed but not feeling wet, under 'water,' breathing. Looking up at his mother who was laughing above him. Sean swam to the top, head out of the bearings. "Mum you can't do that...but this is awesome!"

"A couple of widths then we need to move on." Jenna had moved to the safety of a chair nearer the door. Sean obliged, two widths swam, no different feeling to swimming at home but he was not wet. The second width Sean swam fully under 'water' breathing the whole way. Now at the side of the pool Sean requested, "Give us a hand out?"

"Do you think I am a fool?" Jenna laughed, "No chance I'll see you at the door."

Sean thought, 'Damn no chance of revenge;' he helped himself out and joined his mother at the door. "It is not best to swim with your full clothes on, but they are dry enough although a bit slippery so watch your step..." Jenna was too late as Sean ended up on his backside.

Slippers off they continued to a room on the side of the palace, Sean again noted plain, glass or similar walls to those on the Research Park, typical Earthen. Jenna started, "One of my favourite rooms, the music room. So, you can call a drum kit." A drum kit raised from the floor, "Or a piano," A piano raised from the floor, "And others as you like."

Sean walked to the drum kit, again mainly white, grey, silver, very similar looking to those on Earth except the drums were not actually a skin but solid. Jenna noted Sean was perplexed and said, "No I am not going to go through the instruments, but yes you do not need sticks to play the drums, guitars do not have strings, that's for another day. Drum and piano lower." With that the room was clear again. "Sit here in the middle with me," Sean joined his mother on the floor sitting cross-legged as though to meditate.

"Ed Sheeran, Thinking Out Loud." Sean heard the song clearly all around the room, "Don't just listen, feel it."

Sean looked at his mother, eyes closed really listening, 'oh well he thought' and decided to give it a go. A minute or so into the song and Sean could feel not just the words but air or pressure at certain points as when the word love was sung, he felt a little pressure in his heart area, the word kiss he felt slight air pressure on his lips. So much so he opened his eyes, no one was kissing him. "This is great but spooky!" Sean addressed his mother who was clearly in the zone.

"No patience just like your father," Jenna smiled. "You felt the pressure?" Sean nodded. "So, it is not just sound but in this mode the room is set to interact, and it sends air in the correct places, it can higher or lower temperature depending on set words – it is a glorious feeling. I love it."

Sean looked at his mother, then around the room, the song was still playing, and she was right. "Does this work for many people at once?"

"No, it is best with only one or two and sitting or standing still. I get so much in the zone that occasionally whilst standing I fall over which is why I now sit." Jenna and Sean laughed.

"Move away a bit and watch this." Sean moved away to see his mother now lying on the floor; Jenna instructed, "3D lying part." With that a life size Ed Sheeran was lying next to Jenna and moving as per the video. Jenna copied a couple of moves. "Stop!" The music stopped but the 3D Sheeran was still on the floor. Jenna stood up. "That could be a little embarrassing." She giggled, "But yes you can 3D interact with the video, I often dance with Ed."

Sean laughed, "OK Mum, I get the picture but that is awesome!'

"Now I have embarrassed myself, let's do it together? Beyoncé Single Ladies all three," With that the Beyoncé song started and the singer and the two backing dancers were full size 3D figures. The music was louder; the room was rocking Sean felt.

"Come on, your turn, join in." Jenna was next to Beyoncé copying the moves. Sean although in hysterics joined in for a minute. As the song stopped, Sean said, "Mum that was awesome, Emma and Mush would go mad over this?"

Jenna composed herself then smiled, "I'm sure Emma would also appreciate the songs wording when you are both older of course?"

"Mum, please now I am embarrassed!" Sean chuckled.

Both left the room, although Sean was close to his mother the last hour or so reinforced his love for her. "Put your shoes back on, they should be dry, come on the really best bit!" Jenna was virtually skipping into the garden, Sean following. They were moving along very clean paths between beautifully kept grass or plants with the occasional sculpture, Sean stopped at a Dolphin statue, "You have Dolphins on Earthen?"

"No that came from Earth, that is an Earthen sculpture," Jenna was pointing to a strange statue nearby. Sean looked at it, "It's like a matchstick man running, and it's crap!"

"Don't let your father hear you say that, it is a Bosworth a very famous Earthen sculptor and worth millions!"

Sean thought out loud, "Typical Earthen you have everything and nothing," both laughed.

Sean looking ahead said, "Mum, now I know what you mean." They were entering the stables; Sean knew his mother loved horses.

An aid was holding two horses, "They are ready your Majesty, the back holdalls have refreshments in."

" Thank you Aran. Come here Gloss." With that Jenna was stroking a very large black stallion.

"This is Gloss I call him...well simple look at his coat, he is my favourite." Sean looked and Gloss actually looked like he shone. Sean mounted Droop, so called by his mother as the horse had a slightly longer lip on one side. Droop was smaller than Gloss, but Sean was not as good a rider as his mother.

Mounted they were soon riding around the palace grounds; 'this is a big place' Sean thought. Jenna, who was still pointing things out to Sean from the saddle, then led them to a small stream with a waterfall. Dismounting Jenna said, "This is clear water from the mountains behind the Palace so the horses can drink here, we will have some lunch."

Both horses drinking, Sean and Jenna sitting by the stream also drinking and eating from the back holdalls they had been wearing. "Shadow would love this place; this is heaven Mum. This, I mean my...no our palace is magnificent!"

Jenna was back in serious mode. "I know honey, yes if we could do what we have done today everyday with friends it would be perfect but then you interact with Earthens and it all goes wrong. Visiting this place for brief periods I can live with, but it will soon kick you."

"It is such a shame," Sean thought longer. "Why could we not just move the best bits to Earth?"

"In some ways that is the plan, but as your father has said how do you do it without scaring Earth?"

"Ok so why can't we just have a palace on Earth with a fluid bearing pool, that music room, and horses?" Sean asked.

"Actually, there are smaller versions on the Research Park site I use however, until now we could not show you. Temptation, you would want to show your friends. You know what maybe we can change that now, let's see, I'll race you back!" Jenna was up and running. Sean had no chance, as once on the horses Gloss was obviously quicker and Sean and Droop tried but they lost.

Sean spent the evening FaceTiming his friends, unusual for him he remembered tomorrow would be Emma's play. "Break a leg as they say!" Emma was thrilled that he had remembered.

THE CHAMPION:
(CHAPTER 20)

"Morning you're up early, so are you up for the big event tonight?" Algier asked as he bumped into Sean whilst entering the lift.

"Morning Uncle, what event?"

"The Duel...of course Kain has not told you?" As they exited the lift, Algier continued, "Quick sit here I'll tell you. I don't want your mother hearing, that's Kain's job." Algier giggled, "At Saulten Stadium in the city the World Heavyweight Dueling Championship fight is on. Our Saulten born Mali Syston is the reigning champ and Sheko a Biernite young upstart is challenging him for the honour. It is going to be explosive!"

"Wow! They don't fight to the death?"

"No, it is a professional fight so has rules and safety measures. Look have breakfast and then I will sit with you and explain."

Whilst enjoying breakfast Sean realised that although the boxing was not mentioned Jenna obviously knew – Kain and Algier were hiding around the subject, even Jenna's, "Shall we go out this evening?" Was avoided. Algier had managed to gain Sean's time by suggesting he had had enough of politics, therefore, was having a day off - this was agreed.

A short time later and Sean was in the games room with Algier, "Wow what is this?"

"It is an Earthen board game, similar to chess but 3D. No

time to explain the rules so let us try pool."

"Pool?" Sean looked around and there was a pool table very similar to an Earth table, "Why I've played that!"

"I know but it will be the easiest game to teach as you do know it. I'll break." Algier had removed the triangle from the already set up table and was crouching behind the white cue ball.

"Ok, where's my cue?"

Algier laughed, "No the Earthen way." With that Algier with his mind struck the cue ball, which hit the pack. "I'm red!" Algier's next shot also potted however, his third missed. "Gentle young man." Sean crouched behind the white ball eyeing up the yellow one to the middle. He thought, projected then heard a crash!

"I said gentle!" Algier was laughing, "That was one of your father's cups!"

Sean surveyed the damage, it was clear he had over thought and both the white ball and the yellow he was attempting to pot had come off the table, the guilty yellow ball was sitting next to a cup on the floor.

"Oops, I need to control my power!" Sean apologised.

"That is what we are here for. I'll set up again."

Algier set up again but now with coaching Sean was getting the hang of controlling his thoughts more delicately, although Algier won the first three matches.

"Drinks break maybe?" Algier said after raising his hands having just potted another black.

"Yes please."

Algier and Sean sat on chairs by the window looking out onto the gardens. Algier started, "So professional dueling and combat dueling have the same structure, five rounds of one minute then if there is no winner the sixth is continuous until someone wins. You win by being the first to three knock-downs or a knockout in either the first five rounds or during continuous. Every time you are knocked down you have a ten second count, after each of the timed rounds you have a one-minute break."

Sean thought, "So there has to be an outcome?"

"Yes. The continuous round is brutal as you get the ten second knock down break but no round breaks, you literally fight till you drop."

"That is brutal!"

"It is but well we like fighting together with power and submission. Unfortunately, few fights go to continuous because if say you were two down in the fourth and know you were going to lose most fighters will go down in the fifth. Amateur fights such as kids has the same rules."

"So, people must get hurt. I've seen Dad's power?"

"That is why your father is a combatant and not a professional Duelist, he would not have the control to not hurt someone." Algier paused. "There are safeguards, the bodyguards worn in Professional Dueling have varied sensors on them, heartbeat, perspiration and lots more so if a duelist is sensed to be seriously injured the sensors go off and the fight is stopped, they obviously losing."

"Ok, but what if you fry their brains or just blow them apart?"

"First each duelist wears a helmet, not as protection as such but it monitors both output and input to the brain. 'Brain frying' as you put it is not allowed; the force of your...punch as such is what it is all about. If you try to fry someone's brain the alarm goes off. You lose and vice versa if the opponents helmet picks up too much energy aimed at the brain it will also alarm, the offender is warned or loses dependent on the referee's decision."

"But people can just explode?"

Algier laughed, "As I said that is why professionals have control but also each duelist is handicapped. Each duelist's power is assessed before a duel then given enough TDL to weaken his or her power to eighty per cent. The idea is both duelists at eighty per cent each would have a similar chance as one hundred per cent each however, it is a sport, and no one is meant to get hurt." Algier again paused. "It is not a perfect science as in theory someone could blow and use a lot of power however, the sensors would pick this up and the six referees would jump in to subdue and protect."

"So, if you use full power you are disqualified?"

"No, punch power only thought power to the brain is not allowed. In properly organised professional and amateur duels injury is rare. The odd broken bone and bruising no different to boxing on Earth."

Sean took this in, "In combat though?"

Algier looking uncomfortable, said, "You fight to the death using any power you need. The only rule is once a duelist is down you give them ten seconds, if they don't rise you finish them off."

"Barbaric!" Sean stated. "So, can anyone duel or combat anyone regardless of age?"

"No there are rules, not all challenges are authorised and under eighteens cannot combat only duel. Obviously in organised amateur and professional duels the duelists are in bands, weights etc. so are fair. In combat again depending on the situation you can nominate a proxy." Algier paused, "So let's say a young fit Earthen killed someone's Granddaughter. The Grandfather could challenge the convicted murderer however, as the Grandfather would possibly lose then he could nominate a younger proxy. Once the proxy obviously agrees and is of similar age etc. then they can combat."

"So, if someone say killed my Emma could I ask Dad to combat for me assuming the killer is over eighteen?"

"Yes, if being a normal family, obviously being Royal the

killer would be executed anyway, but you get the picture."

"So, are there many combat duels?"

"Not as many as when I was young. Certainly, here in Saulten it is rare however, in other kingdoms it is still common. Vulten has at least one televised each month, if there are no legitimate duels then life prisoners are given the option to kill another for a pardon." With that Algier reminded Sean about Emma's play back on Earth, Sean left to FaceTime Emma and wish her well before dressing.

Now at the front doors ready to leave for the duel. Sean got into n a square shaped car of a similar size to an Earth car. The car had no roof but a see-through force field. He sat in the rear seat and Kain and Algier in the front seats. In front were two or three other vehicles as was behind, different shapes and sizes but the same silvery grey colour however, all had blue flashing lights, clearly Police.

The motor parade pulled out of the palace grounds, Sean looked out the windows, and initially there were few buildings and little traffic. Upon entering what was obviously the city centre Sean noted the buildings were denser and the traffic busier but nothing like on Earth. All the buildings were the same white and grey, mainly oblong shaped, the only signage was over the doors of what were obviously offices or stores. Each sign was no more than three metres by one metre and were static or video advertising the name and the product.

Algier noted Sean's interest, "Protocol is all buildings are within similar shapes, colour and no unnecessary mess. You will see no advertising boards, even rubbish, plain but clean."

Sean looked, apart from the buildings, plants and trees there were only three-metre-tall posts every fifty metres or so that were road and pavement lighting. "Your drivers are good, with only blue lights they are moving out of the way and stopping at junctions, although I've not seen any traffic lights?"

Algier advised, "Police cars send out signals direct to other cars, they have no choice they automatically slow down and pull over. No need for traffic lights the junctions know the speed, the gaps, the time and automatically allows the correct vehicle to go first stopping the other vehicles. Police and this car being a king's transport get priority over everything. Indeed, I don't think I have ever stopped in this car on the road other than to get out at my destination."

Sean was just about to ask another question when clearly the lighting rules were not always held to. Coming up in front was a great stadium, oval in shape very similar to those on Earth but with a roof. Not only were there a few screens on the side advertising but also laser lights and varied floodlights. Algier added, "For special events such as this the Heavyweight Duel Champion of the World different lighting is allowed."

Kain asked, "Ready Sean, there is a big crowd?"

Sean did not answer as the car pulled up and he, Kain and Algier exited. Police either side but people and camera flashes all around, Sean noted they were actually on a red carpet. "Wow!" Upon entering the stadium, the party was met by varied people, all shaking or curtseying to Kain, Algier and Sean. Finally, they were in a side room with few people in.

"Your Highness a pleasure to see you," A big black man around his thirties was bowing to Kain.

Kain said, "Champ Syston do not be so formal, shake my hand." Syston shook both Kain's and Algier's hands.

Looking at Sean, Syston gave a big smile, "What a pleasure your Highness, you are a strapping lad."

Sean replied, "Thank you, you're a big lad!"

Syston laughed, "Obviously as I'm the Heavy Weight Champion of the World!"

"Mali how are you feeling about tonight?" Kain asked.

Syston replied, "Sheko is young and tough so I will need to be on my guard but I'm confident your subject will still be the champion at the end."

Kain smiled, "I would love you to remain as the champion, but you must look after yourself my friend, do not be too confidant Sheko is powerful." Kain then looked at Sean, "And you get front row seats; Sal please."

Sean looked as Sal joined them, "Come on Sean follow us." With that Sean followed Syston, Sal and others to his dressing room. Syston made a comment about using the facilities and changing then went into a side room. Sal explained, "Each duelist has a manager, coach and first aid present, I'm Syston's first aid this evening. All three are at the arena side, I and the coach can enter the arena during the round breaks."

"You said three, am I not the fourth?'"

"Yes, but as this is Saulten and you are a prince you can join us and watch."

Syston returned to the room, this time wearing a white all in one tight jumpsuit with some subtle grey markings on. Sal continued, "The man with him is an assessor he will watch me administer the TDL then put the guards on and check the vital signs on my tablet to then sign off for duel, watch."

Sean sat and watched the process unfold as Sal had stated. "Your Highness will stand with me. I am Gram, Syston's manager."

"Yes, thank you."

With this Sean, next to Gram, followed Syston, Sal and Hoy (Syston's Coach) to the arena. Sean was stopped just at the side of the arena, Gram next to him; Syston entered the arena with Sal and Hoy to the cheers of the crowd, music blaring and lights flashing. Sean looked around, the arena was oval shaped similar to that on the space station, he was in the middle, opposite was the opponent's group. Looking up Sean could see the six referees in position just in front of the glass, which had thousands of people sitting behind. The roof had varied lights flashing but clearly at each end of the oval were scoreboards showing zeros.

Sean looked and King Bier was sitting above the opponent's tunnel opposite, although he could not see up and behind his own tunnel Sean assumed Kain would be above him. "Oh no! What's that idiot doing out there?" Sean could not stop himself saying out loud.

Gram laughed, "His highness Prince Dain is the commentator, he is quite the celebrity on Earthen on our television." Sean watched as Dain did his presentation piece introducing the duelists, just like a boxing match. Sean did think of trying to trip his uncle over live on TV but held back. Dain completed the introductions and the chief referee spoke to both duelists before sending them to their ends, both now some thirty metres apart from each other. Sal and Hoy spoke to Syston before joining Sean and Gram in the tunnel, a force field materialised in front of them for protection.

All lights went off apart from the arena lighting pointing directly at the duelists and the scoreboards that were red but counting down from 10…at zero everything went green. Sean saw Syston go into defence mode, Sheko was clearly throwing punches. As the round progressed Sean could tell, like in boxing, that some punches were hitting. Syston was more static and Sheko was moving around within his area. At the break Sal and Hoy went to Syston, upon returning round two started. Syston appeared stuck to the floor, Sheko was occasionally wavering as he moved but neither went down.

Round three and instantly Syston went for Sheko, a couple of strong punches and Sheko hit the floor. The lights and scoreboard went red, with Syston's showing a big one score; Sean could hear the cheer from the crowd. Next to the large zero on Sheko's scoreboard smaller red digits were counting down from ten. Sheko got to his feet and went defensive just as the countdown reached two, as it reached zero the lights went green and Syston was attacking hard. Sheko did not go down again.

As Sal and Hoy were going to Syston for the next break Sean heard Gram say, "Tell him to stop playing around, respect the challenger."

Round four, Sheko had different ideas, moving faster he was clearly going for it. Somehow Sheko was going one way, turned quickly and threw three blows at Syston, Syston hit the floor, and Sean heard the crowd gasp. The end of round buzzer went - Sal and Hoy ran to the still fallen Syston.

"As you would say, saved by the bell!" Gram said to Sean but was gesturing with a clenched fist to the now sitting Syston. "Syston needs to finish him now he will not win on continuous."

The fifth round started, Syston defensive, Sheko giving all he could. Then Syston made his move, two quick arm movements then one joint blast, Sheko was unsteady, Syston took ten steps forward, arms joined and clenched, Sheko hit the floor. The arena went red, you could hear a pin drop...everything went green, claxons sounded, and the crowd went wild. Syston had won by a knockout as Sheko had been counted out. Sean punched the air in unison with the grinning Gram. Both remained in the tunnel as first the main assessor called the win to Syston then Dain made the award, a large medal adorned Syston's chest. Syston hugged and shook hands with Sheko before waving to all as he approached the tunnel where Sean was. Giving Sean a wink he continued to the changing room, Sal and Hoy following.

Sean and Gram took in the crowd for a while. Sean took a few steps into the arena to look back and up, seeing his father and Algeir laughing and smiling, their man had won. Gram led Sean to the changing room; Syston was sitting on the table, top undone down to the waist with Sal checking him. Syston seeing Sean called him over. "That looks painful!" Sean was looking at the bruising all down one side of Syston's chest.

"It is but don't tell anyone you have seen me like this." Sean noticed Syston had tears in his eyes as he said it.

Sean laughed, "Of course not, you are ok though?"

"Yes, he will be, a few of broken ribs but he will live." Sal answered for Syston.

With that the door opened, Kain and Algier entered. "Congratulations my friend you remain the Champion." Kain addressed Syston.

"Thank you Sire, it is both a personal honour and an honour for my Kingdom…about that knighthood?" Syston laughed.

"In the bag, it will be announced for the new year!" Kain shook Syston, Hoy and Gram's hands then beckoned Sean to follow him.

A few minutes later Kain, Algier and Sean were in a bar within the stadium joining what were clearly Saultens celebrating they're Champion Syston. Lots of hand shaking and, 'Your highnesses' later and Sean finally hid in a corner with Algier at his side.

"Did you enjoy that?" Algier asked.

"Yes, in a sporting way, but Syston is injured, you don't really notice that on TV."

"He will be fine; indeed, he is about to join the party look," Algier pointed to the door. Syston was entering the room, Sal and Hoy behind him. Sean laughed to himself, Syston got as many handshakes and pleasantries as he and Kain did. An hour in, Syston approached them both, "How much did you win?"

Algier looked uncomfortable, "Young man I'm a Councilor I don't do things like betting." The wink he gave Syston as he left suggested this was not the truth. Syston sat next to Sean, "So what did you think of it?"

"Awesome." Sean paused, "But your injuries are worrying."

Syston laughed, and then grimaced. "Sal has done a good job, temporary for now. Although I'm sure you will never duel, my advice, never underestimate an opponent."

FESTIVE FUN:
(CHAPTER 21)

Awakening Sean was happy, the fight last night was indeed awesome, and Saulten was awesome. He dressed then joined the breakfast table.

"What time of year is it?" Jenna asked.

Sean replied, "Easy, it's Christmas."

"Good, then you have bought all the presents you need?" Jenna asked.

"Oh, mm...I left them on Earth?"

Jenna could see through this, "Luckily I have arranged presents on Earth for Emma and Mush from you. As for anyone here...Sal and her mother Beatrice will take you shopping today to see our city centre."

Algier replied on Sean's behalf, "I'll go with them as I'm sure there are some shops Sean would prefer to go to with me, besides it is holiday time."

Within the hour Sean, Sal, Beatrice and Algier were driven the short distance to the city centre. Sean noted the traffic was busier the buildings denser and there were many people walking between what were clearly shand bars. Again, all the buildings looked alike, only their standard signage giving an idea of what was in store.

The motorcade came to a halt outside one shop; the police escorts were out of their vehicles and standing around the exiting party. The party led by Sal entered the shop, Sean looked around, and it was clearly a clothes shop. The internal layout was similar to an Earth shop, varied clothes around the walls, dummies and hangers. As it was Christmas there was tinsel and the odd Christmas tree but no way over the top. Sean looked at a few items noting many were obviously Earthen but there were Earth clothes as well, these appeared to have a higher price in credits than their Earthen equivalents.

Sal picking up on this explained, "As you know we love Earth culture thereby our shops will sell a mixture of Earthen and Earth products, Earth products because of transport etc. are dearer. Think of a credit like a pound, we do not have money but earn and spend credits no different than Earth currency. We can break plastic no different to your mother!"

Sean giggled, "I don't know Mum's size, so clothes is not a good pick?"

"Let me worry about that, you just watch."

Sean did as was told, some three shops in although all were clothes or related items which Sean would normally hate, watching Earthen life was of interest. People were scurrying around; complaining about the rush, "what rush," Sean could not help thinking. A few people would pass the police guards and speak to Sean; again, all were welcoming to him.

"This one is a bag shop, let me save you." Algier was now addressing Sal and Beatrice, "Sean would like a drink, you two are busy so let me take him across the road." With that Sean and Algier were at the exit, police guards around them. As they reached the road the police guards walked onto it holding what looked like light sticks. The approaching cars all stopped to allow Sean and Algier to cross. "Their police sticks send a signal to the cars which stop them."

Upon reaching the other side Algier led Sean to a similar looking shop to all the others but appeared to be advertising motorbikes on its screen. Sean following Algier walked through the main doors then saw that the inside was different. First there was a front show area full of motorbikes, no different than the outside of an Earth shop – indeed the roof above them was clear so appeared that they were outside. In front was a building that looked as though it had come from Earth, big windows, and posters of motorbikes, advertising the lot. Sean stopped, "Hold on," Then walked back out of the shop, looked Earthen clean and boring, walking the few steps back in and all was cluttered and full of colour, Earth.

"Again, to achieve building protocol all buildings look the same from the outside but in many cases are just shells to hide the real building inside. For standard shops such as the clothes ones we have been in there is no need however, motorbikes, cars, certain bars and the like will be different inside." Algier informed Sean.

Sean took this in but was distracted by the varied motorbikes on show. Most were white or silver including the wheels and tyres. The styling appeared very angular and boxy; none had obvious engines or exhausts. Sean stood next to one very brutal looking trials type motorbike, "Wow, this one is awesome!"

"Good choice Your Highness," The shops manager Henric was approaching. "It is a Girella All Sport utility bike, and it will go anywhere. As you can see it is electric powered so has no engine in Earth bike terms but rides and goes similar to Earth bikes. I am Henric the shop manager."

"Henric my friend, let's show our Prince around." With that Sean was shown varied Earthen motorbikes on the show area, eventually being led into the shop. This was closer to an Earth shop, the motorbikes looked like Earth bikes.

Henric explained, "As you will see your highness these bikes here are Earth bike body replicas however, our power plant is hidden behind what appears to be an Earth engine, touch it." Sean walked up to what was a Kawasaki Ninja replica, but upon touching the varied parts it was mainly plastic feeling, including the engine. "Looks good but feels strange." Sean stated.

"Please don't start Councilor Algier off." Henric was too late.

"I told you. An Earthen bike is nothing like an Earth bike in touch and feel, especially the ride!" Algier was virtually cheering as he spoke.

"The pollution, the noise Councilor." Henric was pleading to no avail.

"Show him the real stuff."

"Of course, this way."

Henric led Sean and Algier to another side of the shop. There were fewer motorbikes, but they stood out. "Earth bikes, look at that Harley it is beautiful!" Algier was on air.

Sean touched the first motorbike, "Yep Uncle Algier is right, the real deal. So, with all your pollution protocols why do you sell Earth bikes?"

"Fossil fuel is still available but only for pleasure riding, although you have to have a special license to ride one within strict guidelines." Henric informed.

"Unless you are a prince like me, I ride my Harley when I like, plus hit the V8 Mustang I have here!" Algier was smiling.

"Obviously your uncle has certain privileges that us normal Saultens do not. The good point being that only selected few Saultens will purchase a fossil vehicle be it car or bike which is why they are at a premium. Are you in the need for another bike Councilor?" Henric was in sales mode.

Sean looked at Algier who was obviously struggling, "Can I have a go on an Earthen bike, the Girella?"

"Yes, follow me." Sean was led by Henric to the rear of the shop, exiting they were in what was clearly a car park area still within the main building.

"Lots of space Your Highness. Note the roof is open as it is a cool clear day therefore, if your uncle wished to try an Earth bike he could?"

"Not today, let us give Sean the fun." Algier was not biting.

Sean was soon astride a smaller version of the Girella he had seen on show, helmet, elbow and kneepads on. "Has your highness ridden a motorbike before?" With a "Yes" being the response Henrics further instruction was made easier. "Throttle and brakes the same as an Earth bike but no gears so no clutch. Just place in gear with the switch on the left and it will go. Note, it will gain speed quick and with no noise, well a low whirring noise."

Sean followed the instruction and was soon riding the motorbike to the end of the car park some fifty metres there and back. After a couple of laps Sean stopped. "So, what do you think?" Algier asked.

"It feels just like an Earth bike but..." Sean thought, "No noise is an issue and is it the tyres? They don't feel soft enough."

Algier laughed out loud, "See I told you Earthen tyres do not have the feel of a good old Earth rubber tyre!"

Sean saw Henric raise his eyes before responding, "I know Councilor however, and Earth bikes cannot slide as an Earthen one can. Shall we show His Highness?"

Sean interrupted, "Yes please!"

Henric pointed, "The other switch on your left moves it from S for solid, to the 2 position not the full 10 and F for fluid setting. You will feel the bike allowing you to go slightly sideways. Watch the turn at the end, I suggest you have your legs down at that point and very slow speed. Do not wiggle or turn on the straight."

Sean took off; the motorbike did feel a bit different. Approaching the turn Sean slowed down, legs out he turned the handlebars. The motorbike appeared to slide in the direction Sean was aiming it, the turn being much tighter. A few more circuits and Sean was getting the hang of it. After the fourth circuit Sean was stopped and dismounted as shown by Henric.

"Look at the tyre, not rubber but an Earthen equivalent. More importantly look at the tread, as you can see it is a mesh but sticking out from the mesh are small soft bearings four across and a hundred or so around the whole tyre." Sean looked and could see this; Henric continued, "The hub is a very strong but localised magnetic generator. Inside the rubber coated bearings are basically metal. When the slide setting is set to S for solid the bearings can only rotate one way, go forward. Upon adjusting the slide setting the bearings can move sideways. Ultimately say when parking you can set the bearings to F and the bike will drive sideways."

"Wow," Was Sean's response.

"In Earthen motorbike racing you can with skill pull up to a bike in front hit the slide switch and right angle overtake it. With the correct setting you can turn a bike on its front tyre. Allowing the rear tyre to full slide keeping the front tyre locked. Obviously a very competent biker can do this. Try a 4 setting."

Sean took off with the new setting, approaching the turn a little over exuberantly, Sean ended up on his backside. Having checked if he was ok by the worried looking Henric, Sean was left to complete some further circuits. 'Wow,' he thought as he was finally cornering at quite tight angles and speed.

"Sean!" Sal shouted, "I am sure you should not be on motorbikes!"

Sean, once stopping, attempted the, "Algier's fault" line but Algier did not want to argue with Sal either. Sean's motorbike excursion was not mentioned in the evening although Algier promised Sean a good Christmas present!

The next morning Sean was at the table eating breakfast. Kain said, "If you recall we are here to formally note the dignitaries, as you call them, time on Earth. Princess Gabrielle is here already as she arrived with her grandfather before the boxing so you will have some time with her today...see some teenage Earthen life."

"I thought Sean was helping me to prepare the Christmas hall decorations today?" Jenna challenged.

"He can first thing then spend the afternoon and early evening with Princess Gabrielle, I am off to the council. Algier let us go!"

Sean noted the strange look his mother gave his father but finished his breakfast to join her in the function hall. The hall was a large room, square, and a glass wall opposite the door end looking to the garden. On the right was clearly a stage. In each corner were tables already set, the middle part in front of the stage was clear. Sean noted the tables had some Christmas decorations but not the walls or solid ceiling. Jenna led Sean to the stage, and then took centre stage, looking out to the hall. "Ok let's see, Christmas theme!" With this the walls came alive. Each wall looked like snow fields, with a mixture of snow animals and snowmen randomly shown. The snowmen and certain animals such as the penguins had Christmas scarfs on. The higher part of the walls going into the ceiling were day going to night sky and stars.

"Christmas tree centre wall, Santa centre clear wall!" A 3D fully decorated Christmas tree appeared as requested with a 3D Santa and Elves also. Sean exclaimed, "Wow this cool!"

Jenna continued, "Now the fun part. Ceiling snow, room animate!" As instructed the hall came to life, the animals moved, the snowmen danced, the tree glistened then the ceiling snowed.

"Wow I feel as though I'm actually in the North pole." Sean was surveying all around with a big smile.

"So that's the decorating done?"

"No, I will work with the staff to complete the table settings and arrange the stage with the band; It's not all easy you know! Of course, you need to get ready for the rest of the day with Gabrielle, shame as I was going to go riding or something."

Sean could sense some tension in his mother's voice. "I 'd love to stay here but seeing Gabrielle is part of the deal, right?"

"Yes, it is but what's the deal" Sean looked a little perplexed. Jenna continued, "Remember tomorrow for the party we will have King Ders and Kiera. Plus, Alex and Det with King Vul. Having that man here in my house makes my skin crawl!"

Sean giggled, "So I will meet all the Kings tomorrow?"

"Not King Ain, he was not part of the visit although invited."

"Sean, good afternoon!" Princess Gabrielle was at their side. Sean looked at her, although wearing what were clearly Earthen style clothes it was not formal attire. The skirt was short, and the top was low, Gabrielle all made up, 'yep,' Sean thought, 'I am going to have a good day.' Things got better as Jeng arrived "I'm yours and Gabrielle's main bodyguard today!"

Within the hour Sean and the girls had exited the motorcade and entered a building. Sean looked around and could see that it appeared to be one big room but with varied sections, the music, although strange to him, was loud. The place was busy with young Earthens.

"This is a teen club, we have food, dancing, games, bowling and because it is Christmas ice skating." Gabrielle informed, "Ice skating is my favourite. Over in the corner let's go." Sean followed Gabrielle; all the teens looked at Sean's party as they walked through. Jeng and the four uniformed Police guards around them kept any from approaching although Sean saw most did tip their heads in acknowledgement of their royalty. Approaching large doors, entering then walking through a corridor they arrived at a dressing area.

"Put this large coat on, do it up and put on these skates, very similar to Earth." Jeng was instructing and providing Sean with his snow wear. Now dressed the party entered the ice area. Jeng continued, "It is like an ice rink on Earth but a round dome shape, the ceiling is dropping snow as are the walls like you saw in your hall however, this is the best bit..." With that Jeng hit Sean with a snowball. Before Sean could react, Gabrielle joined in and another hit Sean. Taking some five minutes to catch the skating Gabrielle, Sean grabbed her. "The floor is moving and yet we are skating, where did you get the snowballs?"

"You are strong." Gabrielle winked as she looked at Sean's arms that were around her. Sean immediately let go. Gabrielle giggled, "Look at the floor closely." Gabrielle was crouching - Sean joined her crouching. "Another version of fluid balls. The difference is they are a lot smaller, because they are on the ice they are cold and have a glue like material so you can push them together to make what appears like a snowball, when they hit they disintegrate giving the affect, plus they are soft similar to our pool balls so don't hurt!"

"Once back on the ice they move around the skates not stopping you so you skate through them, but you can pick them up again!" As Sean was hit by a further snowball. Jeng was now skating away after that comment. The throwing snowballs and skating continued for some time. Gabrielle at one point, realising Jeng was too good and accurate, joined force with Sean to pin Jeng down and catch her in their crossfire.

Skating fun over and they were in the bar area. Drinks ordered Sean sat to survey all around. Apart from the varied staff all the people were young, his Police guards, let alone Jeng were clearly the eldest in the building. "Are adults not allowed here?"

"Correct, it is a teen club so thirteen to nineteen's only apart from staff of which only the least required are here. Normally Jeng and the guards would be barred. But we are royalty." Gabrielle informed. With this Gabrielle snuggled up closer to Sean, whispering in his ear.

"Our adults allow us fun time and within reason we can grow up here, the drink is mildly alcoholic if we want. We can dance to loud crazy music, or just hug and get close..."

Jeng was obviously listening, as she interrupted, "Not too close there are boundaries young lady!"

Gabrielle laughed, now talking normally, "And when alone we can hug and kiss. It was in a similar club in Bier City that I had my first real kiss. How about you big ears?" Jeng laughed in response. "Sean let us dance the Earthen way!" With this Gabrielle dragged Sean onto the dance floor, now alone with no Jeng or bodyguards by their side. Sean watched Gabrielle who started to dance to the music, it was rock type music but every few seconds it seemed to come to a definite stop then start. Gabrielle and the other teens around them would dance, freeze then dance. With Gabrielle's guidance Sean soon had the moves. With the quick dances mastered Sean was ready for the slow dances, or at least he thought. The slow dancing was similar to Earth's, the songs had fewer words but more music however, and Gabrielle was very close. Sean soon got lost in the moment; Gabriele was not only close but moving parts of her body against and all around his.

"My turn!" Jeng was interrupting.

"You can't you are too old!" Gabrielle was defensive.

Jeng gave Sean a look; Sean thought then said, "Of course, sorry Gabrielle but I did say I would dance with Jeng once, may I?"

Gabrielle passed a, "Remember I am a Princess," comment to Jeng before leaving.

"I will dance like on Earth not too close young man." Jeng smiled.

"Oh, that's a shame." Sean responded. In a different way the dance with Jeng was more warming to him.

After a second dance with Jeng, Sean joined Gabrielle at the table. Jeng gave them some distance. "So how are we to get to know each other if you are dancing with her?"

"Jeng is my friend, I am sure we will have more time tomorrow as you are at our party?"

"Yes, I am and yes we will but with you only being here for what another week we should plan things."

Sean thought this was an odd comment. "Gabrielle I would love to spend some time with you but Christmas and all that."

Gabrielle sat upright. "You do not get it do you?" Sean looked perplexed. "This is our opportunity as Prince and Princess to get to know one another. Think. We would be the first mixed royalty pairing in Earthen history."

Sean sat bolt upright, startled even, "What, what are you on about I hardly know you. Besides I'm spoken for!"

Gabrielle gave Sean a disgusted look, "And your duty as a royal, surely you know you should consider someone closer to your position?"

"Oh my god, this is planned or something. No, you would not date me just because we are royal?"

"Why not it is our duty?" Gabrielle was looking perplexed.

"No, definitely no. I'm sorry but you have the wrong idea, I mean you are gorgeous but..." Sean could not finish as Gabrielle had already stood and was leaving. Jeng sat next to him, "I think we will let her go away on her own, follow me." With that Jeng led Sean over the road to another building with a small Earth diner look to it inside. Ordering them both a burger and coke they were sitting in a booth.

"Arranged marriages for royalty are just as common on Earth as here young Sire!" Jeng started. "Chosen suitors may not always be royal but should be of a standing, say a prominent dignitaries daughter or granddaughter, or even a honoured ranked soldier."

Sean thought for a while. "Are you saying Gabrielle, Kiera... even you have been brought into my life for me to find me an appropriate suitor?"

"Possibly Sal, Livia even if you think Earthen ways of numerous wives for differing reasons, but yes your father through duty will have arranged these opportunities."

"Dad, he does not fail to disappoint me. I'm sorry Jeng, I do love you but like a big sister, Emma is the only one for me."

Jeng smiled, "Hey look I'm not after you. Being honest yes given the opportunity to meet a prince of course I thought that, but you are too young for me. I think your father is over thinking this because of your relationship with Emma." Sean's look suggested he needed more. "I have said too much, let's enjoy our burger then you need to talk to your father. Please do not get me in trouble." Sean gave Jeng a hug.

Upon returning to the palace Sean went gunning for his father, only to be informed he was still working. Jenna obviously knew what was going on and decided it was an Algier's job to deal with.

"So, Dad was trying to split me up from Emma then?"

"Oh Sean, no not exactly." Algier was clearly uncomfortable. "As Jeng told you it would be preferred for royalty to marry the right person of station..."

"I get all that royalty crap." Sean rudely interrupted, "I'm not interested in it, but why does Dad hate Emma so? Come on he married an Earthling!"

"That is the crux of the matter. Your father did break all the protocols; no, he shattered them by marrying an Earthling. However, he was in his twenties, at his peak and in control of his feelings. Well kind of." Algier chuckled. "You are nearly fifteen and maybe a little early to be claiming love..." Algier stopped at Sean's disbelieving stare. "Look you are fifteen do you really know Emma is right for you or her you? Kain is not splitting you up but he does want you to meet other girls, even women before you make that decision."

"So, you all think my relationship is just a teen thing..."

"Maybe, you would say on Earth a 'puppy love'?"

With this Sean stood, "What! No, I decide whom I want to be with, I'm not a puppy. Where is Dad I'll show him what for!"

"In hand Algier?" Jenna was now in the room.

"No, your turn I'm off to bed." Algier stood, gave Sean a hug then left.

"And you are part of this?"

"No, but I am aware of the what's and whys."

"Mum no! Of all these...hypocrites you being human I thought I could trust you more."

Sean went to leave but unusually his mother grabbed his arm. "Sit! You know I do not like their ways but I, as you, have to understand both the Earthen way and the responsibilities of royalty. What your father is doing is his way, he does not believe in it, but he wants you to make informed decisions. You and Emma could be too young to be thinking such a long-term commitment."

Sean looked at his mother, rarely was she that straight or defensive with him. "So, you think it is puppy love?"

Jenna thought, "No, I believe in love at first sight. I believe you will know who that person is when you meet them. I love Emma too, you know that, but could you be too young? I'm sorry honey but I cannot answer that, and you cannot blame me or others for thinking that."

"I love Emma, I miss her everyday surely I can only go by what I feel?"

"Yes, but things can change with age, with experiences. Sean, I cannot believe I'm saying this. I was a fifteen-year-old girl and loved many things and boys, well not many, but none are with me now, fifteen is young."

"If you had met Dad at fifteen?"

"Ok you have me on that one but take note of my comments before you judge."

"But you, no you and Dad like Emma?"

"Yes, we both do as I have said. We see you and Emma as a young us. Your father sees all the troubles we went through coming your way, he is being protective."

"His protection always seems to differ from my wants!"

Oddly Jenna laughed, Sean looked perplexed again. "How can I, your parent, answer that honestly? Look we sometimes think what we know is best and will always try to influence our children in the right direction. You are not the only teen who has gone against his parent's wishes, maybe Granddad John should tell you my teenage stories."

"Mum you disappoint me."

A tear came to Jenna's eye, "That proves I am also human and not always right." A big hug was all that was needed to end the conversation.

PARTY TROUBLE:
(CHAPTER 22)

The next morning was Christmas Eve. Kain was avoiding Sean. Sean took every opportunity to glare at his father that he could. Jenna deciding it was best for Sean to help her with the final preparations; Kain found a need to personally meet the visiting kings in the palace outer accommodation. Following two-hour long FaceTime's to Mush and Emma, to whom which Sean repeated his love for her so often, she had asked, "Is there something wrong?" Sean had got away with a simple, "No, I just miss you so much." Sean dressed for the party in a very royal suit with a distinct military look and joined the party in the hall.

"Be civil at least around me or I will deal with you!" Kain addressed Sean in Earthen mode but laughed as Jenna clearly gave Kain a dig in back whilst winking at Sean. Standing at the hall entrance: Kain, Jenna, Algier and Sean were introduced to all entering, 'boy this royalty work can be tiring' Sean thought as the greetings went on and on. The only differences being when first King Ders entered with his entourage that included: Anders, Beatrice and Sal, her cuddle with Sean broke all the stuffiness. King Bier and his group were introduced next, Sean could not help but feel the aura around both the kings he had just met, as indeed his father had in this formal setting.

King Vul's entrance was grander. His entourage led by himself, included his four wives then varied siblings, stood out for both its size and colour. Most already in the hall wore light coloured clothing; Vultens predominantly wore black and all their clothing appeared with a military style. King Vul shook Kain's hand, Kain gave Vul a brief hug – Vul was nearly half a metre taller than Kain. Vul gave Jenna a big hug, Jenna's small frame nearly disappearing completely into the big arms of Vul. "You would look better in Vulten black Jenna, my offer is still there".

Jenna removing herself from Vul's grasp. "I know Your Highness, but I have King Kain trained now and therefore have no energy to train another." Both Kain and Vul laughed at this. Sean also noted his mother had her fingers crossed behind her back whilst saying this.

"Prince Sean. You are larger in the flesh although could do with some broadening out." Vul addressed Sean as he gave him his hand to shake. Sean could not help but freeze, this man was enormous, and his hands were bigger than Sean's head. Meekly holding Vul's hand Sean shook it. Again, Vul and Kain laughed.

"Hi Sean, good to meet you again." Prince Alex gave Sean a hug.

"And you," Was Sean's response.

"Prince Det," Was all Det managed, no handshake.

"I know mono," Was Sean's thought reply to which Det snarled.

With that Sean and party went to their corner to finally sit, Sean noted Prince Dain was already sitting, surrounded by at least five young women. The hall was clearly separated by kingdoms in each corner. The four kings took to the stage, Kain being host made the introductions and welcomes to all. The other three kings reciprocated, all appeared in the Christmas spirit. After the formalities dinner was served, again in each owns kingdom area. After the meal of which Sean skipped at least the third and fifth course, or was it the fourth? He had forgotten; a band took to the stage.

Jeng was the first over to Sean, "And now we mingle."

Sean got up to join Jeng in meeting other people; most were closer to his age. "Are you not here with Daved?"

Jeng replied, "No after what he did here the other day Kain gave him extended leave. Besides we are no longer together."

"Oh, I'm sorry."

"Don't be it was coming to an end; besides I may have a go at you again...NOT!" Jeng and Sean both laughed.

"Your Highness you look very handsome in Earthen clothes!"

Sean turned; the vision of Kiera all dressed up was enough to stump him for words.

"May I have the honour of the first dance please?" Kiera curt-sied.

"Yes, definitely yes." Sean was hooked; Jeng gave him a stare to bring him back down to Earthen. Sean and Kiera danced to a couple of quick songs before getting close for a slow song. 'OMG' thought Sean as Kiera danced like Gabrielle had.

"Changing your mind?"

Sean looked to see Princess Gabrielle standing beside them. "Your Highness of course you must dance with Prince Sean." Kiera was in subject mode making way for Gabrielle to dance with Sean. Gabrielle was making a point, she was virtually stuck to Sean's body, 'maybe I have decided a bit quick' was Sean's thought.

These ended quickly, "Why are you dancing with Gabrielle!"

Sean turned to look at Prince Det, "Naff Off." Sean felt a surge of pain in his head; Det was trying to get into his head. Sean nearly fell over but jolted up hitting Det square on with both hands – Det flew across the floor knocking other dancers over. Det turned on the floor and threw a power punch at Sean who hit the floor. Sean raised then went to attack Det but froze.

"Enough!" Was the bellow from King Vul, now between the sparring teens.

"What is going on?" Kain was now between Vul and Sean.

"Prince Sean attacked me for no reason!" Det claimed.

"Rubbish, you were in my head, you started it!" Sean gave Det a snarl.

"Enough stand like men!" Vul commanded. Sean saw Det stand, quiet but straight, Sean copied.

"King Kain, what have you to say?" Vul addressed Kain; Sean could tell Vul was sizing Kain up in power terms.

Kain stood tall, "King Vul. I will deal with my son."

"He attacked me I wish to duel." Det called.

With this the whole room went completely silent and no movement. "Young sire that may not be the best course of action," Secretary Seth was addressing Det.

"Wait, as Patron of the Dueling Association that was a clear duel request." Dain had joined them.

"Prince Dain, keep out of this." Kain turned on his brother.

"Have you forgotten Earthen ways; it is a clear legitimate request which I support."

Kain turned back, and walked closer to Vul. "I am aware of Earthen protocols however, these are teenagers just having a disagreement, let us keep this in context."

Vul and Kain were eyeing each other, although Vul was the much larger in body, he was obviously aware of Kain and his powers. Sean went to say something, but a pull on his arm by Sal stopped him.

"King Kain, my son has formally requested a duel with your son. Both are within the allowed age grouping and standing. Protocol would suggest this goes ahead." Vul was pushing then trying to lessen the impact, "As per protocol it is only a controlled duel neither will be hurt. Therefore, I, King Vul, formally request this duel in support of my son."

The hall gasped; Sean saw Jenna was now at Kain's side. Kain looked at Jenna, and then at Sean, "So be it, I will have my council arrange this. Both Princes go to your rooms!"

Again, Sean could not respond but was being pulled by Sal to the lift then to his room. "You idiot what did you hit Det for?"

"I told you all, he started it, he was in my mind."

"No one could see that all they saw was you push and use your powers on him, you are being seen as the aggressor."

"That's not fair, anyway why am I to duel that idiot."

"Sean, you have attacked in public, a prince. He has the right to call a duel."

"Dad can stop this, why did he give into Vul."

"I'll answer that, please leave us Sal." Jenna had joined them, Sal left as requested.

Jenna sat next to Sean, hugging him, "You are a fool for reacting to Det even if he was attacking you. Your father can only stop this by taking on Vul in a duel."

"Dad would kick Vul's arse in a duel."

"Maybe, but their fight being kings would be to the death."

"Oh shit!" Sean exclaimed, "A combat not a duel why?"

"You watch but do not learn. If two kings dueled in anger the one that lost would never be able to live with the disgrace, death would be the preferred outcome. Besides as you have often said it is about time you took responsibility for your own actions."

Sean felt his body drop, the enormity of the situation came across him. "If Dad had responded aggressively then he would have fought to the death for me?"

"Yes," Jenna hugged Sean. "Against all my beliefs, my son fighting in a controlled manner with very little chance of injury compared to my husband fighting to the death. I'm sorry honey but in thought I told, no, demanded your father to stand down. Go to bed and think after all we have Christmas in the morning." As Jenna stood to leave Sean went after her, "I'm sorry mum."

Sean woke to Christmas morning, running to the lift upon exiting he was advised to go to the sitting room, not the breakfast room. Upon entering the sitting room Sean could see all present, "Merry Christmas. Have I missed breakfast?"

"Merry Christmas to you. No, we are just having drinks and light finger food, last night's meal was enough. Give me a Christmas hug."

Sean responded to his mother's request with a big hug. "Sean, we will not speak of last night's events today, it is Christmas Day. I'm sure Algier and Anders will resolve the conflict tomorrow, or I may shuffle my council." Sean noted both Algier and Anders (who were present with Beatrice and Sal) drop their heads upon Kain's words. "Anyway, Merry Christmas to you Son," Kain gave Sean a hug.

"Present time!" Sean smiled as Jeng gave him a wink after declaring this. Jeng then went to the real Earth Christmas tree in the corner to issue out the presents. Most presents were small ones, Sean knew that this was all about the family and the thought as he knew most had what they already needed. Opening Mush's present, a history of West Ham United Sean chuckled. Upon opening Emma's Fitbit Sean thought aloud, "Mum what did I get Emma and Mush?"

Jenna giggled, "You will see when you FaceTime them later, and don't forget we will FaceTime Granddad and Grandma later. Thank you for the perfume it has a lovely fresh odour to it."

Sean winked at Sal. "Thank you all for my presents, it was not expected," Jeng was being very honest. "And of course, inviting me for today." Sean thought a hug was needed - Jeng received the hug warmly. With all the presents open Algier stood, "So young man you should have the present from me."

"Oh, sorry Uncle, did I miss it?"

"No, no follow me."

Sean followed his uncle to the door, before exiting he heard, "Algier if it was not Christmas!" Jenna was goading.

Algier led Sean outside to see a large plain box on the path, "I will help you lift the box." As both lifted the box Sean could see his present, "Wow! A Girella motorbike, really!"

"Yes, hiding it from your parents was going to be hard so I told them. Thankfully they cannot divorce an in law, although my head still hurts from your father's response." Algier chuckled. "Helmet on, give it a go but please be careful."

Sean geared up and was soon riding up and down the path. Seeing his parents could see him from the sitting room Sean did think of trying a wheelie but thought, 'no', he would only get Algier in trouble. Some half hour later and Sean was back with all in the siting room.

"My best present ever." Sean announced purposely, giving his parents a look so as they would not comment.

"FaceTime your friends before dinner please." Jenna instructed. Mush was the first call; he loved the signed Arsenal shirt Sean had got him, but he complained that he had actually gone into to buy and handle the West ham book but, "Hey it was for a friend."

Emma's call was just as fun. A big "missing you" numerous blown kisses started the call from both.

"Did you like my present? As I do think you are fit!"

Sean went red and even considered seeing if he could change the redness settings on the screen before answering. "Yes, it is great, it will make me think about fitness. I can pair it with yours so as we can compete...not that you need to be any fitter!"

Emma giggled, "As for your present, it's amazing." Emma was now holding the necklace around her neck to the screen.

"Just like your mother's, real quality gold too, how did you know I liked it?"

Sean went red again; "You have told me once or twice besides the two most favourite women in my life deserve the same thing, although Dad bought Mum's." This worked; Emma was gushing and going on about how wonderful Sean was. Sean thought 'I bet it has the same protection gadgetry as mum's.' The call finally over, Sean went down for dinner. Surprisingly Dain joined them for dinner with his favoured girlfriend, disappearing to his room with her after dinner. Sean sat with Jeng, looking around – his father and mother were in a corner with headsets listening to music together, Sal with her mother and father and Algier sitting with Wort and Lans. Wort and Lans had served the dinner, assisted by Sal and Jenna but also joined in the festivities.

"Your family?" Sean asked Jeng.

"They are all at home in Ainten, I have spoken to them. The chance of spending Christmas in a palace could not be missed." Jeng then addressed the room, "Everyone, it's time for games!"

With that Jeng managed to have them all playing some standard Earth games such as charades, the only break being when Jenna and Sean FaceTimed her parents. The evening ended quite late with all watching or pretending to watch between napping an Earthen version of A Christmas Carol. Sean found this very interesting, him being probably the only one to watch it in full.

DUEL TRAINING:
(CHAPTER 23)

Boxing day and Sean was at the breakfast table, again no one was really eating. "Sean, whilst Algier and Anders go to resolve the situation you will spend time with me."

"A bit harsh sending them both to work on Boxing Day Dad?"

"And whose fault is it?"

"Oops, sorry Uncle, sorry Anders." Both men acknowledged Sean's apology before leaving to see if a diplomatic solution could be had. "Let's go!" With that Sean followed his father outside to see two motorbikes.

"Are we going for a ride?"

"Yes, me and you, gear up, and make sure you put that backpack on. We are going to have a father son day plus a chance to talk." Sean knew a talk was needed but motor biking, 'yes please!'

Both astride their bikes Kain led them to the rear of the palace, gates opened, and they continued first onto clear roads then onto some dirt roads. Kain was pushing but not hard allowing Sean to keep within a few metres. Eventually Kain pulled up next to a ridge. Sean stopped, dismounted and looked up. The ridge was about one hundred metres in height and the end could not be seen either side in length.

"We will climb this ridge. Gloves, boots and more appropriate helmet are in the bike side containers."

Sean did not question this as he and Kain had climbed previously. After gearing up Kain headed to the foot of the ridge. "Eh, should we not have ropes?" Sean thought it was now time to question.

"Why you have climbed before, this will be easy?"

"Yes, but with safety gear?"

"I will not speak to you down here, if you want to talk you have to make it to the top. You see that small ledge sticking out about ten metres up let's head for that." Kain started to climb.

Sean stood still, before he moved, he heard in his head, "Trust me, I love you. You are in no danger." Sean gulped then took the first step, within a few minutes he was on the ledge next to his father. "Now the next ledge about another ten metres, you go first." Sean looked up, then down, then at his father.

"Ok," He was off climbing. Upon reaching the second ledge, again with Kain next to him Sean stopped and looked down.

"Feeling scared? Don't watch." With that Kain jumped backwards off the ledge, Sean screamed. Kain fell a metre or so but then straightened and was now hovering in front of Sean. "We have Air Drift packs on our backs, think Jetpacks. Sorry I made you jump." Kain laughed. "Simply think up and you rise, down and you descend." Kain moved up then down a metre away from Sean in the air.

"OMG – I can fly?"

"Yes, give it a go, try saying up and down rather than thinking it for now."

Sean took a deep breath then jumped off the ledge, the Air Drift unit kept him floating. Sean said, "Up" and he ascended, "Down" and he descended. Hovering next to Kain. "Can I fly like Superman?"

"Yes, but with more lessons. Hovering and the reassurance you have it on your back is all you need for now. We were climbing remember." With that Kain was back on the ledge and climbing up the ridge face. Sean thought 'I could just fly up, no exercise.' Sean landed on the ridge then followed his father climbing. Upon reaching the top of the ridge both stopped for a drink.

"So, you are trying to marry me off then?" Sean decided now was the time to talk.

"No, just giving you options. Your mother has explained this?"

"Yes, but still as my Dad surely what you are trying to do is wrong?"

"In what way is it wrong. Remember you are royal and fifteen."

"Getting on for sixteen. But I get it, why do you hate Emma?"

Kain smirked, "I do not hate Emma, whatever gave you that idea? Actually, I like her very much. It is your problem not mine."

Sean was taken aback by this but thought further. "Accepting that you did this for your own valid reasons, look at the trouble it has caused. I nearly lost Emma before Christmas and now, well the duel is because of it."

Kain thought, "Yes in a roundabout way. I was not to know that Det wanted Gabrielle, he did not show this. Mind you he does not show anything."

"So, because of you I have to fight." Sean was not going to let go.

"Yes. Do not tell your mother I said this, but it will be the making of you as a man."

"Is that your parent or Earthen side talking?"

"Do you wish to challenge me on all of my Earthen ways? I was born and bred here, no I do not wish to ask any forgiveness for that," Kain gave Sean a stare. "I did not expect or wish you to duel however, it is only like say the kickboxing fights you had a few years ago. You were into kickboxing in a big way, until that Hamling kid joined in. You should have let me deal with him." Kain paused. "I am by no ways the perfect father; indeed, I am still learning. My love, support and protection for you are unquestionable. If the duel goes ahead you will be fine, I promise."

Sean looked at Kain, "Then promise me you will love, support and protect Emma in the same way if she is MY chosen one."

"You insult me even to think that I would not. If Emma is the one, then yes of course. Now can we have some more fun?"

"Ok but I'm watching you."

"Good. Let me just make an adjustment to your pack. There, now see that small mount about twenty metres away?"

"Yes?"

"Watch me." With that Kain started to run then leaped into the air. Not flying but cushioned Kain made the last ten metres to the mount airborne. Sean thought 'that was easy', so set off. His run was good; the cushioned jump was better, the distance wrong. Kain bellowed with laughter as Sean landed but slipped backwards down the two-metre-high mount. Looking up at his father, "That's not funny!" Even Sean could not stop laughter coming out.

After helping Sean to his feet Kain said, "Concentrate look there is another mount, me first." Kain ran, jumped and landed spot on. Sean again took a deep breath then set off, this time landing on the mount next to his father. "Cool, can we do more?"

Kain took off; Sean followed both jumping to varied mounts. Some twenty minutes in and Sean asked for a break. Taking on water, "Wow Dad this is crazy, but exhilarating."

"Yes, on Earthen Air Drifting is a sport, we are actually using an old course. It is surprisingly good exercise even though the

Air Drift units cushion the jumps but do not propel."

"Wow I could take this sport up?"

"Yes, but you would need to live on Earthen," Kain stopped and looked at Sean. "Ok let's see who can get to the ridge edge first. You see those mounts to your left some six or seven, there are similar to the right. Pick left or right then when I say go you Air Drift all the way to the ridge edge just beyond the last mount. Left is the easier route."

"I'll take right, I know you want to win so the left was a red herring." Sean said, both then laughed.

"Ready, 3, 2, 1, Go!" With that both took off. Sean felt great as he made every mount landing spot on. Upon reaching the last mount in what felt like seconds Sean made out the place they had started and ran for it, only to be beaten by his father by about fifteen metres.

Both sat on the floor laughing, "I knew you would question my instruction; the left is slightly shorter. Although I am a fully developed man so should have won as I did."

"Can I mush you?" Was all Sean thought of to say.

"One last thing." Sean looked quizzed.

Kain stood and walked to the edge of the cliff, Sean joined him looking down the full one hundred metres. "This is high, but I have my air pack on."

"Exactly come here, let me adjust the pack. Let me see ten, no twenty that should do it."

"Do what?" Sean was now intrigued.

"Jump. Headfirst, backwards or like a sky diver." Kain was serious.

"Jump off the ridge, down there."

"Trust me you have an Air Drift on, enjoy the free fall, do not fight it."

Sean looked at his father, "Ok here goes." Sean moved to the ridge lip, took a sideways look at his father then jumped. The free fall was exhilarating, about seventy metres down Sean felt the Air Drift unit kick in, by twenty metres off the floor he stopped and hovered. "Wow!" He screamed as the unit then landed him safely on the floor. "Are you ok?" Sean felt his father asking in his head. "OMG that was awesome!" Was Sean's unspoken reply. "Can I do it again?"

"Next time, watch this." Sean looked up to see his father's Air Drift unit falling on its own. As Sean's had done the unit stopped about twenty metres from the ground then landed safely. "Watch out below, don't panic." Sean looked up. Kain was now flying towards him in a diving shape with no Air Drift unit on. Sean gasped. Kain about fifteen metres above Sean put out his arms, flipped upright then came to a stop hovering just above Sean. "OMG you can fly?"

Kain descended slowly and stood next to Sean, "No I cannot fly however, I can use my power to stop me hitting the floor. Or even this." With that Kain raised a couple of metres off the floor, then descended back down.

"Wow. So why the Air Drift packs if we can do that?"

Kain laughed, "You mean I can do this with practice, you cannot at present. The Air Drift packs are safer which is why they are generally used. I will train you the other bit one day. Now more importantly, I am going to thrash your butt in the race home."

"You can't say that Dad! Besides racing the bikes that fast is dangerous!"

"Is it? Remember how you do the protective bubble, so if when riding you are about to come off think bubble and you will protect yourself. How do you think we and the car were hardly damaged by that twenty-ton truck?"

"You mean the light I saw, you in a trance was you putting a protective bubble around us and the car?"

"Yes, it sapped a lot of my strength hence the over the top power. Somehow, I light up when mad or at full power. As you do not know the way it counts as your win if you remain within ten metres of me as we reach the palace gates."

Sean did not respond but mounted his motorbike and gave chase to his father. With the empty paths and open road both were moving fast. Never on Earth could you ride as fast as this however, believing in his powers Sean felt safe. Sean could see the palace ahead and hit the throttle, but his father pulled away.

"Damn! What twenty metres?" Sean shouted as he came to a stop at the gates.

Kain laughed, "I will not disappoint you, let's call it a draw. After all you have the smaller power bike so at full speed you had no chance on the flat road to this gate."

"Do you always have to cheat?"

Kain thought, "No but I do always like to win!"

Kain and Sean entered the eating room. "Did he do the ridge jump thing?"

"Yes Mum, it was awesome."

"Really, it nearly gave me a heart attack when he did it to me." Jenna laughed.

"It gave me a red cheek, your mother slapped me hard if I recall." Kain got all in the room laughing.

"You Air Drifted Mum?"

Jenna put on a false scowl, "Really yes, I was young once you know!" Again, all laughed.

"I am sure our master democrats will have good news for us to keep this light atmosphere?" Kain was addressing Algier and Anders.

"I need to get something or be somewhere in the bar room." Algier headed for the door, Sean laughed.

Anders cleared his throat, "I am sorry sire, but it does appear a genuine challenge and...well I better assist Algier." With that Anders headed for the door. Knowing both were still in ear shot Kain shouted, "I will join you both in the bar for your leaving drinks. I am overdue a council restructure," Kain winked at Sean as he followed the two councilors, or was it 'ex councilors' Sean laughingly thought.

"I do not agree with this at all!" Jenna shouted as loud as she could. "However, I am sure you will come to no harm. I need a drink, a large one." With that Jenna filled her glass then Sal's, Beatrice, Jeng and Lan's - who had appeared from nowhere. Sean looked at his mother, "A last drink for the condemned man?" This worked Sean was provided with wine as the others. Although the duel was serious all were able to have a fun evening chatting. Lans again breaking all the rules telling stories of Jenna and Kain when young, Sean found these stories both fun and informative.

The next day Sean felt a clearly more serious tone to the atmosphere, with the instruction at breakfast that Sean needed duel training he was soon in the Palace's small arena. "So, time to kick butt again, remember revenge is sweet!"

"Hi Jeng, am I fighting you?"

"Yes, but serious this time."

"Serious but controlled." Sal was entering with Syston. Sean ran up to Syston, "Wow am I going to train with you?"

"No, I am still injured you know however, I will be your coach. Sal will prepare you including some TDL as this is training so we do not want anyone hurt." With that Sean was geared up and given a TDL shot, as was Jeng. "That should bring you both to fifty per cent power."

"A bit low Sal?" Jeng questioned.

"Training remember; besides I know you can kill. Not sure about him. But don't be easy make him work."

Followed were a few hours of intense training. Sean thought Syston was great, not only providing rule tips but also some moves. After the initial couple of duels Sean could tell Jeng was being serious, their fighting was hard. This was repeated the next day, Sean was clearly being prepared. The difference being Jeng was pushing harder, in one round Jeng hit so hard Sean hit the floor face first, even though this was training as he got up, blood coming from his nose, Jeng continued to fight.

Nearing the end of the session Kain entered. "Drawn blood Jeng, well done. Cease please." Jeng stopped fighting, Sean thought shall I...no, and also stopped. "Syston how is Sean doing?"

"Very well sire. He is struggling to get over Jeng being a girl or even a good friend, but his technique is good."

"He has good power but needs to work on his reflexes, I would have won if as Syston suggests I was also not holding back a little. Although giving a prince a bloody nose is fun." Jeng advised whilst smirking.

"And how do you feel Sean?"

"I'm good, they are right I don't feel scared I have the power but do need to concentrate more. Can I have another go at Jeng?" Sean turned and gave Jeng a stare, but both doubled over with laughter; he did not expect Jeng to just stick her tongue out at him. "Enough we will complete the last session tomorrow," With Kain's word the session was over.

The evening started off light-hearted, most kept away from talking about the coming duel until Dain joined them. "Have you a dueling name young Sean for my introductions?"

"What introductions?"

Dain recoiled, "Oh my dearest sister in law have you not been told? It will be the New Year Eve's big TV event, what with two princes dueling."

Jenna scowled at Dain then looked at Kain, "Please tell me this is not the case, dueling is one thing but not in the eyes of the world!"

Kain was very uncomfortable in his response. "I am sorry dear but even the King's Council has got involved, it will be shown live."

Jenna threw a glass she was holding on the floor then stormed off. Sean saw Dain was about to speak when Anders jumped in, "Maybe it is best we do not discuss this any further."

Kain could not help but turn on his brother, "My son will be called Prince Saul, and it is as simple as that. Goodnight Dain and go!" Dain got the message, bowed and left the room.

NEW YEAR DUEL:
(CHAPTER 24)

The next day was the last training session; the fight was on New Year's Eve the day after. Jeng and Sean were at it; Sal had clearly given them less TDL. Jeng was at her goading best; finally, Sean saw beyond the girl and friend and gave Jeng a hard time. Nearing the end Kain appeared.

"A lot better Sire, Sean is as ready as he can be."

"Good, you and Sal leave the room." Sal looked quizzically at Kain but she and Syston obeyed.

"Jeng you will support, you will know when. Sean we will duel". Sean took a gasp of breath.

"Eh, ok Dad, should you not gear up first?"

"No!" With that Sean hit the floor. Sean rose and fired back at his father; Sean hit the floor with his father's response. Sean got up and went defensive. Although not being directly hit he could feel the force and the repetition of his father's blows on his safety field. 'This is brutal' he thought. Sean felt a break in the attack; taking his opportunity he hit back, clearly seeing his father feel the hit. Sean threw a couple more punches; Kain was going down...no Sean hit the floor again. Sean looked up; Jeng had joined in and was now attacking Kain. Sean saw Jeng take a hit; she ended up lying next to him. Jeng looked at Sean, winked and said, "Let's kick butt!" With that both raised, both throwing punches at the now defending Kain. Kain was clearly on the back foot but holding ground. All of a sudden, "Enough cease now!" Kain ordered.

Jeng and Sean stopped, Kain stood still and quiet – looking menacing. Jeng went into defence mode and Sean copied. Kain appeared to calm down then smiled, "Enough I really do mean enough. That was excellent combatting by you both, anymore and...I would have killed you both." Even Sean could hear Jeng's gulp next to him. Kain walked towards them, giving Jeng a hug to comfort her. Looking at Sean he said, "You are ready son. Do not be afraid of anything tomorrow. With Jeng protecting Jenna and you looking after yourself all will be ok. I'll see you both for a drink later." Kain hugged Sean then left.

"What was that all about? I was fighting my Dad...properly."

Jeng replied, "Shit that was awesome, your father is strong, scary but loving. Do you think he needs a younger wife?"

Sean looked at Jeng, realising she was joking. "I was giving it some, but it did not get him."

"Oh, it did, that is clearly why he stopped as I think we hurt him. Anyone else and he would have killed them. I need the ladies room." Jeng laughed and left.

That evening talk of the coming duel was not allowed, Sean taking a moment with Algier decided a good distraction was to find out more about Earthen, specifically robots or the lack of. "If Earthen is this advanced where are all the robots?"

Algier chuckled, "Before the great war we did have robots however, there were some problems. Of course, I was not around then regardless of how old you think I am." Sean giggled. "The main problem was that we went robot crazy. Our AI and physical robotics were very high tech. I have seen in museums some very good people framed robots that could walk and talk. Anyway, robots in manufacturing were accepted. Once they started to carry out external roles such as cleaning, delivering all seemed good. Then of course with robots carrying out many of the jobs Earthens had done, what could they do?"

Algier paused, "It is believed the first unrests were labour related, without work how do you live in a commercial world? However intelligent or not there are only a certain amount of brain surgeons and the like that can be employed. High numbers of unemployed people together with the global warning, now you see why there was a war. Following the war, once Earthens started to live back on the lands their focus was on building, power and water. Robots were deemed not required. We have very few today."

Sean had to think, super robots were coming for Earth and yet his uncle was talking of them as the past. "Wow we are getting things wrong. Are you telling me you have never seen a real robot?"

Again, Algier chuckled, "Yes I have never used a real robot if you mean advanced walking types. I have as I said seen them in a museum. My thoughts were that however convincing the AI is and indeed the body they are unnerving. Their movement is never as flexible as our bodies and more disturbing...they have no soul. Monstrous things."

Sean laughed; this world was full of paradoxes and contradictions.

New Year's Eve was upon them, with little said during the day Sean arrived at the city arena early evening. From exiting the car Sean could see this was a sellout event, spectators were everywhere. The other three kings had stayed on, King Ain being the only absentee. Sean was led to the changing room quickly. "Sal will be your first aider, Syston your coach. Sean you will be fine, please do not be silly whether win or lose I will support you." With this and a quick hug Kain left with Algier to continue their greetings.

"Honey you know I hate this, but your Father is right don't be silly. I will be with Jeng supporting you." Jenna also hugged Sean then left with Jeng.

"On the table I need to check you over, administer the TDL then get you suited." Sean did as Sal told him. Syston led Sean and Sal towards the arena, before entering he stooped. "You will be fine, don't be scared just concentrate." With that Sean and team were in the centre of the arena. Sean faced Det; Det did not move but just stared at Sean. Dain did his introductions, the chief referee stated the rules, and both combatants went to their area. Syston and Sal said something to Sean, Sean did not hear as he was taking in the surroundings.

With Syston and Sal in the tunnel the arena went dark apart from the oval duel area, the countdown started... 10, 9, 8, 7, 6, 5, 4, 3, 2, 1. Sean was immediately hit and fell to the floor; his scoreboard above was already counting him down. Sean got his thoughts together and went straight into protection mode as the duel restarted. The first round ended; Sean had hardly thrown a punch.

"Concentrate Sean. Look at me, listen!"

"Yes Syston. I'm sorry, the lights...everything caught me out."

Sal checked Sean over. "You seem ok but listen to Syston."

Syston instructed, "Protect this round. Det is too psyched up so will go for it again. His one-point advantage will encourage him. Watch him; see how he moves when he punches. Remember what I taught you!"

"Ok I will."

Sean was ready for the next start, going straight to defensive, Det went straight on the attack. Again, Sean defended most of the round but did watch his adversary. This and round 3 were more even, Syston had advised Sean to move a bit, show confidence but keep watching.

"Ok this is round four. You see his move before he punches, easy when he moves hit him before he launches. Hit him hard," Sean nodded.

The round started; with the advice given Sean hit Det a couple of times. Finally, one got through and Det hit the floor. The buzzer sounded for the end of the round just after Det got up, Syston and Sal was at Sean's side. The scoreboard showing one each, the crowd was cheering.

"Look at me Sean," Sean looked at Syston. "You do not want to go to continuous, this time move as he punches then hit back hard. He will be confused that he missed. Please do it early as you need two knock downs."

"Kick his butt!" Sal said in Sean's head.

Sean laughed in his head and responded, "Ok Sal" telepathically.

Round five started, and Sean was the clearly initial aggressor. Twenty seconds in and Det was fighting back. Sean seeing a punch coming dodged quickly then fired with both arms. Det wobbled but somehow still stood. Sean moved forward, felt the strength within him build then hit out. Det hit the floor, Sean went defensive. Det's countdown got to 3, Det moved but stayed down. 2, 1…Buzzers sounded, the crowd went wild. Lights flashing varied colours, Sean had won.

The referees filled the floor, Sal and Syston by Sean's side, Syston giving a low high five as he was too tall for a full high five. Sal gave Sean a hug. Sean gave a smile; his opponent was still down but sitting with his corners. The chief referee took to the centre, "Ladies and…"

There was a loud crash like noise, and the protective field appeared to shatter, although no actual fragments rained down. Sean out of the corner of his eye caught some movement. King Vul had obviously crashed the field and was floating then landing next to the chief referee. "Hold that call!" The referee froze and stopped his announcement. The crowd went silent.

"Det get up!" Sean and all in the arena looked towards the fallen Det. Det tried to rise but fell back to his knees, his first aid shaking his head. "I said get up, move away from him!" Det's corners moved away, Det stood but looked unsteady.

"See he is up; the fight will continue!" King Vul was in the chief referee's personal space.

"Your Highness please?" Kain had completed a similar move and was next to Vul. Sean noted Syston and Sal took a step-in front of him, "Be ready just in case." Sal said in his head.

Vul turned to face Kain, "My son is standing he will fight on."

"I am sorry, but he was counted out, the duel is over." Kain was not backing down. Sean looked up; Jeng, Anders and Algier were in front of his mother still in the seats above. Sean thought, 'this is going to kick off'. Vul circled Kain, eyes drilling into him. Kain turned step for step with Vul keeping eye contact. Vul stopped; Secretary Seth was next to him, saying something in his ear.

"My friends please, our subjects are watching," King Ders was with the group. Vul looked at Ders, then Kain. Even from this distance Sean could see fire in his father's eyes. Seth again spoke to Vul in his ear. Vul turned to look at Sean; Kain was immediately in his way. King Ders moved between them. "Please there is no need for this."

Vul took two steps back and looked at Seth. "Chief referee, call the result!" Sean felt the relief in the whole crowd as Vul said this.

"Ladies and gentlemen. By technical knockout the duel winner is Prince Saul!" The crowd went crazy but Sean and co kept their defensive stance.

"Wait!" Vul wanted more. Looking towards his son. "Det you have failed me this is treason!" With that he raised his arm and Det hit the floor. The crowd gasped as one, "Leave him we are going!" Sean saw Vul and both Det's corners leave the arena with Seth. Sal was first to react running to the stricken Det. Syston gestured and Sean and he were next to Kain. Sal was busy around Det, stopped, looked up, and shook her head. Sean saw Kain drop his head. Kain took Sean's hand and looked up, "Ladies and gentlemen the duel is over. There will be no celebrations." With that Kain led Sean and party to the changing room.

Sean sat on the trainer's table; Sal was already checking him over. Sean could not hold back his feelings and cried. Kain responded first, "Son are you ok?"

"Yes Dad, did Vul just kill his son?"

Kain was holding back tears, "Yes."

"Surely he can't do that?"

"If he calls it treason then it will not be questioned." Kain was now tearful.

"Sean honey. Are you Ok?" Sean was engulfed in his mother's arms.

"I'm fine mum. I'm not hurt. Well at least not physically." Jenna gave a quick look over her son; only stopping when Sal reassured her Sean was not injured. "Mum can we get out of this place. I want to go home...to Shadow and Emma."

"Yes of course, we will leave now. Algier make the arrangements." Jenna then approached Kain, "And you?"

"I am sorry my love. I need to stay with Algier to sort the backlash out, Sal and Jeng will go with you."

Jenna gave Kain a kiss and a hug; Sean provided a hug as well.

LOSS OF A FRIEND:
(CHAPTER 25)

Sean did not recall any of the flights home, his thoughts were only on the barbarity of King Vul. Chief Inspector Cott drove him, Jenna, Sal and Jeng home. Sean only felt better as he lay on his bed, Shadow by his side. "I can't believe it; a father can kill his own son and get away with it. Earthen stinks!" Although Shadow could not answer him Sean knew he would agree if he could.

The next morning Sean grabbed a drink and an apple. "Mum. I'm going to walk Shadow then see Emma and Mush this afternoon."

"Not having a proper breakfast?"

Sean did not respond he was soon at the lake, watching Shadow jump around in the water was enough of a distraction. Sean felt better. "Ok Shadow, time to deal with the world, let's go."

Sean walked to the path; his mood had improved. Suddenly he felt a force on him and fell to the ground. Sean went into protect mode. Lying there he could not see where the blow had come from. Shadow had disappeared into the undergrowth barking. "No! Shadow come back, come back!" Sean heard a yelp, and as he looked up, saw Shadow flying through the air and landing on the path ahead of him not moving. Sean rose and headed for Shadow. Out of the bushes came a man, between Sean and the fallen Shadow. The man was throwing punches. Sean was still defensive but nearing his unmoving friend Sean cried, "No!!!!" With that Sean pushed out with his arms, the man in front of him disintegrated.

Sean was now kneeling over Shadow, he looked up Jeng was with him. "What has happened?"

"He, he..." Sean was pointing to the remains of the man, "Has hurt Shadow. Come on Shadow wake up."

"Sean. Let me please?" Sal joined them. Sean stood to allow Sal to look at Shadow. Jenna was now holding Sean, Cott beside them. A minute or more past when Sal looked up, "I'm sorry Sean, Shadow has gone."

"No. Do your magic save him!"

Sal started to cry, "I'm sorry I can't..."

"You must!" Sean was crying.

"Sean!" Sean looked away; Jeng was standing a few metres in front of them and was holding a bracelet of some sort in her hands. "Have you..."

Before Jeng could finish her sentence, Sean screamed, "No you!" With that Jeng was knocked backwards. Sean felt a hard slap across his face. He turned to take on his attacker. "Stop now!" Jenna was his attacker. "Sal, see to Jeng. Sean you come with me and Cott."

Sean did not argue and his mother and Cott led him back to the house. Sitting on the sofa, Sean asked, "Please tell me Shadow is not dead?"

"I am sorry Sean, but it looks that way." Jenna sat and hugged Sean.

"I'm sorry Your Highness..."

"Sean! My name is Sean!"

Cott continued, "What happened, who has attacked you?"

"It was Daved!" All went quiet. Sal eventually came to the door and immediately sat beside Sean. "I am so sorry but there is nothing I can do, Shadow is gone." Sean fell into tears.

"Cott please resolve things outside." Cott obeyed Jenna and

left.

Sean sat with Jenna and Sal for some time, all three crying. Sal left to make some drinks, asking Sean if he required anything, "Just tea no drugs!" was Sean's response. With drinks to hand Jenna was first to speak. "This is terrible Sean, I am sorry. I will call your friends; maybe they would be best to visit tomorrow. They will also need time."

Sean thought then said, "Yes please mum. I do want to see them but not now. I need some space." With that Sean went to his room. Although both his mother and Sal popped in every half hour or so Sean stayed in his room holding Shadow's favourite ball. Eventually Sean cried himself to sleep.

"Your father and Algier will be here later. They are upset about the news."

Sean acknowledged his mother then sat at the table. "I will sort school out. You will not attend this week. I will say you are having problems with your medicine."

"Thanks Mum."

"I have asked Emma and Mush to stay away for now, but they do wish to see you. Maybe after school tomorrow?"

"Yes. Will you walk with me today, here and the woods?"

"Of course."

"Wait where is Shadow now, what about…his funeral?"

"Shadow has been taken to the Research Park; it has all the facilities there. Whilst we are walking, we can agree the best for his funeral."

"Can I see him first?"

"If that is what you want, I will have Livia arrange it. Maybe we could go there before walking in the woods?"

"Yes please."

Within the hour Sean was at the research park. Following his mother, Sal and Livia past a hospital area the group entered a small morgue. Cott greeted them and introduced a Doctor

Hinton. Sean could see a shape covered on the middle table.

"Are you sure? "

"Yes Mum." With this Doctor Hinton raised the cover. Sean looked at Shadow and took steps towards him. Leaning over Sean laid his head above Shadow's. "I will miss you," With that Sean cried. Sean was left for a minute or so then Jenna approached, "Are you ready?"

Sean raised, "Goodbye my friend. Please give me some time." With that Sean did not realise how but found himself sitting on a wall outside. "Shall we have that walk?"

With a, "Yes" reply, Sean was driven to the local woods and walked with his mother. Little was said until they found a large fallen tree. "This is where we would stop, may we?"

"Yes honey."

Sitting for a while, Sean gave a chuckle, "Shadow loved here, he would try and climb this log after me."

"I know."

"I would like to spread his ashes in the lake near home?"

"That would be nice. Do you want a ceremony?"

"Not in a church. It sounds wrong but I do not wish to be there when he is...you know. But yes, I would like a ceremony next to the lake."

"Ok. I will have Cott arrange this with Father Dom. This Saturday morning would be good; the other part can be done the day before. If you wish to change this then let me know."

Both sat then walked chatting, Sean felt a little better. The evening past with Sean and Jenna on their own. Kain and Algier arrived home very late. Sean was already in bed with some of Shadow's toys around him.

Sean woke, following the voices he went to the sitting room. Kain was first to respond, hugging Sean then ushering him to sit on the sofa with him joining Jenna who was already seated.

"I am sorry about Shadow. The loss of a friend is hard. "

"Thanks Dad" Sean thought, "Why? What did that thing want to kill me for?"

"Daved..."

Sean interrupted, "Don't say that name!"

Kain continued, "It would appear that he had believed there was something going on between you and Jeng."

"What me and her, never! How could he I'm only fifteen?"

"I'm sure it was not thought in that way, or at least at this point. However, you would certainly in his eyes be a contender due to your position in only a few years. Jealousy is blind."

"No that's crazy he couldn't have surely?"

Kain took a breath. "Sean, we believe he had heard rumours about Jeng and a prince. He clearly got this mixed up by thinking of you and her. I believe Jeng is seeing Prince Alex."

"So, Shadow has died for nothing!"

"No, no. He was doing his job protecting you."

"Is that Dad or the Earthen speaking!"

Sean was shocked, Kain did not respond but fell into tears. Jenna hugged her husband. Sean had never seen his father like this and could not think of anything to say. Sean rose and went to his room. An hour or so later there was a knock on his door, Sal entered.

"Here is some tea, no it is not drugged. May I sit with you?"

"Of course." Sal sat on the bed next to Sean.

"You may not wish to hear this, but your father is doing more to change Earthen than you know. Unfortunately, this will not happen overnight."

"I don't wish to hurt him, but he has to realise what his planet is doing to us."

"He does, I assure you he does. Besides letting him feel it is not a bad thing. Earthen men need to get in touch with true emotion sometimes."

"Wait Sal, I'm sorry. Here I am crying over a lost pet and yet you are hardly over the loss of Millan."

"Don't be silly. As you have been told before love of a living being that can at least show it back in some way will hurt. I am coming to terms with the loss of my loved one."

"You kept it secret, why?"

Sal chuckled, "No, not a secret as such, we just did not highlight it to the world. It was like a game even to us, shall we, shan't we, secret meetings; we were big kids at heart."

"Would you have married Millan?" Sean saw a tear in Sal's eye. "I'm sorry I shouldn't have asked that."

"That's OK. You know talking about him, as I'm sure you will about Shadow helps. And yes, we were talking of marriage."

"I'm sorry I did not go to Millan's funeral."

"It being on Earthen you were not expected to, Kain and Algier represented Saulten as you know. You and your mother with all his Police colleagues at the mass here on Earth were more soothing for me. I do not really recall the funeral but the mass I do."

"Am I right to not wanting to be at Shadow's actual funeral, the cremation?"

"If that is what you want. I'm sure he if he could, he would fully understand." With that Sal gave Sean a peck on the forehead. "You will see your friends after school tomorrow. Night."

The morning was spent with Kain helping Sean to gather Shadow's toys. They were to be boxed and put in the loft. "Sal said you are sorting Earthen out?"

"Yes. I have a plan and indeed a goal. I have been working on it for some time. I will share this with you when closer to the end. It is not something you need to worry about now."

"I thought we would have no more secrets?"

"Sean they are not secrets just actions, plans that until pieced together mean nothing."

Sean spent the afternoon on his own. At 6pm his friends and their mums were at the living room door. All greeted Sean with hugs, Emma's the last and longest. Jenna made a comment and the mums went to the kitchen leaving Sean, Emma and Mush on the sofa.

"Look mate I'm sorry. I don't know what to say." Sean gave Mush a quick hug. "Don't worry mate you just being here helps."

"It is so sad. So shocking, so quick." Emma was also struggling for words. Sean turned, cuddled Emma and said, "Look don't be worried about what you guys say." The three sat and spoke for a couple of hours, each remembering stories with Shadow.

Saturday morning came. Sean and his parents with Sal were waiting in the house. Sean heard a couple of cars pull up then some voices. Gwent, Cott, Livia, Father Dom and Professor Smith entered the room.

Professor Smith was the first to greet Sean, a hug then a message in his head, "Father Dom is human and does not know about Earthen please be careful what you say." Sean nodded.

"Master Saul." Father Dom approached Sean. "I blessed Shadow yesterday at the church. His ashes are in this urn would you like to carry him?"

"Yes Father, thank you." Sean took the urn and held it to his chest. Sal led them all out to the garden path. Standing at the path were Emma, Mush and their parents. Each smiled at Sean, Sean smiled back. Emma took Sean's arm and the group walked to the lakeside. "Sean hopefully you will like what the Research Staff have done?"

Sean looked, the clearing was tidy, grass cut, bushes

trimmed. Looking further Sean could see the bench was different, 'cleaner' he thought.

Cott continued, "The bench is not new it is the old one varnished and cleaned up. We believe many of the character marks would have been from Shadow."

Sean smiled and the others smiled with him. "Look at the plaque on the bench." Emma pointed.

Shadow, run free in heaven,
Your loyalty and spirit will never be forgotten.
Love Sean and Friends

A tear came to Sean's eye, "Thank you that is lovely."

Father Dom led them the short distance to the lake edge. Father Dom said some words then spoke to Sean. "May I take the urn? I believe the ashes are in a small soluble bag that you can put into the lake."

Sean gave Father Dom the urn. Opening the urn Sean removed the bag, held it to his heart then under arm threw it into the lake. All stood still for a while. Father Dom made another blessing then putting his hand on Sean's shoulder said, "Shadow is now resting." With that all left. Only Jenna and Emma remaining.

"Honey, I can see Shadow swimming around in the lake." Sean smiled. "Stay as long as you need, we will all be at the house," A quick hug and Jenna left. Sean looked over and Emma was sitting on the bench, Sean joined her.

"Shadow, I'm sure is looking down and would be happy with this send off and proud of you as I am."

Sean looked at Emma, smiled and kissed her.

NIGHTMARES & TRUTH:
(CHAPTER 26)

The figure was running fast through the quiet, Rome, streets, his pursuers hot on his heels. Vaulting a six-foot fence in his stride and turning the corner, he stopped. A police car screeched to a halt some ten metres in front of him. Two police officers jumped from the car; guns drawn. "Stop or we will shoot!" Although this was shouted in Italian the figure understood and was not about to give up. With a whoosh of his right arm the driver's side door slammed against the policeman crouching behind it, knocking him to the floor. The second policeman opened fire, the figure waved his left hand and the bullets fell to the floor in front of him. With both arms raised the police car moved to the left, then into the air and as it was released it dropped onto the two policemen.

The figure turned to see his pursuers were nearly upon him. Turning again, he ran and jumped another fence and headed for the arches. Coming out the other side he ran towards the middle of the Coliseum. He looked behind but his pursuers had stopped. He heard movement in front of him, and as he turned, he hit the floor hard. Looking up at his attacker, he froze in fear. "Mercy your highness, please!" Were his last words, as he was no more.

"Kain, you did not need to kill him," Algier was the second figure standing above the body.

"He has killed humans and would not have spoken even if tortured. There is no point in him living."

"You can be very persuasive; you could have tried. He may have had information that would have been of use to us."

The two pursuers joined Kain and Algier in the middle. "Sire, there will be many police here shortly."

"Algier and I will leave. You two, with the commissioner's help, will tidy this up."

With that Kain turned and left, Algier following him.

Splash! The water went everywhere, the girls sitting by the pool screamed. Mush came to the surface laughing, "Did I get them?"

"Yes, well and truly soaked them. Excellent dive bomb mate!" Sean, a metre, or so away by Mush's side, was treading water.

"I was enjoying the sun you idiot!" Zandra told Mush off whilst wiping down her wet costume.

"We are going to have something to eat, by ourselves. Let's go Zandra," Emma had also risen from her poolside sunbed and started to head towards the main villa.

Mush was non-repentant and laughing. "That was good, soaked them fully. Now for you!" Sean tried to swim away but Mush was upon him trying to mush him although both were treading water. The high jinks continued for some time until they heard, "Boys. Dinner!"

Sean and Mush exited the pool, grabbed some towels and wiped themselves down as they took the short walk to the main building. The girls, Jenna and Sal were already seated and starting to eat.

"Mrs Saul, your villa is lovely. I can't believe we have been here, what? Two weeks already?"

"It's Jenna. And yes, Zandra this is a lovely place. We have the weather, Tuscany, forests, fields, towns and beaches around us and good friends."

Mush, now sitting next to Zandra said, "Shame we leave tomorrow I've had a great time."

"Your mum and dad have arranged your sixteenth birthday trip to the Grand Prix, so it won't be that bad to go." Emma was being realistic.

"I know. Could your dad not have organised more tickets, Sean, and we could all have gone?"

"Kain thought it would be nice for you, Zandra and your parents to have some time together so we are happy to keep out. Besides we will have a meal or something in a few weeks to celebrate your and Emma's sixteenth, probably on Sean's birthday?" Jenna responded on Sean's behalf.

"That sounds good, I will miss Emma's sixteenth though..."

Zandra interrupted Mush; "It will be good for you and me to be together on your sixteenth and Sean and Emma on hers."

Mush looked at Zandra, then Sean. Sean shook his head—this was enough for Mush to think before falling in and being quiet.

The meal was eaten and after a few drinks and music they decided it was bedtime. Sal and Jenna went to the main house and the boys escorted the girls to the first of the two smaller villas in the grounds of the main villa.

Mush held Zandra, "Good night sweetheart. See you in the morning, or..."

Zandra gave Mush a kiss, "Not now, good night."

Emma smiled, kissed Sean and said her good nights. Within the hour Sean and Mush were in their beds sitting up talking. Having discussed the day's events Mush suggesting they could still sneak into the girl's rooms, but both decided it was time to sleep.

"What was that?" Mush sat up upon hearing a scream.

"Emma!" Sean said no more and was up and running to the girl's villa about twenty metres from theirs. Sean entered the villa; the light was on and Zandra was holding Emma on

Emma's bed.

"It's okay, just a nightmare. Emma is alright." Zandra advised.

"Another one. Let me see," Sal had joined them. Zandra moved aside for Sal to sit with Emma on the bed, Sean still standing in the doorway.

"God, you can move when you want to!" Mush was at Sean's side.

"Is everything okay?" Jenna was the last to arrive but joined Sal on the bed comforting Emma.

"I am fine. Sorry to disturb you all it is just that same nightmare," Emma was talking but clearly distressed. "I'm nearly sixteen and having nightmares, it's ridiculous."

"Don't be like that honey we all have nightmares. Look if Sal stays here with Zandra, how about you come up to the house with me. We can have a hot drink, a natter and maybe fall asleep on the couch?"

"Yes Mrs...I mean, Jenna, that would be good."

Emma and Jenna rose from the bed, Emma gave Sean a cuddle as she passed him at the door. "See you in the morning." Was all Sean thought of saying.

"Sal. I'll look after Zandra if you want to keep an eye on Emma, you being a nurse and all that." As the pillow hit Mush full on, he realised that was a no.

Both boys back in their room, Sean laughed as he said, "Nice try mate but a bit obvious."

"I thought your parents and Sal were...modern and all that. I mean they happily let us drink wine in front of them."

Sean laughed again, "They are but being subtle is not your best trait is it?" Both laughed and eventually the night passed with no further disturbances.

Sean and Mush were up early. Morning swim out the way they joined the women in the main villa for breakfast. "No

Emma?" Sean asked seeing only Sal, Jenna and Zandra present.

"No honey. We sat up and talked for some time, Emma fell asleep in the spare bedroom. I looked in earlier she is very peaceful so leave her be. I, on the other hand, am shattered."

"You do look a bit rough Mrs S." Sean took cover as his mother's eyes hit Mush square on. "Oops I mean...you look great but not as great as normal, Mrs S."

"Thank you for your honesty, Master Green. Maybe you should not eat as much breakfast."

Mush looked at Sean and whispered, "I walked into that one, boy your mum can be harsh when she wants." With that he laughed as did all around him.

Breakfast completed and Jenna 'scrubbed up,' she spoke to Mush, "Look Emma is still asleep. This being your last day with us maybe Sal would take you and Zandra to that lovely cove and bar. Sometime on your own maybe?"

Mush smiled, "Yeah! I mean, yes, but we will all have dinner together later?"

Sal, Mush and Zandra left shortly after, Sean and Jenna were left sitting on the patio. "I don't know why I jumped so much. After all that is the second time this holiday that Emma has woken us," Sean stated.

"Yes honey. Judy told me to be aware of it as Emma has been having the nightmare about Millan's sad death ever since it happened months ago."

"Sal is struggling to keep it under control?"

"Emma is strong minded and without maybe hurting her Sal can only ease it but never take it away fully."

"It's not fair that we continue to lie to her..."

"Lie to me!" Sean looked up—Emma shouted as she joined them.

Jenna got to her feet, "Honey you are up, come and sit down I will make some tea, food maybe?"

"No. Who is lying to me?"

"You need to sit down Emma. Please."

Emma looked at Jenna, went to a chair and sat down, "And?"

Jenna sat next to Emma and took her hand. "Oh, Emma, dear, I am so sorry but for your own good I have allowed my family to lie to you." Jenna had a tear in her eye.

Emma looked taken aback, "You have lied to me, why?"

"Emma, I am happy to take the responsibility of telling you, but you must listen before you judge me, Sean or others?"

Sean looked at his mother; she was still holding Emma's hand and did look very unsettled. "Mum, are we supposed to tell her, what about Dad?"

Jenna ignored Sean. "Emma, please listen before you judge me?"

Emma looked at Jenna; "Yes of course I have nothing but respect and love for you Mrs S."

Jenna gave Emma a hug and stood up. "I will get some hot drinks. Sean, you may be best to at least start as you have only recently been aware yourself." With that Jenna gave Sean's hand a grasp as she headed to the kitchen adding, "I will call your father and let him know."

Chicken, came into Sean's head, but he decided not to say it. "Great, my job, where do I start?"

Emma swapped chairs and now sitting next to Sean held his hand, "Just say it whatever it is please."

"Your nightmare is real." Emma gulped. "You did see PC Millan's death. You were there with me, my dad and others." Sean looked into Emma's eyes and could tell she was remembering.

"We were kidnapped, no, you were kidnapped I jumped on a van. Oh my god why did I do that?" Emma froze for a moment. "Never mind; it was real. Those people, Gill and his lot, were attacking us, they said they were going to kill us."

"Yes, basically Gill and his people wanted to kill my father.

An on-going feud from where my father comes from and unfortunately you and I got caught in the middle of it."

"A feud, yes, but hang on, there were no weapons. The car I tried to escape in lifted into the air, you were fighting in that pit with your arms!"

Sean kept silent; Emma was clearly recalling the events with clarity. "Millan and your uncle were hit but Jeng arrived and helped." Emma sat up straight, "Your father killed them, I mean Gill and the others with his mind."

Jenna returned and placing fresh drinks on the table sat on the other side of Emma. "Yes honey. That is correct there was a fight and PC Millan was killed, Uncle Dain was injured, and Gill and his gang were also killed. There were no weapons as Kain, Dain, Jeng and the others have powers, telekinetic powers, that they use to fight with."

Sean watched Emma's face more closely, it was clear she was becoming more enlightened to the situation, and then came the expected question. "Your father and the others, they are not human?"

Sean chose to answer, "My father and others are Earthens. They are aliens from another planet who have powers, that we, as humans, do not have."

Emma shook, "Your father is an alien?"

"Yes."

Emma took a sip of tea, "I don't know which is worse, the fact he killed people or that he is an alien. Wait!" Sean and Jenna jumped in their seats. "Are you two aliens?" Emma's face became a scowl.

"No," Jenna was firm. "We, like you now, have been brought into another world. I am happy to tell you more of it, but I think you need a moment or two to take it in. Please finish your tea, think for a bit."

Emma listened, all sat without talking for some time. "If Kain is an alien then you are not his child?"

Sean gulped, again his mother saved him. "There is a longer story here but although aliens, their anatomy is virtually the same as ours and therefore together we can...reproduce." Sean could see his mother was struggling.

"I am a mongrel!" Sean went for it hoping to lighten the conversation. "Part human part alien."

His attempt at an ironic smile failed. Emma jumped to her feet, "You are an alien. My boyfriend is an alien!" With that Emma took off running to her room.

"That went well," Sean inadvertently said out loud.

"Idiot, give her some time and we will talk further. I'll call Sal and get her to keep the others away for a little longer." Sean nodded although thinking *a little longer* would not be enough.

One hour later Sean and Jenna decided to take the conversation further, entering Emma's room they could tell she had been crying. Jenna sat on the windowsill next to Emma. "The hills here are beautiful, it is so good to be this high, and you can see the sea."

Emma smiled, "You are not kidding me."

"No, this is a beautiful view."

"Not the view, Jenna. All that you said about aliens?"

Jenna giggled, "I know. I am so sorry honey. Whatever and however the truth is, please understand that I love you. My son can be an idiot and make many bad decisions but loving you is the best decision he has ever made." Both women had tears in their eyes and hugged each other. "Look if you wish to blame someone or argue with someone then it is with me. Not Kain or Sean, after all it was me who chose to allow an alien to enter my life and bring with him the good and the bad of his world. Sean has only been told himself about all this recently and is as lost as you are. I'll leave you two alone."

Jenna stood, kissed Sean on the forehead and left. Sean sat where his mother had just left. "Is it true you have only known for a while?"

"Yes, about a year. Sorry. No, I was not aware of what my dad was or the situation he was in until all the trouble started by Gill." Sean paused and took Emma's hand, "I can tell you more if you want."

"Yes, please tell me."

Sean started, explaining about Earthen and how his father had fallen in love with an Earthling. Missing out some of the details around his father being a king, he did tell of feuds and the medieval ways of his father's world. Sean was happy with his openness and holding Emma's hand all through the conversation felt inside he had done the right thing.

Although Emma challenged many points, she did not argue, she did not judge, she just wanted to understand. Zandra's appearance stopped the conversation. Both agreed to not talk further that evening but to enjoy the last night of the holiday for their friends.

REALISATION:
(CHAPTER 27)

Some kilometres away from the Tuscany villa in Rome the climate delegates were going to their beds. "Mr President, all is clear, you may go to your room." The U.S. President acknowledged his aide, entered his hotel room, closing the door behind him.

Taking the few steps toward the mini bar he took out the whiskey poured a glass then sat down. "How the hell did you get in here?" Kain had entered the room from the en-suite.

"Stay seated, Mr President, I only want a word."

"A word? You had an hour of that when presenting earlier about climate change and you tried to chew my ear off at dinner. This is a security shambles, Chief Mulder, come in!" With that Chief Mulder, the president's head of security, entered the room followed by Senator Virage, his main advisor and friend. Virage closed the door behind him.

"Sire. How may I help you?" Mulder spoke.

"Idiot, this save the planet maniac is in my room and you ask me how you can help me?" The president exclaimed.

"Sorry Sir, I was not talking to you," Mulder added as he bowed to Kain.

"What the hell is going on here?"

"Mr President. I have tried to talk to you the diplomatic way but your ignorance angers me," Kain approached the, now standing, president.

"Pardon, who the hell do you think you are talk..." the president did not complete his sentence. With a look and a movement of his head Kain had thrown the president against the wall where he was now pinned.

"I have had enough. You will listen to me!" Kain was in the president's face. "What I and others are saying about climate change and global warming is all true and at some point, in the future, will affect your planet and mine. At this point in time leaders, as I, or you, as you would call yourself, need to take the right decisions to stop this. Tonight, I will not force you, all I ask is for you to listen for once and change...no, lead your country, and indeed your world, in the right direction."

Kain allowed the president to fall to his feet. The president calmed himself, he looked at his trusted aides, and neither acknowledged him. Looking at Kain he asked, "Who are you?"

Kain walked away then turned. "I am the guy that will ruin your presidency, your marriage, and then happily, slowly, kill you if needs be."

The president gasped; his face full of terror. "No, this is not real, you can't do that, and you can't threaten me and my family. Mulder, shoot him or something!"

Mulder looked at Kain then addressed the president. "I am sorry, Sir, I have and always will serve you but only upon Kain's say so."

Virage spoke, "Mr President, my friend. I am sorry but my service to you is also only upon Kain's say so. You are not the most powerful man in the world; Kain and his people, as I am, are." The president was even more frightened.

"Enough!" Kain said turning back to the president. "I am sorry you have learnt this way however; I do not have time for games anymore. You have heard my speech; you now know how powerful I am. Who I am is not what matters, what you do from now on does."

Kain flicked his right arm; the president flew across the

room ending up on the floor. "How did you do that?"

"My people here will advise and continue to advise you of what to do, take heed of their words. I will not burden you any more in this way once you as your peers already do listen to me and act. My threat is real; do not push me to carry it out. Mulder, Virage, you may educate this man, thank you." With that Kain left the room.

"What time are your parents here?" Zandra asked Emma.

"Sorry, they won't be here until later this afternoon. Actually, I think Sal is picking Kain and my parents up from the airport as they all fly in about the same time."

"Yes. Sal said she would drop Mush and I off at the airport then wait around for your parents. If they are in time maybe, we could say hello to them before flying off to meet our parents."

Mush walked up to Emma, "You okay?"

Emma nodded a yes, then spoke, "Come here!" As she gave Mush a cuddle. "I'm sorry, we will miss your birthday, but we will all celebrate together soon."

"We will miss yours too," Zandra added whilst also cuddling Emma.

"So, looks like Sal and the car are ready. I will miss you both," Sean joined the group huddle.

A short while later, Sean, Jenna and Emma, were sitting by the pool. "How are you honey?" Jenna was inquisitive.

"I am fine, Jenna. Sean explained very well. We have something else in common...being lied to by his family for years." Jenna gulped and soothed Emma with a smile, as Emma added, "I am only joking, Sean told me to say that." Sean laughed, and then looked elsewhere to avoid his mother's glare.

"Really, I am okay. It is crazy but in a strange way knowing the truth is a relief. I thought I was going mad with the nightmares. I don't understand the violence as such or why but I'm sure I will at some point. My parents, how do we tell them?"

Jenna advised, "Sal, Algier and Kain will meet them at the airport and will take a detour and tell them before they all arrive here later."

Sean took his chance, "Maybe we could take a walk to the beach and talk, and maybe I could show you some powers?"

"Okay but don't scare me."

Sean and Emma took the ten-minute walk to the sea to their favourite alcove. It was quiet with very few people around. Taking off their outer clothing they went for a swim, returning to their rucksack of drinks and towels a half hour later.

"So, is swimming your power? If it is, you are useless," Emma goaded.

Sean looked around—the alcove was empty. With that Sean looked at Emma, concentrating he removed the hat she was wearing from her head. Moving the hat a few metres away but still off the ground, floating in mid-air.

"Wow, are you doing that?"

"Yep, with my mind. Watch." Sean flicked his head and the hat did a somersault in the air, flew around Emma at speed then stopped above her. Sean carefully made it land back on her head.

"All that progression for you to move a hat, really!" Emma mocked.

Sean thought, and then thought again. "I can talk into people's minds." With this Sean attempted to enter Emma's head but caught a disturbance.

"What are you doing, are you in my head? It feels weird."

Sean tried again but he could not connect to Emma. "You have the necklace on that I bought you for Christmas? That's stopping me getting into your head."

Emma felt her necklace; "You gave me something for Christmas that does things?"

"Yes, it stops Earthen's reading your mind and can warn Dad and his people if you are in danger," Sean added innocently.

"I'm sorry but you have some strange device on me, and it can track me!"

Sean gulped, "Oops, that didn't come out right. Can I explain while we walk, your parents will be here soon?" The walk back to the villa was interesting; Sean managed to get back out of the hole he had dug. Emma was unsure of the mind reading and worried that Sean could or could not read her mind. The necklace and its needs were understood and kept on.

Upon returning to the villa Emma and Sean joined Jenna in preparing the dinner for the evening. Sean felt comfortable in talking further about Earthen and his father, still missing out the king part. All three were comfortable on the patio when finally, the car pulled up; Emma was first to meet her parents with a big hug. Sean, adding a similar greeting to his father and Algier. "Thank you for preparing the dinner but maybe we can eat in our villa on our own please," Harry Cooper advised as they walked towards the patio.

"Of course," Jenna agreed.

With that the Coopers took some food and drink and headed to the small villa, ignoring the "Sean could sleep on the main couch if you want two rooms?" Shouted Jenna. "They did not take the news well then?" Jenna addressed Kain.

"They were okay, but it is a lot to take in. I'm tired honey maybe we could take some food and eat in our room?"

Jenna did not argue, she and Kain took their food and headed into the house leaving Sean with Sal and Algier.

"We are having a drink young man," Algier opened two beer bottles for him and Sean.

"That bottle's mine." Sal joined them, taking Sean's bottle

whilst smiling.

Sean spoke, "As Mum asked, they didn't take the news well?"

"They were okay but do need time as a family to talk it over." Sal replied.

"Do they know everything including the king bit?"

"No. They understand we are aliens, an idea of our power and the dangers around feuding," Algier updated Sean.

"Wow, tomorrow will be interesting. Dad looked tired, concerned?"

"Yes, he has had a hard time in Rome. Did you hear of the terrorist attack there?"

Sean explained, "No, we have been full of our news here. What terrorist attack?"

"The other night before the climate seminar some buildings were blown up, twenty killed."

"Shit, that's not good, what terrorist group did that?"

"F.A.M.—the Fight Against Monarchy group. They are an Earthen group."

"No—Earthens are attacking Earth again?"

"Yes, although they are probably making a point to your father. He dealt with the situation here, but the trouble is still on Earthen."

"There is terrorism on Earthen?"

"Yes, as it suggests there is a group that are demanding the overthrow of the monarchy. Kain's thoughts are with Vulten, Saulten, indeed the whole planet."

Sean sat for a while and thought on his uncle's words. "Do the Earth leaders know about Earthen now?"

Sal joined in, "No. F.A.M., if it was them, did it in a way to suggest it was an Earth terrorist group, so the leaders are not aware."

"You said F.A.M., if it was them?"

"There are many troubles on Earthen. F.A.M. and a so-called Royalist group called F.F.R.—Fight for Royalism, maybe others," Algier thought before continuing. "Who is doing what or blaming who, we do not know but there have been deaths on Earthen as well."

"And Dad has to deal with this?'

"Yes. Leave him to think; he will involve you and us when required. He may need to go to Earthen soon, I think that is why he is speaking to your mother."

"Are we in danger?"

Sal looked at Algier then addressed Sean, "These are difficult times and, yes, we must be careful and alert. Goodnight both."

Sean sat with Algier a little longer, swigging the beer that Sal had left—few words were said.

Another beautiful morning on the Tuscany coast and Sean woke and went to the pool but swam alone—already missing Mush. Joining his parents for breakfast with Algier and Sal, they awaited the Coopers.

"Good morning all," Harry Cooper approached. "May we join you for breakfast?"

"Yes of course," Jenna welcomed them to the table.

"Judy, and I, have discussed the situation and have agreed to understand more before we comment."

Kain addressed Harry, "Thank you, my friend. Do you want time alone or maybe we could play golf and talk together with Algier?"

"Yes. Golf would be good. Judy, dear, maybe you could spend some time with Jenna. Obviously, Sean and Emma you can do what kids do." Sean thought, although rough, it sounded like a plan.

Plan finalised by Jenna and the men were soon off golfing, she was shopping with Judy and Sal was walking up a mountain with Sean and Emma. "I'll stop here, you two carry on." Sal gasped.

"Funny Sal, there is a bar just here where you wish to stop," Emma laughed but continued walking with Sean. Although counted as a mountain it was more a big hill with a good path to climb their way up. At the top, they could see for miles, greenery and hills one side, and the sea the other.

"What is Earthen like? You were there at Christmas, not Canada?"

"It is quite barren, very open, lots of space. Parts of Canada are a good comparison." This sentence led to a further conversation that continued all the way down the mountain. Picking up Sal on the way they were soon back at the villa.

Jenna and Judy had arrived back earlier, both giggling, both denying the extremely long liquid lunch they had obviously partaken of. Settled in, the men arrived back; Sean noted Harry was grinning ear to ear. "So, no guessing who won then?" Sean asked.

Harry dropped his smile, "Your father did as usual. If it was not for the odd, strange, sliced ball though I would have." Sean looked at his father who averted his stare. "Anyway," Harry continued. "I have decided that we will try and learn your... alien ways before we make judgement." Harry was again smiling.

"No, Kain, you haven't?" Sean looked at his mother thinking that was a strange comment.

"Jenna, dear, if you are suggesting, Kain, has bribed me then yes, it is the case."

"Dad!" Emma shouted.

"No, dear, don't worry. You are speaking to the new Financial Director of the Research Park. A handsome salary, big car and house to go with it."

"A house." Emma was bewildered.

"Yes. Use of the Jameses old house to be exact."

"We are moving to the Jameses house. O.M.G. that's...big!" Emma was smiling.

"So, after all these years I find out my husband is bribe-able?" Judy threw out.

All laughed before Harry responded. "Oh, dear, it is not the money, the car or even the house as such. But finally, after all these years I will have a bathroom of my own from two women. Bliss!"

Again, laughter filled the air. Judy got up and hugged her husband, gave a knowing wink to Jenna and said, "Celebrations, then music, wine and fun!"

REUNITED FRIEND:
(CHAPTER 28)

The next morning came; all were sitting on the patio having breakfast; the men were dealing with hangovers.

"With all your alien magic do you have a hangover cure yet?" Harry asked aloud.

"No. Us Earthen men suffer as you do here on Earth," Algier chuckled at his own response.

"A walk would be good for this," Kain joined in, "Then maybe a round of golf?"

Algier and Harry both nodded their heads in agreement. Judy finished pouring coffee and added, "Don't forget tomorrow is my little girl's sixteenth birthday so maybe there is some girly shopping to do? Then a quiet night later?"

Jenna and Sal agreed, and Emma smiled, "Yes, spoiling me today would be nice."

"And what about me? I don't play golf and I am not going shopping for girly things!" Sean stood to make his point.

"Your problem!" Harry shouted as he, Kain and Algier headed for the car.

"We will take the jeep girls. Sean, you can tidy up if you like, see you later!" Jenna was leading the girls away.

"Great," Sean thought as he sat alone.

Passing the time with some reading, swimming and general messing around the villa. Sean took an afternoon nap. "What! Who! When!" Sean shouted as he woke to some voices.

"Hi, honey we are back!" Sean turned to see the girls clambering out of the jeep carrying bags of stuff.

"Did we wake you?" Emma was next to Sean. "Ahh," Emma planted a kiss on Sean's cheek.

Sean sat for the next hour watching the girls' show off the various items of clothing they had bought, *sleep would have been better* he thought.

"This is what I am wearing tomorrow. Remember we have an early meal then the evening show at that lovely theatre for my birthday," Emma was informing.

"Wow. That looks lovely," Although it did not come out right, Sean knew he meant it. The women sitting and talking for the next hour stretched Sean's patience. "Emma, why don't we go for a walk? We will get back for dinner."

Before Emma could reply, Sean's attention was taken by the noise of a car screeching to halt in the drive. Algier, Kain and Harry all jumped out. Kain did not speak but went straight into the villa followed by Algier. "Kain took a call from someone and rushed us home. Any beers?" Harry was still in lotto winner mode. Jenna provided a beer, not saying anything she looked at Sean as if to say, wait and see. Algier was the first to come out; sitting at the table he took a sip of drink.

"Not good news from Earthen, a terrorist attack has taken place in Saulten City. We believe there are casualties." No one responded but Sean noted their heads drop. Kain joined the group some ten minutes later.

"There are ten dead, some we know personally. It is unbelievable that this could happen in the middle of Saulten City," Kain paused. "Jenna, dear, I will need to go to the space station now to communicate in full and assess my next move."

"Yes, of course, dear."

"Did you say space station?" Judy asked.

"Yes, he did," Algier advised. "The space station is this side of the sun. Our communications and intel will be clearer from there."

"How long does it take for this trip?" Harry asked.

"If we leave now, we will be on the station later tonight," Kain turned as he spoke. "Sean, you would be best to come with me and Algier."

Sean stood but before he could walk Emma had jumped up in front of Kain. "Mr S. I'm sorry, but would this mean you and Sean would miss my birthday?"

"Your birthday party is..." Kain stopped mid-sentence, looking into Emma's eyes. "I am sorry Emma, but this is important and, yes, we will miss your birthday."

"Mr S. I know this must be awful, especially if friends are hurt but I am only sixteen once and I wish to be with Sean." Sean looked at Emma and then his father waiting for the reply. The reply came but from Jenna, not Kain.

"Call me crazy but if Sean has to be involved then why not show Emma, Harry and Judy what it is all about? Let them go to the space station with us."

All appeared taken aback by this suggestion. "Dear Jenna, it could be dangerous for the Coopers," Algier spoke.

Sean saw Emma look at her father. Harry responded to her look, "I don't know what danger there is but if you guys are real then why not show us your spaceship?"

"It is settled then!" Jenna took charge. "Sal. Help the Coopers to get ready. They will need very little luggage, as there will be clothes on the space station. Algier, you can make the arrangements."

Sean looked at his father, who was staring at his wife, opened mouthed—Jenna had won again, Sean noted.

A little later Emma sat next to Sean in one of the cars heading to a private airfield. "Am I really okay in jeans and a t-shirt for space travel?" She asked.

"Yes, of course you are. It is nothing like our spaceships. Think...Star Trek, you can wear what you like."

Emma grabbed Sean's hand, "This is so exciting."

The cars pulled up and all exited, Sean could see a few people around them, one he knew, "Councilor Robare, what are you doing here?"

"Ah, young Prince, I am here for the climate meeting and stayed on to assist our Italian friends. How are you?"

"Wow, stop!" Emma had interjected. "Did you say, young Prince?"

Sean responded, "Ah. There is a little more to the story. Can I tell you on the shuttle?"

"What shuttle?"

"That one." Sean looked at Emma as her eyes left his to look at what appeared to be a helicopter but was actually a spaceship.

"O.M.G., you were not kidding!" Emma exclaimed.

Sean smiled, "Nope, we weren't. Can I take you for a ride?" With that Sean took Emma's hand and lead her towards the shuttle with the others following.

"How do we get to a space station in a helicopter?" Sean heard Harry say as they were walking up the ramp to enter the shuttle.

"I have no idea what you are on about dear, but this is a spaceship," Judy was obviously more open to the surroundings.

"Hi, Your Highness, I see you have a friend with you?"

"Hi Captain Shad. It is good to see you. Maybe you could show Emma the controls a little later?"

"Yes, once your father agrees." Sean followed Shad's look towards his father who had not yet boarded but was talking with Robare.

"Your Highness!' Tell me what that's all about!" Emma demanded.

Shad looked at Sean then addressed Emma. "Young lady, your boyfriend is Prince Saul of Saulten. Kain is the king, my king, our king."

"O.M.G., you are not kidding, are you?"

"No," with that Shad bowed to Sean.

Sean looked over Shad's shoulder, although he did not wish to see her, she was not there. Shad caught Sean's look. "Commander Jeng is not here however, Ensign Jordon is my co-pilot, he will take over and show you later. By the way, Your Highness, you are wrong about Commander Jeng."

Sean looked at Shad, thought then reacted, "I am not looking for her. Thank you for your honesty but it is not required." With that Sean sat down motioning Emma to sit next to him. No more was said as Kain boarded, Shad counted down and the shuttle took off. Sean sat watching Emma's face that was full of amazement.

"Captain Shad, here, we are on a steady course for the space station, you may remove your seat belts."

"Your Highness?" Emma was looking at Sean.

"Yes, I am a prince, what more do you need to know?"

"That is a bit disingenuous Sean," Jenna was standing by them. "Emma, maybe you could assist Ensign Jordon at the helm as, Commander Shad, Sean, Kain and I need to talk."

Emma instantly forgot about Sean, jumped from her seat to join Ensign Jordon at the helm. Sean was led to the rear of the shuttle and, advised to put on his Earthen clothes with crown; he did, as did Jenna, Kain, Sal and Algier.

"I will advise the Coopers, you deal with Emma," were Jenna's words as they went back into the main shuttle cabin. Sean walked towards Emma who was sitting in the pilot's seat; Shad was at the rear talking with Kain.

"Have you flown it yet?" Sean asked.

314

Emma turned to address Sean but before speaking laughed, "O.M.G. what are you wearing?"

"These are my Earthen clothes, a bit bland but this is what we wear."

"Idiot, on your head?"

"Oh. It is my crown." Sean could not make the expression on Emma's face out so added. "Are you okay? This is for real."

"I don't know whether to laugh or curtsy," Emma jested.

"Curtsy would be my advice as it is the way to welcome a prince," Ensign Jordon advised.

Sean looked at Jordon, then back to Emma. "A curtsy it is, my subject...Ouch," As Emma responded with a dig to his ribs. All three chuckled, "Have you fired the lasers, yet they are awesome." With no being the answer, Jordon made the appropriate communications and Emma fired off a couple of rounds. Sean watched as Emma played with the controls, he remembered when he had first experienced the shuttle...This time was better, the continued look of amazement on Emma's face made him feel happy inside.

Finally sitting down Sean informed Emma more about his family being royalty. Emma looked at Jenna, white gown, cape and a tiara, "Your mum looks beautiful...that tiara. Can I have one?"

"I don't know...maybe...why not, I'll ask," Sean was thinking protocol.

All conversation ended as the shuttle landed in the space station, the door opened, and the ramp emerged. Kain stood at the exit, Jenna on his arm—Sean and Emma behind, holding hands. Walking down the ramp Sean ignored the people around them and just watched Emma. "They are all bowing to us, this is unreal," Emma whispered to Sean.

The party stopped, a tall bearded man stood before them, Sean could tell he was a Vulten. "King Kain," the Vulten bowed. "I am Commander Ruzz. I am the commander of the space station and I welcome you aboard."

"Thank you, Commander Ruzz. We shall go to our quarters and meet you on the bridge later."

No more introductions were made, and the party walked to the Saulten welcome room that Sean had been to only some few months previous. As the royal party entered all present in the room stood, bowed or curtsied then continued with their entertainment. Kain led the group to a cleared corner and asked all to sit. Sean went to sit then found himself chasing Emma who had ignored Kain and was walking towards the glass wall for a view out to space. Sean looked back at his father who said in his head, *Don't worry, go with Emma.* Sean joined Emma at the window.

"This is real space, out there. This is awesome!" Emma was in awe of the view.

Sean looked at Emma then outside before answering, "Yes, this is real. This side is space, the other is the sun which, obviously, is blacked out."

"Can I see Earth from here?"

"No, we need to be up higher and around a bit, but I will show you."

"Please!"

"Sorry, dear, but not now. Sean, you need to go with your father. Emma come with me and maybe we can get you looking like an Earthen," Sal instructed. Sean left Emma with Sal and joined his father for the walk to the bridge.

Once on the bridge, Commander Ruzz approached Sean, Algier and Kain, "Secretary Seth is waiting for you in the private com's room upstairs, Your Highness." With this the group were lead upstairs to the com's room Sean had seen previously.

"King Kain, Algier and young Saul, a pleasure to meet you again."

Sean shook Seth's hand; he felt Seth was being honest and not just pleasant. Kain did not welcome Seth in the same manner. "Ruzz, leave us. Secretary Seth, you have disturbed my holiday just to measure my power—we could have communicated from Earth."

"Your Highness that is not true. Your council and I believe you need to be nearer to the situation. Feel your people." Seth was standing tall.

"Do not tell me how to handle my people. Start the communication." With that monitors came alive, the remaining four kings and their secretaries appeared.

"King Kain you called this communication what is it you want?' Vul started.

"My fellow kings, good evening. I have been updated on events on Earthen and wish to take your views on the horrific terrorist attacks?" Kain asked.

"You have shown little interest until Saulten was bombed!"

Sean looked; it was King Bier who had spoken. "That is not correct, King Bier. I have been updated all the time. But yes, a bomb in my capital killing my subjects and known friends is not acceptable. Is anyone aware of who is to blame?"

"F.A.M. was responsible," King Ders spoke.

Kain thought then responded, "Are you sure my friend? My understanding is F.A.M. bomb buildings and do not generally look to kill people?"

"That is absurd, Kain, are you siding with F.A.M.?" Vul interrupted.

Sean watched his father take a few steps then walk towards Vul's screen. "Why would I wish to support a group that plan to overthrow me? If you were a Saulten I would count your words as treason and deal with it directly!" Sean gulped; *Dad was in king mode* he thought.

Vul was not giving in, "For once Kain, I wish I were a Saulten as I would take your offer up!"

All screens took a breath—Seth came to the rescue. "Your highnesses I am sorry to be blunt but there is death and destruction on our planet, and you wish to score brownie points with each other?"

Again, the screens gasped, Sean thought to himself *go Seth*— his thought was wrong. "Secretary Seth!" Kain had turned on Seth, "I do not care for that tone." Sean saw Seth pull back; clearly Kain was putting force on him. Then suddenly Kain twitched and averted his gaze from Seth who gave a wry smile.

"King Kain. I agree my secretary has spoken out of line, but I will deal with him, not you," Vul was strangely smirking as he spoke.

"Gentleman please!" Algier pleaded. "This is going nowhere; we must agree a way forward before we see further deaths in each of your kingdoms."

All was quiet until Kain broke the silence, "I will see my people. I will be returning to Saulten. There is a planned King's Council soon; maybe we can talk before then. Secretaries make the arrangements. Viewers off!"

Sean looked; Seth was smiling at Kain then said, "You are brave or stupid." With that Seth left the room.

Algier approached Kain, "I do not know what has come over, Seth, but he is right. Kain, are you unwell?"

Sean looked at his father—he did look lost. "Algier, please make the arrangements with Seth. Sean, you come with me."

Sean did not speak but followed his father to a small room within the Saulten sector. With the doors closed behind them he was alone with his father.

"Dad, are you unwell?"

Kain smirked, "No. Indeed I have never felt better son."

Sean looked perplexed.

"All is not as it seems. I do not do politics well but deception I do."

"You lied to me for years so I'll second that," Sean could not pull back his words.

Kain chuckled, "You are still young and yet this is thrown upon you. My son. Sean. You know that my love for you has no end and now and over the next week you must trust me and accept my actions and decisions without question."

Sean took the words in, "If that is to be the case then I need to know everything."

"You will however, I am sorry, it is not that I do not trust you, but I cannot let my plans out. Watch what I do, always think the good and take my lead—I need you to promise me you will?"

"Of course, Dad, you don't need to ask."

"You must and will, over the next week, act as an Earthen. You need to be a prince and a would-be king."

"Yes, I will."

"Good, then learning when to talk, who to talk to and who to trust are important."

"I think I know who."

"It is not just Algier, Sal, Anders but sometimes people you do not expect to. Like this woman, doors open."

Sean turned to see standing in the doorway Jeng. "No, not her!"

"Yes, her!" Sean was twisted around by his father, looking in his eyes. "I trust Jeng with my life, no, I would trust her with your mother's life. Listen to her and move on. I will leave you alone."

With that Kain left the room, only Sean and Jeng were left. "Tell me why I should not just kill you!"

"Your Highness, I will not defend myself. If death is your sentence, then so be it."

Sean was taken aback by Jeng's response. "I do want to

kill you, you killed Shadow!" With this Sean took an attack stance.

Jeng knelt before him, "Before you kill me think on what your father has said. Please accept my apology in what happened to Shadow. I was not aware that my actions would lead to such a terrible response by a deranged person." Sean started to circle Jeng, who knelt without movement. "My crime was to fall in love, I and Prince Alex were and are together. Unfortunately, for obvious reasons, we must keep it quiet. Sean, I love your father, your mother and you." Jeng started to cry.

Sean's head was now spinning. Standing in front of Jeng he demanded, "Stand!" Jeng stood. Sean raised his arms, Jeng stood still. Sean felt the tears in his eyes as he moved towards Jeng and gave her a big hug. "I am so sorry, Jeng, I am so sorry, you are right, it is not your fault, please forgive me." Both stood embracing and crying for some time.

"You loveable fool if only you were a few years older," Jeng could not help but to kiss Sean fully on the lips. Sean thought before returning the kiss. Jeng came to her senses first.

"We will forever be friends; it is not to be for us. You have Emma and I have Alex. But our relationship is needed to go forward. I am your father's biggest fan and supporter; together we will help change things." With this Jeng held out her hand. Sean smiled, wiped his tears and shook Jeng's hand. He knew in his heart he now loved Jeng but in a different way.

BIRTHDAY IN SPACE:
(CHAPTER 29)

Sean woke having had a good night's sleep, he and Jeng had returned to the group so late no one was around. Emma! He said to himself. Her birthday! Sean cleaned and dressed as fast as he could then went to the breakfast room. He dropped his head as he realised he was the last one there. "Happy birthday, Emma!" Sean shouted as he gave her the biggest cuddle he could.

"Thank you, may I breathe now?" Sean let Emma go but stole a kiss before sitting next to her.

"Oh shit!"

"Sean!"

"Sorry, Mum, but I have no present. Oops, I said that aloud."

Emma smiled, "It looks like in all the rush all my presents are back on Earth. Anyway, I will get them soon, but having my family, friends and you here with me is all I need. Being in space kind of helps as well." All laughed as Sean received another kiss.

Breakfast eaten, Sean asked, "Is there anything planned for today?"

"Of course," Jenna responded. "We have a meal booked for early evening then the bar later with some music. I would think Emma may enjoy the pool during the day?"

"Swimming, it will ruin my hair."

Sean laughed, "Not Earthen swimming. Let our food go

down and we can go in an hour or so." Emma nodded a yes.

On the hour, as promised Sean led Emma to the fluid bearing pool where both changed into swimwear and stood beside the pool. "That's not water." Emma was being vigilant.

"I know, watch," Sean jumped and with no real splash entered the fluid balls. After submerging he came to the top treading water. "Watch!" This time Sean swam lower, immersing his head fully but with his eyes and mouth open, smiling. Emma looked quizzical before first placing her hand into the pool then dive-bombed Sean. Both heads emerged from the water.

"What is this? It's not water?"

"Fluid bearings to be exact. Don't worry just enjoy, look you can go under and breathe." Sean again immersed his head. Emma copied and both were half a metre under the surface. Eyes and mouths fully open looking at each other.

"O.M.G. it feels like water, I can swim but breathe and talk as well."

"Yep, beat you to the edge."

Both enjoyed themselves for some time, jumping in and out of the pool or just floating fully immersed in the middle. Sean took the opportunity for an under-water kiss. Finally, Emma got up onto the edge and sat there.

Sean joined her. "This is amazing, and I don't feel wet?"

"Technically you could just dress as it cleans as well however, Mum says it's no good for the hair so proper washing is needed."

"O.M.G. look at the time, where did it go? You are right I need to do my hair and get ready for tonight. Let's go!"

"It's hours yet?"

"Exactly which way?" Emma was up and running. With Emma off to get dressed Sean decided to FaceTime Mush, this lasted a further hour or more—Mush missed them both. Sean heard a knock on the door and Jenna entered, "Are you ready?"

"What? No, we have hours yet!"

"You mean a half hour," Jenna had opened a wardrobe. "This would be good for tonight."

"A bit formal."

"It is Emma's sixteenth! You will be formal and wear your crown as well. A half hour, watch the time, I'll be back!"

Sean showered and dressed, standing at the door as his mother reappeared. "Wow, as you would say young man, you are looking good."

"Wow back Mum, you can certainly wear a crown or is it a tiara?"

Jenna laughed, turned and Sean followed her to the welcome room. Upon entering Sean noted all there were formally dressed. Harry had somehow got into an Earthen suit. Judy, Jeng and Emma were not there. Sean grabbed a drink off the side and sat awaiting the birthday girl.

Judy entered the room first, as was her husband, she was wearing Earthen clothes. Jeng followed, Sean's jaw dropped, *was this the first time he had seen her in a dress* he thought. Jeng smiled and moved aside, Emma was behind her. Sean froze, Emma was dressed in a figure hugging white Earthen dress that showed a lot of flesh all around and was wearing a tiara. "You are beautiful!" Sean said aloud as he stood, this was his girlfriend, and all should know.

Emma smiled and took Sean's hand, "Thank you. Apparently, we have a table and meal waiting for us."

Jeng led, Sean and Emma close behind with their parents and friends in tow. The walk was quite a distance and included a lift. As they passed, other ships occupants all bowed as the party approached, the women ahh'ed. Sean knew he had the most beautiful woman on his arm. Once at the restaurant in the bar area, all sat for drinks and a toast. Sean could see Emma loved the attention.

"May I take you to your tables Your Highness?" Sean turned to see the headwaiter addressing him and not his father who was only a metre or so from him.

"Please do." The waiter led the party to a couple of tables against the glass wall that looked out to the stars. "Are there set places?" Sean asked in his most formal voice.

"No, your highness however, these tables are for your guests. You and your lady need to follow me."

Sean looked at his mother; Jenna smiled and nodded. Sean and Emma followed the headwaiter up a short flight of stairs to a small room. In the middle of the room was a table for two already set with candles or at least an electric gadget made to look like candles that looked so realistic. The headwaiter pulled the chair out for Emma to sit first, then did the same for Sean. "The room has a fully interactive music system and this view." As the waiter finished his sentence the room walls went clear, the stars surrounded them on three sides and above.

"O.M.G. that's Earth!" Emma could not control her excitement as she jumped out of her seat to look out at her home planet. "We really are in space."

Sean stood, walked to Emma and took her by the arm, "Of course. Earth is nearly as beautiful as you." Emma smiled, they kissed and held hands all the way back to the table. Four courses later and a good mix of music and chat, Emma had mastered the sound system—both sat looking into each other's eyes.

"This is the best and most magical birthday ever."

"I could not agree more. Waiter, please clear the table." The table was cleared, and the waiter left.

"Chairs and table down," The furniture did as instructed. The room was now empty, just Sean, Emma and the stars. Sean thought, then went for it, "Ed Sheeran please, Shape of You. With effects." The room temperature changed; the music started. "Don't move yet just listen and feel the music." Emma held back but within thirty seconds she was in the mood—both danced closely for song after song under the stars. Sean's reward was the longest most perfect kiss ever.

"I think I need a drink, after all I'm the only one sixteen here."

Sean went red, "Yes, me too. Shall we join the family?"

"Yes, but wait," Emma closed her eyes; "I will picture this moment forever. You have literally given me the stars for my birthday."

Both made the short trip down to their family and friends; it was clear there had been more drink than food partaken. Jenna was the first to greet them, "Hi both, did you have a good time?"

"Yes, Jenna, the best."

"Maybe my young man has learnt something from his father"—Sean went red. "Now you need to learn something from me." With that Jenna took Emma's hand and led her to the dance floor, quickly joined by Jeng, Sal and Judy. Sean laughed and sat next to his father.

"You had a good meal?"

"Yes Dad, it was the best. Thank you." Kain gave Sean a hug.

Sean was awoken by a knock on his door, "Enter."

"Get up son, we need to get to the bridge," Kain was throwing Sean's clothes from last night at him to wear. Sean did not argue but put on the clothes and followed his father. As they exited the Saulten corridor Kain stopped and looked out the window. "Damn! They have ignored me!"

Sean looked out the window; a craft of some sort was leaving the space station. Sean watched as the craft came more into sight, the pointed shape emerging below him got bigger and bigger. Sean's heart sank. "Is that a battleship?"

Algier had joined them, "Yes, a Vulten battleship."

Sean kept watching as the full shape of the craft, guns

and all were evident. The battleship was moving slowly then stopped, the lights on the craft went out. Then a blue haze from the rear and the battleship shot out towards Earth, visible in the distance.

"Is it going to attack Earth?" Sean started to panic.

"No son, it is on manoeuvres, but an unconfirmed one. The bridge, let's go."

All three were shortly in the lift with the doors about to open. "Control Kain, you are ill, remember."

Before Kain could respond to Algier the lift doors opened, the large shape of Commander Ruzz was in front of them. Kain did not speak but pushed past Ruzz, Algier and Sean followed.

Kain spoke, "I wish to speak with Secretary Seth."

"Secretary Seth is still asleep. I am the commander, what is your question?"

Sean watched Kain look at Ruzz, he could tell his father wanted to pull him apart but did not. "May I remind you of who I am. I wish to speak to Secretary Seth now!"

"Don't worry Commander as I am here," Seth had announced himself. "King Kain, what is your concern?"

"My concern. A Vulten battleship has launched, a launch that is unconfirmed?"

"My friend it is just a formality of confirmation, it has been a planned manoeuvre for weeks."

"No battleship planned or otherwise leaves the space station without confirmation. You know the rules Secretary."

"I am sorry, maybe there is a miscommunication here, but its deployment has been planned for months," Seth was looking clearly into Kain's eyes.

Kain stepped back, Algier came forward. "You have broken protocol and I will ask for the ship's immediate return."

"Councilor Algier, you are talking red tape, paperwork, by the time we have noted your concern, maybe take action the manoeuvre would be over. Please let us not make such a thing about this."

"Secretary Seth, shall I call our king?"

"No commander, I am dealing with this." Seth walked towards Kain, "Do I need to involve, King Vul?"

Kain coughed, looked at Algier then back to Seth, "Algier, lodge the complaint." With this Kain walked to the elevator, Sean followed. Doors closed, Kain hit the wall with his fist.

"Be quiet, we are not in a secure area." No more was said; father and son went back to the Saulten area.

"What does this mean?" Sean finally asked.

"I for the first time did not kill someone when I should have." Sean was a little surprised by his father's response.

"You killing, Ruzz, or, Seth, would not have helped?"

"It would have shown my strength."

"But that is exactly what you did not want to do."

Kain smirked, before he could speak Jenna joined them. "That was not part of the plan I guess?" She asked, Kain shook his head. "Is there a danger? Surely this is just a manoeuvre? Another opportunity to wind you up?"

"Maybe, dear, but it is working, definitely not something I expected. I need time to think," Kain walked away to sit on a chair on his own.

"You have a young lady smiling from ear to ear in the day room over there, maybe you should see her." Sean nodded to his mother and walked to the adjoining room. Sean's entrance was met by a big hug and kiss from Emma. Sean sat with Emma and her parents not really taking in the conversation as his mind was elsewhere.

"All please listen!" Kain had entered the room. "There is a change of plan, we will be going to Earthen shortly," Kain stopped. "Yes, young lady, if your parents agree you can come as well." Sean looked to see a big smile on all the Coopers faces

—if only they knew, he thought.

"We will meet you all at the sun ship in half an hour. Sean, Algier with me," Again Sean followed his father without question. Once again Sean found himself in the small room where he had met Jeng the day before. Jeng and Shad were already in the room as the three Saul's entered.

"Shad, fill us in please?" Kain asked.

"The Vulten ship is carrying out set manoeuvres. It is in Earth orbit but hidden, again nothing unusual there. All appears, although not confirmed, to be sticking by protocol as such."

"Secretary Seth has the complaint, he will update us soon," Algier added.

"Now the real situation, Shad?' Kain pushed.

"The battleship is fully loaded, two destroyers attached and ten fighters in each."

"And?"

The Ainten, Dersian and Saulten battleships can be deployed. The Biernite ship has damage since a fire a week or so ago and cannot launch."

Kain thought, "Algier put forward a request to launch our battleship, make something up, like…a joint manoeuvre."

"They won't fall for that Kain."

"Put the plans in then have a com's failure, if they can do it, so can we!"

"Yes, of course, I will do that now," Algier left.

"Shad, the Ainten battleship must not launch. You know what to do." Shad bowed and turned to leave. "Captain, you need to be strong, here on the space station when I have left. I can count on you?"

Shad turned, bowed again. "Yes, Your Highness, it is my honour." Shad then left.

"So how come the bridge is still intact?" Jeng smiled.

"Act like the commander you are please," Kain's smile gave away his intent.

Jeng played along, "Do you wish me on Earthen or here just in case military action is required?"

"You know what is needed...Earthen. I will speak with the Earth council—they will protect the Earth. You two can talk, I need to see someone alone," Kain left the room.

"Surely Vul is not going to attack Earth?" Sean knew he would get more out of Jeng, adding a smile for good measure.

"No, I am sure it is like poker. Bluff and double bluff, even Vul would not act on his own."

"Would your Ainten king not support him?"

Jeng chuckled, "Shad, is good with matches you know."

With that both left to go to the sun ship. Emma greeted Sean with the standard cuddle; she was already trying to board the ship even though Kain and Algier were not present. Jeng took control, the air locks were opened, and all entered the ship. Again, Sean sat next to Emma; he gave the rundown of what to expect— 'listen to the music' and 'take the pill,' was double stated.

First Algier, then Kain, boarded with Jeng at the controls. Launch process activated they were soon in flight. Sean stretched out and held Emma's hand, as the sun ship hit full drive, he wished he had not, Emma's grasp and nails drew blood.

The sun ship started to slow, eventually, to its landing speed; the helmets lifted, and the seatbelts came undone. Sean looked at Emma, "The toilets are in the back." Sean laughed as Emma and her father both raced to the rear nearly knocking each other over. Upon her return Emma sat down, looking very pale.

"Are you okay honey?" Jenna was looking from behind her seat.

"Yes, please tell me we won't be doing that again in a hurry?"

Sean laughed, "You should have taken the pill!" No more was said. All sat back down as the sun ship berthed on the Earthen space station, again Emma and her father were happy to be off the smaller ship.

"This is much better, more room, I can breathe. Wait a minute, is this finished?"

Sean noted Emma was looking around and could clearly see exposed ducting and cables. "Yes, it is an older version of the space station concept and only used as a station to catch the sun ships. It is not meant to be a base as the more modern Earth space station is."

"Are we really the other side of the sun?"

"Yes, and I'm sure we won't be here long before leaving for Earthen. Wait, shush!" Sean stopped, he noted Kain and some people were talking in loud voices, Kain clearly agitated. No words were said but the group followed Kain to a room. The room was plain, no chairs or views. Kain finished talking with the people and addressed all present.

"My friends, I am sorry to advise you that whilst we were in flight..." Kain stopped, "The Vulten battleship released a destroyer. The destroyer is now...hovering over the White House. Viewers on."

With this, ten viewers lit up the walls, all showing varied pictures and angles of an Earthen destroyer hovering over the White House. Sean looked all around, many of the viewers were showing Earth footage, their NBC or BBC logos clear, others could only be Earthen—none had sound on.

"Holy shit!" Broke the air; Emma could not hold her thoughts.

"What is going on?" Harry demanded of Kain.

"My friend, nothing yet. My understanding is the ship is hovering, but no contact has been made. Please stay here with

Jenna and the others. I, Sean and Algier will find out more."

Sean found himself on another bridge but this time a Commander Dune was in charge, a Saulten. "Sire, you were beaten here by another sun ship. Maybe Secretary Seth can answer your questions."

Sean looked and Seth was standing before them; *if Dad won't, I will* he thought.

"King Kain, before you speak you have our deepest apologies. The destroyer we believe is being piloted by a rogue F.A.M. supporter, we were not aware of his plans."

Kain did not speak, Algier again led, "Secretary Seth. I am appalled at your lack of control over your ships and people, no soldiers!" Algier circled the much taller Seth, "Call the destroyer back now!"

Seth looked uncomfortable, "I have tried but the destroyer is not responding, indeed it is in complete communication shut down to us and Earth."

"Then blow it out of the air, you have a battleship out there, it is clearly breaking all protocol!" Sean noted Algier had finally lost it.

"My friend, even if I could do you really think a fully armed destroyer, metres over a densely populated city, would go down without a battle? How many humans do you wish me to sacrifice?"

Algier froze, this time Kain spoke, "Call the kings now. I wish to talk to them." It took ten minutes to arrange but the bridge screen's viewers all showed the kings and their secretaries, plus others. Sean scowled at his Uncle Dain.

"Kain, you have my ear." Sean thought it a surprising opening remark from Vul.

Kain rose, went to speak but coughed. "Are you unwell, my friend?" Councilor Anders spoke.

"I am fine, Earthen food does not agree with me. Your highnesses, you failed to acknowledge my last call and now we have this. At no point have we agreed to show ourselves to Earthlings let alone create such unrest as this."

"I must agree with, Kain!" King Ders supported Kain clearly.

"This is not a vote," King Ain joined in.

"Vul, you are quiet, when it is your ship, your subjects, we are talking of?" Kain was trying to stand tall.

"I am disgraced that my kingdom is being shown in this way however, I believe F.A.M. have infiltrated my army and have taken this action of their own accord. I assure you, Vulten, are not condoning this."

Sean looked at Vul, did he mean it? Was he being sincere? No, surely not. "Then call your ships back." As Kain spoke Sean saw each of the king's viewers go red, each appearing to take a message. As the screens went green Kain continued, "Oh I forgot, you will of course not question the launch of my battleship, it too has manoeuvres to carry out." Kain could not stop a smirk.

"This is preposterous!" King Bier announced. "King Vul, I normally support you however, we must all condone this action. You are not in control of your own fleet! You disappoint me."

Vul's face went red; Sean swore he saw steam coming from his ears. "Give me time and I will sort this!"

"Before you go, I demand the King's Council be brought forward!" Kain addressed all.

"We have one planned in a few weeks on Ainten," King Ain advised.

"That is too long, we need one this week or next. I propose Friday next which is nine days away. I would be happy to facilitate it on Saulten?"

No one spoke for a minute, as all considered a response. Vul took the lead. "I would agree to next Friday but on Vulten."

Kain coughed and responded, "So be it, next Friday on Vulten."

Each king nodded his head in agreement, but Anders spoke, "King Kain, this is all well and good however nine days of a Vulten destroyer above the U.S. capital is too long a time."

Kain turned, "My friend you are correct. I am sure that King Vul and Secretary Seth will take all actions they can to call the destroyer back. If not, my battleship, supported by the Dersian battleship that leaves within the hour, will attack. I take personal responsibility for this course of action as the Earth Secretary—after all it is my job to protect Earth!" All went quiet again before Kain continued; "I am both prepared to duel anyone who questions my authority in this matter and order the loss of human life in the battle if I have to."

Sean took a deep breath, as did all. Algier spoke, "My king, I am sure no one wishes to challenge you and I would also guess that regardless of communications failure the destroyer will know we will attack. Maybe the message will get to it that a King's Council has been called and maybe it will await a decision. Surely those on board do not wish to die unnecessarily?"

King Ain responded, "Chief Councilor Algier, I would agree a direct challenge at this point will serve no benefit. I would suggest your assumption about communication is correct although your inference that the ship will listen to someone of this group disturbs me. It is unfounded however; I believe this would be the best course of action for now. Kain, I will not challenge your decision or role at present but in person and at the King's Council I may change my mind."

Sean watched as each king nodded and ended the communication from his end. Sean watched as Kain went up to Seth, clearly saying something directly into his head. Whatever it was Seth looked troubled. "Algier, Sean with me." Again, Sean followed Kain and Algier to a private room, Algier spoke first.

"I'm up for the delaying bit but a direct challenge? Someone could have called your bluff."

"It was no bluff, I would have accepted a challenge."

"Maybe a little foolish as you have been giving the impression you are unwell?"

"I know but they are still weary of me, besides you and I both know this is a ploy to hold the King's Council. Vul controls that destroyer."

"This and you offering to meet on Vulten walks straight into Vul's hands. He will be strong and well supported there."

"Yes, but that is tomorrow's problem, for now I have at least bought Washington time."

"Are you both sure about this?" Sean wanted to know.

Kain put his arms on Sean's shoulders, "Of course we cannot be certain, but we have our spies and believe we know the enemies' plans. Sometimes you have to go with your instinct or indeed challenge straight on."

"So, if Vul or one of the others had accepted your challenge you would have fought...and to the death?"

"Yes, I would. My life to you and your mother is precious but in the scheme of things when I need to face death I will for my planets and people." Kain hugged Sean and left.

"Wipe your tears Sean, your father knows what he is doing. I assure you his own death is not top of his agenda."

Sean looked at Algier, "How do you know that? Why does he talk to me in this way?"

"My child, Kain is clearly making you aware that his actions may lead to death. I know he has spoken with your mother about this. However, he is still the most powerful Earthen I have ever witnessed, maybe this honesty is also preparing himself for that final fight."

Sean sniffled, "And when will that be, on that Friday?"

"Maybe, maybe not, but you must be prepared to face up to the possibility and support your father, without question."

No more was said; Sean and Algier joined the main party on the shuttle to leave for Earthen.

PALACE RETURN:
(CHAPTER 30)

"Earthen shuttle requesting low flight over Saulten City," Commander Jeng requested.

"Permission granted, your fighter convoy will stay above you, P.A. out."

Sean looked out of the numerous viewers on show around the shuttle. As the shuttle approached Saulten City it stopped, hovering above a large crater that looked completely out of place within the relatively built up surroundings.

Sal spoke aloud, "That is where the terrorist bomb went off and all those people died." There was no response, Sean could see both his mother and father looking but with their heads lowered. Emma grasped Sean's arm in reassurance. As the mood was low Sean could not help feeling disappointed for Emma who was clearly holding back her excitement. Sean could recall his first sight of the palace, the grounds and the people.

Emma and the group refrained from talking until they were in the palace hall. "Please have some refreshments," Wort was handing drinks out with a smile. Lens got to Sean and Emma first.

"Oh, my, you are a beautiful young lady, welcome to our palace." Lens addressed Emma with a big smile on her face.

"Thank you. It looks like an amazing place." Lens gave Sean a quick hug then moved on to serve Judy and Harry.

"Sean, maybe you and Emma should go to your room. I think we all need some time out on our own," Jenna smiled as she spoke. Sean needed no further encouragement, taking Emma's hand, he headed for the lift. Emma's face was full of amazement as she looked out of the glass lift, but again nothing was said. Sean led Emma to his bedroom door, opened it and led her in. Emma turned, checked the door was shut, and then screamed, "Holy crap this place is awesome, sorry, but I have to say it!"

Sean chuckled, "I'm sorry you had to see it for the first time in this mood but yes, let me show you." Sean spent the next hour demonstrating the furniture, the monitors and many other features. Both ended up on the balcony looking at the sunset.

"This is beautiful, magical, like a fantasy," Emma gave Sean a quick peck on the cheek to enforce the message.

"Yes, it is young lady," Both Sean and Emma jumped, as they had not heard his mother come in.

"Your clothes are in the spare bedroom in Sean's apartment. Your mother and I are happy for you to stay here. We were both sixteen once, be as comfortable as you like but be careful."

Sean went red, as did Emma. "Mum, you can't, I mean..."

Jenna laughed, "Goodnight, we trust you both." Jenna then left.

"O.M.G. did she? I mean...no she didn't?" Emma was as spell bound as Sean.

"Maybe you should see your room?"

"Yes, of course."

Sean led Emma to her room, the bigger of the two guest rooms within his apartment. Emma ran into the changing room, the toilet then jumped on the big bed.

"I am in heaven!" Emma shouted whilst rolling around on

the bed. Sean laughed and, waiting until she stopped, sat beside her.

"Maybe you should sleep alone tonight? You could use the bath? It has jets and everything, freshen up after the travel?"

"Yes, that would be best for tonight…but don't think I don't want to…I mean, just not now," Emma blushed.

"I know, goodnight," Sean kissed Emma and left for his own room.

Sean awoke, dressed and met Emma on the balcony, "Have you been up long?"

"Yes, I have watched the sunrise. It is unbelievable, I am on another planet."

"This view is best, over the gardens and then the hills."

"Is it right that that Earthen thing over Washington is unlikely to attack?"

"Yes, as far as I know it is just like a pawn in a chess match—more politics then war. Let's catch breakfast and then explore a bit." Sean was uncomfortable. Although he was closer to the truth, his views on the barbaric Earthen nature were worrying.

Joining all for breakfast, Sean made an unusual comment, "Uncle Dain, I have not seen him, is he in the palace?"

"I believe he has found triplets of the female sort and is spending a little more time in the city," Kain laughed.

"That he is, such a shallow man. We can ask him shortly at the council," Algier informed.

Jenna was in organizational mode, "Whilst Kain and Algier deal with the council I will show Judy the palace. Sean, you can show Emma."

"And me?" Harry chirped up.

"I believe you have the pleasure of my company," Syston announced as he entered the room.

Sean jumped from his chair and gave Syston a hug, "Wait,

you are in military clothing?"

"Yes, I have signed up to support your father," Syston's smile dropped. "Gram and Hoy were killed in the Saulten terror bombing."

A tear came to Sean's eye, "I am so sorry to hear that, I did not know."

"Don't worry my prince, their deaths will not be in vain." Sean looked at Syston who upon uttering these words stood tall; he was a very formidable sight.

"My friend, thank you," Kain was shaking Syston's hand. "Harry, this is our dueling champion, think World Heavyweight Boxing Champion on Earth. He will talk sport but also advise you of our ways today."

Sean looked at Harry who was clearly looking at the size of Syston whilst saying; "Of course I will do whatever this hulk says!" All chuckled at his response.

Emma's tour started with the swimming pools, then onto the music room. "Just like the one on the space station but better, watch." Sean requested, "Ed Sheeran, Galway Girl, 3.D." Emma's mouth dropped in amazement, as the main characters from the song were shown in full 3.D. moving around the room just like on the Earth video.

"O.M.G. can we join in?"

"Yes, it is like being with them."

Emma ran to the female character and started to copy her moves, mostly running around the room. The song stopped, the 3.D. paused, "Again!" Emma asked. The song started from the beginning, but this time Emma ran and sang along, pulling Sean in at certain points. Six songs in, all different performers and Sean sat down exhausted—Emma kept going. Sean watched Emma standing, mimicking and singing with Ellie Goulding—How Long Will I love You. Their eyes met frequently whilst Emma was singing, Sean knew the answer —forever. Emma requested, "Play that song," but before she could pull Sean to the floor he had moved to the door.

"I'm done, let's see something else!" Emma smiled and they were walking around the palace. The games room was next. Upon entering they saw Syston and Harry were there already.

"Hi Dad. Having fun?" Emma asked.

"Be quiet. It's like chess but 3.D. I'm concentrating dear." Harry responded. Sean winked at Syston and led Emma out to the garden.

"What do you think of that?" Sean asked as they passed the Bosworth statue.

"It's good, I love the pose captured."

"Oh, I thought it was crap."

Emma gave Sean a dig in the ribs, "You uncultured fool." Emma stopped, looking at Sean, she said, "Wait, what are you thinking?"

"Nothing," was the response but Sean's eyes were looking around. Capturing Wort out of the corner of his eyes Sean addressed him.

"Wort, where is the Girella please?"

"In the garage, next to the stables. Be careful."

Sean addressed Emma, "Follow me."

"You have a gorilla, a zoo here?"

"No, a Girella, you'll see," Sean smirked. Upon entering the garage Sean saw his favourite Christmas present ever, it looked brutal. Without speaking Sean went to a shelf next to the motorbike and pulled out some helmets. "This one is mine; this should fit you."

"You think I'm getting on that thing with you?" Emma was looking unsure.

Sean ignored her and jumped on the bike, started it and said, "Get on." Emma shrugged her shoulders but obliged. Sean pulled the throttle and the bike took off, exiting the garage with Sean's direction. Sean took it easy at first, manoeuvring around the various garden paths.

"There is no engine noise?"

"Its electric or something. Hold on!" Sean felt Emma's arms tighten around him as he twisted the throttle, the bike sped up, heading towards the woods at the rear of the garden. Upon reaching the woods Sean slowed down as he steered the bike around the smaller, undulating paths.

"Don't scare the horses!" Sean heard as he approached the stream and small waterfall, Jenna and Judy had beaten them there.

"Can we join you for a drink?" Sean asked.

"If it gets my daughter off that thing then yes!" Was Judy's reply. Sean and Emma dismounted the bike, removed their helmets and went to join their mothers by the stream, but Emma veered off.

"O.M.G. horses, they are beautiful!"

Sean assessed the situation; of course, his mother had been riding with Judy. "This is Gloss, Mum's stallion," Sean gave Gloss a stroke on his mane. "This is Droop, my horse."

Emma gave Gloss's head a hug, and then moved to Droop. "Oh, I see," with a smile Emma gave Droop's head a hug too. "Can we ride them?" Emma asked as she joined the mothers at the stream.

"Yes, whenever you want. Have a drink," Jenna replied providing drink.

All sat talking for an hour, Emma jumping up every now and then to feed the horses. "Whatever is going on with the spaceship over the White House is scary...so are their ways however," Judy spoke. "This place is beautiful, and sorry for being shallow, but this royalty thing is amazing."

Jenna smiled at her friend, "Yes, now you see the dilemma. Here as a Queen. Or, on Earth as a wife and mother with real family and friends. Earthen does not compete."

Sean saw Judy and Emma exchange glances before Judy spoke. "Yes, we can see what you mean, do you think it will change?"

Jenna stood walking toward Gloss, "Maybe, no hopefully. We will ride back, be careful on that bike, or would you like to ride with me, Emma?"

Sean looked at Emma, she was clearly thinking of the right decision. Catching Sean's eye Emma responded, "Thanks Jenna but I'll stick with Sean for now, maybe we can ride tomorrow?" With this Sean and Emma put their helmets on and were again on the Girella. As Sean took off, he heard Judy shout, "Be careful on that thing, if you hurt or kill my daughter, I'll kill you!" Although Sean could not see Judy or Emma, he knew it was lighthearted.

Sean steered the bike towards the rear gate, slowing down, he looked at the guards. "Open them, let me out!" Sean noted the perplexed expression on the guard's face, but the gate was opened. Sean twisted the throttle and they were flying down the road, then the track that led to the hills. Sean had recalled the journey he had taken with his father. As the bike went up and down, at points making small jumps Sean felt Emma holding on, not in fear but enjoyment. Sean stopped the bike at the foot of the ridge, both dismounted.

"This place is stunning, wow, look how high and straight upwards it is."

Sean followed Emma's stare, "Yes, me and Dad climbed this on the last visit."

"Wow, it looks dangerous."

"It is but we had special equipment, I will show you another day. Were you okay on the bike? Do you want a go?"

"Yes, it is fun, the faster the better, but don't tell mum. No, you drive, I want to see the scenery even if it is a blur." Both laughed as they remounted the bike and Sean took the same way back to the palace at a slower speed.

Leaving the motorbike in the garage Sean and Emma headed for the dining room to join the adults.

"You're alive, thank god!" Harry greeted his daughter whilst giving Sean a disagreeable look.

The evening passed, as there was no change in the destroyer situation, all were quite lighthearted. Sean noted even his father appeared relaxed. "Sean, we need to talk, let's walk," Kain advised quite late. Sean obliged and walked into the moonlit garden with his father. "Tomorrow you will go to Ainten for the day and stay the night. There is a Prince's Council; basically, our heirs meet every now and then; the idea being they get to know each other before one day they are all kings. Obviously, you have not been before, but they have met every six months or so."

"Oh, okay. Will I be safe?"

Kain smirked, "Probably not as they are mini kings, but you are more powerful than any of them."

Sean gulped, "Oh..."

Kain interrupted, "I am only jesting, you will be safe, Jeng and Livia will be with you. Although what I said about your power is true."

Sean thought, "It will be great to see Livia and yes, I feel safe with Jeng around. Can Emma go?"

"No. Protocol is one prince with one advisor. Livia will be with her older brother, Prince Wil Ders, then, Prince Trev Biers, and, Prince Sebast Aint, with their advisors. Prince Kruge Vul, Vul's eldest son, will be with, Prince Alex, his advisor, and you have, Jeng."

"Okay, I met them all at the Christmas do you know," Sean stopped then said, "But I did not spend much time with them."

"Let us hope it does not turn out the same. Kruge, is not really the type of Vulten to be messed with, he is much older."

"Yes, there is quite a difference in our ages. I am the youngest."

"Sean. This meeting and what you talk about will not have depth, as it is more social however, I need you to look into their eyes when a final decision is made."

Sean gave a quizzical look, "What decision?"

"It will be led by the one you will not expect but you will know when. Upon your return, we do not need to say things directly, but we need to feel the truth." Kain looked at Sean and smiled "You will be fine as, Jeng, Livia and Alex, will look after you. Have a good sleep before you go and have fun."

Sean watched after his father as he walked towards the palace, thinking *this is strange, why not be clear?* Sean followed Kain, leaving the lift a floor below. Sean entered his room, it was dark, but he saw light from under Emma's door. Sean walked towards the door, stopped, thought then went to his own bed.

PRINCES' AGREEMENT:

(CHAPTER 31)

"Wake up sleepy head!"

Sean opened his eyes. Emma, fully dressed, was by his bedside. "Apparently you are on a trip somewhere today and tonight, Jenna told us at breakfast."

"I missed breakfast?"

"Yes, and I suggest this uniform," Jeng was entering from the walk-in cupboard room. Jeng placed the uniform on Sean's bed; Emma gave him a quick kiss and both women left. Sean washed then dressed. Looking in the mirror, he saw his clothes were very military style, still white top and blue trousers, but with more emblems around them. They were also of a heavier material.

Sean said his goodbyes and boarded a small shuttle. Jeng sat next to him, as she was not flying that day. "We are staying at my uncle's, unfortunately my parents are no longer with us," Jeng added with a small tear. "In the back is some food, a bacon sandwich I believe Jenna made for you." With that Jenna pulled the sandwich and a flask from the bag she had, Sean thought *I like this kind of in-flight meal* before tucking in.

Although the flight was relatively quick compared to Earth travel for such a distance, Sean did have a chance to look out of the viewers. Saulten was quite baron, the ocean empty and Ainten, at least where they were landing, was forested. "Home," Jeng smiled as she led Sean off the shuttle across a small clearing, along a path sided by tall trees, to a small group of buildings.

"Uncle Pal, Auntie Dors, it is great to see you again." Sean watched as Jeng was engulfed in the arms of her family. Sean noted both were in their fifties probably and that Pal had similar features as Jeng, he must be Jeng's blood relative.

"We have another prince amongst us, welcome Prince Saul," Pal shook Sean's hand, and Dors curtsied. Pal led Sean and Jeng to a building, although remote and in the woods, it still looked like other Earthen buildings, bland and square but at least it was brown in colour.

As Sean and Jeng entered he was met with a big hug. "Hi Sean," Prince Alex gave Sean a smile, then turned to Jeng. Sean was surprised as Alex hugged Jeng then kissed her, especially as Sean was aware there were others in the room.

"Your first meeting little Prince," Kruge said with a smile as he shook Sean's hand.

Sean stood tall, looked around and then said, "I am the youngest but not the smallest." Before Kruge responded Livia took him off his feet.

"Sean, I have not seen you for some time, how are you and your parents?"

"Hi, Liv. As good as they can be at a time like this."

"Yes, obviously, come and I will introduce you to the others."

Sean knew all the princes; the only two new people were Jude and Mart, Sebast and Trev's advisors respectively. Sean noted they all welcomed him warmly; the first hour was for drinks and small talk before Kruge called the meeting. All sat around a large table, princes at the table, their advisors just behind.

"My fellow heirs, first a formal welcome, especially to Prince Saul." Each nodded their heads as Kruge continued. "We have a short agenda although it will take some time. We will discuss the present situation of terrorist attacks here and the situation on Earth. After that we will have a private meeting for the heirs only."

Sean watched and listened as the four heirs (as he was now calling them) discussed quite frankly the terrorism on both Earthen and Earth. Sean kept quiet most of the time; Livia and Jeng were allowed to speak and filled in many questions. Sean was quite surprised to feel all the heirs appeared concerned with the Earth situation; none seemed to support what was happening. At one-point Sean could not hold back and innocently asked, "If you are all against this, and so say your fathers, then how has an Earthen destroyer ended up over one of our major cities?"

"That is a bit too direct a question," Sebast replied.

"I am sorry but all this politics, deceit and the like hides a very dangerous situation that surely can be stopped?" Sean noted the uncomfortable looks on the other's faces; Jeng gave his arm a reassuring stroke.

Sean noted that before Kruge spoke he had looked to Alex. "Sean, although we are open here sometimes direct questions do hurt. We have our opinions and they are real however; we are not in power and can only act and plan for the future. Our fathers, on the other hand, still think and act as our troubled ancestors had to in building this world. Are they wrong? Are they different? Yes, but only to our views. Change, especially cultural, does not happen overnight."

Before Sean could respond Wil interjected, "Our fathers are split. Some want to stay, as others do not. I feel there is no appetite to invade Earth at present, the more pressing issue is here on Earthen."

"Then call the destroyer off." Sean looked straight at Kruge. Sean jolted backwards; realising Kruge was attacking him by thought. Sean responded hard. Kruge also pulled back but then pushed harder. Sean went to stand when Jeng pulled him up and away from the table with her arms.

Kruge was now standing as were the others but had stopped his attack on Sean. "You need to control your emotions young Prince!" Were Kruge's words.

"You attacked me first!" Sean was in fighting mode; he could feel anger swelling inside.

Livia stood between them, "Boys please. Sean, you will apologise to Kruge for insulting him with your suggestion that he or anyone here has control over the destroyer!" Sean looked at Livia, although her tone was harsh her smile looked sympathetic.

Livia said in his head, *Don't be a fool you are amongst friends!*

Sean thought and Livia moved aside. "I apologise for my outburst Kruge."

Again, Sean was taken aback by Kruge's response, "No apology necessary my peer. The drinks are on me as we need a break."

All took refreshments for an hour. "Have you calmed down Sean?" Alex asked him whilst they were on their own.

"Yes, I think so."

"Don't think so you fool, there could have been a fight. My brother is more traditional Vulten bred then me, he could have fought properly."

"So, could I!"

Alex laughed, "Oh my friend now I see why you and your father are so powerful. Too much human spirit in you both. Please don't wind my brother up again?"

"I don't intend to."

"Heirs, we shall meet on our own!" Kruge declared as he walked towards the exit. Sean looked at Livia then felt her and Jeng's voice in his head both saying *control yourself*. Sean nodded his head and followed the heirs to a small opening in the woods some one hundred metres from the buildings.

"Heirs, this will be brief but also away from other ears,"

Kruge again led.

"This facility is secure Kruge." Sebast assured.

Kruge ignored this and motioned for all to stand in a small circle, Sean was next to Kruge. "Heirs. We are in troubled times however; we believe that the time to act will be soon. I am personally against war and will do all within my power to stop it." Sean could not help but lift his eyebrow at this statement. Kruge continued, "I believe in a better Earthen. I believe in certain forces that are pushing towards this. My oath to you all is that I will fully support any action required and indeed take action when required to support this change."

With this Kruge extended his right arm, fist clenched, into the middle of the circle. Wil followed, placing his arm in the same way, his fist touching Kruge's, "I make the same oath to you all." Sebast and Trev responded in the same way.

Sean looked in all their eyes, thought of his father's words, extended his fisted arm touching the other four, and, "I make the same oath to you all but include Earth protection!"

All nodded in support. With no further words the group broke up and started to head towards the building. "Stop him, over there!" Came a shout. Sean knew the voice was Jeng's; there was movement in the bushes closer to him. Sean took off towards the bushes; within a few metres he caught a shape running from him. Sean was quicker, as the shape turned to defend, Sean hit the figure flat on with a power punch, and the figure hit the floor. Sean was over the figure and pressing him down with force, now joined by Jeng, assisting him.

"Turn over but do not fight!" Kruge was next to Sean as were the other heirs. The figure turned over; it was Jude. Sebast shouted, "No, Jude, not you. Jeng check him."

Jeng leant over felt Jude's pockets and pulled an electronic device from one. Holding it up Jeng pressed a button, then another, and the oaths of the heirs was played back.

"Has it been sent?" Wil asked.

Jeng looked at the device more closely, "No, it is a recording device not a transmitter. I assume it would be taken to a transmitter for long range distribution." Jeng turned and was looking into Jude's eyes. Jude nodded a yes, to confirm Jeng's thoughts.

Jeng stood, moved back, dropped the device and crushed it with her foot.

"No Kruge!" Sean saw Sebast restrain Kruge who was clearly going to attack the fallen Jude. Again, Sean was surprised.

Sebast turned and with, "You have let me down!" Took direct action on Jude.

"He could have lived, maybe tell us something?" Alex had arrived.

"What would he have told us that we don't already feel?" Kruge first addressed Alex then Sean. "Well done young prince, you are quick and powerful. We shall meet again." Kruge bowed to Sean, shook Sebast's hand and left with all the others except Sebast, Jeng and Sean.

"I will tidy up here, you two go—the evenings activities are cancelled."

Jeng gave Sebast a hug then collected their belongings from the building, Jeng and Sean boarded a shuttle and left for Saulten. Halfway into the flight Sean addressed Jeng. "I assume Kruge meant that Jude was advising one of their kings?"

You don't learn, do you? Jeng said into Sean's mind. *Yes, Vul and Biers are believed to be behind much of what is going on. They want trouble, they want war but even on their lands the younger people do not have the same appetite for war.*

Will this be resolved or come to a head at the King's Council on Vulten?

Probably. You did well today, following your father's guidance.

A SHOWING OF POWER:
(CHAPTER 32)

Sean and Jeng were late to the palace. Sean, not seeing anyone slept alone in his bed. The next morning Sean was first up and dressed; he looked into Emma's room; she was still asleep. Deciding not to wake her, Sean went to the breakfast room alone. Wort was first to join him, then Lens. "Please don't feed him that much," Jenna had joined them. Giving Sean a hug, "I thought you were staying on Ainten?"

"Yes...but no, there was some trouble. Nothing to worry about Mum but we decided to come home early."

"And you have something to tell me son?" Kain had entered.

Sean looked at his mother and then back to his father, "Yes, all is okay, and I believe I have found friends." Kain gave Sean a knowing smile much to the annoyance of Jenna.

"Is there any change in that awful Washington situation?" Judy asked as she entered with her family.

"No, I have been watching all morning. The destroyer is just hovering, no contact." Wort informed.

"I, and Algier, need to go to council, maybe you all could go into the city?" Kain stopped. Then looking at Harry. "There is nothing you can do here but just sit and worry so please take the opportunity to explore."

Harry agreed. Breakfast eaten the Coopers, Jenna, Jeng and Sean were heading towards the city. Sean sat looking at Emma; her expressions to the views of this new world were interesting to see. Sean was happy to visit all the shops the Coopers wished, Jenna was a great tour guide, although she missed the motorbike shop.

"Why don't you take Emma skating with Jeng? We have enough guards and wine bars to entertain us for a while."

Sean took his mother's words as an instruction and was shortly booted up and skating with Emma. "Wow, these skates are amazing," Emma was a natural and soon flying across the ice, even the Earthen naturals looked jealous. Sean stood to one side, *Emma looks brilliant,* he thought. Grace and beauty soon turned as Emma had found out how to make snowballs, joined by Jeng they both attacked Sean. Two against one, Sean had no chance, although one particular well-aimed shot caught Emma smack on the head; Sean laughed but felt guilty at the same time. Skating over, the three joined the others in the Earth themed diner for the remainder of the afternoon; all keeping up to speed with Washington as everywhere viewers were showing live pictures.

Although all were back in the palace dining room, no one wanted food, much to Lens' annoyance. Kain and Algier came in quite late. "Sorry dear but these things go on. Algier, let's have a drink," was Kain's welcome. Wort was already on the case and walking towards Kain with a tray of drinks when he suddenly stopped, and the tray and glasses smashed to the floor. "Are you okay Wort?" Kain asked. Wort's response was to raise his arm and point at the main wall viewer. Sean had seen this and took in the viewer.

"Dad, why are they going towards the destroyer?" Sean asked as the B.B.C. screen was showing three dots approaching the destroyer. No one responded until the camera zoomed into the dots.

"My god, they're two F15 fighters and an RC135 reconnaissance plane!" Harry clearly knew his aircraft. "What are they doing?"

Kain ordered, "Idiots. Algier, get me Virage!" All continued to watch the U.S. jets approach the destroyer in formation, circling the destroyer but keeping a distance.

"Sire, I am sorry the president gave the order whilst I was carrying out other duties. They are not to attack just to monitor and try to contact our craft."

"Virage, you disappoint me, how have you let him do that?"

"He is the president; they will carry out his orders Sire."

"And you mine!"

Algier interrupted, "Sire, do not be so harsh on Virage, you know the president is hard to control." Sean saw Virage take a reassuring breath, but then the main screen took his attention. A door had opened on the destroyer and out flew three fighters, Sean's heart sank.

"I want the U.S. aircraft mission control now!" Virage looked busy then a third screen popped up, it was the U.S. control centre. Sean listened.

"Recon one, we will keep our distance. Our fighter support wish to go to engage mode if required." The RC315 pilot spoke.

"Engage mode authorised but do not attack unless provoked." Control responded.

"Virage, call them off!" Sean heard Kain command but continued to watch the screen.

The three Earthen fighters were now above the three U.S. craft, appearing to track them. One Earthen fighter accelerated in front then down and around the three U.S. craft, very close to each as it spun.

"Hold your fire, Recon One, and support, wait...call off, return to base!"

"Affirmative!" As the first F15 banked left an Earthen fighter flew in above, without warning, two laser shots were fired and the F15 blew up in a ball of flames.

"Oh my god!" Emma was first to scream.

"Kain stop them!" Jenna was next to scream.

"Fighter down—I will engage." Sean heard the pilot then saw the remaining F15 turn sharply, flip and start to round upon one of the Earthen fighters. Two rockets left the F15 heading straight for the Earthen fighter, exploding into flames as they hit the craft's force fields.

"Shit! What the hell is going on?" The pilot's dismayed voice was heard. With two Earthen fighters heading towards him the pilot evaded for some two minutes. The Earthen fighters were clearly faster and more manoeuvrable but the F15 was giving them a run for their money. The F15 pilot was good, evading a couple of laser shots at him, even managing to fire a couple more rockets. He could not evade them any longer as both Earthen ships finally hovered above him; another ball of fire extinguished a brave pilot and his aircraft.

Sean and the cameras moved to the RC135, which had continued its circling and was still been tracked by the third Earthen fighter. "Recon one, the mother fuckers!" With that the biggest ball of fire was seen as the RC135 lit up. Sean's heart sank further, he looked to his father who bowed his head. Looking back at the screen three Earthen fighters were hovering in formation above the White House adjacent to their mother ship destroyer.

Sean saw another viewer open, Robare appeared in it. "Quicker, Robare, I need them now!" Kain demanded.

"Yes, Your Highness, a couple of minutes. Do you wish them to engage, over the city?"

"If need be, they take that destroyer down. Algier, inform the kings we will attack, get ours and the Dersian battleships on full alert. They have my permission to attack!"

"Kain…no…there will be thousands of deaths!" Harry was next to Kain. "Look, they are moving!"

Sean watched the main viewer; the three Earthen fighters circled the White House then went back into the destroyer, the doors of which then closed. Kain ordered, "Let ours circle but in perception mode." The B.B.C. screen picked up more shapes approaching the destroyer. Again, the camera zoomed in, there were five British Spitfires. No, Sean, realised, these were Earthen, Earth Council fighters. The Spitfires did a few circles around the destroyer then pulled off and disappeared into the distance.

"A bit dramatic but it made a point," Algier addressed Kain.

"What the hell is going on? Where did those Spitfires come from?" Harry was imitating the voice of the T.V. presenter.

"They are Earth Council Fighters in perception mode, not Spitfires. I am sure the destroyer is aware we would have attacked. There are twenty more only a few minutes away," Kain advised. The show of Earth Council strength had obviously worked as the Earthen destroyer had called its ships back but the B.B.C. was totally confused. Sean listened to the T.V. presenter who had war specialists piping up.

"Incredible what has gone on here, how five old Spitfires scared off spaceships that took out three of the most up to date military craft we have?"

"Maybe they did not see them as a threat?"

"And our fighters were?" The debate continued.

"Get the president!" Kain ordered Virage. "Only you and him!"

Within a couple of minutes, the U.S. President was in the viewer, looking very disturbed.

"You are a fool. You now have a better idea of our, no, my power. I made you a threat last time we spoke, this time there is no threat," Kain walked close to the viewer. "I will do as I said I would. Unless you prove it, to me, by listening to Virage!"

The president wiped his brow, "I don't know who or what you are, but I will listen to your advisor once you promise me this thing will go away from my city!"

"I cannot, at this point, promise that. Evacuate your city if you have not already done so but do not attack or approach the destroyer above you in any way, unless I, or Virage, tell you to do so."

The president thought, "I will work with you for now but if I feel there is a need to take action I will!"

Kain smiled, "Mr President, I applaud your wish to defend your people however, I assure you, I and my people are best to do so, we are on your side."

The President gave a brief smile, which was quickly wiped off by Kain's next command, "Virage, kill him if he disobeys me again, viewer off!"

Sean gulped; Harry was the first to speak, "Kain, was that the American President, surely you can't talk to him like that?"

Kain looked at Harry, Sean could see his father was in full Earthen mode. "My friend, I will talk to who I wish to, how I wish to!"

Before Harry could respond the cries from Judy were heard. Seen looked at the main viewer, the pictures had moved to fallen debris on Washington. All looked horrific, the worst he saw was the remains of an F15 engine still on fire outside the Lincoln Memorial having taken half of the roof off—Lincoln was sitting looking over the fallen F15. "They are saying two hundred dead including the aircraft crews. Kain, no," Jenna was in the face of her husband.

Kain looked uncomfortable, "I am sorry, dear. The situation is calm for the moment, but I must plan my next move. Algier with me." Kain and Algier left.

There was little further talk as all watched the viewers, the death toll hit the two hundred mark, and Washington resembled a war zone. Jenna deciding all should go to their rooms early. Sean and Emma FaceTimed Mush, "Scary as hell!" Was his main point, "When you coming home?" Was his last question.

Sean lied, "Oh, as you can see, we are in Canada," the viewer was doing the perception bit. "Dad is not in Washington, but he may travel there so we are a little closer than home, but we are all safe."

Call over, Emma looked at Sean, close to tears. "He is right, this is scary. I don't want to sleep alone tonight. You will hold me?"

"Yes, of course."

Sean stood and headed towards the large sofa. "No. I will get my pyjamas and see you in your bed." Sean went to his bed, brushed his teeth and waited for Emma. Emma came in, approached, then slipped into the bed, gave Sean a kiss then laid her head on his chest—both finally fell asleep.

THE CHALLENGE:
(CHAPTER 33)

Sean awoke; Emma's beautiful face appeared to be smiling whilst laid next to his. Sean gave her a kiss, seeing her eyes open, he kissed her again. "Good morning," Sean said.

"You too," but "Oh no!" As Emma put her hand to her mouth. "Bed breath and I bet bed hair!" Were her last words as she took off towards her own bedroom. Sean chuckled to himself but also washed and dressed finally catching Emma at the door to leave the main room.

In the lift Sean spoke. "Hey, we have woken up together before many times, you have slept over remember."

Emma, now all clean and fresh, responded, "I know but not in this way," ending the sentence with a smile.

Sean thought about a response but soon found them both in the breakfast room. Sean caught Judy's eye. "Good morning. Are you two okay?"

"Yes, Mum. Besides all the troubles I managed to sleep well."

"Yes, you do seem to have a happy demeanour about you…" Sean thought this was a funny comment as Harry stopped halfway through it.

Sean looked up as Harry gave him a strange look, before Sean could respond Judy interrupted. "Harry, if Emma is happy leave her alone, have some more tea."

Sean sat with Emma in the seat away from the table but overlooking the garden, Lens provided some food. "What's wrong with your Dad?"

"You are a fool, you really are." Emma giggled.

Sean went to reply but was interrupted by a big, "Hello both!" as Sal entered the room. All three embraced, Sal joined them on the seat, explaining she had been visiting her parents in town.

"Hi, Mum."

"Hi Mrs...Jenna." Sean and Emma both greeted Jenna as she joined the, now four, on the sofa.

"You look worried, Mum?" Sean asked.

"Sorry honey. Your father and I had a long talk last night." Sean's eyes followed his mother's gaze to see Kain sitting with Harry. "As usual I do not know what he is planning. He is a bit distant."

"He has a lot on his mind, Jen," Sal gave Jenna a hug whilst responding.

"Wort said there is no change on Earth," Emma added.

"That is good news although the death toll rose to two hundred and eighteen." Sal advised.

"That is terrible," Sean went to answer Emma but stopped as he heard his father having a coughing fit. Both Sean and Jenna went to Kain.

"I am okay, sorry, Sean, we have to go to the council. Say goodbye to, Emma. Honey I will see you later." Kain ended with a kiss to Jenna and headed for the door. Sean caught a fleeting kiss from Emma and joined Kain and Algier in the car for the ride to the council building.

Walking through the main doors, and through the corridors Sean was met with people bowing. Kain seemed keen to get to one room in particular. Sean noted his father was still coughing. Approaching the room Sean, Kain and Algier entered, Algier closing the door behind them. "Are you well, Sire?" Sean looked to see a very old looking slightly stooped man in the corner.

"Good morning Doctor Krips, but, no, I am dying," Sean froze at his father's response.

"Oh dear, then you better have some medicine." With this Sean watched Krips go to a cupboard, remove a bottle of whiskey and pour four glasses. He gave the first to Kain, then Algier and finally approached Sean. "Oh, my word you have grown. Old enough to drink?"

"No doctor. Dad, are you dying?" Sean ignored Krips.

Kain laughed, sat against the table and looked at Sean. "I am in the best health ever however, the world believing I am ill is of use."

Algier, also laughing, joined in, "Dying ah. A bit of a move up from being unwell and hiding your power?"

"I know however, I have decided today will be very entertaining. Doc. pour me another and then when we go into the council chamber you will announce my impending death. Greydust condition will be the prognosis."

"Yes, of course, all that coughing sounds good to me. How long do you wish to live for?" Krips was pouring more whiskey.

"About a week or two should do it." With this, all three men laughed aloud.

"You are not drinking?" Krips words woke Sean from his thoughts.

"I'm only fifteen."

"Silly me. Look young Sire I brought you into this world so I think I can advise you. Have the whiskey."

"What? You brought me into this world? I was born on Earth!"

"I know. I was there you fool. You were born in the Research Park hospital. Sal and I delivered you. Of course, your mother played a part. How is the wonderful Jenna?" Sean gave a smile;

the first whiskey went down in one. Sean coughed and spluttered, Algier gave him a pat on the back.

"We will go in first. Sean only the four of us in this room know the truth. You must not think it or show it, for once you are in on the deception." Sean took in Algier's words, nodded and followed Algier to the council chamber. The chamber was full, all the chairs at the table were taken apart from Algier and Kain's, and Kain had not entered yet.

"Nephew, hope you are unwell!" Sean looked at his seated uncle as he passed to go to his seat. Sean gave no response but glared at Dain. With Algier and Sean seated they were waiting for Kain.

"Is his highness coming?" Barlo asked.

"Yes, he is with Krips," Algier informed.

"Hopefully he is still unwell..."

"Wipe that smirk from your face brother!" Kain was approaching the table, Krips in tow. Kain stood at his chair then went to address the councilors before coughing uncontrollably. Krips' pat to the back and stethoscope to Kain's chest Sean thought was a bit over the top. But his father did look poorly. Kain sat after Krips' instruction.

"My friend, you are really not well?" Sean looked up and Anders was speaking, looking very concerned.

"Krips, please advise my council."

"Oh, yes, of course. My council, I have some bad news for you." Sean bowed his head but looked around the table, he knew what was coming. "Our king has Greydust disease."

Sean heard the ahh's, mixed in with some no's. He focused on Dain. Dain looked sad but said nothing. "No, my friend no," Sean looked up to see Anders had risen from his chair and was next to Kain, his hand on Kain's shoulder.

"Yes, my friends, my council. I have the disease which took my father," a tear came to Kain's eye. Sean thought *go dad,* this was convincing, clearly Anders was not in on this ploy.

"My brother, thinking of our father is sad," Dain was clearly trying to be nice. "The disease can be quick; do you have any idea of time?"

With this Sean decided to join the fun, shooting a thought into Dain's head he cried, "My father is dying and all you care about is when!"

Dain flinched as he caught Sean's force in his head, then thought back, hard. Sean was taken aback as he felt his uncle's force in his head, it was hurting. The hurt stopped as Sean heard the noise of Dain hitting the floor—Algier and Irnside above him.

"Leave him!" Kain standing, ordered.

"He cannot use his powers in this way in the chamber, he was attacking the young prince," Irnside still had Dain pinned to the floor.

"Leave him I said!" Kain was now above Dain, who was allowed to stand. "Now you are standing, and Sean is ready maybe you would like to try again?" Kain looked at Sean.

"With pleasure, go for it Uncle!" Sean stood, glaring at his uncle.

Dain looked at Sean then addressed Kain, "No, Sire, that would not be necessary, besides he is a child in the eyes of the law."

"I am not though," was Kain's strange response. Dain looked uncomfortable then threw a glare at Kain; Kain went to respond then stopped with a coughing fit. Krips was between the two brothers. Sean looked at Dain who was clearly enjoying seeing his brother ill.

"Leave me!" Krips moved away from Kain. "My brother, for your information I have but a week to live." The gasps of shock filled the air, Sean could not help joining in with the group gasp. Sean noted Dain was nearly smiling. "Therefore, I have decided to clear up some things before I go. That thing is you my brother!"

Dain froze, Sean could see that even though Kain was stooped and looking poorly, Dain was still scared. "My brother, I believe you have been behind many of the recent disturbances. The attack on my life, twice. The car crash and my neighbour shooting me. But worse the cause of the duel my son had to endure with Det."

"Sire, I am sorry, but there is no proof or even truth to these allegations." Irnside was in advisory mode.

"I, your king, need proof?" Sean could feel the room go tense. Barlo went to say something but even looking ill the glare from Kain's eyes stopped him. "My brother. I do not know what is to become of this world however, I am not leaving it without dealing with you. I have despised you all of my adult life."

"Brother, are you mad?" Dain retorted.

"No, I am angry. Guards!" With this command some ten guards entered the chamber, weapons drawn. "My brother. I deem your actions as treason and formally challenge you, we shall duel!"

Again, all gushed, Sean joined in for real, *Dad was going to duel Dain?* he thought to himself.

"Sire, no!" Dain was clearly distressed, "I am your brother?"

Kain went to respond but again suffered a coughing spree. "You are no brother of mine. Guards, suppress him and lock him away." Two guards pounced upon Dain, one raising his hand weapon and placing it to Dain's arm, fired. Sean watched as Dain went to struggle but stopped, he was like a rag doll as the guards took him away.

Anders was the first to speak, again at the side of Kain, who had sat in what was Dain's chair. "Kain, no, please, your brother. No, not in your state?"

"My friends," Kain stopped, composed himself then addressed his council. "My councilors. My life has been a mix of feelings, Earth and Earthen. I came into this world as an Earthen, and although enjoying Earth, I will leave this world as an Earthen. Anders, I wish the duel to take place this Friday before the King's Council." Kain raised then left with Krips.

"Councilors please!" Algier took control of the murmuring voices. "Our king has spoken; his challenge is legitimate, and we must now prepare for this. We will adjourn for an hour to gain our thoughts then return to discuss and arrange the details. Anders, please check that Dain is locked away and is sedated further with TDL, plus, provide advice. Irnside, you must go with Anders." Algier said no more, grabbed Sean and led him back to the room they had previously been in. Again, Sean noted the mood was totally different; Kain and Krips were sipping more 'medicine'. Algier joined them.

"So, ten out of ten for your acting Dad but dueling Dain to the death?"

Kain smiled, "Dain is no threat to me, my hate for him is real. Do not be concerned about the duel however, the presence, on Friday, of the kings here in Saulten city will be interesting."

"The King's Council is in Vulten?" Sean quizzed.

"Is it now? Algier, you are the politician, get it moved to here."

"Oh, yes, the kings will not be able to resist it. Well done my nephew."

"May I just add something," Krips, clearly a bit sozzled, spoke, "I know we are all in on this, you obviously have not informed Anders. Jenna?"

Sean's heart skipped a beat, Kain's face dropped. "No, Dad, please don't tell me Mum does not know?"

"I may have overlooked that part," Kain was clearly distressed.

"You idiot, you will have to tell her, or I will!"

"No!" Sean froze, Algier was rarely this direct. "Although this hurts me tremendously Jenna or anyone else especially the Earthlings will not be able to hold out if mind searched. They will have to be left as they are and believe Kain is dying."

Sean beat his father to another whiskey shot before sitting. "Dad, I can't lie to Mum, even Emma, in this way. Stop this." Sean looked up at his father, Kain's eyes were full of tears but the fire in them glinted.

"I am sorry, son, but Algier is right. If the king's sense any of this my plan will not work. They must think I am ill, and they must come to Saulten. This is the only way." Kain stood and approached the small window, looked out, then turned to address Sean, "I am sorry, but we continue the deceit to all other than us four."

Kain left with Krips, Algier stopped Sean at the door; closing it and said, "Sean, Friday will be a terrible day, but it must happen. You must support your father, lying to Jenna and Emma is best for now. You wanted to be involved, you want to understand power. Now you see the kind of things your father must do. Be strong."

The car ride home was quiet, Kain with Krips said no more however, the viewer was on and the Saulten news was reporting the rumours. *King Kain dueling with Dain, Is Kain really dying?*

The car pulled into the palace, the guards meeting them, all were sombre. Kain led them to the sitting room; Jenna was first to greet them, straight into Kain's arms. Sean looked at his mother, she had clearly been crying. Sean was engulfed in hugs from Emma, Sal and Jeng—all were tearful. Sean cried as the truth inside was killing him. Kain addressed all. "My family, my dear friends, I am sorry the news has come this way but yes...it is true. Please leave me time with Jenna." Jenna gave Sean a big hug then left, with Kain, for their room.

Sean could not make out what his friends were saying; all

were being polite around him, caring.

Algier saved him. "Let him breathe, Kain advised us earlier. Maybe a walk or something would be good, get some air?"

Sean said, "Yes, thank you all, yes, I need some space." Sean headed for the door. Judy and Harry both were hugging him on the way. Sean looked back, Algier was holding Emma back. Ten minutes later and Sean was on a bench looking back at the palace. Specifically, at the top, his mother and father's apartment. Thoughts were flying through his head, *Dad must be telling mum, and he cannot keep this up surely.* Then his thoughts changed to *Oh no*, for the first time ever in his life he was not happy to see Emma.

"How are you?" Emma cuddled Sean as she sat next to him. "Surely this planet has modern medicines, Kain can be cured?"

"No, no. It is a disease from the wars and there is no cure," Sean was feeling awful in uttering his words. Emma clearly taking Sean's awfulness as unhappiness. Emma did not need to speak but sat for some time holding Sean. Finally, Sean was summoned to his parent's room. Sean's heart shrunk upon seeing his mother, clearly distressed with Sal attending to her.

Jenna motioned for Sean to sit with her. "I am sorry, I did not think of you."

Sean could hardly breathe with the cuddle from his mother. "Mum, I'm okay, well, as okay as I can be."

"Good, you must be strong." Although his mother was speaking Sean could tell she did not believe her own words.

"This duel, of your father's is mad. With all that is going on he turns into an Earthen."

"He is an Earthen, and a king," Sean hurt as he spoke.

"Jenna, I think Algier needs to speak to Kain, shall we use the bathroom, freshen up?" Sal asked.

Jenna ignored this, "You and your council are more important than my marriage, my feelings!"

Sean looked at the approaching Algier, Jenna's words made him look smaller and very awkward. Kain spoke, "Honey you are being unfair, I will talk to my councilor, Sean with me."

Sean found himself on the balcony with Algier and Kain.

"You have kept your word, Jenna does not know," Algier had tears.

"Why can I not just go out and kill everyone?"

Sean was a bit taken aback by this comment from his father. "Kain I have no doubt in your powers, but control, support and diplomacy will make the better long-term path. Your, our, hurt for the present will have to be endured."

"Jenna, our friends, this is killing them."

"They are strong, they will be okay. Besides I have good news." Sean thought there could be no good news. "It appears the other kings cannot resist it. It has been agreed, the King's Council will be held in Saulten City after the duel. I do believe Vul thinks Dain has a chance you know."

Kain allowed himself a smile. "Well done, my friend. Sean, Friday will be hard but having it here in Saulten will help our preparations and security. My deceit is worth it."

"Friday cannot come quick enough," Sean said. "Is Vul in charge of that destroyer, is Washington safe until then?"

"Yes, to both," Algier gave a reassuring smile.

COMBAT PREPARATION:
(CHAPTER 34)

Sean awoke with Emma by his side and decided he liked these new sleeping arrangements. "If I kiss you will you run off again?"

Emma smiled, "Nope, you will have to get used to the ugly me."

"Oh, I think I'll have to join a dating site." Sean took cover from the flying pillows as he went to the bathroom.

Both dressed and they joined the others in the breakfast room, Kain and Jenna being the last in. "Good morning you two."

"Morning, Mum."

"Morning, Mrs S."

Jenna smiled, "I need to talk to your mum and Kain, your father. Please both go and enjoy yourselves this morning. Nothing is going to change in a few hours."

"Are you sure, Mrs S?"

"If ever you marry my son you will call me Jenna?"

Emma and Sean went red. "Yes, Jenna."

"Good, then I need a quick word with you before you go out."

Sean watched as his mother and Emma walked to a corner of the room, both soon sniggering. *Dad's told mum* he thought, Sean looked at his father, noting Algier was doing the same.

Kain looked at both and said in their heads, *I don't know what you two are thinking but no I have not told her, clear your thoughts. Sal is an amazing nurse.*

No Dad, you didn't? Not the drugs. Sean replied through thought.

Kain spoke aloud, "I know this is a shock but, please, for me, go about things as normal. All have some time together. Sean please take Emma out, show her the ridge."

Sean stood, took Emma's hand and headed to the garage. "Here, wear this backpack today." Sean handed Emma the pack whilst she was putting the crash helmet on. Both suited up and climbed on the Girella; Wort had provided lunch and instruction on how to use the bikes satnav to get back to the palace.

The Girella flew across roads, then paths, Emma was egging Sean on with reassuring hugs whilst holding on. Within no time they were at the ridge. Both swigging water they looked up. Sean asked, "You fancy climbing?"

"Not really is there not a path or something quicker to get up there? The view would be awesome?"

"Oh okay. You see that backpack; it is an air drift pack. Think Jet Pack, we can fly up there!"

"O.M.G. never, show me?"

Sean gave Emma a quick demonstration, and after a few attempts a couple of metres off the floor they were ready. Holding hands, they both shouted, "Up!" Both took off vertically taking the one hundred metres or so height quickly before landing on the ridge edge.

"That was awesome, can we fly?"

"Kind of, watch me." With this Sean started to air drift, upon stopping, showing off, he explained to Emma the principle of jump and float, not fly. Again, Emma was quick to learn, and both were soon air drifting across the ridge top from mound to mound. Some hour later they stopped for refreshment.

"This is incredible, more exercise than you think. Wow, look at the view."

Sean joined Emma at the edge, she was right. Saulten City and the Palace were visible in the distance but the general flat and green landscape with few buildings did look inviting. "Shall we go back, but maybe slower? Wort has put in a long route that will take us through a village and things, so he told me."

"Yes, that would be fun. How do we get down, do we just jump off?"

"Yes, let me check your settings. Whatever you do you will stop twenty metres from the ground and float the remainder."

"Even if headfirst?"

"Yes, it will stop at twenty then turn you and land you, just jump out from the ridge a distance."

"Here goes!" With this Emma jumped and heading for the ground headfirst before finally stopping and landing safely. Sean could hear her cry of joy from above, he thought, *Yeah why not!*

Taking his air drift off Sean threw it out to descend and land next to Emma below. Emma was shouting, Sean ignored her. "Watch out below!" He screamed as he dived off the edge, soaring downwards. Just before the bottom he summoned his powers and glided right side up to hover just on top of Emma. "Why are you laughing? You are supposed to be impressed by that." Sean queried as he lowered himself to land next to Emma.

"Your Mum said you would do that."

"The bitch, she spoilt my fun. Did she tell you about the air drift kits and everything?"

Emma was killing herself with laughter, "Yes, she did, but hey, don't be so mad it was still very impressive. Come here my hero." Sean argued no more; the kiss was enough to silence him.

Mounting the bike, they were off, Wort was right, the bike led them back a slower path. Both enjoyed the scenery more at the sedated pace. Their helmets had microphones so they could talk easily. As Wort had said they approached a small village. The buildings were the typical square Earthen ones however, the externals had more furniture such as chairs and benches outside, people and kids were sitting or talking. Sean stopped outside what was clearly a shop. Keeping their helmets on they both entered the shop. It was like a typical Earth local store with odd house bits, food, papers and drinks on display.

"Sire the natural berry juice is a must to try." Sean was taken aback as the shopkeeper addressed him.

"How did you know I am a prince?"

"Wort from the palace said you might pass by. Of course, you have full credit here so please try what you wish."

"The berry juice is best. I like the appleden flavour," a young girl was next to Emma.

Emma smiled, "We will have a couple of appleden juices please." The shopkeeper grabbed the juices; the girl was staring at Emma. "May I help you little one?" Emma asked.

"Yes, are you an Earthling?"

Emma and Sean laughed, "I am but I'm not so different to you."

"Can I touch you?"

"Leave the princess alone Suki. I am sorry Your Highness my daughter is inquisitive."

"No, don't be, look grab her a juice as well and maybe we could sit on the bench outside and chat?"

"Father, please, please let me sit with the Earthling?"

"Yes of course if Your Highness agrees?"

Sean realised the shopkeeper was addressing him. "Yes, we must. Suki is it? Call me Sean and this is Emma."

Sean and Emma took the drinks and sat with the little girl talking. Suki was amazed to be sitting next to an Earthling, Emma allowing her to stroke her hair having removed the crash helmet. It was not long before another few kids, parents watching, joined them. All were polite and although Sean was human and a prince, Emma was the real attraction, the real deal, he thought.

A young lady approached them. "Thank you, Your Highnesses," she said as she curtsied. "The children do not see royalty often, let alone aliens from Earth."

Emma giggled, "Sorry that was rude, I forget I'm an alien here."

"Your mother, such a beautiful queen, has been here a few times. Unfortunately, not as often more recently which is why the younger children are so enthralled."

Sean responded, "This is a lovely village, you are not so far from the palace."

The shopkeeper joined them, "Yes that is correct indeed some of our town folk work at the palace. I provide some of the fresh veg. My privilege to provide for our king."

"Your service today and the berry juice is wonderful, maybe we could invite you all to the palace at some point. Or eat here, do you have a restaurant?"

"That would be such an honour," the lady responded. "We have no restaurant, but you would be welcome in any of our houses, or as you say on Earth, a barbeque?"

Emma laughed, "Yes that would be great, we will arrange that at some point. Suki, you would love the palace."

"Wow, Daddy, I am going to be a princess!" Suki was in her father's arms.

"That would be wonderful your highness, although I would

assume after the King's Council and the..." The shopkeeper stopped.

"Look what happens this Friday happens however; you have my word we will have our meal together at some point."

An older woman approached, "May I?" she asked as holding Sean's hand. "Your father is a great king, please tell him of all our support in this difficult time."

Sean was taken aback; these people were generally worried about Kain. "Thank you, I will pass on your kind thoughts to my father later." Both Sean and Emma gained more hugs from not only the kids but also the adults before finally leaving the village on the Girella.

In a quiet moment later, Sean was sitting on his own with his mother, having told her about the villagers. "Yes, I did go there a lot, they are lovely people. They remind me of Ireland in a way. The older lady sounds like Hildu, a renowned teacher here in Saulten. I have eaten with her, she is lovely. O.M.G. what do I tell Mum and Dad?" Jenna added which made Sean jump.

"Granddad and Grandma...tell them what?"

"About Kain, his illness, his..." Jenna stopped.

Sean thought, *Dad has clearly not told her it was not real.* "Maybe wait until after Friday, as you said, nothing will happen until then."

"Yes, that may be best, get Friday out of the way first." Then Sean's gut wrenched as he heard his mother's words continue. "Please be strong for me, I can't keep this facade up any longer, I just want to cry and hold your father forever." Jenna had tears, Sean felt so uncomfortable, and Sal came to his aid.

"Jenna let's have a drink, a real one," both left Sean's side. Sean looked up at his father who had been talking with Harry for some time. "You...git!" Is all he could throw at his father's head. Sean felt the twinge as Kain fought back.

"Ladies and gentlemen, please listen," Kain was addressing

all. "I have spoken with Harry; I know Jenna has spoken with Judy and their decision is to stay here. Although I feel Earth would be safer." Kain stopped, took a deep breath and continued, "The next few days, especially Friday will be difficult and, I am sorry to say, dangerous, especially to Earth people without powers. Tomorrow and the days after Jeng, Sal and Syston will provide you equipment and details on how you can at least attempt to protect yourselves. Obviously, you have the protection of me and my people at all times."

Harry looked uncomfortable as he spoke, "Sorry, my friend, but when you are gone, not just me and my family...what about Earth?"

The mood dropped, Jenna sat next to Sal, holding her arm. Kain looked at Jenna and then replied, "Once I have gone, Sean will be king. My council, especially Algier and Anders, will support Sean, therefore I am sure the support for Earth will continue. We all need rest. Jenna please." No more was said, and Sean was soon in bed holding Emma.

The next morning all were asked to wear Earthen clothes, the mix of white and blue clearly showing they were of military style. The Coopers, Sean and Jenna were taken to the palace small duel arena. Sal, Syston and Jeng were to be their trainers.

Jeng was first to address the 'humans' as she called them. "There are two types of defences, well, one defence and one attack device. The first are these helmets, although quite flimsy looking they are very tough. They will help stop people attempting to get into you heads and, well, frying your brains."

"Completely?" Emma questioned.

"No, it depends on the power of the attacker. You must all be aware that if a fight, or a battle breaks out then Earthens will look to defend. Our powers, focused on one or two objects can be lethal however, with a battle of many thoughts flying around and many people, we too can be overcome."

Jeng put the helmet down then pulled from her waist holster her gun. "This is where the laser guns you will be provided with come in handy. In battle, in general, you can take out an opponent with a gun."

"Give me the biggest one going!" Was Jenna's surprising response. At this point all, including Sean, to his amusement, were provided with helmets and guns. For the next hour, the trainers showed them how to use the helmet, its effectiveness and fire the laser guns. Sean, completely missing the point, thought firing the guns was more fun than using his powers.

Refreshments taken, all were confident in the helmets and at least at holding and aiming the guns. Sean looked at them, *would they shoot someone*? He thought. Looking at his mother again he decided *yep!*

"Sal, may I have your assistance please?" Sal joined Jeng at the front of the group.

"So, the helmets will protect you, we will work on them more later. The lasers, well I am not going to show you how they can kill us but do need to show you something else. Most important for you Sean." Sean saw the glint in Jeng's eyes, she was up to something. "Sal, ten metres please. Stun or kill?"

Sal walked away from Jeng ten metres and turned, "Stun would be most appreciated."

Jeng laughed, "Did you miss my last birthday present, ah, yes, kill!" With this Jeng raised the weapon and aimed it at Sal. Sean went to stop her, Syston held him back, "Watch and learn!"

"Ready, go for it, three blasts," Sal was eying Jeng.

Jeng fired the first shot, Sal went into defence mode and the laser bounced off, the next two shots dispatched in the same way. "As you can see an Earthen focusing can stop laser shots therefore try and shoot them whilst they are not directly concentrating on you or when they are in attack mode with their guard down. Sal please."

"Still on kill mode?"

Jeng fell backwards before responding, "Sal, please, you are not supposed to be fighting back. Double kill mode if possible." Jeng gave a smirk, "Three shots ready?"

Sean watched as Jeng shot the first laser, Sal did not go defensive but volleyed the laser with her arm away from her—again the following shots were dealt with and Sal survived.

"Wow," Emma was first to speak. "You guys can deflect lasers, we're fu..."

"Emma language!" Harry was still the father in charge. "Emma is right, Jeng, we have no chance."

"One on one," Syston now spoke. "No chance. However, as Jeng has said in a battle or with many things going on, yes you do."

"So, we shoot you in the back and all's okay?' Harry chirped up.

Jeng asked, "Jenna, please, with your gun."

Jenna joined Jeng. "Stand where I was," Jeng instructed as she moved away from Jenna.

As she passed Sal, she threw a thought punch at her, "Bitch," was all Sean heard from Sal.

"Okay Jenna is ten metres facing Sal, I am ten metres behind her. Jenna you have used lasers before, so I trust you. Although remember that time when that last special perfume was on sale and you bought it for Sal? I know you really wanted it."

Jenna laughed and joined in the fun. "Looks like you are cooking today my friend." At this point both Jenna and Jeng raised their weapons. Sal appearing to focus on Jenna. Jenna and Jeng both fired, Sal did not go defensive instead standing still and with no arms, diverted both shots.

"Wow!" Emma screamed; Sean agreed.

Jenna fired two more, as did Jeng not at the same time—six shots were diverted, Jeng's without Sal even looking at her. "Finished?" Sal asked, as Jenna and Jeng said yes Sal raised her arms; both went flying on their backsides. All three were laughing hysterically; Jenna and Jeng got up and hugged their friend.

"Impressive, but I am not sure it has made me feel any more comfortable," Judy spoke.

Jeng continued instructing, "Look, you have to know everything and be prepared for it. The next few days will show you how and when to fight. You do have a chance but must be clever. Sean of course you can fight the Earthen way. Syston will put you through your paces tomorrow. For now, let's play with the lasers."

With that all took the next few hours to shoot and block out attacks. Sean decided to give the laser bending a go after a few practice attempts. Emma chose to shoot him, thankfully it was with a training laser, but the sting to Sean's chest hurt, not once, but a few times. Emma was clearly enjoying this too much, so Sean put her in her place, Emma could not sit down for an hour after as she hit the floor so hard. Although Sean was very apologetic Emma accepted, he was still learning to control his powers however, the, "You're sleeping on your own tonight!" Put him in his place.

The evening meal was quiet, Anders and Beatrice Doogan joined the group, Sal was much happier with her parents around. There was no talk of Kain's illness; Sean could not help but feel this felt a bit surreal. Thankfully, Emma did not keep to her word.

The following day followed the same pattern with the humans learning their new skills. At one-point Sean took a break to sit and watch his mother and Emma taking laser shots at varied targets. "They are good," Jeng joined him.

"Good teachers, do they really have a chance in a fight?"

"Yes, in a battle if they keep their senses however, you need to be at your best. I am a confident fighter, yet I would not take you on in a serious battle. And now with your father..." Jeng stopped. Sean looked up, did she know, and *no* he thought. "At his peak, no one could touch but now, I admit I am worried."

"Don't be, he will be fine."

"Earthen is rubbing off on you. You know, I, Anders, even Syston, have offered to proxy fight for Kain."

Sean was a little shocked; "You would fight to the death for Dad?"

"Without a shadow of a doubt," Jeng had a serious look.

"Could I?"

"No, not until you are an adult, at eighteen."

"What if I decided to just do it?"

"If you fought without permission, within the protocols you would be imprisoned if not killed."

"Although I don't care about Dain, is he drugged and in jail still?"

"Kind of. As he was challenged and could run, he is locked up, but not in jail, he's under house arrest. If you can call that room with the three triplets a house let alone a home. Anyway, he will be drugged if they thought he was going to flee. Of course, he can train. Remember Sheko, he is training him."

"The boxer type guy who fought Syston?"

"Yes, an advantage to us as they are professionals, not military fighters."

"On the day would he be drugged?"

"No, not when it is to the death. He and Kain will be seen as equals so no handicaps."

"Are they equal? We are all of the same blood."

"Strange, but no, it is clear Dain has nowhere near your father's or even his father's power. Indeed personality, looks, everything, he fails on," Jeng chuckled.

"Ouch!" Both looked up; Emma had clearly shot Jenna on

the backside.

"Sorry Mrs S., sorry!" Emma was laughing, Jeng and Sean joined in with the laughs. Training over and an early meal was called for. Again, Sal and family joined in.

"There has been no more action on Earth?" Judy asked, although the permanent viewer showing the live pictures of the destroyer still over Washington was clear.

"No Judy, all is the same," Kain sat and looked at the viewer next to Judy. "Robare and Shad please!" There was a slight delay then two viewers came up.

"Sire all is quiet here. Washington has been evacuated," Robare was first to speak from one of the viewers.

"You have spoken to the Americans and Virage?"

"Yes, Sire, the president has no appetite to push you any further. The Spitfires are hard to explain though."

"It is better than Earth thinking we are fighting each other."

"Yes Sire. May I pass on my best wishes?" Shad spoke.

"Yes, thank you my friend. Is the Ainten battleship able to launch?"

Sean heard a laugh from the corner of the room, Krips had joined them—Sean had not noticed. "My money is not, am I right that that Vulten, Ruzz, could not get onto his own bridge a couple of times lately?"

Shad chuckled, "Doctor Krips, for an old man, do you hear everything?"

"I may be old but not incompetent young captain. Of course, I vaguely remember your grandfather, great man, he was the lead designer on the spaceship and the battleships. I'm sure a skill that has passed onto his family."

Sean joined the laughter from all, Shad went red. "Doctor, please, what are you suggesting? Sorry I must go as I think Ruzz is trapped in a toilet somewhere." All laughed louder as Shad turned his viewer off.

"More medicine, Sire?" Krips was at the whiskey counter again.

"No, please, good doctor, my husband needs to stay sober over the next couple of days."

"Oh, I'll have his share then. Algier, Harry, is it? And Anders, come let's talk." With that all the men left, Kain as well.

"A doctor and he drinks like that?" Judy quizzed.

"He is one hundred and ten years old, let him do what he wishes," Jenna advised.

"A hundred and ten, O.M.G. I'm going to take up drinking!" Emma spoke too soon as the wine bottles were shared out. Sean sat with the women for a while then moved to the men who were in the games room. On entering Sean noticed Harry was looking totally perplexed at the 3.D. chess set, Anders was sitting smug next to him.

Kain and Syston were playing darts, but with their minds. Algier and Wort were sitting smiling, empty bottles ahead of them. *Krips looked dead,* Sean could not help but think.

"He is okay, he gives up after an hour or so and kips. Amazing really, he can sleep anywhere, at any time," Anders advised as he moved and sat next to Algier.

Sean chuckled and joined the sitting three at the table. Sean did not take any alcoholic drink but listened to all the talking. Anders was clearly not in on the Kain dying scam, neither was Wort who at one point stated, "I should not lose a child before I go."

Sean looked so quizzical that Algier shot in, "Wort thinks of Kain as his, after all, with all the duties' of your grandparents Wort and Lens virtually brought your father up."

"Yes, that's right, that is why he is such a great man. I taught him all I know," Wort had a proud smile.

"Time for bed gentleman. Krips' snoring is now unbearable." Was Kain's instruction.

Sean went to bed feeling happier but was upset there was no Emma. 'What have I done now he thought. *Maybe I should go and see her in her room.* His thoughts did not last long as Emma came falling through the door. "I'm an honorary (hiccup) woman you know," Emma slurred as she entered.

"You are drunk!" Sean shouted the obvious.

"I know (hiccup). Our mums are worse. I think I challenged Jeng to a drinking game. Big mistake, big mistake."

Sean laughed, "Surely our mums have not let you get into this state?"

"Oh, they know we have drunk before (hiccup)," Emma then collapsed on the bed fully clothed. Sean did not know what to do; he had seen Emma tipsy before but not drunk, not in his bedroom. He decided to try and make her more comfortable as she was on the edge of the bed.

Emma shot up. "How dare you (hiccup) you can't take advantage of a drunken girl. I thought you were..." Emma did not finish the sentence and did not sleep next to Sean; she spent most of the night next to the toilet.

Sean was first up; Emma had managed to get into the bed, still fully clothed. Sean checked she was breathing then went downstairs. Lens was first up after him.

"Morning Lens, you did not drink so much?"

"Oh, dear I can drink all those girls under the table, actually I did. How is the wonderful Emma?"

"Not good, sick all night. She is on the bed out like a light."

"Oh dear. We have a very good Earthen hangover juice recipe. I will take her some up."

Sean chuckled as Lens disappeared to the kitchen. One by one the drunken troops emerged. Judy and Emma last, hand in hand. Little food was eaten but the hangover juice was going around well, only Sean had not drunk too much.

"Jeng were you trying to kill my daughter last night?" Judy

started with a laugh.

"No Judy, she did not need much encouraging."

"Please tell me I won otherwise this headache was not worth it." Jenna asked.

"No, you did not and you being a queen...terrible example," Judy was still laughing.

"Sal won, but you cheated again somehow?" Jeng turned on Sal.

"Who me? Never, just water while you drink helps."

"And whatever was in your hip flask," all the women fell about with laughter, Emma had ratted Sal out.

"Friends please," Kain started. "Tomorrow is Friday, this morning would not be good to train but maybe later. May I suggest you all spend time together and we will meet later. Jenna dear, a walk maybe?"

"Of course, but someone give me my sunglasses!" Jenna added as she joined Kain on his walk. Sean looked at Emma, "Mush first, then maybe a walk or something?"

"Yes but no motorbikes!"

"You were sloshed, absolutely gone and your mum let you?" Mush was on the viewer.

"Yes, please don't shout it hurts."

Sean and Mush laughed. "What are you then a T-totaler, did the guys not drink?"

"Oh, they drunk but, no, I only had a few. Whiskey is awful!"

"Whiskey, O.M.G. I'm on my way to Canada get me a plane quick." Again, all three friends laughed.

"How is Zandra?"

"We are great, Em, thanks. However, she has gone back to the Philippians, they want to be with their family if the aliens attack."

"Why do you think they will attack?" Sean asked.

"Oh, come on you are closer than us. Why else are they here?"

"Surely if they were aiming to attack it would have happened by now?"

"Who knows Emma, it's weird they have made no contact. Or is it like the X files and the government knows and us normal people are kept in the dark?" Mush was on a roll, "Do you think they are green and scary?"

"Who knows, Mush, but we have to have faith in our leaders."

"Really, Em, ours is okay but the yank? He could be dangerous. Did you see how they blew up the fighters. But where did the Spitfires come from and why did they not blow them up? This is crazy!"

Sean joined in, "Mush, can we drop it for now please." This was agreed and the next hour was less worrying, just updates on friends back home in Aville. Viewer off, Sean and Emma headed downstairs, the palace appeared empty. Finally, they found Lens pottering around the kitchen.

"Has everyone gone out?" Emma asked.

"I think so, it is a big place. How about some time with me?"

"Yes, that would be nice, maybe we can cook?"

Sean looked at Emma indignantly for suggesting this, but thankfully Lens was on his side. "Oh no dear I was thinking of exploring. I know a beautiful place, not far, the guards will drive us. I don't get out of the palace often you know."

"Oh yes of course," Emma had changed her mind.

The journey was about an hour; both Sean and Emma enjoyed looking out the windows, seeing more of Earthen. Most was flat with small towns but plenty of greenery and sun. Approaching some hills, the car meandered around the bottom before, through the front window, a lake could be seen.

"Blue lake we call it. Yes, the water is a clear blue," Lens announced.

Sean noted it was quite sparse but there were boats or the like on the water. "Can we swim or something?"

"Oh yes we will go to the small marina."

It was not long when the car stopped. Sean, Emma and Lens exited. "This place is beautiful!" were Emma's first words as she took in the view.

Sean looked around, surprisingly it looked fairly Earth like. The building appeared to be made of wood as was the small pontoon, but the boats! "Wow!" Sean screamed as he rushed to the pontoon edge. There were strange looking boats on the water; one was a kind of jet ski but with two round loops, one top to bottom and the other around the middle; the rider was fully visible within the non-enclosed loops. The jet ski skimmed across the water but flipped on the centre bar spinning three sixty degrees on its side a couple of times then spun over on its front. The rider was literally doing cartwheels whilst moving forward quick on the water.

"Would our young prince wish to have a go?"

Sean looked at the approaching man. "Would I? Yes!"

Sean and Emma were led to the changing rooms, both emerging in similar Earth type wet suits. A brief instruction, the jet spheres would float even on their bottom once turned on, but when on the move by use of the handlebars or body movement they would spin, go upside down, with the rider strapped in.

The man advised, "Have fun, you will get wet just try not to hit each other or anything else as you can lose sense of direction whilst spinning around."

Sean waved to Lens, who was drinking tea at the small pontoon bar and sunning herself.' Then he hit the throttle, the jet sphere took off, gliding across the water. Sean looked behind; Emma was following. Seeing there was no other craft near Sean leaned to his left, as the side bar hit the water Sean could keep going straight but at a 45-degree angle. A twist of the handlebar and the sphere turned still at 45 degrees. A harder pull to the left on the handlebars and the sphere dug in, and then turned sharply. Forgetting to straighten the handlebar the sphere continued the turn, three back full circle twists later Sean stopped. A big grin on his face.

Looking up he could see Emma coming towards him a bit too fast, as she got closer, she must have panicked and turned too sharply. Emma and the sphere went headfirst into the water and it spun on its axis three or four times but ended upright some thirty metres from Sean. Sean took off towards the stationary sphere.

"You okay, Emma?"

"O.M.G. that was awesome, my head is killing me though. I think I'll take it easy!"

Sean not having the constraints of a hangover hit the throttle, within half an hour he was spinning the sphere sideways, upside down, anyway he wanted. Stopping for breath he could see the lake was empty, Emma had clearly gone back to the pontoon. Sean headed towards it. It was clear he was the only one on the water and all the other people, around thirty in number were on the pontoon.

"Let me tie you up your highness," The man was grabbing the sphere as Sean undid his belt and jumped off.

"Are all the others not going in the water?"

"They will now, after you are off the water it is safer." The man laughed. With this Sean noted the other people were getting onto various crafts. Sean walked over to Lens, who was asleep, Emma was sunbathing, although sat up as Sean approached.

"Apparently you were so mad out there they should have thrown you off the water. However, as you are the prince, all your poor subjects had to get out instead," Emma laughed, Sean went red.

Both now sipping soft drinks, watching the water activities, Sean spoke, "That was really awesome though!"

"Yes, it was but I was not prepared for it, breakfast or what little I had of it is back there in the toilet."

"Ha ha, you got sick again!" The squirted sun cream hit Sean full in the face, conversation stopped.

Having sat in the sun for some time Lens finally woke. "Did you have a go dears? You both look very dry. Never mind we can go and eat somewhere; this water business is hard work you know."

Sean and Emma giggled but followed Lens to the car, thanking the pontoon man as they left. Again, watching out the windows the car headed back towards the city but stopped in a small village. "This is where we were the other day," Emma stated as they got out of the car. "Look, up there is the shop."

"Oh, my friend, it is so lovely to meet you." Sean turned to see the old lady, Hildu, who they had met before, welcoming Lens with a hug. Hildu then welcomed Sean and Emma before leading them into her house, then to her garden.

"Hi my, Earth Princess!" Suki jumped into Emma's arms; Emma gave the little girl a cuddle.

"I am sorry, Your Highness," The shopkeeper said.

"Don't be, and please call me Emma. What is your name?"

"I am, Eric, the shopkeeper."

"This is Coral, my daughter, you met the other day," Hildu advised. "And, Fred, my son in law, Coral's husband."

Introductions over, Sean and Emma were made very welcome as they sat for lunch under the canopy in the garden. Sean noted the food was mainly vegetables but there was some meat, all was delightful and crisp in taste. The conversation was light, although Suki was not; she sat on Emma's knees most of the time.

"Hildu taught your father, she was what you would call his

head mistress," Lens informed. Hildu started to tell some tales of the young king then at one point mentioned Glad Smith.

"O.M.G.!" Emma exclaimed. "Professor Smith our deputy head?"

"Yes dear. Glad and I are good friends, indeed I trained her," Hildu said proudly.

"No. I meant Smithy is an Earthen!"

The table laughed; Lens spoke. "You did not know?"

"No, actually I don't know who else is an Earthen?"

"You know most by now of those around us," Sean thought. "Maybe Cott and Gwent?"

"They are aliens too?" Emma went red as all laughed. "I'm sorry I mean Earthens."

"And of course, the dearly departed Carnell, a very dear friend of ours," Hildu added.

"And Mrs Carnell, the old wom...I mean that lovely lady was an Earthen," Emma had corrected herself.

"Yes, sadly she died a hero as that young Millan chap did in service to King Kain." Lens face dropped upon seeing Emma's reaction. "Oh, dear you did not know?"

"No Lens I didn't but it makes more sense now. Mrs Carnell died in her house the day Gill kidnapped you?"

"Don't mention that name, if your father had not dealt with him I would!" Hildu obviously disliked Gill.

"Mum, please, these things happen. Mrs Carnell had a great life and died with honour," Coral was trying to help.

"Oh, that's good coming from my own daughter. A great life, you mean old. Are you thinking of the inheritance dear?" Hildu turned on her daughter but with a smile.

The afternoon led to early evening, Sean felt he and Emma did not want to leave but that they had to. Having said their goodbyes, they were soon back at the palace. Joining their family and friends in the dining room, but not eating. The mood was tense; all were on edge, although Kain was very confident he would succeed the next day's duel.

THE DUEL OF DUELS:
(CHAPTER 35)

This time Emma woke Sean by kissing him. Sean, opening his eyes, he thought he was in heaven. Emma went to her room to dress, Sean his. Again, the clothes laid out for them were military, including holsters for guns. Sean coming out of his bedroom caught Emma standing in the main room looking in a mirror. "I feel like an all action girl" Emma smiled as she pretended to draw an imaginary gun from the holster at her side.

"If wars were won on looks you would beat all," Sean added before holding his warrior.

"Do you think we will have to fight?"

"I hope not, but you will be safe with me."

"How do you ki...I mean hurt people. I'm not sure I can?"

Sean thought. "You do what you have to. I recently think of the git that killed Shadow and then whatever I do, I do."

"Yes, maybe I will try that."

Both went to the breakfast room, all present were in military clothes, all already had their weapons. "Good morning you guys. Here are your guns," Jeng provided Sean and Emma with their weapons.

Kain stood tall, "My family, my friends. I cannot both apologise for bringing you into my troubled life and thank you enough for your love and support." Jenna stood by her husband. "Today will be dangerous, I am sorry to say but if there is trouble, shoot first!" With this Kain dropped his head, kissed

Jenna then led the party to the waiting vehicles for the trip to the arena.

Before exiting the car, Jenna put her helmet on, Emma copied her. As Sean went to put his on, Kain stopped him. "No, you are an Earthen and a powerful one at that, you do not need a helmet. They are protective but can also hinder your power out. I, Jeng, Sal, indeed all us non-military Earthens, will not have helmets on." As they exited the cars Sean could see his father's point. Jeng, Sal and others were not wearing helmets however, the general troops of which there were many were fully uniformed, with helmets, guns and machine guns, all lasers of course. The Coopers were also in full battle dress.

There were no formalities as the party were led to a holding room beside the changing room. Sean could see amongst the many people they walked past that other military guards were present, the black coloured troops obviously Vulten. The group were left to talk amongst themselves. Emma by Sean's side, Sean watching his father who was with Algier and Anders. The door opened and in walked King Ders with a group of some fifteen people, again the guards in full uniform and fully armed. Ders spoke with Kain, it looked quite lighthearted if not reassuring from where Sean watched. Sean gave a quizzical smile as Ders left winking at Sean on his way. *Funny,* Sean thought.

"Hey, you need to come with me," Jeng was with Sean and Emma. "Sorry just me and Sean. You will remain here, Kain and Jenna will be left in the changing room on their own for a short period then you will be shown to your seats. Come on Sean." Sean gave Emma a peck on the cheek then followed Jeng to a quiet corridor; they were the only ones in it.

A door opened, Jeng gushed then ran in its direction, and Prince Alex was welcomed. Sean approached the caressing pair. "Eh hmm."

"Oh, sorry Sean," Jeng blushed.

"Prince Sean, good to see." Alex shook Sean's hand. "I am here in a formal role to offer you my support as an ambassador to the new king. Especially as you would be so young."

Sean pulled his hand back, "What? That is not required as my dad is going to win!"

Sean caught Jeng pulling a face, then fell in. "Of course, if the worst does happen then your support will be welcomed."

Sean saw Alex wink, "Please pass my support on to your father, and wish him good luck from me." With that Alex turned and left. Sean followed Jeng, he had the message. Upon entering the changing room only his father and mother were present. Kain clothed but with his top pulled down to his waist showing his chest was sitting on the trainer's bench. Jenna sitting next to him was cuddling him. As Sean and Jeng got closer Jenna let Kain go, tears clearly in her eyes.

"Nothing to worry about Your Highness, some pecs there Kain," Jeng tried to lighten the atmosphere. It worked as Kain chuckled, then said, "Yes, not bad for a nearly fifty-year-old, but it is my mind that counts, not my body." Even Jenna chuckled.

"Sean, you will sit in my seat with your mother, Jeng and the others. Syston is my coach, Sal my first aid." As Kain spoke Syston and Sal entered the room.

"Prince Alex wishes you well and confirms his support," Sean advised.

"Good, that is good. Sean take your mother and look after her. I will see you all soon."

Jenna gave Kain a last hug and kiss, Jeng followed with the same but not as intensely, Sean could not stop hugging his father. Having left the changing room, hand in hand with his mother Sean stood tall, he was going to make his father proud whatever happened.

Taking his seat between Emma and Jenna, Sean looked around the arena. Algier was next to Jenna with King Ders next to him and Anders. Opposite were King Bier, Ain and Vul, all sitting together. Sean caught Vul's eyes, Vul went to communicate, and Sean fired back a strong, no!

Sean then looked around further, the arena was full, and soldiers were at every entrance and at strategic points in the walkways. It was clear there were more Saultens than other troops. A trumpet type sound caught Sean's attention; below him Kain entered the arena, with Sal and Syston in tow, the crowd cheered. Opposite Dain also entered, to a lesser cheer.

Both parties in the middle looking at each other, the chief referee spoke on the microphone. "Ladies and Gentlemen, our kings," The referee said as he bowed. "This is a duel, a duel to the death," the crowd hushed at this point, "There is no belt as the prize here is greater than I have ever seen before, or certainly of more recent past." The referee stopped, turned to Kain and bowed again. "Your Highness, do you wish to speak?"

Sean looked at his father; he was not the man from the changing room. Stooping Kain went to take the microphone, and then stopped as he coughed. Both Sean's hands went into pain as Emma and Jenna were holding him tight. Kain waved no. Sean swore he heard the kings opposite laugh. The referee turned off the microphone and went through the rules with the two combatants, now face to face with each other. Sean looked at Dain; he did look in good shape, full of confidence. Kain was still 'hamming it up' Sean thought. Formalities over, the referee had left the field of play and both combatants were in their areas. Last words from their seconds and both were standing alone looking at each other. The first countdown started, Sean felt Emma and Jenna again through his hands. As the count hit zero Dain attacked first, Kain went defensive. This continued for the whole of the first round, as the combatants were seen by their seconds Sean heard a voice.

"Kain, you are a king fight like one!" Vul was standing opposite. Sean went to stand, Jeng sitting behind held him down.

The second started in similar fashion, but halfway through

Kain attacked—his efforts looking poor. The crowd gasped as Kain was hit and went to ground, the countdown started. Sean thought of the rules. If Kain did not get up after the count his opponent can approach and finish it. Again, Sean went to stand, Jeng pulled him back harder. Kain coughed, stood and went straight into defence mode. Round two ended.

Sean turned to Jeng, in her head he said, "*I will if I have to, my dad is not dying here today!*"

Jeng responded back in his head, "*No. If your father does not die but loses then all protocol will be against you. If you intervene you will be attacked by all.*"

Sean thought but did not respond, round three had started. Dain was moving more; Kain was attacking more, neither appearing to get a good shot in. Round three was even. Round four started, Dain attacked hard, Kain went to defend but was caught and hit the floor for the second time. Again, the crowd let out a gush of awe. Sean felt Jeng hold him again. Kain rose and went defensive, and then it happened. Sean, even from this distance could see the red in Kain's eyes, followed by a smirk. Kain raised his arm, Dain hit the back wall. Kain raised both arms and threw his brother along the wall. Then holding his brother in mid-air like a rag doll, Kain released three shots; all could see the body take them hard. Dain was released and hit the floor. The arena went silent; the countdown was the only noise. Even before the countdown hit zero, Kain was walking towards his fallen brother.

Zero, the crowd again let out a gush as Kain was now over his brother. Dain moved, raised an arm to fight but could not. Kain circled his brother then looked into his eyes. Sean could hear his uncle's words, "Brother, surely not. I love you!" Kain looked at his brother, then turned and headed back to the arena centre.

Looking up he declared, "I have won, but I will not kill my brother in cold blood!"

393

There was no sound; time appeared to stand still until the referee entered the ring. "Sire, I am sorry, you know the protocol, this is a duel to the death."

"I will not kill my brother." The arena erupted with noise, some ah's then some boo's. Sean was confused.

"Quiet!" All went quiet. Vul had glided into the arena centre, a few metres from Kain. "Kain, you called this duel; you must follow protocol!"

"Must I? Why?"

Sean looked at Vul; he was clearly confused at Kain's response. "You must, it is protocol. If you do not, then you will be deemed the loser and lose your kingdom."

Things got worse; King Ain and Bier joined Vul and Kain. Bier spoke, "Not only your kingdom, but your life, as you dueled to the death!"

There was movement to Kain's left as King Ders joined the group in the middle. "My fellow kings, please wait. Let us consider!"

"Kill your brother now and all will be as it should!" Vul was looking at Kain.

Sean caught sight of someone to Vul's right—Prince Alex was near his father. "Kill a family member as you did father?" Vul was still confused but turned to his son, then took a step back as Prince Kruge joined his brother. "Do you wish to kill us both father!"

"What is going on here. My sons, stop this!"

The two Vul's response was not as expected, both took up attack stances. Seth joined the feuding Vuls. "My sires please, this is of no benefit. Secretaries please." Each of the kingdom's secretaries with Algier, joined the group in the middle. All Earthen hierarchy was in the arena centre. Jeng moved from behind Sean, she was soon next to Alex.

Alex gave Jeng a kiss then looked at his father. "Earthen is changing, the non-allowance of love amongst differing races and the unnecessary killing of loved ones is no more."

"We all second that!" The arena had three more heirs in the middle.

Sean heard in his ear, "Go now, I will protect your mother and Emma." Sean knew the voice was Livia's, without a second thought he was in the arena. Standing looking at the kings, all looked confused, their sons surrounding them.

Algier spoke, "Sires, maybe we can discuss this, surely an arena of death in front of millions here and on screen is not the best place for this?"

"It is old man. We the youth of Earthen wish to speak up!" Kruge looked powerful as he spoke. His brother and Jeng beside him both tensed to fight.

King Ain broke the silence, "My son, what is going on here?"

Sean looked at Prince Sebast as he spoke, "Father. I am with Kruge and the other heirs, we no longer wish for this brutal world."

Sebast dropped his head, paused then looked at his father straight. "I will fight with Kruge and my fellow heirs against you,. If I have to!"

The arena crowd all screamed at once in shock. All five heirs were in fight stance. Seth spoke, "Our kings, you must stand down. Listen to your heirs."

Vul could take no more, a loud, "NEVER!" bellowed from his mouth as he struck out at his two sons. Kruge and Alex both flew across the floor, Sean felt the power even though he was not its focus. Jeng was first to respond, hitting Vul full on. Vul fell backwards but did not hit the floor, he stood and focused on Jeng.

"NO!" Was Sean's roar as he hit Vul side on, Vul flew across the floor but managed to throw a punch back at Sean, who felt it but did not fall. Sean went for a second shot as Vul stood. Vul dodged Sean's punch, and went to throw his own, but again he hit the floor. Kain was attacking—no one else moved. Kain walked towards Vul.

"You will not kill my son as you brutally killed yours!" Kain placed both arms together and even though ten metres from Vul, he screamed and punched out. There was a flash, and Vul was no more. Kain turned on Bier and Ain, Sean could see fire in his eyes.

Ders was beside Kain and spoke first. "There needs to be no more blood loss, please surrender." Biers decided this was not to be the case, before he could fire his power; Ders and Kain floored him—he moved no more.

King Ain looked at the two other kings—Sebast stood beside Kain. "Father, no, please?" King Ain was confused but did as Biers did, he was slain by the two kings and his own son. The arena went quiet, it felt like forever. Sean looked around, three kings had been slain, two bodies, one non-existent. Kain still had fire in his eyes—no one was talking.

"Ladies and Gentlemen, people of Earthen. I, King Ders, renounce my throne with immediate effect."

Sean looked at Prince Wil. Livia his sister was now next to him, and she gave him a hug. Wil returned the hug then stood by his father. "I, Prince Wil, heir to my father's throne will not accept this and offer our kingdom to the people of Dersian." Both turned, walked to their secretary, threw their crowns to the floor and knelt before the secretary. The crowd erupted for a few seconds, then stopped as the other heirs moved. First Prince Sebast renounced his kingdom and offered his kingdom to his people. Prince Trev followed, both kneeling at their Secretary's feet. Kruge followed suit, renouncing his throne and kingdom, he knelt to Secretary Seth. All eyes were on Kain, he was not moving. Sean felt people at his side; Emma and Jenna were beside him. Jenna gave Sean a smile; Sean walked towards Algier, stopped and waited for his father.

"People of Earthen. I am the last King!" Kain called out. "I will not renounce my throne, yet." All gasped as Kain started to walk, not towards Algier, but towards Dain, still laying prone on the floor.

"I make no apologies for my last act as the last Earthen King." Kain raised his arm and threw a punch at Dain. Sean could see the air disturbance five metres or so between Kain and Dain. Dain looked up and his head exploded.

The crowd screamed. Sean looked at his father, the fire still in his eyes, showing no remorse. Kain approached Algier, the fire in his eyes calmed. Kain knelt before Algier, threw his crown to the floor. "My friend, I give you what you and my people deserve. I renounce my throne."

All eyes were on Sean as he knelt beside his father. Throwing his crown, he said, "I. Prince Sean. Heir to my father's kingdom, renounce my throne and give it to the people of Saulten."

As Sean finished his sentence the crowd erupted with joy. Formalities went out the window as all in the middle stood and hugged each other. Sean hugging his father first, and then Algier. Jenna and Emma joining the group hug. All was mayhem for a few minutes, Livia and Jeng also hugging Sean. In the madness, Kruge grabbed Sean's hand. "Your father is a legend Sean. Hopefully because of him and us, Earthen will be a better place from now." Sean gave Kruge, then Alex, a hug.

Seth was on the microphone, all stopped to listen. "People of Earthen. I and my fellow secretaries with Chief Councilor Algier will tomorrow take the steps to arrange our change to democracy!" The crowd cheered, "For tonight however, all please celebrate as Earthen is liberated!" Sean was nearly deafened by the roar of the crowd in appreciation. Kain gave Seth a big hug, then motioned his party back to the relative quietness of the changing room. Kain sat on the trainer's bench, Sal trying to check him over, although fighting for space as Jenna was hugging him and not letting him go.

"Excuse me everyone, may I talk!" All stopped to look

at Krips, who had clearly started the drinking celebrations. "There is good news and bad news." Sean thought, *What?* Krips continued. "First is the little matter of Kain's impending death. Sadly, my prognosis was wrong, no deceitful. He is as fit as a fiddle and not going to die!"

Sean looked at his mother; she turned and looked at Kain. "It was a lie? A deception that you were dying?"

Kain looked very uncomfortable. "Yes, dear. I had to. Vul, and everyone had to think I was vulnerable." Sean swore he saw fire in his mother's eyes as she slapped Kain hard around the face, then laughed and gave him the biggest longest kiss Sean had ever seen. Thankfully Emma was to hand to copy Jenna but without the slap, Sean felt good.

"Eh hmm. Please, if I still have some integrity may I remind you of the destroyer on Earth? What is their reaction to these changes?" Krips brought them back to their senses.

"Yes, Algier, get the secretaries, we must make contact with our troops!" Kain was already heading out of the changing room, Sean and the others followed.

THE FINAL BATTLE:
(CHAPTER 36)

All were soon in a cramped com's room to the side of the arena. Seth had joined them. Various viewers were shown on the screens, the destroyer was still motionless over Washington. "Sire, I mean sir, who cares," Shad was confused. "The Vulten battleship is still in attack mode as is the destroyer. However, I have control over the space station, Commander Ruzz and his crew have been taken poorly. Food poisoning, I think." Shad ended with a smile.

"Commander, this is your secretary speaking," Seth was addressing the viewer that the Vulten battleship commander was in. "Commander you are aware of the changes here, you will call the destroyer back and come out of attack mode." Sean could see the commander in the view.

"Secretary Seth, I will call off my ship. Crew stand down, we will return to the space station. However, the destroyer is truly not under my control."

Another commander in a Saulten uniform appeared in another screen. "I can confirm the Vulten battleship has dropped its shields, we will remain on attack mode."

"Yes commander, the Dersian battleship also." Algier acknowledged.

"Get me that destroyer!" Seth was getting impatient, no viewer opened, what did open caused a cry from all; the destroyer fighter doors opened and out flew all ten fighters. Each fighter opened fire on various Washington buildings. Capitol was hit first as the roof erupted in flames, then the Washington memorial took a direct hit, crashing to the ground. Sean looked, the White House, as yet, was not damaged, but the destroyer was ascending above it.

"Now Captain!" Was the order from Kain, as another viewer came up to show a com's room, obviously on Earth as Sean could see Robare at the Captain's side. Sean looked at the screens as many more dots were approaching from the distance, as they appeared closer to the destroyer, they were a mix of F14s and Spitfires. Sean cried with joy; they were the Earth Council fighters. All watched the screens as the fighters danced with each other, lasers discharged, lighting up the sky. Every now and then a brighter light caught as a fighter was hit and blew up. Sean looked; many were Vulten fighters, but some were the Earthen fighters.

The air battle continued, Sean thought how strange it looked, Spitfires chasing alien fighters, with lasers firing. Another alien fighter blew up, an F14 flying through the debris of its target. A Spitfire got hit and went down, clipping a tall building as it exploded in flames on the ground. A second Spitfire and F14 took out the fighter that had slain their sister Earth fighter. Sean saw two larger laser shots as both the Spitfire and the F14 exploded together, the destroyer had joined the battle. "Sire, the destroyer is high enough to fire its main weapon!"

Sean looked at another viewer; the destroyer was higher above the White House, but still firing deadly lasers at the Earth fighters. The dots in the air were lessening. All of a sudden there was a bright light and a massive explosion. As the light and flames cleared the Vulten destroyer was not there, then two other destroyers flew past. Algier was the first to scream with joy. "Our destroyers have taken out the Vulten one. Washington is safe!"

Just like in the arena, the room went mad as all hugged each other, no more so than Harry and Judy who were so relieved that Earth was no longer under threat. Sean in Emma's embrace still watched the screens. The two new destroyers hovered above the White House. Sean saw a few more laser shots as the last of the Vulten fighters were taken out. The destroyers turned in formation, their hyper drives lit, and they took off into space.

"Wow, look!" Emma let Sean go and was pointing at another screen. A single Spitfire and two F14s in formation flew low across the White House, twice, then headed for home.

"How the hell are we going to explain this to Earth?" Algier expressed in a happy tone.

"Sire, Virage here!"

"Try sir from now, but go-ahead, Virage," Kain responded.

"As I said before, thankfully most of Washington is deserted although the building damage is major."

"We will support the Earthen Council in the rebuilding of the great city," Seth advised.

"Thank you," Kain responded to Seth. "Until we get home, you have a difficult job my friend."

Virage chuckled, "Yes. There is obvious great sadness here, but confusion is giving it a run for its money. Shall I kill the president now?"

Kain laughed, "No, we, no, I, no longer act like that. Help him to help his people. Thank you. Robare, you have some explaining to do, but my gratitude to you and Captain Shad has no end." Shad and Robare acknowledged Kain's thanks and the viewers went out.

"Well. I'm having a drink; can someone actually explain what has gone on here?" Harry shouted.

"At the palace when we have time to think, but, yes, one drink here now would be good." Kain was laughing more than he ever had.

As the group left the stadium they were met by the cheers of the people, the short walk to the cars took some time. Just as Kain was about to get into one car he stopped. "Please let her through." The guards parted and Sean could see Hildu.

Kain gave Hildu a hug as she spoke, "Kain, you are not only the most powerful Earthen ever seen, and great king, but a visionary. A true hero, your people, no sorry, your ex-people, love you. Thank you."

The party were in tears of joy all the way back to the palace. Wort and Lens had decorated the great hall; food, drink and the whole palace staff were present as another party kicked off. Sean looked at the varied screens, it appeared Earthen was full of parties—people, troops, police all dancing together.

Kain made a point to hug nearly everyone, then took Jenna outside alone. Algier approached Sean, "Outside please." Sean with Emma on his arm followed Algier outside to the garden; they sat on a bench together. "A hell of a day!"

Sean chuckled, "Yes, uncle it was. I'm still not with it all?"

"It's simple," Emma interjected. "We have just witnessed independence on Earthen."

Algier chuckled, "Yes, in simplistic terms, that is the case."

"So, we no longer are royalty. I was getting use to this place," Sean said sarcastically.

"Don't worry. Your father will remain the Earth Council Secretary, although reporting to me." Algier chuckled. "All of the crown's public estate such as the council building will go back to the state. However, the families' personal wealth of which the palace is, remains with you. No longer a prince but a good bank account should see you get by."

Sean and Emma laughed. Algier stood, "Ah, what a beautiful young couple."

Emma blushed, "Thank you Algier."

"No, no, not you two, look." Sean and Emma rose to see his father and mother not that far ahead of them kissing. "We had better break it up, your father wishes to talk to you Sean. I will fill you in Emma."

Algier stayed with Jenna and Emma, Sean and Kain moved towards the Bosworth statue. "You do not appreciate this I hear?" Kain started.

"No, I think it is awful."

Kain chuckled. "My son. I have my biggest apology to say to you." Sean held his father's hand. "I had this vision for years. My goal was to never to have you face the decisions I have in life. Earthen had to denounce its kings before your sixteenth birthday at least. By the way son, happy birthday."

Sean thought, "O.M.G. in all the fuss I forgot today is my birthday!"

Kain smiled and continued. "I, for many years through making trusted friends, the opening of Saulten borders, the acceptance of mixed marriages, planned for this. The involvement of great young people such as Livia, Sal, Jeng, Alex and more recently Kruge, proved my goal was right. The journey was not always as planned, Millan, Carnell and even Shadow are sad losses." A tear came to their eyes. "Vul and his allies started to get wind of my plans. Hence the introduction of Gill, your fight with Det, my brother stabbing me in the back, all were part of this. It was never really about you son, but me."

Sean gave his father a hug, Kain continued, "Even more recently I was behind the setting up of F.A.M. Vul set up the F.F.R. in response, and used them to ashen the F.A.M. name by killing in their name. F.A.M. did not kill. My biggest ally, although it was not obvious, is Seth."

Sean took a breath, "Yes, I can see that now, he hated being led by Vul?"

"Yes, as did Vul's own family. Vul killing Det, oh so tragic, was the time that Kruge joined us. Although Alex was already on our side, I needed all the heirs."

"You did not need the kings?"

"No, sadly my peers are still of the old days, enjoying their power and privileges. Oh, apart from Ders, with such a loving a persuasive daughter as Livia, he had no choice but to join us. The others, I was happy to kill."

Sean looked at his father, their eyes started to glisten, "And Dain, he had to die?"

Kain eyes went dark, tears followed. "For all the good I wish, I am still Earthen. Your uncle despised me, and I, he. Yes, he died, not for the cause, but for me."

Jenna was just in time to hold her husband, Sean was held by Emma. "Look, the sunset is beautiful. Our home is just behind it," Jenna pointed to the low sun, and again kissed Kain.

Sean looked at his parents and then spoke to Emma. "You know what? This was as much about the Earth as it was Earthen."

Emma smiled, "Oh, you are still an idiot—it is only about one thing. Look."

Sean looked over to his father and mother both still embraced, then looked back at Emma. "What?"

Emma giggled, "It was all about love!"

With that they kissed.

The End

"Thank you for reading, Enlightenment: Earths. I hope you enjoyed it and you follow me on Amazon/Facebook/Twitter/Goodreads!" Ken Kirkberry

ABOUT THE AUTHOR

Ken Kirkberry

Ken Kirkberry books:

https://www.amazon.co.uk/Ken-Kirkberry/e/B0722YXS97/
ref=sr_ntt_srch_lnk_1?qid=1523824003&sr=8-1

https://www.facebook.com/ken.kirkberry.9

@KKirkberry

BOOKS BY THIS AUTHOR

Enlightenment: This Earth (Boook 1)

Young adult sci fi adventure, book 1 - Earth based. Sean finds out his history which leads him to find an alternate world. A world in which he and his family have power and position.

Enlightenment: Another Earth (Book 2)

Sean moves to the alternate world of Earthen. Ravaged by apocolyptic and robot wars, and advanced global warming. This alternate Earth is more technically advanced, but more dangerous.

Enlightenment: Collliding Earths (Book 3)

Earthen and its Kings show their power. Earthen civil war is beginning, but this soon spills over as Seans Earth becomes the target.

The Figure

Gritty New York cop story. A mysterious Figure is assasinating members of the infamous Carnello gang. Can Detective John Mercer and colleagues stop this murderer before gang war engulfs the city.

The Equals

Mix of crime and horror. Police officer Vicky Lloyd stumbles across a strange murder scene and is paired up with the mysterious Matt. The murder investigation leads Vicky into the dark world of vampires, a world she never knew of. What is her secret, can she stop the rampaging vampire vile.

Deadvent Calendar

Fast paced action adventure. Special Agent Sharon Mansell has to race across the world to catch the murderer(s). Every other December day is a murderous event, from sniper shootings to bombings. Sharon is against the calendar, are the murders linked and how.

Printed in Great Britain
by Amazon